THE GENESIS FACTOR

Paul C. Guest

First published in 2024 in Great Britain

Copyright © Paul C. Guest 2024

The moral rights of the author are asserted.

No part of this book may be reproduced, stored in a retrieval system, or transmitted in any form or by any means, electronic, mechanical, photocopying, recording or otherwise, without the publisher's and copyright owner's prior written permission.

This book is a work of fiction apart from references to actual historical reports, Biblical texts, locations and certain scientific or medical breakthroughs. In the case of characters, any resemblance to actual persons, living or dead, is purely coincidental apart from a few individuals. In these cases, permissions were obtained.

ISBN-13: 979-8321906354

Cover design by Paul C. Guest

'There were giants in the Earth in those days.'
Genesis, Chapter VI

For Brian

Prologue

Lompoc, California
Summer, 1959

On the day that would change his life forever, the boy gripped the rope and rappelled downwards into the crack in the Earth. The soft chalky surface gave his once-white sneakers a non-too-steady grip as he bounced and dropped slowly into the alien depths. The rope felt stiff and cut into his hands. Now was a bad time to wonder why he didn't wear gloves. Also, something smelled like a badger's butt down there. The feeling began to grow in his mind that this was a stupid idea, but it was too late now. Instead, he did what he always did when he felt scared. He imagined that he was a daring, swashbuckling movie legend like Errol Flynn, Tyrone Power or John Wayne, or all three rolled into one. He immediately felt braver and then his chest swelled with pride at the urging of the three up above.

"Brian...Brian...Brian."

He was getting close now. He could feel the space closing in as if the bottom was looming. Just one more second and –

He ran out of rope.

Gravity took over as he fell flailing for a handhold in the dim light. Before he had taken one breath he hit the powdery earth below with a loud thud, forcing all of the air out of his lungs like a suddenly deflated balloon. The others reacted as one might expect of three concerned friends.

"Damn Brian. That was outtasight," called Tim, through cupped hands.

"Yeah man. Cool move," sniped Tony, the self-proclaimed leader of the gang of four.

Tony's younger brother Pete was also on the verge of laughter, until he saw that his friend wasn't moving. "Hey man, you okay?"

No response.

Tim suddenly now realised that this could be serious. "Brian?"

Brian's sheepish face emerged slowly from the gloom as he sat upright, drew in some dusty swirling air and spluttered. "I fell."

"No kiddin' Sherlock," said Tony. "Well, whaddaya see down there?"

"Not much. It's kinda dark."

"Okay we're comin' down with the flashlights," Pete announced.

"Okay but be careful. The rope ain't long enough."

"Guess you found that out the hard way," remarked Tony.

Pete said, "we'll pull the rope up and tie this other short bit to it to increase the length."

They had been friends forever. Tim and Brian Sullivan had settled in the sleepy California town 9 years before with their parents. Their father, a master sergeant in the US army, had been transferred to Camp Cooke training base. This was renamed in 1958 as Vandenberg Air Force Base, the first missile base of the United States Air Force. Tony and Peter Blake had come to Lompoc with their parents the same year. Their father had been hired as a surveyor to work in the Johns-Manville diatomaceous earth mines situated in the southern hills of the city. It was somewhere near this site where the boys had come across the cavernous opening while on one of their jaunts through the hills. The discovery occurred when Brian had stumbled and nearly fell into a hole they had never seen before.

The boys reckoned that the combined efforts of the earthquake from the previous month and the recent heavy rains must have exposed the opening. It was not noticeable a few weeks beforehand when they had last passed by this way. Having spotted the dark entrance, they couldn't resist the temptation. They returned the next day with ropes, shovels and flashlights, all 'borrowed' from their fathers' work sheds, to begin the exploration of the crack in the Earth. They lived for these little adventures.

Brian had volunteered to go first by climbing down through the narrow opening, which was more like a fissure, using the long rope which his brother had tied round the base of a dwarf mountain pine tree. Now the other three came down one after the other on the extended rope which now reached all the way to the mud on the cave floor. They found Brian standing in the same spot where he fell. It was a tight squeeze with all of them down there in what appeared to be an angular pit around 30 feet deep, 10 feet long and 3 feet wide. The dank odour of wet earth, possibly combined with some kind of dead animal smell, permeated the small cavern. Brian was not concerned about the cramped space or any animals, dead or otherwise. He was staring transfixed at a spot on the long wall some three feet from the floor of the pit.

The others noticed his stare but were too unnerved to speak. Tony dusted off his britches and shuffled around in the direction Brian was staring, squelching through the mud as he did so. He flicked on his flashlight and gasped. "What the heck is that?"

"Looks like a stone wall," Tim suggested. He looked over his shoulder at Pete and Brian, almost as if silently imploring them for a second and third opinion. Pete and Brian responded by shuffling forward for a closer look. None of the boys had really expected to find anything of interest. But now it seemed to them as if they had found the mother lode. They examined the bone-coloured stone, which was exposed over a two-foot square area through the chalky dirt covering.

After a moment, Pete said, "this stone doesn't look like it belongs here. It looks like granite." He peered closer and brushed some of the dirt away with his hand and stopped short. His eyes suddenly locked in place and his eyebrows lowered. The rock seemed smooth to the touch as if it were polished. But the part that was the most striking was that the wall was also sparsely covered with small, faded notches that looked like symbols or some form of writing. "Guys, help me clear more of this away," he managed.

The other boys pitched in using their hands to brush away the loose white chalky dirt and they scraped away the larger chucks of rock with the shovels. By now, a cloud of dust had amassed in the crevice and all four boys resembled ghostly apparitions. Pete wondered if they should really be breathing this in. After several minutes, they had exposed a long stretch of what appeared to be a wall made from at least three large cut stone slabs. Each slab was approximately 4 feet long by 6 feet high and seemed to fit together so closely that there were no gaps between them. Also, it didn't seem that any form of mortar had been used. It now looked as if the structure had edges which appeared to be recessed into the soft dirt surrounding it. This meant that they had uncovered one side of what looked like a small rectangular building.

After what seemed like a minute of stunned silence, Pete said, "guys, I think we better get some help with this. Looks like it could be significant." He thought for a moment and then looked up. "Besides, the way we have loosened all of this dirt could lead to a cave-in."

The other boys all looked nervously around them. They clearly hadn't considered this possibility.

"I don't think we should tell anybody just yet," Brian said. "What if there's buried treasure in there?"

"Yeah man, why don't we just explore it ourselves and see what we can find?" Tim said persuasively.

"If there is treasure in there, we won't get any. We're just kids," Tony said. Tim reluctantly nodded in agreement.

"More than likely, it's just bones or somebody's remains," Pete said. "It could be a sarcophagus although I thought the Indians that lived around here, the Chumash, buried their dead in mounds."

No one spoke for 10 seconds and then Brian asked, "what's a sarcophagus?"

Tony gave a muted chortle and groaned, but it was clear from his expression that he really didn't know either.

"It's like a coffin made of stone or rock," Pete responded. "The ancient Egyptians used to bury the mummies of the pharaohs in them. Didn't you pay attention in history class?"

"Are you serious? Let's get the heck outta here," Brian looked worried now.

Tony looked like he was going to be sick.

Tim suggested, "if it is a sarcophagus, there could actually still be something of value in there. The Egyptians buried the pharaohs with all of their worldly possessions."

"Are you kidding?" Tony said. "If there's a dead body in there, I'm getting the heck outta here."

"He's right. Let's go call the police," Pete suggested.

"Yeah, let's go," Tim said.

They got the heck out of there.

Police Chief Ron Thompson was the spitting image of the up-and-coming country music star, Johnny Cash, except for the fact that he couldn't sing or play the guitar and had no sense of musical rhythm. Another distinguishing feature about the man was that he had a constant suntan on just his left forearm. This was because he always dangled this arm from the open window of his Chevrolet Biscayne Police Pursuit Car, even in the wintertime. It just seemed to be permanently attached to the outside of the car door. This was the case as Thompson questioned the boys, occasionally waving the arm for emphasis and patting the side of the car. He wasn't happy.

The boys had bicycled hell bent for leather on their Raleigh 'Space Riders' toward the police station when they had seen the Chief cruising around the Memorial Park where the flower festival's first annual bikini contest was under way. The scent of the many varieties of flowers that filled the surrounding fields and bedecked the festival parade floats was carried on the slight breeze. The boys frantically flagged down the Chief and Brian stammered out a quick summary of what they had found, with the other boys nodding occasionally and saying, "yeah, that's right, uh huh." The black and white Biscayne was still idling. The boys lent over their handlebars toward the sheriff's open window in anticipation of the man's next words.

"You say you found a dead body in the hills?" Chief Thompson said in an accusative tone. He dipped his Wayfarers, revealing baleful bloodshot eyes.

Pete now realised that he should have been the one briefing the chief on what they had found. Brian tended to muddle the truth from time to time. "No, we found what looks like a side wall of a building... or something," he explained. "It could be a sarcophagus."

"A sarko-what?" the Chief said in a pained tone.

"A sarcophagus, Sir," Pete said. "It's like a stone coffin. We learned about this sort of thing in Mister Clark's history class."

"You boys been drinkin'?" Chief Thompson quizzed, trying to recover some of his pride for not knowing what the word meant. "I ain't got time for this sort of thing."

"No Sir," Tony implored. "It's just like he said. And it has strange markings on it."

"Wha...?" The Chief squinted his eyes in pained concentration.

Tony thought, *it looks like he's gonna fart*.

"What kind of markings?" The Chief asked in a tone that made it clear he wanted this matter over and done with.

"We don't know Sir", Tim said. "But it could be some kind of hieroglyphics."

It was obvious to all of the boys that the Chief didn't know what this word meant either by the blank expression on his face. To cover the fact that he was out of his depth on this one he said, "okay, I'll get on the radio and get that lazy excuse of a Deputy, Ned, to join me and we'll go check it out. One of you will have to come along and show us the way."

The boys immediately turned to Pete.

Pete shrugged. "All right Chief. I'll go."

Tony, who had been blatantly checking out at the bevy of bikini beauties in the park during the discussion, turned back to the others and beamed, "sure beats the heck outta the old grandma-style swimsuits."

The contestants on the stage did a 360 degree slow turn for the applauding audience. A voice was announcing the names of the contestants over a garbled public address system. The words were completely unintelligible.

The rest of the boys turned red. Chief Thompson put on an air that he had never even noticed the young ladies in the first place.

After visiting the site with Ned and Pete, Chief Ron was truly perplexed. To him it looked like a stone rectangular building, probably made thousands of years before by the Chumash or some other Indians that he knew had inhabited this area back then. He decided that he could do nothing at this stage and contacted the local universities at Santa Barbara and San Luis Obispo, to see if they had any experts on Indian artefacts that could come to Lompoc and check things out.

Eventually, a team including two archaeologists, a geologist and a pallid scarecrow of a man with an undisclosed title arrived on the scene the following week. All of them were reported to come from the Smithsonian Institution in Washington DC. The head archaeologist, Dr Marvin Chatterwick, a lanky grey-bearded man in his early fifties, directed the excavation from a green and white striped canvass deck chair. His assistant, a young graduate student with close-cropped blond hair named Graham Johns, carried out the hard labour. Johns dug into the soft earth surrounding the pit using a standard garden shovel while the geologist, a rugged suntanned man named Simon Hancorn, sporting a white cowboy hat and a pair of Oliver Goldsmith limited edition sunglasses, casually picked over the occasional rock and jagged pottery shards and placed these in sealed bags for analysis at some later date.

Dr Chatterwick and the pale man observed the proceedings with occasional remarks and suggestions. The latter spoke in a slight German accent. By the end of the first day, they had removed about 6 feet of the covering dirt and had widened the pit considerably. However, it was clear that they were going to need more help as the stability of the ground around the structure was questionable.

As the next day was Saturday, they were able to employ 6 miners from the Johns-Manville mining company to assist in the digging. By 12:00 noon the miners had reached a chalky layer about 15 feet down which appeared to be formed out of a different material from the earth above. By 4:00 P.M. they had completely uncovered two sides of the structure and the lid, leaving huge piles of dirt surrounding the now enormous pit. They had also left a small two-foot-high mound on the exposed corner to allow access to what appeared to a lid on top of the structure.

Although they were exhausted from a full day's work, the miners were spellbound by what they had unearthed. They all now shuffled about uncertainly covered in white dust. The archaeologists and the geologist were also entranced by what they had found, although there was a slight look of confusion on their faces as if they had just uncovered a flying saucer. That is, everyone except the pale man. His expression was different. He regarded the structure with cool calculating eyes.

It was a large, elongated cube, measuring 12 feet long, by 6 feet wide and 6 feet in depth and made out of three polished granite slabs on each long side with a larger single slab at each end. Topping the structure was a 6-inch-thick flat lid measuring 12 by 6 feet that appeared to have been cut from a single piece of granite.

"What is a granite sarcophagus doing in these chalky hills and how did they get it here?" said Hancorn, gazing across the hillside. "Looks like it was built purposefully on this flat section of hard ground," he sputtered excitedly as he held his palm down flat and moved this in a circle pattern as if he were polishing a table top. "Then they covered it with a large chalky mound around 15 feet high. That was noticeable when we hit that different layer about halfway down. Over the years it must have become covered in layers of earth and, most likely, by the frequent mudslides that these hills are known for. Constant seismic activity and heavy rains must have eroded a weaker section of the deeper chalky layer and the overlying mud, giving the hollow section that those kids discovered."

"How old do you think it is?" asked Johns, shaking his head almost as if in denial.

"Judging from how deep it was in the ground, this has to be at least 8,000 years old and probably more like 10,000," replied Hancorn.

"That's impossible," lectured Dr Chatterwick, his beard wobbling from side to side. "The indigenous people of that period didn't build anything like this."

"Well, I'm just telling you the facts as I see 'em. Of course, we can try and confirm the age by radiocarbon dating of some of the wood fragments that we found spread over the various levels. But if the Indians didn't build this thing, then someone else did."

Johns asked, "what about the image carved into the lid?" They had all noticed the faint carving on the lid along with the other strange markings scattered over the structure. The picture carved into the granite lid suggested that the sarcophagus contained –

No way, thought Johns.

"Probably just for decoration," explained Dr Chatterwick. "Maybe it's intended as a warning. You know...to stop looters and grave robbers."

Johns considered this possibility but said nothing.

The sunburnt man's brow furrowed as if in concentration.

In the remaining hours of daylight, the group from the Smithsonian Institute and the miners set about opening the structure. The sunburnt man then used the sharp end of a knife which glinted in the sunlight to trace along a small distance of the boundary between the lid and the body of the sarcophagus.

"*Wunderbar,*" he mumbled to no one in particular.

The others looked on in silence.

"Please remove this," he said, clearly indicating the lid with a pointed finger. He then stepped to the side and attempted to slide the knife back into his pocket. He didn't notice that it missed and fell noiselessly to the soft chalky ground, with a small billow of powder.

At first, the men could make no headway in moving the giant lid. It appeared to fit flush onto the underlying stone blocks and there appeared to be no way to insert a tool for prying the lid open, as the sunburnt man had just found.

Hancorn stepped back, crossed his arms and offered, "if my calculations are correct, and based on the fact that granite has an average density of 166.5 pounds per cubic foot, this lid has to weigh around 6,000 pounds. We are going to have to concentrate all of our efforts on one corner and try and slide it open at an angle." The 6 miners nodded and crowded into position at the front corner and pushed with abrupt, synchronized motions to the repeated cadence of, "one, two, three, push," directed by Hancorn. On the fourth push, the lid moved about one inch with a dull screech. The miners gathered themselves again and continued pushing. Each time now, the lid moved about two inches with an accompanying bone-jarring screech. They had exposed a small section of the darkness within.

"Crow bars and wedges," ordered Dr Chatterwick. The miners worked as a team without any need for further direction now. Two of them heaved with the crow bars, while two others continued to push with their hands. The remaining two gently tapped in wooden wedges to lift the lid in concert with each movement. After several minutes, they had shifted the lid by approximately two feet exposing a diagonal space big enough for several men to peer inside at once, although none of them did so. The opposite two-foot portion of the lid was now overhanging the higher level of unexcavated earth on the far side.

The sunburnt man said to the miners, "okay, we won't need your help anymore." The miners looked shocked and then crestfallen, as if to acknowledge that they wouldn't be seeing this through to the end. One man looked like he was about to complain until Dr Chatterwick fished out wads of 100 dollar bills and fanned them out for the miners to see. They each grabbed a single note from Chatterwick's hand. Now they were content. Not bad for one day of work. That was more money than they normally received for even a whole week of working in the mines. Together they trudged off down the hill towards the town, laughing, joking and already forgetting about what they had uncovered.

Two pairs of eyes looked down on the workers. The eyes belonged to two boys huddled together behind a dense patch of chaparral shrubbery about 100 feet further up the hill. They had been there all morning and had watched the entire proceedings. They both readjusted their crouched positions to get a better look at what was happening below. They could now see the men from the Smithsonian Institution clearly and the newly shifted lid of the sarcophagus. Something was happening.

But Pete was worried. Throughout the proceedings, he had been wondering if the team from the Smithsonian should have taken more care in excavating the site. He supposed that they may have already lost or destroyed some valuable small artefacts or clues with their destructive digging methods. Surely, they should be going slower, being more careful as they unearthed the site. Why the rush? Archaeology was supposed to be a slow careful science. After all, whatever was buried in there wasn't going to go anywhere.

"That one guy looks like a dried-up tomato," whispered Brian, gesturing toward the sunburnt man.

"Shush, they'll hear us," cautioned Pete. However, he agreed completely with Brian's observation.

"Don't worry, they seem too interested in what they're doin'," Brian answered.

"You could be right. Let's try and move a little closer so we can see what's inside."

Brian nodded and said, "okay."

The boys crept forward.

The four scientists approached the open side of the sarcophagus. They stepped onto the mound of dirt that they had left piled near the open corner. The inside of the structure looked dark and foreboding in the late evening gloom. What was in there?

Johns flicked on his flashlight and pointed it inside.

After a split second four men caught their breath at the same time. As they stared in silence, it seemed like the wind and other sounds from the earth had ceased. The sound of a camera hitting the ground outside the chamber could be heard with a dull thud and a tinkling of broken glass.

"Jeepers creepers," whispered Johns.
Chatterwick and Hancorn stood frozen.
The sunburnt man smiled.

"What was it? Could you see?" mouthed Brian in a nearly silent whisper.

Pete responded with a slight shake of the head and raised shoulders. The two had brazenly moved to the edge of the pit so they could observe the top of the sarcophagus which was now situated about 30 feet below them. They had both caught a glimpse of something inside the structure before the light went out, but it was too fleeting to see what it was. Pete motioned that they should withdraw, using a come-hither hand gesture. At first, Brian looked reluctant and started to shake his head. Then he paused, nodded and they both crabbed back to their original position. There was about 30 minutes to go before sunset.

"Let's just wait 'till they leave," Pete said.
"Okay. Ya got any gum?"
Pete shook his head.

There was a lot of activity over the next few minutes. Johns heaved his agile body over the edge of the sarcophagus and slid inside. Moments later his hands appeared and held out a dark terracotta-looking covered jar, about the size of bowling pin. The sunburnt man took this greedily and placed it on the ground at his feet. Then the hands appeared again holding another jar and the sunburnt man repeated his actions from moments before.

To Pete, the two jars appeared to be more or less identical, and each contained inscriptions and maybe even pictures. Strangely, he thought he recognized something on the jars. Maybe it was a pattern that he knew. His eyes narrowed in concentration and then he recoiled in shock. *It couldn't be.*

There was a repeating pattern on both jars, and this was comprised of a single symbol. One quick glance at Brian's wide-open eyes and perplexed expression told Pete that he had recognized it as well. Pete reached over quickly and covered Brian's mouth with his hand to stop him from yelling out inadvertently. He knew that this was a possibility because he felt like doing the same thing himself. With his hand still over Brian's mouth, Pete shook his head imploringly, silently willing him to calm down. After a moment Brian started to breathe properly again. Pete took his hand away and began to breathe in and out normally himself. He realised that he had been holding his breath while he was trying to fathom what he was seeing.

The scientists prepared to leave the site just as the sun was setting over the western wall of the canyon. The fresh scent of mountain pine needles was now more noticeable as it wafted on the evening breeze through the valley. Brian and Pete watched the scientists and noted that the sunburnt man took something from the jars.

They're not supposed to do that, Pete thought. *That's not the way archaeology is done.*

As three of the men scrambled out of the pit, Johns stayed behind and placed the jars back in the structure and covered the opened edge of the sarcophagus with a tarpaulin. He then weighted this down with rocks and he scrambled out of the pit, nearly slipping on the soft chalk near the edge. He caught up with the others and the four of them moved off silently down the hill.

After waiting a few minutes to make sure that no one was coming back, the boys climbed down and skidded into the pit by the sarcophagus. Brian didn't hesitate and immediately pulled off the tarp so that they could see the image on the top more closely. Having done this, they climbed back up to the rim of the pit for a better view.

It was now twilight, but they could see the markings on the exposed long side of the sarcophagus since these were now etched in stark relief by the soft illumination of rising moon. They boys could see the figure on the lid but thought nothing more of it. They scrambled back down again to look at the sarcophagus more closely and climbed up onto the mound situated near the open corner. Then Pete switched on his flashlight and they both leant over and peered inside.

The boys recoiled in concert upon seeing the hideous thing inside, and then they bravely drew themselves back to see once again.

"Dang! What is it?" Brian uttered.

Pete said nothing. He couldn't speak.

The remains inside were amazingly intact for something that had been entombed for untold thousands of years. The body was laid straight and appeared to stretch the entire inner length of the sarcophagus, indicating that it was around 8 feet long. The broad shoulders appeared to be around two and a half feet wide. The leathery skull, which was directly below the boys' view, was around two feet in length, with a low sloping and unnaturally high forehead. The mouth was wide open as if it had died screaming. Inching further into the open end of the structure, the boys could see that the mouth contained not one, but two rows of large teeth in both the upper and lower jaws.

"That's just not right," Brian sputtered, gesturing in the general direction of the mouth.

Pete still said nothing but acknowledged his friend's denial with a quick nod.

They both continued to examine the contents of the gloomy container and the body inside.

The skin on the body's head was wrinkled and tanned and the hair was long and coarse, appearing to be a dull red colour. They could also see the enormous hands, and each contained exactly 6 fingers.

"Okay, that's wrong too," Brian said, shaking his head in denial.

The rest of the body was wrapped in what appeared to be a gum-covered fabric. Pete realised that this must have been used as part of some kind of mummification process. *This was a mummy! A giant mummy!*

There were other objects positioned in the case, including several intricately carved stone objects, seashells, a massive axe that appeared to be made of bronze, as well as the two jars they had seen earlier. The boys saw all of this in a time span of 10 seconds. It was only for this short span because Brian suddenly panicked and started to climb out of the pit. "Let's get outta here."

Pete started to follow but then he paused as he saw something shiny by the side of the sarcophagus. He stooped down for a better look and then blinked in surprise as he realised what it was. He picked it up quickly and stuffed the object in his pocket. Then he and Brian turned and made their way quickly down the hill together. In their haste, they hadn't remembered to replace the tarpaulin over the open end of the sarcophagus.

Early the next morning, they returned with their brothers, Chief Thompson and Deputy Chief Baker. It took the boys a long time to convince the Chief to come with them when they had approached him at the station, since he didn't believe much of their story. They told him everything except for the part about the symbols on the jars. Both boys had agreed that it was best if the others saw this for themselves.

"There ain't no such things as giants, boys," the Chief growled. "Just in fairy tales." Nevertheless, he had to check it out because something funny was going on up there in the hills last night. He had seen lots of lights but assumed that it was the Smithsonian bozos working late. "Alright, let's check it out. Come on Ned, get that fat behind of yours up outta that chair and put it to work protectin' the public."

"Yessa Chief," Ned exhorted with an inherent weariness. "My behind's all yours."

"Not a pleasant thought, Ned."

As they approached the pit, they knew something was wrong. There were footprints around the site, and the digging equipment was gone. Brian and Pete had both realised their mistake about leaving the tarpaulin off the sarcophagus in the middle of the night, but could do nothing about it. They were certain that when the Smithsonian scientists returned, they would have quickly ascertained that someone had been at the site after them.

Pete and Brian were both stunned to see that the heavy lid was completely removed, lying on the on the far side of the sarcophagus. They both ran, jumped up onto the mound and practically dived with their bodies halfway into the sarcophagus. "Empty!" they chorused in anguish.

"It was in there," Brian said in a frustrated tone as he pulled himself from the edge of the sarcophagus. "I swear it was there."

"Yeah Chief, it was there." Pete said still dangling halfway over the edge of the stone structure. "We're not making anything up."

Chief Thompson realised that the boys were genuinely upset about something, so he said calmly, "let me take a look."

The Chief and Ned both climbed onto the short mound and examined the inside of the stone structure. Looking closely, the sheriff noticed something odd. He squinted his eyes tight and then nodded imperceptibly. "You see it, Ned?" he asked casually without looking at his partner.

"What? I don't see anything Chief. It's completely empty."

"Not completely, Ned. Look closely," the Chief said

"I still don't see what you mean Chief," Ned exclaimed.

Pete also hopped up on the mound for a closer look and immediately realised what the Chief was talking about. "I see it Chief. A large stain in the bottom."

"That's right boy, you'd make a good cop someday. Now we don't know for sure if there was a body in there, but something sure was. Ned, you're a waste of space."

"Aw shucks Chief," Ned complained. "I saw the stain. I just didn't think it was important."

"Everything's important at a crime scene Ned."

"I didn't think this was a crime scene," Ned mumbled.

Pete said, "Chief, I think I know how the stain got there."

"Okay, let's hear it," the Chief said.

Pete explained. "It must have come from the resin used to mummify the body. It would have seeped into the rock and discoloured it."

"I'm not sure what was in there," the Chief said, shifting back into his authoritative mode again. "But it's not there now." *And whatever it was, it sure was big and shaped like a human being,* he thought to himself.

Chief Thompson, Ned and Pete climbed down from the unexcavated portion of the mound to join the others. Tony and Tim, who had been quiet up until this point, now scrambled up on the mound to check it out for themselves. After a moment of quiet contemplation, Tony turned back to look at Brian and Pete and said, "you guys swear that there was a giant body in there?"

"We swear," Brian and Pete said together.

Tim didn't say anything. He knew that his brother was too scared to lie.

"He's not lying, and neither am I," Pete said. "Take a look at this," Pete said as he climbed up onto the raised level of earth past where Tim and Tony were standing on the far side of the sarcophagus. "This is what the giant looked like," he said as he pointed to the image on the massive fallen lid.

The rest of the group followed Pete and fanned out around the lid. Collectively, they all opened their mouths in awe except for Chief Thompson. Something else about the situation bothered him. He couldn't figure out why the scientists had removed the body and the tomb contents. *Were the Smithsonian clowns trying to hide something? Had they found something of importance buried up here?* He had some telephone calls to make.

Two days later Chief Thompson called the Smithsonian Institution and asked to speak to the man in charge of the excavation in Lompoc. The receptionist told him that Dr Chatterwick only made a brief appearance after he returned to the Institution the day before, but hadn't been back since that time. The Chief then asked if any of the other members of the team were available and was given the same news.

The Chief was a details person and didn't like to let anything, no matter how insignificant, go unquestioned. "What about the fourth man on the expedition? I'm sorry, I didn't catch his name."

Her next words caused the hair on his arms to stand up. "There was no fourth man. It was just the three of them."

"But, I saw him."

17

"Sorry Chief Thompson. I meant there was no fourth man from the Smithsonian. Whoever this was, he must have been from another institution. It often happens on projects where someone is seeking the Smithsonian's archaeological expertise. I just don't have any information on who that would have been in this case."

"Okay," the Chief sighed but still not satisfied. "Could you ensure that when any of them returns that you have them contact me? I need to follow up on a few issues."

"Sure will, Officer Thompson."

After the call, the Chief still felt uneasy. His instincts told him there was something wrong, but he couldn't figure out what it was. And then, as is common in a policeman's life, over the next few weeks he became busy on other projects. The case file gradually shifted to the bottom of the pile, and he soon forgot all about it.

As it turned out, he never received a telephone call back from any member of Chatterwick's team. However, this was not too unusual considering that they were all dead.

Chapter 1

Cambridge, England
June 21, 2007

Jim Hawkins didn't care that he was about to die. Death would be a welcome release after what he had been through over the past two hours. Almost every muscle in his body ached. He could feel his racing heartbeat throbbing in his temples. He had been punched, kicked, stepped on and smothered. His entire body was covered in bruises and abrasions, and now he couldn't breathe.

He was too old for this kind of punishment. Right now, he should be sitting on the sofa in front of the telly watching Manchester United take on Chelsea like the other 10 million-or-so football fans in this country. Instead, he had chosen death by torture.

He strained upward through the deep muscular pain racking his shoulder and wiped the sweat from his forehead. Now he could see again. But he needn't have bothered. He should have known they would still be there. The four of them had positioned themselves carefully around him to cut off any attempted escape.

He made his move. He thrust his right hand out toward the face of his nearest attacker. The speed of the sudden movement belied his presumed shattered condition and enabled him to catch the man momentarily off guard. The stalker instinctively protected his face using one of his heavily muscled forearms as a shield.

Perfect!

Hawkins parried the man's thick wrist and executed a powerful neck-breaking, clothesline assault which resulted in the man being flung heels-over-head into another of the attackers. The crushing impact knocked both men down but, to Hawkins' disquiet, they managed to regain their footing almost immediately. The man with the large forearms rubbed his neck and smiled at Hawkins. His eyes seemed to say *you'll pay for that* as he shuffled forward past his three partners and back into the fray. The others followed his lead and moved to spread out their formation with the intention of trapping their victim.

Hawkins inhaled deeply to gather some much-needed air. Then he hurled a stiff right cross toward the face of the man moving in on him from the left flank. But Hawkins had no intention of striking the man. He was trying to provoke the right response. Something he could use to his advantage.

His gambit worked. As the man brought up his arm to block the punch, Hawkins aborted his strike and grasped the man's wrist firmly. Then he twisted his hips, stepped in with his right foot and crushed the man's fingers in the vice-like grip of his left hand. The man went down and slapped the ground, in a frantic attempt to escape the sudden pain.

Hawkins quickly stepped behind the man without releasing his grip so he could use him as a human shield against the others. This strategy would only work for a moment. But a moment was all he needed.

Then one of the men managed to manoeuvre around his fallen comrade and let loose a pile-driving punch towards Hawkins' midsection. Hawkins released the man on the ground and was able to avoid the blow. He pivoted to the left and grabbed the man's extended wrist. Without pausing, he brought his other hand palm-side up beneath the man's fingers and then bent his assailant's wrist and arm backwards. While keeping his hold on the man, he stepped powerfully at a 90-degree angle and propelled him towards the man with the big forearms who had been trying to move back into an attacking position.

But now Hawkins was starting to feel winded again. And his attackers were clearly not going away. The man that he had just sent flying hit the ground, rolled to his feet, and turned back towards the action while 'Forearms' moved quickly to his side. The other two men angled wide, flanking Hawkins. Then, one of them managed to grab him by the shoulder. Just as Hawkins attempted to move, he was grabbed around the neck by another man. Then they were all on top of him.

He was relieved it was over. He was completely exhausted and found he couldn't breathe properly. He also felt that at any moment he would puke his guts out. None of this was surprising considering that the men were currently attempting to crush the vital juices from his body by piling on top of him. There was also the overwhelming combination of sweat, bad breath, feet, and other non-identifiable odours emanating from the tightly packed bodies of the four men.

"Stop!" a booming voice commanded.

There was a moment of stunned silence except for the wheezing of Hawkins' laboured breathing. Then, the four men began to unstack themselves systematically from his squashed body. Hawkins felt like an insect that had just been splattered onto the windshield of a speeding lorry. The man with the big forearms was the last to step away. As he did so, he added insult to injury by pinching Hawkins playfully on the right bum cheek. "Nice going you crazy Aussie bastard," the man whispered.

After what seemed like several minutes, but was only a few seconds, Hawkins slowly peeled himself up from the floor, with all the dignity he could muster. As he was rising, he noticed that the world was spinning just a bit faster than normal. Then he stooped with his hands on his knees and once again considered the need to vomit.

"Okay. We'll give him a moment to get his breath back and move on to the weapons," the voice announced without emotion.

He groaned inwardly as he turned slowly and gazed through eyes blurred by sweat toward the voice. He focussed on a serious-looking, solidly built man with hands that looked like they belonged on a 10-foot giant. The man's features were hard as if chiselled from granite and his dark eyes regarded Hawkins as one might look at a fly floating in their bowl of soup. But there was one striking inconsistency about this man that might make an outsider stop and consider that something strange was going on. The man with the big hands was dressed in thick, white pyjamas and a pleated navy-blue, long skirt.

As he slowly began to breathe normally again, Hawkins scanned the room to take in the scores of other men and women who, strangely enough, were all kneeling in straight ranks along the edge of the mat as if emulating Japanese Samurai warriors. Like the large man before them, they were all attired in similar pyjama outfits and some were also wearing the skirts. The pyjamas were Japanese keikogis, or gis for short, and the skirts were actually traditional wide-pleated trousers called hakamas. The hakamas were only worn by those who had achieved the rank of black belt or above.

To the untutored, all of this might appear to be the gathering of a group of extreme wackos in the midst of a kinky adult pyjama party. But to those in the know, it was the Annual General Meeting of the British Aikido Association. Hawkins was more inclined to agree with the 'wacko' hypothesis.

Aikido is a modern Japanese art that teaches its practitioners to harmonize with and redirect any attacking force, no matter how powerful. Hawkins always smiled at the oft-used analogy which compared aikido to the way a flexible willow bends and yields to the force of the storm while the stiff oak tree may break as it attempts to resist the wind. This was all very useful until someone came at you with a big stick or a knife. That was about to happen right now.

"Okay Jim, grab your bokken and pick a partner," the granite-chiselled man commanded. Sensei Jack Major was currently the highest-ranking aikido expert in the United Kingdom with a 6th-degree black belt. He was an imposing figure and made no attempt to hide this. In fact, Hawkins sometimes felt that this man thrived on his ability to intimidate and unnerve people. "Let's see you perform the kumitachi. And remember…keep it lively!"

Hawkins moved on his not-so-steady legs to the centre of the mat accompanied by Richard Jameson, the muscular man with big forearms. After a moment of silence, they began to carry out the 5 kumitachi, or sword-against-sword techniques. The entire room of aikido practitioners watched as the two men tried to clobber each other with the wooden swords. Both moved almost quicker than the eye could follow with a dynamic swirling of their hakamas as they lunged, turned and parried using their bokkens at a blistering pace. The dull clunking sound of wood against wood echoed loudly throughout the gym along with periodic piercing shouting noises, called kiais.

Hawkins was the better swordsman, with an electric sharp energy to all of his movements. However, the objective was not to win. It was to blend and harmonize, while maintaining perfect technique.

"Stop! Now grab your jos for the kumijo techniques," Sensei Major said, sounding almost as if he were falling asleep. However, this was far from the truth. He had been following every movement intently and was more than impressed by the crisp precision and display of techniques.

Hawkins and Jameson now returned to the mat with the jos, which were basically hard wooden fighting staffs approximately 4 feet in length. Now the audience watched as the two men whirled their jos through the air like low-flying helicopters to clash and absorb and redirect the force of each movement. Again, the voluminous room resounded with wood clunking and smacking noises as they executed their strikes and thrusts aiming for heads, midsections, and knees. There would be dire consequences if someone made a mistake. Neither of them did.

Then there followed an extremely dangerous series of tests with Hawkins carrying out empty-handed techniques against an attacker who came at him with a real knife. Hawkins only made one mistake when he nearly grabbed the knife blade instead of the attacker's wrist as he had intended. When Sensei Major finally stopped the class and made the announcement that Hawkins had passed, the sounds of clapping and repeated calls of, "yeah Jim!" and, "youdaman!" were heard across the mat.

Although Hawkins was overjoyed with the result and grinned stupidly at his supporters, he couldn't help feeling that he really needed a place to lie down.

Although Hawkins liked to believe that his life was currently taking the non-violent path to enlightenment, this had not always been the case. In fact, at one time he had been involved a violent situation of terrifying proportions. As a young man just out of school, he had joined the First Battalion Australian Commando

Regiment, and took part in a covert mission during the first Gulf war, a mission that was never officially publicised. This was because as far as the international community was aware, Australian forces were only deployed in this conflict as part of the multi-national naval and ground support operations, under the auspices of the United Nations. Officially, Australia's war in the Gulf was uneventful and there were no casualties. Unofficially, two Australians commandos, who weren't even supposed to be there, were killed in action.

On a joint operation with three members of the British Special Air Services, Hawkins and two other Australian commandos successfully infiltrated enemy territory and provided critical intelligence on a potential biochemical weapons plant in the desert near Basra that was thought to be developing a weapons-grade variety of the smallpox virus. Hawkins' specialty was in the use of electronic surveillance and tracking devices which he and some of the other team members managed to place at several strategic locations in and around the site. Once the true nature of the plant was identified using the surveillance equipment, the tracking devices were initialized pinpointing the target for destruction by a stealth bombing mission.

For Hawkins and the others, the problem occurred during the ex-filtration stage of the mission. Nine miles from their recovery zone, they encountered and were pinned down by 30 to 40 Iraqi ground forces who were heavily armed. In the ensuing fire fight, more than one dozen of the Iraqi soldiers were killed along with both of Hawkins' compatriots and one of the British soldiers. Just when it seemed that all was lost, Hawkins and the remaining two Brits were rescued by two US Apache attack helicopters that erased the remaining hostile forces in a fierce air-to-ground extermination.

Hawkins had nightmares for years over the horror of the battle and the incredible loss of life, on both sides. One of the surviving Brits was named Richard Jameson who would later become one of Hawkins' best friends when he moved to Cambridge to take up his post-doctoral position in the Department of Archaeology. Through some unspoken agreement, neither of them had ever discussed their experience in Iraq. They both decided to forget about that stage of their lives and move on. Then Hawkins had the bright idea that they should take up aikido as a possible route to this quest. His friend had agreed wholeheartedly. From that point onwards, Hawkins believed that he had left his violent past behind him.

The Prince Regent is a popular pub frequented by tourists in Cambridge during the summer months because of its prime location between Regent Street and the expansive green called Parker's Piece. However, on this night, most of the space within and just outside the pub had been taken over by the aikido group who were carrying on in the usual tradition of celebrating heroes and success by drinking themselves senseless. Some were still dressed in their pyjamas and, *ipso facto*, had clearly not even showered for the occasion.

His Sensei, sporting a rising sun headband, was up to his usual parlour tricks of reading palms of the aikido students and other patrons of the pub. Hawkins didn't really believe in this sort of thing but his teacher seemed to be on top form by offering up snippets of very specific information to his bewildered subjects. Things that he couldn't possibly have known about. Although Hawkins had seen this on many occasions, he still wondered what the trick was.

Trying unsuccessfully to maintain a low profile, Hawkins had already received several congratulatory cuddles and sloppy kisses from female members of the club and, to his dismay, even from some of the males. By 11:00 P.M., his body and mind were in severe pain from the day's events and so he begged off with a quiet goodbye to Richard and some of his other friends in the immediate vicinity. His Sensei gave him a thunderous pat on the back and remarked, "you dun good today, Jim. You truly deserved to get your second dan grade. Besides, your weapons were phemon…phenonem…um…quite good."

Hawkins was pleased to note that his teacher was not completely immune to the effects of alcohol. Wincing from his newest pain, a dull ache in his left shoulder where the man had 'patted' him, he said, "thank you. It was the closet I've ever come to death without actually dying."

"Oh that was nothing. Just wait 'til the next test," Major remarked.

"I can hardly wait," Hawkins said as he made his way out of the pub. As he left the building, few of the remaining aikido group even noticed his departure as they carried on in pursuit of alcoholic oblivion.

Stepping onto the pavement of Regent Street, Hawkins was partly revived by the cool night air. The noise of the pedestrians and light traffic brought him back to reality after the false sense of security of the pub environment. He noticed that the foreign language students were out in force and late night lovers were cuddling in earnest, lightly buffeted by a summer breeze scented with jasmine.

He turned and headed away from the town centre and trudged in the direction of his home. Before long, he was moving past the towering majesty of the gothic-style Catholic Church of Our Lady and the English Martyrs on the corner of Hills Road and Lensfield Road. Hawkins had always thought that the building looked menacing in the night-time gloom. After a 10-minute walk, he eventually crossed over Station Road which led to the busy Cambridge Train Station and he walked on past the family run Centennial Hotel.

After passing several houses, he turned and mounted the three short steps to his mid-terrace three storey Victorian townhouse where he lived alone. He groaned as he inevitably tried the wrong key in the lock, fumbled in the darkness for the correct one and then dropped the whole lot in a loud jingle on the steps below. After searching on his hands and knees in darkness for half a minute, he found the keys, inserted the correct one and entered through his solid wooden door and closed it behind him. The lights were off as he had left them. Just as he was reaching for the light switch, a massive dark shape lunged at him from out of the darkness.

Chapter 2

Cambridge, England
June 21, 2007

Hawkins was knocked back into the door as two massive thumps struck both sides of his chest simultaneously. Then he felt the hot, stinking breath of his attacker followed by something very wet slapping him in the face.

"Brandy! Get down girl!" he said strictly. "Haven't I told you about a gazillion times not to jump up on people." He pulled himself upright from his slumped position against the door and flicked the light on. The dog had settled down now, but it was clear that she wanted some attention.

Brandy was a fawn-coloured Great Dane that Hawkins had raised from a puppy to the present 195 pounds of solid muscle. She was now two years-old and was eating him out of house and home.

"Brandy, what am I going to do with you?" he said ruffling his dog's natural floppy ears. "You want something to eat?"

The dog emitted a *woof* from the depths of her throat and wagged her tail. This was one of the few circumstances that led to the massive animal eliciting some kind of bark – feeding time. The only other occasion was when she insisted upon some quality playtime with the Frisbee.

Hawkins wasn't even sure if Brandy knew what the word 'food' meant or if she merely responded to the tone. She certainly didn't seem to know the words for sit, lie down, find me a girlfriend, or anything useful. Nevertheless, Brandy was probably his best companion.

There had been a few women in his life, but none had been able to put up with his lifestyle. At least that was the most common reason. Sometimes he just wondered if they thought he was a boffin and would therefore have nothing of real interest to discuss like what happened on *Eastenders* last night or the latest scandal on *Celebrity Big Brother*. He had given up worrying about it though. He was still hopeful that Miss Right would come along eventually.

As an archaeologist specializing in ancient civilizations, he was the proverbial globetrotting academic. Apart from his teaching duties at the university, and occasional local field research trips, he spent more time in other countries than he did in the United Kingdom. In his home country of Australia, he had completed his undergraduate degree in archaeology at the University of Sydney, where he developed a fascination for prehistoric civilizations. Then after his brief stint in the Australian Commandos he pursued his interest in archaeology in the United States, where he worked towards a PhD degree at the University of California, Los Angeles, specializing on the effects of climate change on ancient civilizations. After finishing his PhD, he relocated to the University of Cambridge in the United Kingdom, where he became an affiliated lecturer and academic researcher in Old World civilizations.

Now, more than a decade later, his field research had taken him to more than 60 countries in Europe, Asia and Africa, including a handful of Central and South American countries. Recently, he had been involved in investigating the artefacts associated with the remains of the three-foot-tall human-like species dubbed 'the Hobbit,' after JRR Tolkien's fictional face of dwarves. These had been found in 2003 in the Liang Bua limestone cave on the Indonesian island of Flores. There were at least 7 of these miniature individuals dating from 94,000 to as recently as 13,000 years ago. This made the Hobbit the longest known surviving relative of modern humans, lasting even beyond Neanderthal man who disappeared around 30,000 ago. Because the remains of *Homo floresiensis* were so young, geologically speaking, they were not even fossilized. In fact, scientists were hopeful that some of the long leg and arm bones could even yield DNA and provide new evidence on human evolutionary history.

Scans of one of the female skulls allowed scientists to digitally reconstruct the long-decayed brain of *Homo floresiensis*. At around 400 cubic centimetres, the brain size of this species was less than one-third of that found in normal sized humans. Despite the small brain size, the possibility that this species was intelligent was supported by the finding that a region of the brain normally associated with self-awareness, part of the prefrontal cortex, was around the same size in *Homo floresiensis* as in modern day *Homo sapiens*. Likewise, the unusually expanded temporal lobe area of the brain suggested a high level of cognitive processing, and the sophistication of the stone tools and other artefacts that had been found along with the remains of these creatures had surprised some scientists.

Even more intriguing was the fact that Flores islanders told detailed stories about the existence of little people called the Ebu Gogo, loosely translated as "the grandmother who eats anything". The Ebu Gogo were described as small and hairy and prone to murmuring to each other in a strange language. They were also known to repeat anything said around them in parrot-like fashion. Interestingly, the latest legends dated to around 100 years ago, raising the possibility that some remnant of this small species of humans might still exist in the unexplored rainforest of Flores or other Indonesian islands.

Hawkins ruffled Brandy's floppy ears once more and made his way to the kitchen to get her some food. She went through a 25-pound bag of dry dog food every two weeks, and he occasionally gave in to her voracious appetite by providing other tasty treats such as raw beef steak, lamb, eggs and even cottage cheese.

"Brandy, you eat enough for a family of saltwater crocs," he said as he poured approximately one pound of the chow into her fishbowl-sized doggy dish. She wagged her tail and gave him that adoring, lovable look that was typical around feeding time. He picked up the dish and walked with it to the conservatory at the back of the house, which had been taken over by the dog from early days. He set the massive bowl down in front of the French doors. The giant dog sauntered over to the dish and began to tuck in.

He left his faithful pooch to her dinner and made his way upstairs to the sounds of, *wumpff, chomp, chomp*, emanating from the conservatory. He noticed that his legs still felt wobbly as he scaled the steep steps. He was approximately halfway up when he suddenly remembered something.

He stopped, leaned back down the stairs with his hand on the side rail and called out, "Brandy! Don't tip the bowl over this time!"

Silence.

Then after a three second pause, *wumpff, chomp, wumpff.*

He shook his head in helpless acceptance and continued up the stairs to his bedroom. He started to undress when his weariness suddenly took over and he flopped face-first onto his king-sized mattress. He immediately fell into a deep sleep.

He awoke suddenly and bolted upright to what sounded like a scud missile coming through his bedroom window. When his senses cleared, he realised that the noise was the telephone ringing. He would have to turn that damn ring tone down. As the mental fog of deep sleep rapidly dissipated, he turned to look at the bedside digital clock display. It was 6:02 A.M. He had been asleep for almost 6 hours but he still felt like death warmed up.

He fumbled for and picked up the telephone receiver. "Hello," he said in voice that was halfway between irritated and sleepy.

"Jim?" a familiar voice said. "Hope I didn't wake you."

"No, I had to get up to answer the phone anyway," he joked, now that he realised who he was talking to, David Englehart, his PhD student.

"You okay?" David asked cautiously. "You sound a bit more geriatric than usual."

"Well, I'm not quite ready for the old age pensioner's home if that's what you mean. Besides, you did wake me up at 6:00 in the morning. I am not usually at my best 'till 3:00 or 4:00 in the afternoon."

"This might spark your interest though. We've just broken through into another layer on the dig site in Wandlebury."

Hawkins was suddenly wide awake. "And?" he asked tentatively.

"Jim, this looks like it could be the big one."

Chapter 3

Gog Magog Hills, Cambridgeshire
June 22, 2007

The early morning silence was shattered by the deep rumbling growl of the 1969 Chevrolet Camaro Super Sport that glided brazenly down Hills Road. A small cluster of wood pigeons scattered clumsily in abrupt flight as the gaudy American car bore down upon their position. The few pedestrians, who were out at that time of day, turned their heads one by one to stare at the sleek lines of the impressive burnished brown car, with its shining chrome intake vents on the bonnet and thick white go-faster stripes along the sides. A withered blue-haired woman walking a Jack Russell Terrier snorted in disgust at the noticeable Doppler shift of the deep purring engine noise as the car went past her and carried on dismissively down the road. She was tempted to give the driver, who was obviously rude and thoughtless, a piece of her mind.

If Jim Hawkins was aware of the effect that his thunderous flashy automobile was inflicting on pigeons and people, he didn't appear to be concerned. This was because he was lost in the moment, which he liked to think of as the perfect synthesis of man and machine. Not many other people thought of driving a car in the same way, but Jim Hawkins was not an ordinary person. And the 1969 Camaro was no ordinary automobile.

He had acquired the unique classic sports car from an American serviceman who was on a short stay at RAF Lakenheath. Lieutenant Grant Collins had shipped the Camaro over from Arizona but decided not to go to the trouble of shipping it back to the US when his tour of duty was over. Because he and Hawkins had become fast friends through frequenting the same pubs, and he knew of Hawkins' fond appreciation for classic cars, he sold it to him at a bargain price. Since that time, Hawkins had kept the Camaro in finely tuned condition and polished regularly.

After the brief drive down the Cambridge-Haverhill Road, Hawkins turned into the small unpaved car park on the south-western edge of the Wandlebury Estate. Having left the main thoroughfare for the quiet country road, he felt as if he were suddenly intruding on the sanctity of the grounds, especially in his less-than-subtle vehicle.

The Wandlebury estate contained the remnants of an Iron Age circular hill fort, surrounded by a 110-acre country park, popular with the locals and tourists alike for its walking trails and wildlife. But more than this, the hill fort has long been the subject of many legends usually centring round the giants Gog and Magog, after whom the hills took their name. Stories were even told that the remains of these giants were buried nearby. Another theory put forward by Iman Wilkens' book *Where Troy Once Stood* suggested that Wandlebury and surrounding areas were the actual battlegrounds for the ancient siege of Troy and not Turkey, opposing the claims of Heinrich Schliemann's famous archaeological discovery and Homer's descriptions in *The Iliad*. As for its early history, Neolithic and Bronze Age artefacts have been found in areas surrounding the hill, although the exact nature of the people and settlements before this time are largely unknown. It was because of their interest in this time-period that Hawkins and his team of archaeologists were carrying out an intensive excavation there.

Hawkins eased the Camaro to a stop in the nearly empty car park, oblivious to the marvelling stares from the three people who were waiting for him. David Englehart was smiling broadly as Hawkins pushed the door open and climbed out of the Camaro with an audible groan. Based on David's expression, Hawkins surmised that there had already been some discussion prior to his arrival and that probably had something to do with the amusing combination of martial arts and the elderly. Even though Hawkins was technically still a young man at 39-years of age, he supposed that to David and the rest of the younger generation, he was as good as extinct.

David had an athletic youthful build and stood just under 6 feet tall, with dark tousled hair and a perpetual cheeky grin on his face. Apart from his PhD work in the lab and in the field, he spent most of his time at the gym working out. It hadn't escaped Hawkins' notice that exercise and other sporting activities seemed to be a common pursuit of many students these days. He supposed that this was because most of them needed to achieve some balance with the academic side of their lives. David had participated in most of the usual physical activities in his 25-year lifetime with a heavy emphasis on the combative sports of wrestling and boxing. As a teenager, he even had a decent amateur boxing record with 30 wins and 4 losses. Hawkins knew that David was proud of the fact that he had never been knocked out. Hawkins had jokingly told his student that this was only because of his exceedingly-thick skull.

Hawkins knew the man standing next to David very well, as they had been collaborators over the last 10 years. Zoran Radovic was a geologist from the former Yugoslav republic of Croatia. He was a lanky 6'5" with a rugged angular nose, dark hair, and a two-day growth of stubble on his chin. Hawkins had met him several years before as part of an international team comprised of Croatians, Italians, French, Germans, British and Americans carrying out extensive excavations at a 5,000-year-old Sumerian burial site near Eridu in southern Iraq. They had formed an almost instant liking for each other. A solid friendship had naturally developed between them when Zoran came to England and joined the Geoarchaeology subgroup of the Archaeology Department at Cambridge University.

Not long after his arrival in Cambridge, Zoran was seeking an inexpensive, effective means for getting around the city which was constantly congested with traffic. So, Hawkins introduced him to the concept of the motorcycle. He helped Zoran to purchase a banana yellow Triumph Daytona 900 and gave him a few riding lessons. Zoran was proud when he managed to pass his test on the first attempt and became a licensed motorcyclist. Now, he and the Triumph were never seen far from each other. Zoran even went so far as to refer to it as his Dragi, which translated in Serbo-Croatian as 'sweetheart.' He was now leaning with one elbow on the motorcycle and smiling towards

Hawkins. He held his black and yellow striped helmet in his gloved hands and was still wearing his matching leathers.

The final member of the team was a visiting 32-year-old American molecular archaeologist named Lori Davis. She had clearly grown up along a beach somewhere in Southern California based on her looks alone. She was tall, strawberry blonde and still maintained a slight suntan even following her first dark, cold, and drizzly winter in Cambridge. Her face displayed soft features, and this was juxtaposed by the sharp discerning gaze of her deep blue eyes. Hawkins furtively noted that she also looked fit, most likely from regular surfing and swimming as part of the beach lifestyle. However, any misconception of her as the typical surfer type disappeared when she spoke. Hawkins had heard that she could also be a bit abrasive towards male scientists who failed to afford her the respect she deserved. She was already an authority in her chosen field and clearly knew the subject better than most long-standing academics.

Molecular archaeology involves the analysis of DNA and other biological molecules such as proteins, recovered from animal and plant remains, to aid in reconstructing the past. The key to success was in the careful collection and preparation of the biological specimens to avoid contamination or destruction of the samples, which would otherwise render any molecular analyses useless or misleading. Lori was present on this occasion to ensure that did not happen.

Hawkins didn't know her that well, but he had a lot of respect for her sharp intellect and trusted that she was an indispensable member of the team.

"You're movin' kinda stiffly there Jim," David teased, not being able to resist the verbal jab at his supervisor.

"Nothing that a whole-body transplant couldn't fix," Hawkins retorted. "Anyway, let's have a little respect please. You really need me to be in the best of moods if you want me to look over the next draft of your thesis."

David smiled. He knew when to shut up.

"What happened, Dr Hawkins?" Lori asked in a neutral tone. "Have you had an accident?"

Maybe she isn't so abrasive after all, Hawkins thought.

Zoran answered for him. "I think my friend is ironically suffering from the aftereffects of a lesson in the way of harmony – the art of aikido. Did the grading go well, Jim?"

"Well, I passed," Hawkins said. "But I wouldn't say with flying colours."

"He's just being modest," David said. "I'm sure he left them all knocked senseless and bleeding on the mat."

"It was the other way around, actually," Hawkins responded.

"It sounds the same as any other martial art," Lori offered. "It seems to me that they all just promote violence as a solution to any problem."

"But aikido is not your typical martial art," Hawkins responded hastily, taken off guard by Lori's generalization. "Personally, I enjoy it more for this spiritual side and not the...uh...martial part." His argument sounded weak, even to him.

"That's just as lame as men saying they only look at Playboy for the articles," Lori stated flatly.

David made an attempt to come to Hawkins' rescue. "We do...I mean not me personally...of course I don't look at Playboy at all...I just... oh crap!"

"Solid point," Hawkins commented.

David looked sheepish.

"Well, let's get to it then." Hawkins couldn't think of anything else to say.

The scientists made their way silently around the circular trail encompassing the remains of the hill fort. Then, after traversing approximately one-third of the circumference, they left the path and approached the site situated on the far side of a small clearing. They arrived to find the three undergraduate assistants, who had been waiting at the site for them, in the middle of an animated discussion at the near end of a freshly excavated pit.

"I'll bet you it was put here by the same people who built Stonehenge," remarked Gary, the most vocal of the students.

"Naw. I think its Trojan," commented Craig, although with less confidence than his fellow student. "Maybe we'll find Achilles or Hector buried in there."

"Achilles wasn't even Trojan, you numpty," Gary retorted.

"It might even be a woman," interjected Nancy, a slender Irish girl with freckles and flaming red hair. "Most ancient civilizations also buried females in tombs, you know."

"The first rule of any science…," Hawkins announced as he approached from behind them, "…is to let the theories come after the facts, and not before. Let's just see what we've got first."

"Sorry, Dr H," Gary said. "I guess we got carried away."

"Yeah, we're all just excited by the discovery," Nancy added.

Now Hawkins felt guilty for his well-intended but slightly chastising remarks. After all, the three graduates had probably carried out most of the hard work here and had done an excellent job of excavating the site. "Can't say I blame you –" his voice trailed off as his eyes took in the object on the far end of the pit for the first time. After lingering another moment to absorb the fine details of the massive stone and earth-covered structure, he said, "let's take a look at what you've found so far."

As a group, they moved across to the tables containing the containing the artefacts recovered from different levels of the excavation. "Let's use the site map as our guide to go through this layer by layer," Hawkins suggested. "David, can you do the honours?"

David nodded and immediately reached to the nearest table for a large folder containing several maps, each showing the successive levels of the excavation. It was also evident from the presence of the Canon EOS Digital camera near the folder that the excavators had made a photographic record as each layer of the site was uncovered. David opened the map folder and withdrew a 24" X 24" clear sheet of Permatrace paper, which he then placed over the same sized sheet of white graph paper containing a light blue grid pattern for orientation purposes.

Then he cleared his throat and began his explanation. "This is the primary map corresponding to the first stage of the dig. As you know, this area was identified as a potential site after several aerial surveys revealed what appeared to be a circular mound in this undeveloped area between Wandlebury Hill and the edge of the Gog Magog Golf Course. This is the feature here," he said pointing with his forefinger at a faint dashed circular figure in the far corner of the map. The others crowded around him for better viewing. "It appears to be around 20 feet in diameter. We confirmed the results of the aerial survey using the magnetometer, which showed a decreased magnetic susceptibility of the overlying soil above the suspected area of the...uh...tomb."

David flipped through the Permatrace sheets to pull out another map marked with various features. "Surrounding the mound in the shallow surface layers we found what appears to be fragments of Roman pottery, a few Roman coins and small bone fragments, probably from birds and reptiles. We also found several pollen grains." He systematically pointed out the locations of the objects on the map and gestured toward the contents of the first tray to indicate the actual items.

He pulled out another map and said, "then, at a depth of around two feet, we found several iron objects including a ring-headed pin, knives and what looks like the head of a hammer. As before, we found pollen grains and a few other biological materials that could be used for dating purposes. Then a little deeper we found similar artefacts including a bronze axe head and what looks like part of a knife. None of this is too dissimilar from the Bronze and Iron Age artefacts that have already been found surrounding the hill fort itself."

He drew out the final sheet of paper and continued his explanation. "Then we reached what appeared to be a late Neolithic Period layer at around four feet down where we found several polished bone needles and pottery shards, some stone tools including grinding implements and axe heads, flint knives and part of a crude bronze axe head. At all levels we used the water flotation technique on selected samples of soil to identify any biological artefacts including light bones, insects, charred wood, and seeds. There should be plenty of material in there alone to keep Lori busy doing her molecular thing for weeks."

"Looks reasonable so far," Hawkins said. "Closer scrutiny of some of the artefacts that you found in the descending strata should tell us more about what we are dealing with here. However, I would say that this appears to be the strongest evidence so far of Neolithic occupation at this site. What's your best guess for an approximate date associated with the finds in the lowest level?" Hawkins asked.

David answered, sounding almost apologetic. "Of course, we will have to wait for the pollen grain, seed analyses and radiocarbon dating for a more precise date, but I would guess that it's around 5,500 years old."

"I agree Jim," interjected Zoran. "That fits with this being a megalithic passage tomb that was commonplace for that time," he said gesturing toward the mound. "Although, it would be the first one ever found in this part of the UK."

Hawkins turned to look at the structure. "How much of it would you say is below ground level?"

David answered. "We thought you would notice that. It appears that the original craftsmen who built the tomb dug down into the earth to a depth of around 6-feet before assembling the stone slabs on the top. You can see what we believe to be the foundations of the structure in the intersecting internal trench that we dug along the side there." David pointed at a deep narrow trench which appeared to reveal the lowest levels of the stony mound. "And this section houses the entrance passage," David said, now pointing to a protruding section of the mound.

Hawkins now looked closely and scrutinized the large stone slab covering the entrance slope. The massive stone appeared to lie at an angle of around 30 degrees from the horizontal. It appeared to be a solid piece of granite approximately three feet wide and four feet long. "Zoran, how heavy do you think that entrance slab is?" Hawkins asked deferring to the geologist's area of expertise.

"Well, we think it is around a half metre in depth, so that would make it around 1,400 kilograms. Or, for those of you that still use the imperial weights system, around 3,000 pounds."

Hawkins responded by stating the obvious. "We're going to need help."

By 11:00 A.M., the temperature at the site was a scorching 90 degrees Fahrenheit. All of the workers in the exposed pit were wearing Australian bush hats except for Lori who sported a San Diego Padres baseball cap that was turned around backwards on her head. The archaeologists had also enlisted the aid of four construction workers that were often employed by the University during the winter months for archaeological digs requiring additional manpower. Such projects usually involved the use of large earth moving equipment including diggers and bulldozers. These machines are normally used for sites which are buried deeply to remove the overlying layers of earth or rubble that are of no archaeological interest. Once this has been accomplished, the more precise slower paced work of the archaeologists can begin.

However, it is more difficult to find this kind of help during the summer months because most construction teams are too busy with their normal work. Hawkins was able to get past this problem by calling on one of the regular crews that he had worked with over the years. It also didn't hurt that the leader of this team was Hawkins' wartime buddy, Richard Jameson.

Richard and his team didn't need to use any heavy equipment on this occasion. Instead, they employed a system of crow bars and brute strength to gradually ease the top end of the entrance slab several inches up and away from the mound. The hardest part of this task was to get the slab moving in the first place since it was wedged so tightly into place, having been in its current position for over 5,000 years. At the point when the slab was sufficiently elevated, the workers tapped in several thin wooden wedges to secure it in place. Once this was accomplished, it became an easy matter for them to steadily increase the angle of the opening using their crow bars and then by tapping in other wedges of increasing thickness. Then after a few more mighty tugs with the wrenches, the inner face of the stone slab finally cleared the edge of the tomb.

After this, the workers easily manoeuvred the slab into an upright position against the angled stone block below. The stone did not fall through because the original builders had cut a supporting inner sill into the slabs surrounding the entranceway. The gaping dark entrance was now exposed for the first time in over 5 millennia.

"That's great guys," Hawkins called out from the edge of the pit, trying to stay out of the way. David, Zoran, Lori, and the others were fanned out surrounding him so that they could all observe the proceedings. David and Zoran were also busy making copious notes on this basic method of tomb entry, each focussing on their own respective areas of expertise. "Now see if you can walk it back at least a few feet from the entrance to allow easy access," Hawkins called out to the workers.

Richard nodded and issued the instructions to his crew, imagining that he was captain of a pirate ship at sea. "Alright lads, put yer backs into it."

This phase of the process was relatively simple. Richard and his crew were able to rock and walk the slab away from the mound and onto the main floor of the pit, which the archaeologists had dug to the same level as the bottom of the entranceway for this very purpose. Now the repeated sounds of strained grunting and the heavy thumping noise of shifting stone could be heard as Richard called out the cadence to his crew, "one, two, three, heave, ho." Using this method, they manhandled the slab all the way to the side of the pit.

"Great job you guys," Hawkins said marvelling at how easily they had moved the large stone block. "There's a case of Australian lager in the cooler over by the artefact tables. Why don't you have a few cold ones, chill out and relax for a while. We'll need you again to seal it back up at the end of the day."

"Australian lager?" Richard retorted. "What ever happened to good ole English beer? I can't believe you brought that cheap kangaroo swill."

"I'm trying to broaden your horizons, you Pommy lowlife," Hawkins tried to reason with his friend. "Anyway, thanks a lot. You men did a great job. We'll take it from here."

"Yeah, okay." Richard said like a small child who had just been told that they weren't going to Disneyland after all. As he and his men climbed from the pit towards the cooler, Hawkins and the others could still hear him muttering faintly, "he brought us Australian lager boys, after all that hard work. Geez."

Hawkins shook his head and smiled at Richard's antics. Then he turned and said to David, "it's all up to you now."

David crouched low as he approached the entrance. He felt a strong sense of euphoria and a slight out-of-body sensation. He was living every archaeologist's dream to discover and enter an undisturbed tomb. He imagined how Howard Carter must have felt as he entered Tutankhamun's tomb in Valley of the Kings at Thebes in 1922. The interior of this igloo-shaped tomb was an order of magnitude smaller than that of the Egyptian boy king. Also, he expected that any human remains would most likely have turned completely to dust after all this time. However, he wasn't sure if the fact that the tomb appeared to be well-sealed would help to prevent that. He switched on the 6-cell Maglite flashlight that he had purchased the day before at Halford's just for this occasion. Then he moved tentatively into the darkened entrance.

Examining the walls of the entranceway closely, he could see that they consisted of 8 roughly cut granite slabs stacked on all four sides to form the sloping rectangular opening into the tomb. He reckoned that each of the blocks weighed in the region of 2,000 pounds each. He wondered to himself where the stones had been quarried from. And, more importantly, how had they been transported and then finally erected here.

He recalled that the blue granite stones that were used to make up the inner circle of Stonehenge in Wiltshire weighed around 4 tonnes each. Amazingly, those stones were quarried almost 250 miles away in the Preseli Mountains in southern Wales. Also, the large upright stones, which each weighed a colossal 50 tonnes, were transported from Marlborough Downs 20 miles to the north.

"David," Hawkins called from just outside the entrance with the others. "Give us a verbal commentary on your movements and observations for the record. Remember not to swear because these proceedings could be read by other archaeologists, and even school children, in the years to come."

"No swearing? Me? I never use profanity," David exclaimed innocently. "Damn! Crap! Bugger! I just banged my head."

Everyone outside the entrance smiled at the banter between the supervisor and the student. But it was obvious from their expressions that they were all feeling nervous excitement in anticipation of what they might discover.

"Okay, I am in the passageway," David said needlessly. "It's constructed of large granite blocks, similar in composition to the entrance slab but only around half the size," David's voice echoed from the tomb. "They are smooth to the touch," David called as he ran his palm against the blocks on the right side of the short hallway. "Even at the joins between the blocks. It appears like they have been polished."

Those listening outside now craned their heads to hear what David was saying. Hawkins diligently recorded the narrative, scribbling with a pencil onto a notepad. He now regretted not joining David inside the chamber. But this was his student's discovery. And it was too cramped for both of them in there.

Back in the tomb, David turned his head to confirm that the left side of the chamber was equally smooth when his eyes did a double take. He squinted his eyes to see better and then paused for a second before speaking. "Uh, there appears to be markings on the second block on the left side of the passageway just before the inner chamber. I think it could be writing of some sort."

"What kind of writing?" Hawkins called out as he bent down to peer inside the passageway.

"I dunno," David replied. "Looks like hieroglyphics but not the Egyptian kind."

Unable to restrain himself any longer, Hawkins crouched down and shuffled into the chamber behind David. "Let me see."

Etched into the stone, Hawkins could see four separated horizontal lines of markings which were comprised of wedge-shaped stick figures and geometric objects orientated in different directions. Some of the stick figures looked like they could be animals and others were strikingly similar to letters used in the English language, such as 'V' and 'Y.'

"This is strange," Hawkins said. "It reminds me of Sumerian cuneiform and there seems to be other symbols here as well. But this shouldn't be here in England."

"Shall I go on?" David asked.

"Yes," Hawkins said. "See if you can access the central chamber. I'll wait here." Hawkins crouched down and recorded the events of the last few moments on his notepad using his own small flashlight to illuminate the page. "Remember to keep up the commentary."

"Okay." David response was slightly muted. "With this quick inspection, I can't see anything of further interest in the entrance passage," David announced. "I'm moving through into the central chamber." He moved down the passageway to peer into the gaping central chamber.

"The ceiling of the inner chamber appears to be dome-shaped like the inside of an igloo," David continued. "The blocks appear to have been fitted together without mortar although I can see a fair amount of soil in some of the cracks, most likely having seeped through from above."

He paused for a moment and then said, "in case you're wondering, I'm purposely waiting to examine the floor of the chamber. This is mainly to make sure that I carry out a complete survey before I get too side-tracked to do this job properly."

Yes, this kid is a real pro, Hawkins thought. *What self-discipline!*

"What's that idiot doing in there?" Gary said, looking around at those outside the tomb.

"The construction of the ceiling is remarkable," David called out. "It's circular. There are stone walls on opposite sides of the inner chamber. The blocks in these walls are smaller than those which make up the ceiling and the entrance hallway. I would guess that each weighs approximately 400 pounds. This gives the inner chamber a long rectangular shape, approximately 15 feet long, 5 feet wide and 8 feet high."

Hawkins inched forward behind David. He could see the reflected light from the domed ceiling, but he couldn't make out anything else beyond David's body.

"Okay, I'm now examining the floor of the chamber," David continued. "I'm stepping down onto the floor. It appears to be just a flattened layer of earth. And there are several objects in here."

No one breathed. Hawkins was the first to recover. "Okay David, what can you see?" He was waiting with his pencil poised ready above the notepad.

The rest of the group had all shifted so that they were packed together near the tomb's entrance, straining to hear the next words from David's mouth.

"I can see several completely intact ceramic jars lined up by the walls. Most of them look like they are still sealed and similar in appearance to the canopic jars used in Egyptian tombs, only these seem to have unornamented lids. Some of them are imprinted with the same writing style that we saw on the slab in the entrance passage. And... uh... some also contain crude images of animals, people, trees, and some other stuff."

Hawkins couldn't believe his ears. This discovery was turning out to be even more significant than he had imagined. "David, is there anything else?"

"Yeah," David responded in a breathless tone. "I was saving the weirdest part for last."

Everyone outside the chamber exchanged glances and Hawkins gazed intently into the tomb.

"It looks like a big statue wrapped up in sheets," David said. "The head is on the far side of the tomb so I can't make it out completely yet."

Hawkins started to feel uneasy. Something wasn't right.

"There is a large 5-foot long sword lying on one side," David said, bravely carrying on with his reporting. "It appears to be made of bronze. Lying near this is what looks like a bronze axe head, minus any kind of handle. Then, partly covering the statue on the other side is a large bronze shield with a concentric ring design like record grooves. There is also a bronze knife on the same side as the shield."

David paused with his commentary for a second to gather his thoughts and put the unexpected findings into some kind perspective. "I guess that the presence of the relatively advanced bronze weaponry blows our bright idea that this could be a Neolithic tomb right out the window. I don't understand it though. All of the other artefacts outside and the stratification suggested that this should be much older than Bronze Age."

But Hawkins had stopped listening. He had now eased his way forward behind David, just on the verge the internal chamber. His mind was racing as he said, "David, check the statue."

David nodded in the dim light and stepped carefully around the massive object toward the far end of the tomb.

"Alright, it appears to be a statue of a tall, emaciated man wrapped in filthy looking discoloured greyish brown cloth. I don't see any sign of a base so maybe the statue wasn't meant to stand upright."

The back of Hawkins' neck began to tingle.

David said, "I'm moving toward the head. The surface of the statue is exposed there. It looks kind of wrinkled, grey and –"

Hawkins stiffened but remained silent.

Then David broke his promise not to swear.

Chapter 4

New York City
June 22, 2007

    William Merrick regarded the lavish interior of the private elevator that was silently ferrying him down to street level and he felt nothing. He found it strange to finally realise that he had become indifferent to it all. He was currently the fourth richest person in America with a net worth of just over 20 billion dollars. He spent most of his days now in his 4,000 square foot full-floor Park Avenue penthouse in the heart of midtown Manhattan. Over the years he had also accumulated several other properties scattered throughout the world along with a fleet of private automobiles, two airplanes, three yachts and a helicopter.
    Although he had many financial interests, his favourite was a pharmaceutical company, which he had named Merrick Incorporated. The company focussed on development of novel drugs. This involved intensive screening of natural products, such as plant extracts, and the analysis of centuries-old traditional treatments including Chinese herbal remedies and Ayurvedic medicines. By 1995, Merrick Incorporated had 8 block buster drugs on the market. In 2001, the company moved into the exciting area of stem cell research. Such treatments offered a means of replacing lost or damaged tissue in cases of degenerative disorders like rheumatoid arthritis and Alzheimer's disease, and may also provide a way to slow the aging process.
    He had achieved almost everything a man could wish for in a lifetime. He had travelled the world, having visited more than 100 countries. He owned houses or villas in 6 of those countries and he had homes in several major USA cities including Miami Beach Florida, San Diego California and Seattle Washington. He had also amassed various priceless collectable items including great works of art, rare coins, stamps and even superhero comic books from the golden and silver ages. But most important of all to him was his remarkable collection of

classic automobiles all from the 1960s, his favourite decade. This included a 1960 Ford Thunderbird, a 1962 Jaguar XKE, a 1966 Chevrolet Corvette, a 1967 Pontiac Firebird and a 1969 Rolls-Royce Phantom VI. But he couldn't remember the last time that he had the opportunity to take any of these cars out on the road. He was now 84-years-old, unmarried and had no children. There had been plenty of women over his long life but he hadn't found anyone special. So, instead, he had devoted his life to his projects.

One of the major interests which developed during his twilight years was on the rise and fall of ancient civilizations. For him, the most exciting discoveries involved the belief system and legends of civilizations such as the Egyptians, the Maya, and the Inca and what appeared to be a widespread quest for eternal life. He believed that there must be some underlying truth to these legends. He had earnestly sponsored archaeological projects in the Middle and Near East which occasionally turned up snippets of information, corroborating some of the biblical accounts at ancient cities including Jericho, Judea, and Jerusalem. He had even funded projects aimed at discovering the true location of the Garden of Eden. The latest findings by a British archaeologist named David Rohl suggest that the garden once lay in a river valley near the Sahand Mountain in north-western Iran. But the information that Merrick was seeking, still eluded him.

"Here we are sir," Manuel Rodriguez stated in a monotone as he wheeled Merrick out of the 1960s style elevator through the ornate black and white marbled lobby. The handsome Latin American man pushed the wheelchair-bound Merrick past Cyril, the building's slightly overweight security guard, and out onto the pavement of one of Manhattan's busiest thoroughfares.

Merrick and Rodriguez had been together for 24 years ever since they first met at the ruins of Teotihuacan near Mexico City. Merrick had been one among the thousands of tourists that day that flocked regularly to the ancient city to walk around and scramble up the marvellous pyramids and temples, basically just so they could say that they had been there. He had been walking in a crowd along the Avenue of the Dead towards the Temple of Quetzylcoatl and listening intently as their young, green-uniformed guide detailed the architectural wonders of the city. Suddenly, Merrick had been jostled as a small boy brushed past him and began to run away though the crowd.

The tourists had all been warned about the gangs of young pick pockets in the area, but it never occurred to Merrick that it could happen to him. Just when the boy looked like he was certain to clear the crowds and get away, Merrick saw a flash of green swoop in on the young culprit like a whirlwind. Merrick was stunned when he realised that the whirlwind was their guide. He couldn't understand how he had managed to cover the distance so quickly. The guide plucked Merrick's wallet from the boy's hand in a lightning-fast movement and then gave him a swift, but gentle, kick on the behind and sent him grumbling in mildly-outraged protest to continue his day's work elsewhere.

Then, young Manuel Rodriguez had returned the wallet to Merrick and said in accented English, "he was just trying to feed his family Senor. It was not personal."

Merrick was so taken by Manuel's character and the masterful way he had handled the situation that he invited him to lunch. Over tacos, enchiladas, and frijoles, he listened intently as Manny described his early life attempting to survive as an orphan on the streets of Mexico City. Like his hero the Panamanian boxing legend Roberto Duran, Manny had learned that fighting was the key to survival on the streets of a rough city. And he discovered quickly that he had a raw ability for this because of his unnaturally fast reflexes. He eventually transferred his talents to the boxing ring where he successfully tore through most of his opponents. They had nicknamed him 'el Flash Verde,' the Green Flash, presumably due to his uncanny speed and the fact that he always wore the Mexican sporting colours of green and white for his bouts. However, unlike Duran, Manny longed for a future that didn't involve fighting, and he looked for opportunities elsewhere.

Next, Manny described how he had taught himself to read and to speak English by hanging around the tourist sites. It was there that he developed a strong interest in the cultural heritage of his country and, from then on, he couldn't get enough information to read on the subject. He was fascinated by the accomplishments of the Aztecs, Toltecs and the older Mayan and Olmec civilizations that arose further to the south. When he turned 16, he applied for a tour guide position at the ancient city of Teotihuacan. The interviewer was impressed by Manny's knowledge and he told him that he could start work the next day.

By the end of lunch, Merrick had come to a decision. He offered the young Latin American a position on his personal staff.

Manny accepted the offer without hesitation. He couldn't let such a golden opportunity pass him by.

Manuel Rodriguez sported his custom made Collezione Italia dark-green three-button suit as he wheeled Merrick down Park Avenue. He smiled to himself thinking about how far he had come. He was more-or-less a bodyguard and personal assistant to Merrick, even though he didn't have a proper job title. But in many ways, he was like the son, or grandson, that Merrick never had. There was nothing that he wouldn't do for the man who had so selflessly given him the opportunity for a decent life.

But sometimes Manny couldn't help but feel tormented by demons from his past. There had been much more to his former life in Mexico City than he had ever told the aged billionaire. He hadn't always been the sort of person that Merrick now believed him to be. On some occasions, he had been forced to do things that he had known were wrong. But as his thoughts returned to the present, he realised that none of it should matter anymore. It was all safely in the past. Besides, it looked like it was going to be a beautiful morning for their walk in the Park. He had no way of knowing that the past would soon come back to haunt him.

Chapter 5

Gog Magog Hills, Cambridgeshire
June 22, 2007

The dark Stygian depths of the tomb exuded an oppressive aura of veiled malevolence. The stale air was dry and permeated with miniscule swirling particles of dust, and possibly other animal or vegetable matter of unknown origin. The other-worldly luminosity generated by the flashlights created dancing, threatening shadows, as if some unseen presence warned all to leave at once. There were 5 bodies crowded together in the dome-shaped sepulchre. One of these had been dead for untold millennia.

The four tomb raiders stared in stunned silence at the giant mummified body on the earthen floor of the chamber. Under the almost hallowed glow from their flashlights, most of the massive form of the mummy was visible. To all of those present, it appeared to be a human of gigantic size. The body stretched across most of the length of the chamber floor which meant that it would have to be around 8 feet tall if it were standing. The deep chest alone rose around 18 inches from the floor and, like most of the remains, it was swathed in a coarse cloth that had turned a brownish-grey colour over time. The long arms, although withered with age, were stretched out flat and looked like they had been immensely powerful in life with a thickness in proportion to the overall size of the body. But the scientists noticed something even more bizarre about the gigantic form. Something that their eyes had still not accepted. It had 6 large fingers on each hand.

This seemed so unnatural that it almost appeared as if the giant sprouted a bunch of bananas from its plate-sized hands. As if this wasn't enough, those in the chamber had also noted that each of the giant's enormous feet terminated in a matching set of 6 elongated toes.

And then there was the giant's colossal head. This was around 20 inches long from the broad bearded chin to the top of the crown. The craggy eye orbital and cheek bones were large and protruding and the nose was broad and sweeping. The mottled forehead was unnaturally long and sloping to give the overall appearance of an elongated, withered egg. The scalp was covered sparsely in long, coarse, reddish-brown hair, and the closed eyelids covered eye sockets that appeared to be larger in proportion compared to those of a normal human, each being around the size of a snooker ball.

But the most extraordinary feature about the giant was that which the four scientists now regarded a feature that could induce nightmares. This was the large, partly opened mouth which contained two upper and two lower rows of grotesquely-stained teeth. None of them had ever seen anything like it.

David was the first to speak. "Does anyone else here feel the urge to visit the dentist...like, right now?"

Zoran responded, "no, but I was thinking of calling a psychiatrist."

"It's incredible," Lori intoned, her eyes still fixed on the body.

"It is incredible," Hawkins commented. "But, there's something wrong about all of this."

"You mean besides the dead giant dude with the bad teeth and a surplus of fingers and toes?" David posed.

"Yes, besides that. The problem is that nothing seems to fit. None of this should be here."

At first Lori thought that Hawkins was questioning his own eyes but then she was struck suddenly by the true intent of his words. "You think that all of this could be a hoax?"

"The possibility did cross my mind," Hawkins acknowledged. He turned and noticed for the first time how close she was to him in the tight confines of the tomb. Then he realised suddenly that everyone was waiting for him to continue. "As scientists we have to question everything and, in this case, there are many inconsistencies."

"You're referring to the artefacts, aren't you Jim?" Zoran asked.

"Yes," Hawkins said, realising that Zoran had noticed the same apparent problems. Forgetting for a moment that they were all standing so close to the mysterious giant in the middle of the haunting tomb, Hawkins found himself going into lecture mode. "To put it simply, the dates of the artefacts do not seem to match up. For example, the presence of the bronze weapons and the shield suggest a date no older than 2,100 BCE, which is the accepted date for the beginning of the Bronze Age in Britain. But we have an estimated date of 3,500 BCE for this tomb, based on typology and stratification. That leaves us with a glaring discrepancy of at least 1,400 years.

"Also," Hawkins continued, "the style of pottery in the tomb suggests a date corresponding to the middle Bronze Age, which began at around 1,400 BCE. This creates an even bigger disagreement of over two thousand years. Not to mention the problem of the 700-year gap between the pottery and the weapons.

"Then there is the appearance of writing on the jars and on the tomb walls." Hawkins paused momentarily while he gathered his thoughts. "That shouldn't be here under any circumstances. Megalithic engravings usually consist of common motifs such as axes, circles, projecting rays, arcs, chevrons, serpentines, and spirals. Nothing like this script has ever been found at any of the ancient sites in Britain or northern Europe. One would have to go to the Middle or Near East to find anything even remotely like it. In fact, the oldest forms of primitive writing are now thought to have arisen in the Harrapan region of the Indus valley at around 3,500 BCE, which is close to the date that we have assigned to this site."

"So why couldn't writing have developed in ancient Britain and the Indus Valley at around the same time?" David asked.

"It just doesn't seem likely. Otherwise, we would have found more examples of this script, including even more evolved forms, in the succeeding ages. But there is nothing. It's almost as if it appeared suddenly on the scene and then disappeared just as quickly."

After a momentary pause for Hawkins' remarks to sink in, Lori offered a solution that surprised everyone with its brilliant simplicity. "Unless the authors of the script were travellers."

When it didn't appear as if anyone was going to say anything in response, Lori continued. "They could have come here from a more advanced region where writing and other aspects of civilization developed much earlier, such as the Indus valley or Mesopotamia."

"Of course, that could be the case," Hawkins allowed. "It could explain why there are so many other features and characteristics of this site that appear to have come from a different time and location. There have never been any megalithic structures or tombs found in this part of the United Kingdom," he continued. "Also, the style of the structure itself doesn't seem to fit with anything found elsewhere in the UK or northern Europe. The use of precision cut granite slabs is more reminiscent of the south American limestone structures like those found at Ollantaytambo or Sacsayhuaman in southern Peru or those located on the Giza plateau and in the Valley of the Kings in Egypt. "Then, of course, there is the finding of a purposefully mummified body in the United Kingdom," he said, finally shifting the conversation back to the biggest problem of all, literally.

"Yeah, that really put me off my lunch," David commented as he returned his attention to the astonishingly large body lying across the floor of the tomb.

"You and me both," Zoran added. "I almost lost my biscuits."

"Cookies," David corrected.

Hawkins smiled at the ability of his two friends to sustain their repartee, even under the strangest of circumstances.

"It appears that the body was deliberately embalmed with the specific purpose of preservation," Hawkins said. "We can't tell for sure without a proper forensic examination, but I'll wager that the abdomen has been opened, many organs have been removed, and the emptied body was then probably covered in natron to speed up the dehydration process. The remains of the organs might be present in some of these surrounding jars. The fact that this chamber was tightly sealed, combined with the probable use of a strong desiccant in the chamber itself, would have assisted in keeping all of contents dry for long-lasting preservation. But of course, the only ancient civilizations known to have practiced the art of mummification that I can think of are the Egyptians, Japanese, Chinese, Tibetans, Aztecs, Maya, Inca and Chachapoya.

"Finally, we come back to the matter of mummy's gigantic size," Hawkins continued. "There have never been any documented archaeological finds of human remains with a stature over 7 feet tall, let alone 8 feet, as we have here. At least, not any credible reports."

"Well...," Zoran interjected, "there are descriptions of giants in the *Bible* and the *Koran*. The most famous of course was the Philistine warrior Goliath, who was slain by the shepherd boy David. The books say that Goliath was one of the last surviving members of a race of giants called the Rephaim. And as for his height," Zoran paused for effect, "there have been several conflicting claims, but the *Book of Samuel* states that the Philistine giant stood 6 Hebrew cubits and a span. That translates to around 9 feet tall."

"So maybe what we have found here goes some way towards substantiating the story of Goliath and other giants that have been described in ancient myths," David observed.

"Maybe," Zoran said. "But the story of Goliath might even stand on its own. The biblical chronology places him at around 1,000 BCE and there was a recent discovery in Goliath's supposed hometown of Gath that actually supports this. A pot shard dating to around 950 BCE was found bearing a Proto-Semitic inscription, consisting of the names 'alwt' and 'wlt' which are etymologically similar to 'Goliath.'"

"How do you know so much about all of this?" David asked

"I read once in a while," Zoran said, smiling broadly at David.

Lori interrupted before David could think of a comeback. "Zoran, are there detailed descriptions of these giants?" She paused and then added, "In addition to their size?"

"Yes, as a matter of fact there are," Zoran spoke in a tone that suggested he had just realised something important. "Some of these giants were described as having 6 fingers on each hand and 6 toes on each foot!"

The other three scientists were shocked by this revelation. But none made any comment.

Zoran continued. "In the *Book of Chronicles* it says that Jonathan, the son of David's brother Shimea, slew one of the 6-fingered giants who was described as being the son of another giant."

"Did any of them have weird teeth?" David asked.

"Well, no," Zoran admitted. "But there are other sources that made this observation. There were numerous reports in the 1800s and early 1900s from people who claimed that they came across the remains of giant skeletons in burial mounds, caves and tombs in the Americas and other parts of the world. Some of these discoveries were chronicled in newspapers. It was claimed that some of these skeletons had unusual characteristics such as elongated skulls, polydactyly and extra rows of teeth. There are hundreds of internet sites describing these kinds of finds, some a bit more fringe than others. But there is very little archaeological evidence remaining from any of these discoveries which, of course, has led to considerable doubt about their validity."

"What's polyduckly?" David asked.

"That's polydactyly," Zoran corrected. "It comes from a Greek word meaning 'many fingers.' It is an anatomical abnormality of having more than the usual number of digits on the hands or feet."

"Thought so," David lied.

"What actually happened to this evidence?" Lori asked, returning her attention to Zoran's earlier comment.

"Well, I can remember the details of one of these cases," Zoran said. "In the early 1900s, several giant red-haired mummies were found buried in a cave near Lovelock Nevada, by guano miners."

"Guano?" David asked, incredulously. "They were buried in crap?"

"Apparently so," Zoran went on, unperturbed. "But I think the guano came long after the giants had been interred from bats that found their way into the cave. The discovery substantiated the local Piute Indian legends about a race of red-haired cannibalistic giants that lived in the area. However, the archaeologists of that time seemed reluctant to investigate the matter any further and most of the remains were simply discarded by the miners. The rest was salvaged by some of the locals but then most of this was destroyed when the shed that they were being stored in caught fire. One of the skulls was recovered and is now on display with some of the other Lovelock Cave artefacts at the local county museum. The skull measures approximately one-foot from crown to jawbone, which suggests that the intact skeleton would have been more than 7 feet tall."

"But that kind of height is not so unusual," David commented. "There are plenty of 7-footers around today. That's probably the average height of the tallest players on American men's basketball teams."

"Of course, you're right, David," Zoran replied. "And there have also been a few cases of giants with pituitary disorders who were around the same height as our giant. The tallest and most famous of these was Robert Wadlow who died at only 22 years of age in the 1940s at the staggering height of over 8 feet 11 inches."

"I've heard of him," David said. "But, if I remember right, Robert Wadlow and most of the other pituitary giants suffered from skeletal problems such as severe arthritis and bone deformities. Most of them were barely able to stand up straight at all. In fact, Robert Wadlow had to be fitted with leg braces and he could only walk around by using a cane."

"That's right," Zoran corroborated.

"But that's not the case here," David maintained. "Apart from the fact that he's dead, our giant looks like he was fairly healthy and well proportioned. Maybe he's a 'natural' giant."

"You could be right," Hawkins said. "It doesn't look like he shows any of the debilitating side effects associated with acromegaly or pituitary gigantism. However, we won't know for sure until we can carry out a proper examination of the body."

"But natural giants don't really grow as tall as this, do they?" asked Lori, gesturing at the enormous figure before them.

"Not usually," Zoran answered. "But there was one exceptional case in the mid-1800s," Zoran went on. "His name was Angus MacAskill. As I recall, he emigrated from Scotland with his family to Nova Scotia at a young age. He was said to have been of average height until he began a massive growth spurt at the onset of adolescence and then he continued to grow until he was in his mid-20s. He ended up at a height of around 7 feet 9 inches, with a body weight of over 400 pounds.

"Unlike most of the pituitary and acromegalic giants, MacAskill was well known for his incredible feats of strength. It was claimed that he lifted a ship's anchor weighing 2,000 pounds to chest height, carried barrels weighing over 300 pounds under each arm for great distances and accidentally pulled the bow off a dory when fishermen pulled back on the stern as a joke. Fortunately, he was famous for having a 'mild and gentle' manner and he was always helpful. I remembered his story specifically because the *Guinness Book of World Records* listed him as the tallest natural giant and the strongest man that ever lived."

"Sounds like old Angus would have made a good drinking buddy," David suggested.

"No doubt," Zoran said, wistfully.

As Zoran concluded his narrative on the famous Scottish giant, it dawned on Hawkins that they had an arduous task ahead of them. "Okay gang, we have to get this show on the road while we still have some daylight left. Then we can find out what we're really dealing with here. First, we need to record all of the tomb contents *in situ* using sketches and photographs, making sure that everything is detailed on the site maps. Then we need to get other experts out here to view the site for validation and to authenticate the finds. Then, after that, we can transport everything to the appropriate labs for analysis. It will probably take us around 5 or 6 days to do everything by the book."

"Do we need to take the tomb apart to get everything out?" David asked.

"I don't think so," Hawkins answered. "The entrance passage appears to be large enough so that we should be able to remove everything, including the mummy, without any disassembly of the tomb structure."

Lori said, "I would like permission to take some of the more critical samples for molecular analysis while they are still in their original positions in the tomb. That way we can minimize the risk of losing any valuable information."

"Okay Lori, if you can get together a list of everything that you need, you can work together with David on that one," Hawkins offered.

"So, when do we inform the media about this?" David asked.

"We should wait until we have verified some of the more important aspects of this discovery first," Hawkins said. "Considering the controversial nature of these findings, we have to proceed cautiously."

Chapter 6

New York City
June 22, 2007

    Central Park is a large rectangular recreation area measuring approximately 4 square miles, situated roughly in the centre of Manhattan. It serves as an oasis for the Manhattanites who wish to escape from the urban sprawl and skyscrapers that New York is famous for. It has appeared in many movies and television shows making it one of the most famous parks in the world. It is visited by more than 25 million people every year from around the globe. The Park was originally designed by Frederick Law Olmsted and Calvert Vaux in 1857 who envisioned that it would be a place where people of all social and ethnic backgrounds could go and mingle. It is difficult to imagine, but the entire area where the Park now lies was once a treeless, rocky swampland.

    Today, Central Park is highly landscaped containing more than 26 thousand trees, 58 miles of pathways, two ice-skating rinks, a wildlife sanctuary, playgrounds, several artificial lakes and wide sweeping grassy areas for various sporting pursuits. The 6-mile road circling the park is popular with joggers, bicyclists and skaters especially on the weekends, early mornings and evenings when automobile traffic is prohibited.

    The rumours about crime today in Central Park are vastly exaggerated. It is true that there were periods when the Park was deemed to be unsafe and had a reputation of crime like the rest of New York. However, as crime has declined in both the City and the Park, these perceptions have mostly become outdated. In fact, there were less than 100 crimes committed within the boundaries of Central Park in the year 2005 making it one of the safest parks in the United States.

    Today was not going to be one of those days.

    Anna Flores felt uneasy as she jogged through the Park before beginning her often taxing day of work in the City's financial district. She felt that she stood out a little bit too much today in her lime-green, tight Lycra jogging outfit with the words 'KISS ME QUICKLY' written across the back. She usually liked attention but right now she didn't want to attract too much of it.

Normally she ran with two of her workmates, Maria and Tara, but today they were both ill from last night's party at the office. There was just too much alcohol involved. Since Anna didn't drink that much, she was the only one of the three still capable of carrying on with their usual morning three-mile loop which crosses through the Park at several scenic locations. She peered around herself in all directions as she moved swiftly along the path like a cautious deer. The only other signs of life that she had encountered were the morning birds that she could hear bustling in the trees and the old man in the wheel chair with his attendant that she had passed about a minute before.

The old man had nodded curtly to her as she passed and his charming Hispanic attendant with the piercing brown eyes had wished her a friendly 'buenos!' She had smiled broadly and jogged onwards thinking that he she would like to get to know this guy. He was also a snappy dresser in that dark green designer suit.

The sun had already warmed the Park and she felt energized by the morning heat. She quickly became lost in her thoughts about the work that she had to do later that day in the office, mentally planning her tasks so that she would have time to step out for lunch and meet her mother. She didn't see the three men standing by the bushes as she rounded a curving section of the hexagon-patterned pathway until she was just abreast of them. She noticed that they all seemed to be looking furtively back and forth along the path. Immediately she felt an inner alarm go off as she tensed and picked up her pace to get past them quickly. But as she reached the spot where they were standing, she heard one of the men say, "hey baby, lookin' good." Then the closest one jumped up and grabbed her roughly by the arm, stopping her dead in her tracks.

"Hey you freak, let me go!" The words flew out of her mouth before she could stop them. She frantically tried to pull free but the man, a large hatchet-faced oaf with a bad case of halitosis, maintained a vice-like grip on her.

"Come on baby," he said. "Why don't you stay here and we'll do some exercise with you?"

"Please, I have to go to work," she implored as she tried to pull free again. She was completely defenceless. She thought that she had mentally prepared herself for moments such as this but now she didn't really know what to do. She looked around beseechingly, hoping to see someone, anyone that could help. She felt her heart thumping in her chest when she realised that she was completely alone with these men.

"Let's take this chica into the bushes," said the baby-faced man with a spider web tattoo on his forehead.

She did the only thing that she could think of as the hatchet-faced man pulled her by the arm off the pathway. She tried to scream. But she never got the chance. The sound emerging from her throat was immediately stifled as he pulled her in tight to his chest in a one-armed bear hug and clamped his other hand mercilessly over her mouth. He then lifted her completely off the ground and carried her, legs kicking wildly though the air, to a spot behind a large rambling bush. Then the baby-faced man flipped a large knife out of his pocket and moved in close. The blonde suntanned man wearing the Gold's Gym tee shirt, who so far had done nothing, was giggling in anticipation.

"Man, she is a babe," beamed the hatchet-faced man. She noticed that he had the heavily-muscled look of a regular gym user.

A cold fear hit Anna as she was flung to the ground. The baby-faced man held her legs to stop her from kicking and the blonde man sat on her by straddling her rib cage. His massive weight compressed her ribs and the air supply to her lungs was nearly cut off. She desperately wanted to tear herself away but the hatchet-faced man was now pinning her arms down and she had nothing to fight back with. Even though her mouth had been released, she still couldn't scream because of the great weight on top of her.

The blonde man said, "okay baby, hold still now."

This is not me that this is happening to, she thought. *It is not me that's here in this situation*. She tried to disappear within her mind, to go somewhere else far away from this place. She just hoped that, whatever happened, it would all be over with quickly.

Suddenly she heard a whooshing sound, then a sickening thump and the weight from her chest was gone. She was stunned when she realised that the man at her head had released her arms and she also felt the weight lifted from her legs. Anna opened her eyes and her first thought was that she must be dreaming. Incredibly, she could see the man in the green suit squaring off to face two of the men. The blonde man that had been sat on top of her ribs now lay about 10 feet away on his back, writhing in agony and clutching a shattered, bleeding nose.

Now that she was free, she scrambled up from the ground and stepped back wondering whether she should run away or try to help her defender in some way. But she became rooted to the spot when she saw the man in green move quickly into a boxer's crouch and launch two tremendous left and right punches into the hatchet-faced man's ribs. This was followed up immediately with a pounding right cross to man's left cheekbone. The force of this punch snapped the hatchet-faced man's head around and caused him to pirouette backward into the prickly bush behind him with the sound of snapping branches.

The man in green now turned and moved towards the baby-faced man who was waving the knife back and forth in front of him as if he had to fend off a wild hoard. "Stay back or I'll cut you," he threatened non-convincingly. "I swear I'll cut you."

The man in the green suit didn't answer. Instead he lunged directly toward the outstretched knife as if he intended to impale himself on the end of it. Anna screamed. But then she saw her defender pivot swiftly to the side and grab the man's wrist with the speed of a striking cobra. He then rotated clockwise and snapped his left elbow backwards into the assailant's chin. The attacker responded by dropping to the ground like a lead weight, having let go of the knife as well as his consciousness.

Then she saw the blonde man with the busted nose rise groggily to his feet. He took one look at the scenario with several disbelieving blinks of his eyes and then he turned and loped off in a staggering run through the park with his hands held over his bleeding nose. The man in green simply watched as the blonde man weaved through the park, only to lose his balance, hurtle headfirst into a stout tree trunk and ricochet heavily to the ground. Then after a few seconds, the blonde man agonisingly pushed himself to his feet again. Once more he covered his nose with both hands and then somehow managed to scramble over a small hillock and then he was gone.

Without any further thought about her attackers, Anna said, "thanks for stopping them. I thought they were going to kill me."

"I'm just glad I got here when I did," the man said. He seemed unflustered by what he had just been through.

"What made you come back in this direction?" Anna asked. "I saw you leaving the park a few minutes ago with that man in the wheelchair."

"I saw them lurking behind the bushes when we first passed this way and they looked like they were up to no good. They didn't spare us much of a glance but when we saw you come jogging by in that, excuse me...outfit, and heading in their direction, we thought that they would probably try and cause you some trouble."

Anna was blushing now and seemed completely oblivious to the fact that she was standing so close to the semi-comatose bodies of two men. She said, "I'm really sorry. I should have known better than to go jogging alone wearing something like this. I guess you just don't realise that these sorts of things can happen until it happens to you. What's your name?"

The man in green smiled but then he turned serious and said, "it is probably better that I don't tell you my name. We are going to have to leave before the police arrive," he said, gesturing toward the figure in the wheelchair on the nearby pavement.

The old man saw that he was now the subject of conversation, waved politely and called out, "I hope that you're alright, sweetie?"

"Yes fine thank you," Anna shouted back. "I am forever in your debt."

"We're just glad to see that you're okay," the old man responded.

Anna turned back to the man in green and said, "surely the police will know that you were just protecting me. I'll tell them everything that happened."

"It wouldn't happen that way. I would most likely be arrested and charged with the use of excessive force in stopping these men from attacking you."

Anna looked around her at the battered condition of the man sprawled awkwardly in the bush and then she saw the other body kissing the ground. She said weakly, "I see your point."

The man in green continued, "please don't tell the police much of anything about us. Also, could I make a polite request that you change our descriptions sufficiently so that we cannot be traced?"

She was mystified but she said, "okay. You got it. But will you call me sometime?" The words blurted out from her mouth before she could stop them. But she knew that she might never get the chance again. He had the most piercing brown eyes.

"Maybe sometime," he said smiling as he turned to walk away.

"Wait!"

He stopped, turned back and waited.

"What about that guy in the bush? He doesn't look good"

"He'll be okay," he replied, looking almost apologetically at her. Both men had started to move but still resembled roadkill.

Dios mio! she thought as she watched the man in green turn and walk back to the old man in the wheelchair. She watched him wheel the old man quickly around the bend in path and then he was out of sight.

Then she sank to her knees with a moan on the grass-covered lawn, bent forward and vomited.

Chapter 7

Gog Magog Hills, Cambridgeshire
June 23, 2007

The ivory-coloured granite slabs of the tomb caught the warming rays of sun for the second consecutive day after being buried for 55 centuries. The summer swelter had already raised the temperature of the pollen-laden air beyond barely-tolerable levels. Three Englishmen and one Australian waddled one-by-one down the passageway toward the cooling darkness of the central chamber. The Englishmen responded to the shocking contents of the tomb in different ways. One choked out a single expletive and then stared transfixed with a mixture of horror and confusion. Another, simply said, "oh my word," and then felt for the arched wall of the chamber with one hand to ensure that he wasn't dreaming. The third gazed intently around the chamber, taking his time over the entire scene. Then he turned to the Australian and said, "quite a discovery you've got here, Jim."

The aged, slightly rotund man who had spoken was Professor Stanley Green. Stanley had achieved more in his career than most scientists had never even dreamt of. He was one of the world's most successful field archaeologists, with many significant discoveries to his credit and he had appeared as a special guest on various radio and television talk shows. He was also currently enjoying fame and fortune as the leading archaeologist on BBC1's television program *Time Explorers*. And he was the head of the Department of Archaeology at Cambridge University, which made him Jim Hawkins' boss.

Hawkins had decided to move things along carefully by calling Stanley and the other two archaeologists out to the site to verify some of the main features of the discovery. He had chosen his closest and most discrete colleagues in an attempt to avoid any pre-emptive news reports about the discovery until the appropriate time. But the main reason for his extreme caution was to ensure that everything was legitimate and not just part of some elaborate hoax.

Although Stanley was well-versed in many aspects of archaeology, he had achieved fame and fortune as the world's foremost expert on ancient weaponry. With the aid of the other archaeologists, Stanley surmised that all of the pieces represented the oldest examples of bronze weapons discovered anywhere around the world. It was clear that the civilization responsible for producing these items developed the ability to smelt copper and tin for the production of bronze weapons and tools, long before the accepted date of introduction in the British Isles. This suggested that Lori Davis had been right. The weapons, at least, must have been brought here from somewhere else. According to Stanley, the eastern appearance of the weapons suggested they originated from somewhere between south-eastern Europe and southern Iran.

The heavily-encrusted axe head lying on the giant's left side was vaguely reminiscent of ancient Persian designs, although it was approximately twice the normal size. It was symmetrical in two planes with a long cylindrical butt, an elliptical socket and a blade that broadened in a dulled convex cutting edge. A small amount of white powdery material appeared within the butt, the only remains of a handle that must have degenerated long ago.

The gigantic sword, also positioned on the giant's left side, was similar in style to a handful of swords dated more than 5,000 years-old, found near the Taurus Mountains in south-eastern Turkey. The blade and hilt of this sword had been cast in one piece and measured more than 5 feet in total length. Although it showed a similar degree of encrustation as the axe head, it was completely intact. The blade was double-edged, long and tapering with a central ridge, culminating in a now blunted point. The hilt was shaped like a flattened pawn-like chess piece with a protruding hand guard that angled down towards the blade. The same elegant style had been reproduced almost entirely for the two-foot long knife lying on the right side of the body.

The massive shield was perhaps the most interesting of the bronze artefacts found within the tomb. This was mainly because it resembled some of the earliest examples of shields discovered in Thracian tombs in present day Bulgaria which have been dated at more than 6,000 years-old. Also, the shield must have been used extensively in battle because it showed numerous scars and dents, presumably from absorbing countless impacts from Bronze Age or Neolithic weaponry.

With this in mind, the three visiting archaeologists turned their attention back to the mummy. Their superficial examination suggested that it was a genuine human-like body of gigantic proportions. As far as they could tell, it had been mummified in manner similar to the ancient Egyptian style as Hawkins had already surmised the previous day. However, all of the scientists agreed that confirmation of its authenticity required a complete laboratory examination.

The final stage of the investigation concerned the large storage jars housed along the edges of the tomb. It was at this point that Hawkins noticed something strange had come over Stanley. The usually cool star of *Time Explorers* began to perspire as he moved along the line of jars examining each one carefully. Most of the jars were sealed and appeared to be similar in shape and size with a height of two feet and girth of one foot at the thickest point. The two jars that were not sealed appeared to contain a salty residue which may have contributed to the dry air that still permeated the chamber.

Then the archaeologists came to a set of jars decorated with crude images of humans and giants. Stanley drew out a digital camera and began recording images. Hawkins assumed this was for his own interest since the tomb and contents had already been photographed extensively by David. As Hawkins looked at the images on the jars he was struck by how much they reminded him of Egyptian reliefs and palettes showing huge differences in size between the gods, pharaohs and their subjects. He also recalled that there were ancient Sumerian tablets which revealed seated gods and kings who appeared to be somewhere between 50 to 100 percent larger than the humans who brought them offerings. Up until this time, Hawkins, like most other archaeologists, had considered that such depictions were just down to artistic license and a way for these ancient civilizations to show that their rulers were superhuman.

The last jar near the giant's head seemed to draw the most interest from Stanley. It contained an image of crudely-drawn man and woman sitting on opposite sides of a tree and there appeared to be a solitary giant and jagged lightning bolt – or was it a snake? – in the background. Hawkins thought that this image was similar to that of the famous 'Adam and Eve' Neo-Sumerian cylinder seal, currently housed at the British Museum in London. The seal was thought to represent the famous Biblical figures sitting around the Tree of Knowledge in the Garden of Eden along with the serpent of temptation behind them.

But there was another set of images on this jar. Surrounding the Garden of Eden picture was a well-known repeating symbol. Like most people in the western world, Hawkins immediately recognized this as the swastika, the adopted sign of the Nazi Party and Adolf Hitler's Third Reich. But he also knew that the swastika was actually an extremely old symbol dating back thousands of years and was associated some eastern religions. Again, this fact appeared to connect the tomb and its contents with ancient civilizations that lay to the east.

The archaeologists finished off their examination by testing whether the jars contained anything. This was accomplished by gently rocking them and noting the various differences in inertial weight between them. Several jars appeared to weigh more than 20 pounds indicating that their contents could be quite substantial. However, as most were sealed, examination of the contents would also have to await opening under careful laboratory conditions to minimise any further losses complicated by their state of decay.

The scientists left the tomb. Once they emerged outside into the blazing light of day, Stanley appeared normal again. He said loud enough for everyone to hear, "well Jim, you should be pleased."

"Why is that?" Hawkins wondered what Stanley was on about.

"Thanks to you, they may need to rewrite the history books."

Back in his office two hours later, Professor Stanley Green assembled a report of the discoveries along with several digital images into an e-mail message. He spent 30 minutes polishing the message, trying to get the wording just right. After all of these years, this looked like it could finally be what they had been searching for. Naturally, Stanley slightly embellished his role in the discovery. After he was finished composing the message, he pressed the send key. Then he sat back in his chair and waited for the reply.

Cheltenham is a spa town in the county of Gloucestershire, located about 80 miles west-north-west of London. The town is positioned on the edge of the Cotswold Hills and has a national image of being a posh place to live. It has been a holiday and health spa resort since the discovery of a mineral springs there in 1716. The Latin town motto of the town is: *Salubritas et Eruditio*, which translates as 'Health and Education.' Cheltenham is probably most famous for the Cheltenham Gold Cup, the 'Wimbledon' of British steeplechase horse racing.
    Cheltenham is also the site of the British Government Communications Headquarters, the GCHQ. The GCHQ is an intelligence agency responsible for information security. It reports to the Foreign Secretary and interacts with Britain's other well-known intelligence agencies, MI5 and MI6. In collaboration with the US National Security Agency (NSA), the Canadian Communications Security Establishment and the Australian Defense Signals Directorate, the GCHQ is also responsible for operation of the ECHELON system.
    ECHELON was originally developed for use during the Cold War. The capabilities and activities of this system are suspected to include monitoring of radio and satellite communications, telephone calls, fax messages and e-mails throughout the world using computer automated analysis and sorting of the intercepts. This is more commonly known as electronic eavesdropping. It has been estimated to intercept a staggering three billion communications every day. It is believed to be capable of searching for hints of terrorist plots, drug deals as

well as political intelligence reports. Captured signals are processed by a series of supercomputers programmed to search messages for specific addresses, content, key words, phrases, names and even voices.

ECHELON has proven successful on many occasions in the monitoring of domestic and international crimes. In the early 1960s, it was used for the initial discovery of the fact that the former Soviet Union was stockpiling missiles in Cuba. It was also used to gather information that led to the capture of the terrorists who hijacked the cruise ship Achille Lauro in 1985 as well as those who were responsible for the West Berlin La Belle discotheque bombing in 1986.

However, the power of ECHELON has also been used for less than noble purposes. Some critics claim that it is also being used for commercial theft and invasion of privacy. One of the first scandals to hit the press about ECHELON was the disclosure by the NSA that it had eavesdropped extensively on telephone conversations held by Princess Diana just before her death. It has also been alleged that the Bush Administration extended the use of ECHELON to domestic surveillance in 2002.

At 15:07, July 23rd, 2007, an e-mail message was captured by a geostationary satellite before being relayed to its intended recipient in the United States. The message had been automatically flagged in transit as being of potential interest to national security by the GCHQ arm of ECHELON. Over the following days, it was systematically passed along secure lines to appropriate operatives in the GCHQ and other agencies for human review in order to determine whether any action needed to be taken or if the message should be ignored as unimportant.

The process of removing the contents of the tomb began later that day. David spent this time cataloguing and mapping the location of each artefact on an enlarged map of the tomb with the assistance of Gary, Craig and Nancy. Some of the smaller artefacts were also catalogued and bagged for later analysis including all of the pollen, burnt wood chips, pieces of fabric and small bones. These items could all be used to give a precise dating of the burial chamber.

Over the next two days, Professor Green assisted in removal of the jars. These were transported to Hawkins' laboratory in the Archaeology Department for storage and analysis. The jars were designated for the environmentally-controlled room to assist in preservation of the contents.

The weapons were removed on the fourth day and taken to the same lab. All of these appeared to be in good condition despite the encrustation that had gathered on them with time, like a cancer replacing healthy skin. The shield was in the poorest condition, although most of this was thought to be due to the damage that it sustained prior to entombment. The general state and stoutness of most of the artefacts helped to make their removal and transport an easy matter.

On the fifth day, Hawkins, Zoran and Lori assisted David and the others in removal of the giant mummy. This required a great deal of planning and involved the use of a long expandable support stretcher that Hawkins had managed to obtain from one of the University workshops. Hawkins, David, Zoran and Craig carried the stretcher through the passageway and placed it on the left side of the mummy in the space previously occupied by the sword, axe head and storage jars. Then they began the slow and careful process of expanding its width and rolling the mummy incrementally on its right side and back down again until it was loaded fully on the stretcher.

The men carefully hoisted the stretcher and attempted to manoeuvre it back through the cramped passageway. The task was not made easy due to the fact that the mummy weighed in excess of 250 pounds, even though it was partly dehydrated from the mummification process and the inevitable decay over time. Most mummies weigh only around a quarter of their original body weight and Hawkins guessed that the giant had weighed around 400 pounds when he was alive! *So why was the body as heavy as it was?* They would have to investigate this later.

Following a great deal of trial and error, they opted for a technique that involved repetitious small forward movements and a systematic readjustment stage. The men rested the 'feet end' of the stretcher on the smooth blocks of the sloping passageway and then shuffled their feet forwards with the co-ordination of a drunken centipede. Then they reset their positions to begin the next cycle. Hawkins and Zoran bore the major portion of the burden since they were lowermost in the chamber while David and Craig guided the stretcher from the upper end of the passageway.

After a number of bruised knuckles, bumped heads and a modest amount of swearing, they managed to shift the mummy out of the tomb into the evening twilight. Gary and Nancy immediately rushed over to support the middle region of the stretcher. Looking like 6 pall bearers, they lifted the stretcher up to shoulder height, walked forward and slid the body into the back of a van containing makeshift rollers. Once the stretcher was carefully positioned, Gary locked the rollers into place.

Hawkins wiped his brow and said, "that went much better than I thought it would."

David carefully secured the entrance to the tomb by covering it with a tarpaulin and then he hopped into the rear of the van with Gary, Craig and Nancy. Their job was now to ensure that the mummy remained stable during the 5-mile journey to the lab.

Hawkins climbed into the driver's seat, turned the key to start the engine and eased the large swaying vehicle away from the site towards the main road.

Zoran followed the van closely on his motorcycle with the helmeted Lori perched behind him and clutching the tall Croatian tightly around the waist. The two vehicles headed towards Cambridge in the fading light of the midsummer evening.

None of them had noticed the three dark figures who had been watching their every movement closely from beyond the trees.

Chapter 8

Cambridge
July 5, 2007

David Englehart peered through the microscope at the ancient piece of stained linen and felt his eyes suddenly go out of focus. He tried readjusting the instrument by twisting the eyepiece but it was no good. He glanced over at Zoran and found the older scientist gazing vacantly at a flat screen computer monitor. "Hey sleepy head," David said with a sigh. "We'd better call it a night."

Zoran gave a sudden jerk and peered back at David through blood shot eyes. "Okay. I guess this has waited more than 5,000 years to give up its secrets. A few more days won't matter."

David nodded numbly. They had been working at this frantic pace for almost two weeks, going flat out to examine all aspects of the discovery. They were racing against the clock to explore every possible angle before the story leaked out. Now, they both realised that they would need to get more sleep or they risked making costly mistakes. There had been a close call earlier that evening. David had almost chopped off one of his fingers while taking a cutting from the linen cloth that was used to wrap up the mummy. Even worse, Zoran had accidentally deleted 10 pages of graphs and text on geological survey data, simply by pressing the wrong key on the computer keyboard. Fortunately, he was able to recover the data when he remembered, after 15 minutes of self-reproaching panic, that he could retrieve everything simply by selecting 'undo' from the program's edit menu.

The time factor was important but enough was enough. Besides, the project was nearing completion. Hawkins had co-ordinated the workload by issuing assignments that matched everyone's area of expertise. David and Zoran were in charge of preparing all of the samples from the mummy and the artefacts for radiocarbon dating, typological classification and other analyses. Lori was naturally in control of all of the molecular experiments including the protein and DNA tests.

Hawkins had arranged for the initial examination of the mummy to be carried out by a medical expert from Addenbrooke's Hospital, Dr Nicholas Walsh. Hawkins and Walsh had known each other for several years from the intense games of squash that they had played together on the courts of the Hospital's Sports and Leisure Club. But the most important thing about Walsh was that he could be trusted to maintain a secret, as long as he was supplied with a bottle or two of single malt Scotch whisky, preferably of the Talisker or Tobermory variety.

Walsh's examination established that the mummy was genuine, and whoever had prepared the body seemed to know what they were doing. As Hawkins had already surmised, several internal organs had been removed through the abdomen but Walsh discovered that the brain had also been extracted. This was most likely done in a manner similar to the ancient Egyptian method of drawing the organ out in pieces through the nose using a long metallic hooked instrument. The mummy's body proportions, facial features, bone thickness and muscle tone, suggested that it had been a natural giant. The length of the body came out at 8 feet 2 inches. Incredibly, X-ray analysis revealed that the extra-large skull had a brain capacity of over 2,000 cubic centimetres but this was in proportion with the size of the body. This compared to a brain size of 1,400 cubic centimetres for an average human male of 5 feet 10 inches.

The additional digits on the mummy's hands and feet appeared natural with every indication that they had functioned normally in life. The extra row of teeth was embedded directly behind the first row in jaws that were slightly wider than normal. From the apparent wearing of the teeth, both layers appeared to have been used equally in life. Another potentially interesting finding was the recovery of a small amount of material that appeared to be dried meat from indentations of the molars. This was sent to Lori at the Addenbrooke's Hospital Laboratory of Molecular Biology (LMB) with the hope that she might be able to determine what the giant had eaten for his last meal.

The examination also produced a few surprises. The first of these regarded the heavier than normal weight of body, which they had already noted during the transfer process. Apart from the removal of several organs, this body was mostly intact. This suggested the dehydration stage had not been done properly or omitted for some reason, or it had not worked as expected.

The second surprise came when Dr Walsh was able to identify a potential cause of the giant's death. A large deformation at the back of the skull, and a protrusion of bone within the brain cavity, indicated that he had received a massive blow to the back of the head. The size and shape of the injury suggested that the weapon used was most likely a stone object, weighing around 10 pounds. Also, there was a deep stabbing wound to the lower back, which must have pierced the left kidney. Traces of flint were found in and around the point of entry. These findings suggested a scenario in which the giant had been brought down from behind by an attacker using a flint-headed spear. Then, after falling face first to the ground, he was unceremoniously clubbed to death by someone using a heavy stone to cave-in the back of his skull.

But the biggest surprise came when Walsh re-examined the head to learn something about the giant's age at the time of death. There are essentially two time-dependent human characteristics that forensic scientists use to establish a body's age with some degree of accuracy. The first of these is the extent of wearing of the tooth material called dentin. The second is the degree of closure of the natural sutures holding the individual skull plates together. In this case, the extreme wearing of the dentin and complete closure of the sutures suggested that the giant had been at least 80 years-old when he was killed.

As part of their role, David and Zoran sent samples that they had prepared from the mummy and artefacts for dating at the Oxford University Radiocarbon Accelerator Unit. The dates that came back from Oxford for the various different samples were all similar, providing good corroborative evidence that they were reasonably accurate. The bird and rodent bone samples recovered from the pit and inside the tomb yielded dates of 5,660 years. The linen samples taken from the giant mummy gave a date of approximately 5,590 years and bone samples from the body itself were practically identical with a date of 5,570 years-old. These results were also similar to the microscopic pollen dating test that David carried out. He found that the grains taken from the tomb and surrounding pit were comprised mainly of elm, oak, ash, linden and alder pollens. The relative proportion of each pollen type, referred to as the pollen spectrum, corresponded to the known vegetative climate of Britain 5,500 years ago.

The work carried on as the days rolled by. Most of this was routine, but there were some aspects that were simply bizarre. Two days after the giant had been removed from the tomb, Zoran and David had returned for an internal inspection of the chamber, where they discovered something had been buried and covered with patches of red ochre beneath the spot where the mummy had lain. By carefully digging into this spot, they uncovered a spread of wing bones from a large bird. A colleague from the Department of Zoology helped them to identify these as belonging to a variety of *Gyps fulvus*, a griffon vulture. The significance of this had the scientists baffled.

Zoran and David had devoted most of their time to studying the different container jars found within the tomb beside the giant mummy. After carefully examining the exterior surface each jar, they systematically and carefully opened them in order to determine what was inside. As guessed by Hawkins, some of the jars contained the decayed remains of the mummy's organs. Several of the jars were empty and some were filled with cereal grains such as wheat and barley, which were typically in use during the late Neolithic Age in England. One contained several pieces of dried meat and they sent some of this to Lori in hopes she could identify the type of animal that it had come from.

There was considerable excitement when they discovered that two of the jars contained clay tablets of various sizes. These had been imprinted with the same script found on the tomb wall. They took rubbings from the tablets and the wall and sent these away for linguistics analyses. The initial findings indicated that some of the symbols were similar to the ancient Harappan script of the Indus civilization. The linguistics experts said this couldn't be deciphered easily because it was a dead language. However, they ended on a positive note by saying the Cuneiform-like writing that was also present might be partly translatable.

Then they came to the final jar. They had come up with two different nicknames for this which they used interchangeably. The first of these names was the 'Nazi jar' due to the presence of the swastika symbols. The second was the 'Adam and Eve jar' because of the resemblance of the figures on the jar to the supposed biblical characters. Out of all of the jars, they had eagerly anticipated the opening of this one. But they were immediately disappointed. The jar contained seeds. There were about 30 of these all together. They were medium-sized with hard brown-coloured outer casings. Not knowing or really caring what else to do with them, David and Zoran decided to send some to the Department of Plant Sciences for identification. They were surprised when Plant Sciences couldn't provide them with an exact answer. They were told the seeds were similar to those of the modern date palm tree. After learning this, they sent some of the seeds to Lori at the LMB to see if she could shed some light on what these were using her molecular techniques.

The telephone in the office rang abruptly, startling David and causing Zoran to spill a small portion of the grain sample that he was re-bagging in preparation to go home. David picked up the telephone and was surprised to hear Lori's voice.

"Hi David," she said cheerfully. "We've got some results."

David turned to Zoran and said, "it's Lori. She has some answers."

Zoran simply nodded and came forward.

David switched on the speaker phone, set the receiver down and said, "we're all ears."

Lori said, "well, you and your ears had better sit down."

Chapter 9

Cambridge
July 5, 2007

"Why don't we start with the seeds?"
"Sounds good Lori," Zoran replied.
"Fire away," added David.
"We were able to extract sufficient nuclear DNA from the seeds and our gel-sizing test showed this was relatively intact."
There was a pause as David and Zoran digested this technical beginning. David knew that something didn't sound right but his thinking was still clouded from his present state of exhaustion. Then it dawned on him. "Shouldn't the DNA have been at least partly degraded? After all, the seeds are so old."
"That was my first thought too," Lori said. "The only thing I can think of is that maybe the core of the seeds gained protection from their hard outer casing."
"Hmmm," David mused, still not convinced.
Lori resumed unperturbed. "We sequenced several genes from our seeds' DNA and found that it was 95 to 99 percent similar to *Phoenix dactylifera*, otherwise known as the date palm."
"That's just what the plant guys told us," David observed.
"I know. And that's all I can tell you for now. Except Pavlos thought that we might be able to add something to this if we could germinate some of the seeds."
Pavlos Konstantinou was a Greek Cypriot student, working toward his PhD degree in plant genomics. Lori had recruited his help in to analyse the ancient seeds with the promise that he could use some of the results towards his PhD thesis.
"But Lori, that's crazy," David gave his expert opinion. "It'll never work."
"Why not?" an accented, robotic voice responded.
David was shocked into silence. He had no idea that Pavlos was there with Lori. He looked at Zoran for inspiration on a way out of this mess, but the tall Croatian merely shrugged. David

decided that his best recourse was to back paddle. "Well...uh...it's very difficult to get ancient seeds to germinate. There have been very few successful attempts. The most extreme case of growing ancient seeds was carried out by a group of Israeli scientists. They managed to germinate a 2,000-year-old palm tree seed discovered near the Dead Sea. But the seeds that we found are almost three times that age. If you could germinate these, you would have an instant *Nature* paper and it would be 6 o'clock news material."

"Then we should write the paper," Pavlos replied unperturbed.

"I think Pavlos could be right," Lori added.

Zoran jumped into the conversation. "Do you mean...you did it? But how?"

David was stumped. He couldn't think of anything intelligent to say. Part of this was due to the fact that he now felt more than a little foolish after his ill-timed lecture on the difficulties of cultivating ancient seeds.

Lori explained what they had done since Pavlos was not known for his verbosity. "To start with, we looked up the Israelis' work and then followed their published procedure as closely as we could. Around 10 days ago we soaked the seeds in hot water, covered them with a seaweed fertilizer and planted them in pots. And now we have three seeds with healthy looking sprouts growing out of them and some of the other seeds seem to be following closely behind. Pavlos is really excited."

"Yes, I am excited," Pavlos chimed in mechanically.

David noted that the Cypriot's tone was like Schwarzenegger's terminator on Valium. "Okay that looks like *Nature* paper number one is in the bag," he said, trying to recover his poise. "Do you have any other results? What about the samples from the jars?"

"I don't know if amazing is the right word but we did get an unexpected result on the identity of the dried meat," Lori said. "The sample looked like it had been cured, as in the preparation of beef jerky."

"So it was beef then?" Zoran asked.

"No, it wasn't beef. Even though the DNA was fragmented in this case, we were still able to amplify a few informative stretches of DNA using PCR. And the sequences appeared to encode the human forms of certain muscle proteins."

There was a moment of silence as Lori's words sank in. "Did you say human?" David asked in disbelief. He glanced over at Zoran who was also visibly shaken by the news.

"Yes," Lori answered succinctly. "And we also know that he had actually eaten some of this shortly before his death. That's what the residual material was between the giant's teeth. Our sequencing results showed that this contained DNA for the same human muscle proteins."

David's stomach churned. That pepperoni pizza that they had earlier didn't seem like such a good idea now. He realised that Zoran also looked a little bit green around the gills.

"He was a... a cannibal?" Zoran asked.

"It certainly looks that way," Lori replied.

No response.

"You guys still there?"

Zoran replied, "yes we're here. Maybe you should just continue with your report. Are there any other surprises?"

"One or two."

"Okay take it slowly then," Zoran said. "We're still trying to get over the last one."

"Man, you guys are wimps," Lori began. "We did manage to get some useful information on the mummy's blood. For one thing, we identified the blood type using the bone samples that you sent. A little known fact is that blood typing can also be used to establish bloodlines for identification of human origins and migration patterns. A study that analysed blood types from allied soldiers on the Macedonian front after the First World War found that the A and B blood types formed a continuous gradient from north-western Europe through the eastern Mediterranean towards India. This suggested that India may have been the cradle of civilization for at least this one part of humanity.

"Our mummy came out as B positive," Lori said. "This is consistent with the idea that he originated from somewhere in the Middle or Near East. And you will be pleased to learn that we used two different strategies to confirm that he is human. First we sequenced several blood proteins from the giant and compared these with sequences from orang-utan, pigmy chimpanzee, modern humans and even some extinct human species including Neanderthal and Cro-Magnon. The results proved conclusively that our giant contains human-like blood proteins."

"So... he's not an ET then?" joked David.

Lori carried on as if she hadn't heard. "Then we looked at mitochondrial DNA that we had extracted from the bone samples. More specifically, we used the first hyper-variable region of the mitochondrial genome."

"What does that mean in English?" David interrupted.

Zoran politely echoed David's protest. "Lori, keep in mind that our understanding of molecular genetics is remedial, at best."

"That's okay," Lori said. "You don't really need to know that much to understand the take home message. But I'll try to keep the explanations basic. The mitochondria are like the powerhouses, or batteries, of our cells and they contain their own DNA. This is separate from the much larger genomic DNA in the cell nucleus. However, the mitochondrial DNA evolves approximately 10 times faster than the DNA in the nucleus and the hyper-variable region undergoes the greatest rate of change of all. Even between modern humans, this region is highly-variable with an average of around two percent. Molecular archaeologists have used this to their advantage to explore the evolutionary relationships across species as well as between modern species and their ancestors. For example, the average number of differences over this region between humans and our closest known living relative, the pigmy chimpanzee, is about 14 percent."

Lori paused in her explanation at this point to check on her listeners. "Are you with me so far?"

"Yes," Zoran said.

"Absolutely," David added.

Unbeknownst to Lori, Zoran began to mime the act of hari-kari and David was slumped on the desk.

Lori carried on with her explanation. "Good. This approach has also been used to establish the relationship of modern humans with Neanderthal man. This showed a difference of around 6 percent, which is approximately three times greater than the variation between humans and almost half as much as that between humans and chimpanzees.

"Now, as I am sure you already know, the combined fossil and molecular evidence has suggested that modern humans first appeared around 150,000 years ago and the supposed common human-chimpanzee ancestor has been placed somewhere between 5 and 6 million years ago. Using these parameters to calibrate the timelines, it can be estimated that the common ancestor between us and Neanderthals lived around 550,000 to 690,000 years ago. In other words, humans and Neanderthal have been separate species for more than half a million years."

"And now you have done a similar comparison to establish where the giant sits on the human family tree?" Zoran asked.

"Exactly," Lori said. "To cut a long story short, we found differences of around two percent, which is essentially within the normal human variation. From this it would seem that the giant sits on the same evolutionary branch as modern humans."

"But can you be sure he is completely human?" Zoran asked. "Can we rule out David's man from Mars hypothesis?"

"Thanks man," David retorted.

"Well, the results suggest that he is either completely human or he co-evolved with humans from a common ancestor who lived around 150,000 years ago. But if we wanted to, we could narrow this down further by looking at other more highly-conserved gene sequences."

"Is it worth doing that?" asked Zoran.

"Great question," Lori said. "We've already had a quick look at some of the more obvious candidates. For this we sequenced the genes for insulin, glucagon and somatotropin. In case you didn't take biology 101, the last one is also known as growth hormone. All of these gave identical sequences to the equivalent regions of the same genes in humans."

"So that settles it then?" asked David.

"Not quite. There was one anomaly. We routinely visualise the sequences, never mind the details, to confirm that they are the right size before we carry out sequencing. In this case, the sizes all checked out fine but the fragment representing the giant's growth hormone sequence gave a signal that was approximately 10 times more intense than the same sequence from normal humans."

David and Zoran looked at each other with dawning realisation.

"What could cause that?" Zoran asked.

"The most likely explanation is that the giant has multiple copies of the growth hormone gene, maybe up to 10 copies. Assuming that at least some of these surplus genes were functional, he would have been producing massive levels of growth hormone. This might be the explanation for why he grew to such a giant size."

"But wouldn't that make him grow abnormally with bone problems and other deformities like in the case of pituitary gigantism," Zoran asked, logically.

"Not necessarily," Lori said. "Not if high levels of the hormone were secreted throughout his life, including when he was developing as an infant. In the early 1980s, genetically-modified mice expressing high levels of the human growth hormone gene from birth actually grew to two or three times their normal size so they appeared almost as big as rats. But they were just big mice."

"Amazing!" Zoran uttered.

"Yikes," exclaimed David. "But if they could do that with a mouse –"

"They could do it with just about anything," Lori finished.

After this, neither Zoran nor David were capable of absorbing any further information.

Lori seemed to sense this and said, "okay, gotta go. The molecules are calling."

They mumbled their thanks, minds reeling.

Hawkins stopped by the archaeology lab just after 11:00 P.M. to find David and Zoran on their way out. Although they were both physically and mentally drained, they were still excited enough to update their team leader on the latest results. However, they soon realised that they hadn't really understood much of what Lori had told them after all. Because Hawkins had some background in molecular biology he decided to give her a call just to check on some of the most confusing aspects.

He called her from the telephone in the office as David and Zoran wearily left the lab.

She picked up the telephone on the 10th ring.

"Hello, Lori Davis speaking."

"Lori, it's Jim."

"Oh hello, Dr Hawkins."

"Just calling to check a few facts that the boys didn't quite understand," Hawkins said.

Lori laughed and said, "that's okay. I don't understand some of the things that they talk about either."

For the second time that night, Lori patiently explained the results from the key experiments that she and Pavlos had completed. Hawkins realised that she must really enjoy talking about her work as she gave an abbreviated account of what she had told the boys. Hawkins stopped her only twice to ask questions. The first concerned the newly sprouted seeds. The second was about the giant and the multiple copies of growth hormone gene. Like David and Zoran, he was astonished by both of these points. As Lori finished her summary, he had finally made up us his mind about something.

"I think it's about time we announced our preliminary findings to the media. I'm satisfied we've really got something solid here."

"Are you sure?" Lori asked, already thinking of a million other experiments that she could do.

"Yes, I think so. After all, what harm can it do?"

Chapter 10

New York City
July 6, 2007

The dashing celebrity Los Angeles anchorman, Dan Oughton, beamed a sincere 'you-can-trust-me' smile at the camera and began his teleprompter-guided delivery in a velvety voice that was well-recognized across America.

"And now we bring you a report of what could turn out to be one of the most important archaeological discoveries of the century. This discovery has been made by scientists from the University of Cambridge in England."

The image on the television screen switched to a still shot of King's College Chapel, one of Cambridge's most spectacular gothic architectural features.

"Two weeks ago, Dr Jim Hawkins and his international team of archaeologists unearthed a stone tomb near the famous Iron Age Wandlebury hill fort just 5 miles south-east of Cambridge."

The image changed to a panoramic shot of the site sheltered near a thick glade of beech trees. It then zoomed in on the impressive tomb, a giant igloo-shaped mound comprised of stone and earth. A man sporting a Dryzabone bushman's hat stood with arms folded across his chest near the opening. The words 'Dr Jim Hawkins Archaeologist, University of Cambridge' were superimposed in bold white letters across the picture. Beside him were two male figures clad in khaki-coloured safari wear, one of average height and one exceptionally tall, and a slender female with flowing strawberry-blonde hair, wearing a lavender-coloured top tucked into blue jeans.

"The incredible reports have now been confirmed that the tomb contained a mummified human body of gigantic proportions – a body which stretched the tape measure at an incredible 8 feet 2 inches."

The screen shot changed to reveal the partly-shrouded mummy stretched on a long metal table.

"This is the largest substantiated example of ancient human remains ever found. It is also one of the tallest humans on record with measurements that could be verified. The tallest, of course, being the 8-foot 11-inch giant, Robert Wadlow, who died in the year 1940."

A still shot now appeared showing the famed 'gentle giant' from Alton Illinois, towering over two men of normal stature. Neither man exceeded the height of Wadlow's waist, giving the appearance of children posing with their father.

"This finding gives some credence to the possibility that the giants of legends actually existed in the distant past, such as Goliath of Biblical fame. Besides his great height, the Wandlebury giant had two other unusual features."

The scene changed back to the body lying on the table and focussed on the unnatural-looking large greyish hands.

"It had 6 digits on its hands and feet, a condition known as polydactyly –"

The image moved and zoomed in on the giant's face partly revealing the somewhat daunting opened mouth.

"– and it had a complete extra row of teeth on its upper and lower jaws. The experts have said that this is reminiscent of a rare dental disorder called polyphyodontia in which multiple layers of permanent teeth can erupt one after the other or side by side with existing dentition."

In his Park Avenue penthouse suite, William Merrick was hunched forward in the wheelchair and listened intently, staring at the television screen. Manuel Rodriguez sat on the plush oversized couch near Merrick. His normal rock-steady disposition was still apparent, but he felt ill at ease.

"Dr Hawkins has confirmed that the tomb dates to around 3,500 BC, which makes it the oldest found in the eastern part of the United Kingdom. And there were also other surprises housed within the tomb. Several artefacts were discovered which appeared to be thousands of years ahead of their time."

The television image revealed Dr Hawkins striding across the dusty site, looking vaguely reminiscent of the Indiana Jones character from *Raiders of the Lost Ark*. Then the image changed to the stark contrast of a sterile laboratory. The camera panned across the partially encrusted Bronze Age weapons which appeared as if they could be as old as the Earth itself.

"The unearthing of such Bronze Age weapons in a Stone Age tomb is equivalent to finding a flintlock rifle buried inside a Roman villa."

Merrick frowned. He thought that was a stupid comparison to make. The camera image then returned to the inside of the tomb and fixed on the soft red earth where the giant had lain.

"Perhaps one of the most mysterious discoveries was something which had been found beneath the body of the giant. This was the remains of a vulture's wings. The scientists have suggested that the people who carried out this entombment may have had some ritualistic purpose in mind but the actual significance remains to be determined."

Merrick shifted uncomfortably. He knew the significance. The camera finally settled on a collection of the ceramic jars.

"The tomb also contained 18 large storage jars. Most of these were sealed and the contents are currently undergoing further examination. Some of the jars contained dried meat and cereal grains which might have been part of the giant's diet. And another pot contained seeds thought to be from a tree which became extinct several thousand years ago."

The cameraman pulled in for a close-up view of the jar, focussing on the crude picture of the male and female figures standing near a small tree. The camera angle was chosen so that none of the encircling swastika symbols were in plain view. This decision had been made by the head of the news coverage team. The camera then panned to a laboratory table displaying a small cluster of the large brown wrinkly seeds.

"The researchers are studying the seeds further to identify their nearest relative in the plant kingdom."

The camera pulled back to reveal the same young woman who had been involved in the discovery of the tomb along with a stocky, swarthy man with a clean shaven head. Both were wearing long white lab coats and worked diligently at a bench where the seeds were displayed.

"And now to our UK correspondent, Jonathan Quilliam, for a live interview with the scientists who made the discovery."

"Thanks Dan. I am here with Professor Stanley Green, Head of the Cambridge University Department of Archaeology which was responsible for this remarkable discovery...."

Merrick stopped listening. His brow felt cold and clammy and he realised that his limbs were trembling as if he was coming down with influenza again. And then he felt a tightening pain near his left shoulder, which began to radiate outwards down his left arm and across to other parts of his body.

"You okay sir?" Manny asked. "Do you need your medicine?"

The words seemed to snap Merrick back to reality. Almost immediately he became focussed on his surroundings again and the pain in his chest began to subside. He lightly dabbed his forehead with a monogrammed handkerchief. After a few more seconds he trusted himself to speak again. "Yes, I think I'm alright now. For a moment there it felt like I was…. It must have been the impact of the news story."

Merrick was being honest, but not completely. He hadn't expected the report to have such a strong effect on him, because of the simple fact that he had already known about the discovery. He reasoned that it must have been the shock of finally seeing everything in its amazing context.

Manny regarded Merrick closely. He wasn't sure if the man was simply putting on a brave face and covering up for a more serious physical ailment. "Are you certain?"

"At my age you can never be certain."

Manny peered at Merrick closely. When he was reasonably satisfied that all was relatively okay with his boss, he said, "I have to admit that if I hadn't seen the discovery of the giant with my own eyes, I wouldn't have believed it."

"Why not?" Merrick followed up.

"Like most people, I thought that giants only existed in legends," Manny replied.

"Well, now we know there is some truth to the legends," Merrick said. "But we're not talking about the giant beings of mythology with the ridiculously-exaggerated heights of 50 to 100 feet tall. This is about the existence of actual stocks or races of very tall people in antiquity that stood somewhere between 7 and 9 feet tall, something which I don't find so hard to believe considering all of the cases of gigantism in recent times. But the revelation that giants existed in the past is only half of the story."

It took Manny a moment for the words to sink in. "What story?" Merrick told him.

Manuel Rodriguez walked briskly along Park Avenue seemingly unperturbed by the bustling hordes of pedestrians. As he passed by the many fancy hotels, businesses and extravagant store fronts that graced the famous Manhattan thoroughfare, his thoughts returned to the past. A past that he knew he could never escape from.

He entered the Park in the late afternoon when the shadows from the trees stretched long across the green open expanses. He walked for a few minutes along the winding pathways and finally sat on a sheltered bench by one of the Park's many lakes. The water's dark glassy surface was dotted with about one dozen remotely-piloted toy boats with tall white triangular sails. The boat pilots, mostly youngsters with adult supervisors in attendance, were scattered along the far shore. For a few moments, Manny was at peace. He gazed almost longingly at the tranquil scene but then turned his attention to the matter at hand. He dialled a number that he had committed to memory several years before. After a conversation lasting two minutes he hung up.

Chapter 11

Cambridge
July 6, 2007

Wednesday nights were Hawkins' favourite of the week. That was when he taught his beginners aikido course and, after most classes, he and a few of the students would go for a bite at Mama Amalfi's in the Grafton Centre. They used these occasions as a wind-down period and often discussed some of the more interesting aspects of the evening session. But Hawkins preferred it when the conversations turned to other subjects and he was constantly impressed by the fact that many of them led such interesting lives. It made him wonder about his own life, which seemed to be on hold. On this occasion, the usual crowd had to beg off in order to attend other functions. So he went alone.

As he entered the shopping centre and boarded the escalator ascending to the second level, he noticed a familiar figure ahead of him. She was clothed in a light grey blouse and a short snug fitting Levi skirt. Even without seeing her face, he knew it was her. He toyed with the idea of inviting her to eat with him. But then he recalled her less-than-friendly attitude the last time that they had been in each other's presence. He continued watching, considering his options, as she reached the top of the escalator.

He had been prepared to have a sit down meal by himself, even though he knew that this was a sad thing to do. He justified eating alone with the proviso that he knew the owner, Francesco, and they often had a decent chat together about the Bay of Naples area where Francesco was from. Hawkins had been a frequent visitor to this part of Italy due to his interest in the archaeological sites at Pompeii, Herculaneum and Paestum. But he also appreciated that it was an extremely beautiful place, dominated by the still dangerously-active Mount Vesuvius and boasting the picturesque islands of Capri, Ischia and Procida, and the world-famous rugged Amalfi coastline which has appeared in countless films as a site of dangerous car chases or as a scenic backdrop.

When he reached the second level, he saw Lori rush toward the cinema. He surmised that she was probably late for a date. He turned toward the restaurant and sat at his usual table by the open archway so that he could 'people watch' while he dined. As it turned out, Francesco wasn't working at the restaurant that night. His usual waitress, Antonella, said that Francesco was actually back home with his ailing mama in Positano, a picturesque cliff-side village on the southern shore of the Sorrentine Peninsula.

Antonella brought him a large plate of spaghetti Bolognaise and some pizza bread saturated with garlic. He twirled some noodles onto his fork with aid of his carefully positioned spoon, raised this to his mouth for the first mouthful and then promptly spilled the bulk of it back onto his plate, eliciting a small splattering of tomato sauce.

Lori was standing at his table. "You know that if you eat too much Italian food that you are going to lose that youthful figure of yours?" she said smiling down at him, hands on hips.

"Don't worry, I'm not really eating," Hawkins said without missing a beat, "as you can see."

Lori smiled at that. "Mind if I join you? I was supposed to meet a couple of friends for a movie but they either stood me up or went in without me."

"Now why on Earth would they do such a thing?"

"I'm not sure," Lori said sounding genuinely puzzled. "Maybe because I was 20 minutes late, as usual, and the film had already started."

"Yes that might do it," Hawkins observed, sagely. "Please take a seat."

Lori pulled out the chair and sat.

Antonella, who had noticed the encounter between Hawkins and the young lady with an ever increasing smile on her face, appeared at just the right time with a menu and smoothly handed this to the newcomer and gave Hawkins a conspiring wink. She was amused to note that Hawkins looked slightly panicked at this.

"Oh, I'll just have a starter portion of the spaghetti with tomato and basil sauce, please," Lori said without looking at the proffered menu but she gave Antonella a charming smile.

"Ah, that's Lelio's speciality," Antonella said. "I will have it here in less than 5 minutes."

After Antonella left to place the order Hawkins asked the obvious question first. "So, have you eaten at this restaurant before?"

"Yes, many times."

Hawkins was instantly absorbed by her eyes which appeared to be glistening, reflecting the flickering light from the candle on the table.

Lori continued. "I love Italian food and this is the best Italian restaurant in Cambridge. My mother is Italian and she used to cook pasta with all kinds of different sauces for us all of the time. I just came in here after the disappointment at the cinema to order a takeaway, then I thought I recognized you sitting over here by the window." She paused for a moment. "Do you come here often?"

Hawkins answered, "almost every Wednesday, after teaching a beginners' aikido class."

"Oh, the aikido thing…. Look, I'm really sorry for my comment last week about men and martial arts. It wasn't very fair."

Hawkins was momentarily taken aback. He hadn't expected anything like this from someone who he had associated with such epithets as the 'Ice queen'. "That's okay. I have to admit that it was probably a valid point about most martial arts, anyway."

"Well, teaching must be fun," Lori said, inviting more conversation on the subject.

"Yes, and sometimes it's just plain funny," Hawkins said smiling. "You're welcome to come along anytime you like and watch the class. You know…to see if you are interested."

"I've always wanted to take some kind of self-defence course," Lori said.

He couldn't believe she was actually considering it.

"Aikido is great for that. But hopefully you will never find yourself in the kind of situation where you need to use it."

"Oh, I'm sure that will never happen."

On the other side of the restaurant, two tall men dressed in black sat down at another candle lit table. The slightly shorter of the two men had a long jagged scar on the left side of his face and he had the steel grey, steady eyes of a surgeon. But just by looking at the man it would be difficult for anyone to gauge his actual profession. The cut of his suit suggested that he was some kind of businessman.

The second man was approximately 6 foot 5, with broad shoulders and looked as if he might have played rugby at one time. He had short military-cut blonde hair and a jaw that was so square it looked like it belonged on a cartoon character. His face was not a friendly one. It seemed to have a perpetual frown as if he had given up on learning how to smile years before.

Both men attempted to order traditional German beers from the young waitress using halting English in thick Bavarian accents. After being informed that this was, in fact, an Italian restaurant, they both decided with some misgivings to settle for a Peroni Nastro Azzuro.

After receiving their beers, the tall blonde man took a tentative sip straight from his bottle and immediately slammed this down on the table and winced in disgust. After watching this reaction, the man with the scar pushed his own beer away and sat back in his chair. They spent the rest of the time pretending not to watch the couple on the other side of the restaurant.

Lori's pasta arrived when Hawkins was almost halfway finished with his spaghetti. He had been eating from his plate only sporadically to ensure that he still had something left so that Lori wouldn't have to eat alone.

"You mentioned your family before," Hawkins began. "What do your father and mother do for a living?"

"My father does stem cell research at the Salk Institute in San Diego," she answered in between mouthfuls of her pasta. "They are focussing on degenerative diseases and exploring stem cell repair strategies using either implantation or activation of endogenous stem cells."

"Fascinating." Hawkins had kept up with some of the developments in this exciting field, but he couldn't think of any further response, let alone an intelligent one.

"And my mother is a senior lecturer at UC San Diego," Lori continued, unknowingly letting him off the hook.

"Does she lecture in science?"

"Yes, she used to do research and now she teaches pharmacology to undergraduates."

"Do you have any brothers or sisters?"

Lori's face winced involuntarily and Hawkins realised with a sudden jolt that he might have blundered into dangerous territory.

After a long agonising moment for both of them, she said, "I had a brother but he was killed by… in an accident." She lowered her glance, clearly upset but not to the point of tears.

Hawkins lay his fork down, reached across the table and placed his hand gently on top of hers. It seemed like the right thing to do.

Lori looked up with a tight smile and glistening eyes. "I'm sorry, that shook me for a moment. It happened so long ago you would think that I would be over it by now. But I think that I'm still haunted by what happened."

"No, I'm sorry. I shouldn't have pried."

"You weren't prying. You just asked a typically normal question."

Hawkins felt like he should offer more words of comfort but he couldn't think of anything else to say. Then he noticed that the moment had passed and she quickly pulled herself together, drawing herself upright in her chair.

He slowly took his hand from hers and said, "why don't we talk about something else?" He attempted to roll up more of the slippery pasta onto his spoon but seemed to be struggling now more than ever.

"You really haven't mastered that yet have you?" Lori said smiling.

"I usually do a little better than this. There must be something different about the pasta tonight," he joked. "It seems to be more slippery than usual. I wonder if Luigi is using too much olive oil."

Lori smiled again. Then her expression seemed to grow more serious. "You know what we were talking about a minute ago?"

Hawkins stopped eating. "Yes?"

"I'd like to tell you all about it some other time, if you'll let me."

"Are you sure you want to?"

"Yes, but you'll have to get me drunk first."

"It's a date then," Hawkins said a bit too quickly, immediately regretting his choice of words. "I mean not a date…but…you know."

Lori laughed when she realised his predicament. "Are you always this articulate?" she asked smiling.

"Actually, this is me at my best."

Chapter 12

Cambridge
July 7, 2007

The soft glow of the flat screen monitor illuminated the small attic room. The drone of a low-flying jet and the noisy merriment of the pub crawlers nearby could be heard faintly through the opened windows. Jim Hawkins sat hunched over his home computer, hands poised over the keyboard, trying hard to remember what he had just been about to tap out. It was no good. His brain was fogged with fatigue. He scanned the text on the screen to see if he could gain some clue from the last line that he had written. Utter gibberish. "Nice goin' Drongo," he mumbled to himself. Since his brain had obviously decided to shut down, he might as well do the same with the computer.

He had more than 100 publications to his name but it hadn't been easy. He had gone through varying degrees of brain-wracking agony in writing each one of them. He would rather be out in the field. But in academia writing papers was absolutely essential. Researchers were under constant pressure to publish their work in order to sustain or further their careers. This was why he was currently driving himself to a state of exhausted madness in trying to add finishing touches to just one of the multiple papers on their discovery.

His telephone had not stopped ringing following the first airing of the discovery on TV news programmes. Not only had he been pummelled with non-stop questions from other archaeologists, he had also received countless requests for further interviews from British news networks and newspapers such as *The Independent* and *The Daily Mail*. He had even had offers from American, Canadian, Japanese and Australian TV stations for personal interviews on the remarkable findings of his team. Now, the pressure was on to ensure that all tests were carried out correctly, all of the facts were accurate and this was reflected in the publications.

Hawkins stretched his arms towards the ceiling to loosen the kinks that had started attacking his mid-thoracic region from sitting so long in one position. Then he brought his arms down and breathed a deep sigh. As he reached forward to shut down the computer, the telephone rang dully from beneath a pile of papers on the desk. Fumbling reflexively for the telephone with his right hand, he sent his forgotten coffee mug tumbling over the edge of the desk. It didn't hit the floor. He looked down and then groaned in abject disgust to see that it had actually fallen into his wide-opened briefcase releasing a sizeable volume of cold coffee. He picked up the phone and grunted, "hello."

"Dr Hawkins?" Lori Davis asked carefully. "I was betting that you'd still be working."

"Uh...yes. Sort of."

"Is everything okay?" Lori asked. "You sound a bit tense."

"I'm fine. Just a little tired, I guess."

"Well, David and Pavlos are both here with me on speakerphone and we've got something that might just wake you up again."

Silence.

"Are you there?" Lori asked.

"Yeah, I was just doing some damage control," Hawkins said as he cradled the phone between ear and shoulder and began to pull coffee-soaked documents from his briefcase.

"What?"

"Nothing. What've you got?"

"We were looking at DNA sequences," Lori began. "Then we had an interesting idea that panned out. Do you remember the autopsy results which suggested the mummy was at least 80 years-old at the time of death?"

"Yes...."

Lori continued. "Well, since this didn't seem to fit other indications on the body, we worked out a way of determining his age. Have you ever heard of Leonard Hayflick?"

"Uh...no," Hawkins admitted.

"Hayflick carried out some landmark studies on aging in the early 1960s. He simply placed cells taken from a human fetus into a Petri dish to see how many times they would divide and multiply. The answer was: around 50 times and then the cells died. Then he repeated the experiment with cells taken from a 70-year-old person and the cells divided only around 20 times before they died. He reasoned that most human cells are capable of dividing only around 50 times from the time we are born. This led to the idea that there must be a molecular clock inside all cells that tells them when it's time to die."

"Interesting," Hawkins said. "So what is this molecular clock?"

"The telomeres," Lori responded. "These are protective cap-like structures at the end of each chromosome. The analogy that has been used is that they are like the plastic cuffs that protect the end of your shoelaces which stops them from fraying. In reality, they are short DNA sequences which are repeated thousands of times. For most of the cells in your body, the telomeres get shorter each time a cell divides. When these cells reach the limit of 50 divisions, or so, the telomeres hit a critical short point and the cells can't divide any more. This leads to aging, diseases like cancer, and death. In effect, the telomeres are like ticking time bombs inside our cells which limit the human lifespan to an absolute maximum of around 120 years."

"You said 'most cells' act this way?" Hawkins interjected.

"Yes, that's right. There are some cells that actually have full length telomeres throughout the lifespan. But these are exceptional types of cells such as sperm, ova, stem cells and most cancer cells. These special cells are characterized by their ability to divide not just 50 times but thousands of times or even indefinitely. For all intents and purposes, they are immortal."

"But why don't the telomeres in these special cells get shorter?"

"Simple," Lori replied. "They contain an enzyme called telomerase which helps to maintain the telomeres at, or near, their full length. This lets the cells go on dividing. In the case of cancer cells, this is bad because these cells grow out of control and can kill you. In the case of stem cells, it's good since our bodies use these new cells during development and in later life to replace old and damaged tissue. For sperm and egg cells it is also good because these cells have to remain young to pass on DNA with completely intact telomeres to the offspring."

"Let me see if I have this straight," Hawkins said. "If you look at the telomeres of any cell that doesn't normally contain telomerase, say a muscle or bone cell, you should see relatively long telomeres in a baby, and shorter ones in someone who is much older."

"Exactly," Lori remarked. "I had to explain that to David several times before he got it."

"She used a lot of big words Jim," David's said plaintively.

Lori continued, undeterred. "All of this brings us to the point that we tested the length of the telomeres in DNA samples taken from the giant's skin cells. To make sure that the test was working, we also analysed skin cell DNA from a human fetus, a teenager, a 5,000-year-old Egyptian mummy with an apparent age of 40 at the time of death, and an 82-year-old man. As expected, the fetus had the longest telomeres, the teenager and the Egyptian mummy had intermediate lengths, and the telomeres in the 82 year-old were the shortest."

"And the giant…?"

Lori hesitated. "My first thought was that we must have made some kind of mistake."

Hawkins didn't believe that Lori was the sort of person to make mistakes.

"The telomeres from the giant were the same length as those from the fetus," Lori said.

"What?" Hawkins' spine was tingling.

She rephrased her last statement. "The giant's telomeres were fully intact…. "Dr Hawkins? Are you still there?"

"Yes. I just had to think," he said trying to kick start his brain again. "Are you sure about this?"

Pavlos spoke up. "Dr Hawkins, as sure as my name is Pavlos Konstantinou, the results are accurate. We will repeat the test using other tissues from the giant but I believe we will find the same answer."

Who does this guy think he is? Hawkins wondered. *And why does he sound like a robot?*

Lori chimed in, "I think that Pavlos is right. We were very careful not to mix up any of the samples. As incredible as it seems, this result is real." In fact –"

Lori broke off the conversation and Hawkins was suddenly confronted by a deathly silence over the telephone.

"Lori?"

"Hold on Dr Hawkins." Lori said with a note of alarm in her voice.

Through the speaker phone, Hawkins heard Lori say "Pavlos can you go check that out?"

Then he heard David's voice saying, "I'll go too."

"Okay," Lori said to Hawkins. "They are just going to see what's going on. We should be the only one's here but we heard something outside the lab."

"Could it be the cleaner?"

"They usually come around much earlier," Lori replied. "But it is probably noth –"

"Lori? What's going on?"

"I don't know," she said – now frantic. "Hang on!"

Hawkins heard her push her chair back, followed by quick steps moving away. He waited tensely for her to return when suddenly he heard two rapid fire bangs and something that sounded like crashing metal. Then he heard a sharp scream from Lori. This was followed by more crashing noises and the sound of breaking glass.

"Lori! David!" he yelled into the phone. He received no reply but could hear rustling sounds and mumbled voices –

And then silence.

Chapter 13

Cambridge
July 7, 2007

Hawkins was on the telephone for 6 long minutes with the exasperatingly patient dispatch operator. After voicing his concerns that the call was taking too damn long, and throwing in a few other expletives to drive the point home, he was assured that several police units had already been sent to the site. When the operator had finished plying him for information and requested that he remain at his residence for a return telephone call, he hung up and waited as instructed – for three seconds.

He hurriedly scrambled down the stairs, snatched up his car keys, bolted out the front door and jumped into the Camaro. After reversing none too carefully from his driveway, he stamped the accelerator pedal to the floor and launched the car like a screaming rocket down the road, leaving two long streaks of rubber to mark his point of departure. It was less than two miles to the LMB at Addenbrooke's Hospital, but that was like light years for Hawkins in his present state of mind.

Along the way, he streaked through two sets of red traffic lights, nearly sideswiped an old Citroen DS 21 crossing a junction and drew numerous glares of outrage from other motorists. He was also caught by three speed cameras for driving at speeds of 78, 82 and 72 miles per hour, in a residential zone. Nearing the end of the hair-raising journey, he took a risky shortcut by going the wrong way around the Addenbrooke's Hospital roundabout. The Camaro slid and then swayed wildly as he cut the steering wheel sharply to negotiate the final small roundabout near the LMB building where he skilfully manoeuvred it almost sideways to a skidding halt. There were already several police cars and an ambulance present with lights flashing.

He dashed from the car and then practically flew up the two short flights of steps to the glassed-in front entrance of the building, where he found a burly policeman frowning down at him.

"What's your business here sir?" the policeman growled.

Hawkins huffed, looked pained and said, "I'm Dr Jim Hawkins. I'm the one who called in to report this. Those three people up there are members of my research team."

"Right. I see Dr Hawkins. But I can't let you in because this is a crime scene. I am going to have to ask you to leave."

"I'm not leaving until I find out if they're okay," Hawkins said firmly.

"Sir," the policeman reverted to professional calmness, "please return to your home and someone will call you."

Hawkins was frustrated. There didn't seem to be anyway of winning this guy over. "Can you at least let me know if everyone is okay? It sounded to me like intruders were in the lab. I heard fighting and objects being smashed."

"I'll tell you what," the cop began, now sounding slightly more sympathetic to Hawkins' plight. "Why don't you wait here for the Chief Inspector. I'll let him know that you're here and he can have a word with you and take your statement. I think it would actually save him some time, anyway."

"Hawkins let his head sag with the small victory. "Okay, thanks. Please let him know that I'm waiting." He turned and padded back towards the Camaro.

"Will do," the policeman said. He started to pull out his radiophone to call his boss when he noticed that Dr Hawkins wasn't wearing shoes.

As a building, the Laboratory of Molecular Biology, known as the LMB, was stark and unappealing with a brown and white 4-storey façade and plain uncompromising windows. In this sense, it fit perfectly with the other drab units of the Addenbrooke's Hospital complex. Of course there had been some attempts to make the building more attractive. These included the incorporation of a white helical fire escape on the left hand side and, more recently, by the addition the Medical Research Council building on the right, which incorporated a modern-looking, all glass front entrance. The Medical Research Council supported the LMB in aspects of administration and other services. Situated next to this was a grey-coloured monstrosity that looked like the command deck of 1940s battle ship. In actuality, it was a lecture theatre named after the Nobel Laureate Max Perutz, but its sheltering bulk also provided the cover for a multitude of bicycle racks.

Despite its appearances, the LMB has had a distinguished history since its inception in 1962 on the Addenbrooke's Hospital site. Amazingly, it has produced no less than 13 Nobel Laureates including such greats as the aforementioned Max Perutz along with John Kendrew for studies on protein structure, Jim Watson and Francis Crick for discoveries on the structure and genetic transfer of DNA, and Sydney Brenner, John Sulston and Robert Horvitz for work on the regulation of organ development and programmed cell death. Also, several biotechnology companies have been established following major contributions from the LMB. It appeared to be a breeding ground for some of Britain's best scientists. Currently, the building housed more than 60 research groups in the areas of cell biology, neurobiology, endocrinology, protein and nucleic acid chemistry and structural studies.

After nearly 20 minutes, a man who could only have been the Chief Inspector came out of the building and marched briskly down the steps to meet Hawkins, who was still waiting shoeless in the Camaro. Hawkins started to get out of the car but the man waved him back.

"Why don't we sit in your car Dr Hawkins?"

Hawkins thought that sounded like slightly unusual police procedure but he just nodded and eased back into the driver's seat.

After he opened the passenger door and settled into the well-maintained bucket seat the man said, "I have an addiction for American classic cars. You just don't see many of them around anymore. At least, not like this one."

Hawkins immediately warmed to him, and not just because of his interest in cars. The man seemed to have a genuinely honest yet strong face a bit reminiscent of the screen legend Paul Newman in his later years. He appeared to be around 60 years-old but had obviously kept himself in good shape over the years.

Strangely, Hawkins noticed that the Inspector was examining him with a knowing expression on his face. But before Hawkins could think any more about this, the Inspector's commentary on the car had resumed.

"1969 Camaro 350 Super Sport?" the man asked after a brief examination of the car windows and interior.

"That's right. You do know your cars."

"It's my only real hobby these days," he explained. "Anyway, allow me to introduce myself. I'm Chief Inspector Ian Sanderson and I'm in charge of the case." He reached into his top pocket and pulled out a business card which he handed to Hawkins.

"Chief Inspector Sanderson, how are my friends upstairs?" Hawkins said as he placed Sanderson's card in his coat pocket and withdrew one of his own cards from the Camaro's glove box to give to the inspector.

"Brace yourself for some bad news Dr Hawkins," Sanderson said with an apologetic expression. "We've identified one of the victims as David Englehart, your PhD student. He's suffered a concussion and has a few bruised ribs. They should be bringing him down any second to get him to the emergency room. If there is a bright side, there's no better place to be injured than just a 200 feet from an A & E."

Hawkins was both surprised and relieved to hear the news about David, but he still had the overwhelming sense that the worst news had yet to come. He managed to respond, "okay."

Sanderson continued. "The other male, identified as Pavlos Konstantinou, appears to have died from two gunshot wounds to the head and torso. I am sorry to have to tell you this."

Hawkins was stunned and sat quietly digesting this information for a full 10 seconds before he said, "I didn't really know him."

When the inspector said nothing, Hawkins continued, "I did hear what sounded like two gun shots over the telephone speaker."

"What time was that?" Sanderson asked immediately.

"Around 11:05 or 11:10," Hawkins said weakly. "I didn't think to check the time."

"Don't worry about it Dr Hawkins. Can you tell me what else you heard?"

Hawkins nodded. "I was talking with the three of them over the speaker phone about some experiments when Dr Davis heard a noise and Pavlos and David went to investigate. Then, after a few seconds there was another noise and Lori left as well. Then I heard loud banging noises and the sounds of a struggle. This may have lasted about 20 seconds and then I heard glass breaking and the gun shots. I think that was when I heard Lori scream. That was when I called 999." Hawkins paused for a moment before asking the next dreaded question, his stomach knotted in apprehension. "Is she okay?"

"We don't know," Sanderson said, looking puzzled.

"What do you mean?" Hawkins asked.

"She's missing."

Five minutes later, two paramedics brought a barely-conscious David out from the side entrance of the LMB into the parking area on a roll away stretcher. David waved feebly at Hawkins who responded with a wave of his own. But David was quickly whisked away to the austere Accident & Emergency building just across from the LMB on the opposite side of the parking lot. The building was lit up like a Christmas tree as if it had been busy with other accidents all night long. Hawkins wanted to talk with his student but first he had to accompany Inspector Sanderson up to Lori's lab to assist in the investigation.

On their way into the side entrance of the building, Hawkins and Sanderson were passed by two paramedics manoeuvring a gurney containing a motionless body, completely sealed in a black zip-up bag, down the steps. Hawkins couldn't believe that the spirited young man he had just been talking to on the telephone was now dead. He couldn't help but feel somewhat guilty for not having the chance to get to know him. But the vision of the body bag also filled him with dread as to what might have become of Lori.

The corridor outside the lab looked like it had been the scene of a small explosion. Cupboards, filing cabinets and bookshelves had been overturned or knocked into disarray. The contents, including chemical and equipment catalogues, files and various items of stationary, were scattered all over as if a small tornado had swept through the hallway. Two of the filing cabinets had large indentations where the metal had obviously encountered a large pounding force. Hawkins didn't even want to consider how that had happened. It was in the corridor about 10 feet from Lori's lab door that Hawkins spotted the chalk outline on the floor, partly covering a few scattered catalogues.

Pavlos.

Hawkins and Sanderson silently stepped past the grotesque marking and into the lab. They were met by two large-bodied policemen and a plain-clothed auburn-haired woman with a digital camera. It was clear that they had finished what they had been doing for the time being and were just waiting for Sanderson to return.

"Everyone," Sanderson said by way of introduction, "this is Dr Jim Hawkins and he was in telephone contact with the people in the lab when the attack began."

"I recognize Dr Hawkins from the news program on the discovery of the Wandlebury giant," said the woman. "Incredible, by the way." The policemen merely nodded but seemed to be aware of the news.

Hawkins finally understood the reason why Sanderson had appeared to recognize him earlier. Because he had become so caught up in the events of this terrible night, that he had entirely forgotten about his brief appearance on television just the day before.

"Dr Hawkins we know about the basics of your research, but what specifically was going on in this lab?" Inspector Sanderson asked.

"Dr Lori Davis and Pavlos Konstantinou were carrying out molecular analysis on some of the artefacts from the tomb, including samples from the mummy itself. They were actually looking at proteins and DNA in those samples to learn more about how to classify them."

"So in your opinion Dr, is there anything in here worth stealing?"

"I'm not sure... I don't think so. These were just small samples brought here for analysis. The mummy and all of the other large artefacts are being stored downtown in the Department of Archaeology."

For a moment, Inspector Sanderson looked visibly shaken. He raised one eyebrow in a pained expression and said, "where exactly?"

"Wha –?" Hawkins stopped as he suddenly realised why the inspector was asking. "Main building, second floor, secure lab G."

Inspector Sanderson nodded, picked up his radio, pressed the speak button and relayed the message. He sent two units immediately to the archaeology lab.

"Do you think that they may have hit that lab, as well?" Hawkins asked.

"It's just a possibility," Sanderson explained. "We can't be sure of anything until we know what they were after."

Hawkins looked around the lab helplessly. He couldn't imagine what the thieves would want with the meagre amount of samples in this lab.

Sanderson continued. "Do you notice anything missing? Anything at all?"

"The problem is I haven't actually been to this lab for some time but I do know what they were working on. I don't see anything obvious on the benches. Can I look through the refrigerators and freezers?"

Sanderson glanced toward the stocky policeman who said, "it's okay, Chief. They've already been dusted for prints."

Sanderson said to Hawkins, "okay, but open them from the edge and use some lab gloves, just in case."

Hawkins nodded, pulled on a pair of large vinyl gloves and went through the small under-bench refrigerators and freezers systematically. He spotted several racks containing tubes of DNA and protein extracts that had been taken from the original samples, but there was no sign of the samples themselves. He didn't think that they could have all been used up. Lori was far too clever as a scientist to commit such a basic error. He informed Inspector Sanderson about the results of his search.

"What about data?" Sanderson asked. "Did Dr Davis and the others record their work anywhere?"

Hawkins strode to the office, followed by Sanderson. They both noted that the speaker phone was still switched on. "She would have had her lab book by the phone as we were going through the results," Hawkins pointed out. He opened the drawers of the desk and peered inside. "It's not here." He noticed that the computer was still logged on. After tapping a few keys, he frowned and then checked the computer disk space by going into the control panel. "It's been wiped. The intruders must have downloaded everything and then wiped it."

"Okay Dr Hawkins," Sanderson said. "I think that about covers it for now. I have to ask you if you have any idea who would carry out such an act. Do you have any enemies or competitors that you know of who might be responsible?"

"Enemies?" Hawkins was stumped. "I don't think so. At least no more than your average archaeologist. I can't begin to think who could have done this, or even why they would do it."

"Well, I don't think it's a coincidence that this lab was hit after the feature that appeared on the news describing your find. The perpetrators must have been interested in something they saw."

"But they're just artefacts. Nothing of real value. Maybe the weapons and even the mummy itself could be valuable enough if they were stolen for someone's private collection."

Sanderson responded. "Is there anything else that you might have overlooked."

Hawkins' mind was reeling.

"For example, could there be anything that might have commercial value?" Sanderson prompted him.

"Well the only other thing was the seeds and the sprouts," Hawkins said. "But I can't see why anyone would want those."

"Sprouts?" Sanderson asked with raised eyebrows.

"Yes," Hawkins replied. "Dr Davis and Pavlos were able to get some of the ancient seeds to germinate in plant pots. The finding of the seeds themselves was featured briefly on the news program."

"Yes, I remember," Sanderson said. "The seeds. But there was no mention of germinating them on the program."

"No, that's right there wasn't. We wanted to keep that part quiet until we were certain," Hawkins explained.

Sanderson's detective instincts were telling him that there might be something here, so he persisted along the line of questioning. "And do you know where those seeds would have been kept in the lab Dr Hawkins?"

Hawkins responded by asking a question of his own, "you didn't see anything like that when your people were searching the lab?"

"No, I don't think so," Sanderson replied. "McLeish!" he called out to one of the men who had remained in the lab. "Did you notice any sign of seeds or plant pots containing a few baby plants out there?"

The large policeman named McLeish stepped to the edge of the office and poked his head inside. "We did find some pots and a bit of dirt over there in the corner," he said gesturing with his thumb behind him. "But there weren't any baby plants that we could see."

Hawkins and Sanderson followed the policeman to the corner and saw several broken pots and a spattering of rich, dark soil dispersed across the bench top. McLeish was right.

The baby plants were gone.

Chapter 14

Cambridge
July 8, 2007

The extent of the crime was not as bad as Sanderson had feared and appeared to be limited to the LMB site. He had received an update that the Department of Archaeology had been quiet all night with no signs of any intrusion. Nevertheless, he left a guard posted there for the time being just as a precaution. Also, Sanderson sent Officer McLeish to check with the Addenbrooke's Security Department just in case there had been a closed circuit camera pointing at the LMB entrance. There was a chance that the intruders had been captured on film.

Deepening swirls of turquoise and salmon painted the eastern sky, heralding the imminent sunrise as Sanderson and Hawkins walked across the parking area to the A & E. They entered the brightly lit building and Sanderson made the appropriate inquiries of the young woman on duty at the front desk. She told them they would be allowed a short visit with David as the doctor had just finished with him. He was listed as stable and recovering. As they walked into the small room, Hawkins saw that David was awake.

"Hey Jim, how are you?" David asked, sitting virtually upright in his bed. "Hello again, Inspector –"

Hawkins could see that David's ribs were wrapped in bandages and his eyes had a glazed look to them.

"– Sanderson," the Inspector finished for him. "Don't worry. Your memory is likely to be a little iffy after what you've been through tonight. You were barely conscious when we first met."

"Most importantly, how are you David?" Hawkins said as he sat down on the edge of the long narrow bed. Sanderson eased himself into the only chair in the room.

"Well, not too bad considering what happened," David said. "I think they're planning to release me in the morning."

"Are you up to talking about what happened?" Sanderson asked.

"Yeah, of course." David said. "I wanna help you guys get those bastards. How's Lori?"

Silence.

After a moment, Hawkins began haltingly, "David... we assumed that you knew. After they killed Pavlos and dealt with you, they must have taken her."

David's eyes drilled into Hawkins. "Why?"

Sanderson interjected, "that's what we aim to find out. Can you give us a quick rundown of everything you remember?"

"Okay," David said as he winced suddenly and touched the tightly-wrapped bandage on his head.

"Take it slowly," Sanderson urged.

David began. "While we were speaking with Jim, uh Dr Hawkins, over the telephone about some results, we heard a noise in the corridor outside the lab. At first I thought it might be the cleaner but then we heard the sound of several people moving through the corridor outside the lab. Most nights, Lori and Pavlos had been the only ones working late so we were a little surprised. I just figured that someone who worked along the corridor had brought some friends with them while they finished off a late-running experiment. That sort of thing happens sometimes. Lori suggested that Pavlos check it out and I decided to go along too. When we stepped out into the corridor, I think we surprised them. There were four men."

"Can you described them?" Sanderson asked.

"I think so," David said. "Three of the men looked similar: tall, blond or brown hair, Caucasian. They were wearing what looked like black tracksuits as if they had bought them off the same rack. One of the men had a long scar on the left side of his face. He seemed to be the leader, because he did all of the talking. The fourth man stood out from the others. He looked Latin American, and was shorter than them, around my height. He was also dressed differently. He had on a dark green business suit."

Sanderson looked up from his notes "Go on, you're doing great."

"Pavlos asked them what they were doing here this time of night," David said. "At first the men didn't respond. They just walked towards us trying to look nonchalant. Then the leader asked if this was where Lori Davis worked. I remember thinking that this was all wrong and Pavlos asked them to leave and make an appointment to see her during the normal working hours. But just then, Lori came out of the lab behind us. She said something to the effect of 'hey, what are you doing here?' and then the men moved fast. One of the tall ones pulled out a large black handgun and clubbed Pavlos with it. Pavlos was hurt but he didn't fall. Then he yelled something in Greek that didn't need translating and, before I could blink, he had grabbed the man in a bear hug and picked him up off the ground. But one of the others kicked out Pavlos' legs and sent him down in a heap while he was still clutching the first man.

"While they were engaged with Pavlos, I managed to whack the leader in jaw which put him down. Then as I turned back to try and help Pavlos, I saw the man in the green suit move like a blur. He fired a right cross at me which I managed to block but then, far quicker than I thought humanly possible, he followed that with a left and right combination to my ribs that knocked the wind out of me. The guy must have fought in the ring because he knew what he was doing. Before I could get my breath back he put me down with what felt like a sledge hammer to the left side of my head. I managed to roll slightly with the punch but it was still powerful enough to put me down. As I fell, I must have hit the filing cabinet with the back of my head and lost consciousness. But, as I was falling, I thought I saw one of the tracksuit guys… well… he just shot Pavlos while he was still on the ground. The last thing I remember was hearing Lori scream.

"Then I woke up when the police stormed into the building," David finished. "That was when I saw Pavlos lying dead on the ground with two bullet holes in his chest and blood was all around. I couldn't see Lori anywhere and I must have lost consciousness again. I remember seeing you Jim, as they carried me out of the building and then I threw up a few times while they were patching me up in the hospital."

"Can you remember any other details about the men?" Sanderson asked.

"Yes," David said, looking like he had a mental breakthrough. "I think the track suits were Adidas."

"Uh...they will probably get rid of those so that might not turn out to be too helpful," Sanderson said. "Can you remember anything else about their physical characteristics?"

David thought for a moment and closed his eyes. "All of the men in the tracksuits had crew cuts and one could have been bald. The guy with the scar spoke German because I heard him say 'scheisse' when Pavlos grabbed the guy with the gun. They all looked mean except for the guy in the green suit. Even when he was kicking my ass. It's strange but it didn't even look like he wanted to be there and he looked worried."

Sanderson had no more questions after that.

"David, you should rest now," Hawkins said. "Save anything else you can think of for tomorrow."

"Yes, thank you David," Sanderson added. "You've been very helpful."

"What were they after?" David asked.

"Samples from the find, it seems," Hawkins answered.

David sat forward suddenly, hurting his ribs in the process. "Ow! Crap! Is the mummy in Arch lab okay?"

"Yes they haven't touched anything else. It just seems that they were interested in some of the small samples that you guys were analysing," Hawkins said. "And they took the seedlings."

"Strange," David commented as he carefully lay his head back down on the pillow and closed his eyes. It was clear that he was no longer capable of any more rational thought. But with eyes still closed he managed one more question. "We're going to catch these guys aren't we Inspector?"

The inspector said, "we're going to do our best."

As David drifted off, he remembered thinking that really wasn't the same thing.

Chapter 15

Cambridge
July 8, 2007

The atmospheric gloom of the sudden morning rainstorm couldn't have been more appropriate. It served to reinforce the already clouded, sombre mood of the two men in the car. Hawkins drove back to the hospital, wipers going full tilt, as the Camaro was hammered by rain from the surprisingly heavy cloud burst. He had just updated Zoran, who was sitting in the shotgun seat, on the harrowing events of the night before. Like Hawkins, Zoran had been working at home when the incident had occurred. The tall geologist absorbed the information quietly, mulling over the details.

Arriving at the hospital, Hawkins piloted the Camaro to a splashy halt in one of the extra wide parking bays in front of the A & E. The two men dashed from the car into the building to avoid getting soaked. After Hawkins filled out the necessary paperwork at the front desk, David walked with feigned nonchalance into the lobby as if he didn't have a care in the world. But Hawkins and Zoran weren't fooled. David was bravely attempting to conceal his injuries. The head injury didn't appear to be too serious and was only swathed in a single clean bandage. Presumably, this was meant to protect the stitched wound on the back of his head. But it was clear that David's ribs were troubling him as he walked while holding his torso with a slight stiffness.

"Don't look so worried guys. I'm gonna dance again."

"You should take it easy for a while," Zoran cautioned.

"Bollocks," David observed. "Let's go find the wankers that took Lori and kick some ass!"

"We don't even know where to look," Hawkins said. "The investigation hasn't got that far."

David nodded, acknowledging that minor hitch. But he still kept a determined expression fixed on his face as the three of them exited the building. The rain had eased off slightly during the few minutes that they were in the ward. Zoran climbed into the Camaro's small back seat so David could ride in relative comfort in the front. Hawkins turned the key and the car came to life with a resonating roar.

As Hawkins manoeuvred the Camaro around the convoluted road system that led out of the hospital site, Zoran leaned forward and said, "how is that head of yours, David?"

"The head is fine. The only part of me that isn't fine is a burning need to settle the score with those guys, especially that Mike Tyson wannabe who used me for a punching bag."

"You really think he knew boxing?" Hawkins asked.

"Yes, because I'm no slouch and he kicked my ass from here to Timbuktu. I'm not making excuses but I think I underestimated him by assuming that he was just an ordinary thug. Before I could react he had me dead to rights. He was fast, lightning fast. I could hardly see the punches coming. And the way he moved and power of those sledgehammer punches he hit me with... that can only come with a lot of ring experience."

"Which one shot Pavlos?" Zoran inquired.

"The leader. One of the creepy, tall crewcuts dressed in black," David clarified. "That guy was pure evil."

"They are all equally guilty of murder and kidnapping," Zoran said.

David was silent for a moment and then said, "maybe not."

Zoran's eyebrows arched in confusion. "What do you mean?"

"I'm not sure," David allowed. "But I thought that I heard the man in green object when they shot Pavlos. He said something to the leader along the lines of: 'you didn't have to do that'."

Hawkins didn't know what to make of that. None of this made any sense. "You didn't hear anything else, did you?"

"Yeah," David said, surprising himself as another memory came flooding back. "I heard something else before everything went dark. Just two words – seeds and plantlets. I think this was their primary objective."

"But that's crazy," Zoran commented. "What could they want them for? And why kill for them."

"Good question mate," Hawkins said. "That's what we need to find out."

He pulled the Camaro into his driveway, turned off the ignition and said, "why don't you both come in for an espresso and we'll talk it through?"

"Works for me," David said. "Coffee sounds good right now."

"Me too," Zoran agreed.

They emerged from the car into what had now become a light drizzle. Hawkins stepped to the door and used his key to open it. He took one step inside and then just as quickly retreated and slammed the door shut.

While David and Zoran were both standing with mouths agape and trying to work out what was going on, Hawkins shouted at his front door. "Brandy! Down girl! I'm coming in with an injured man. It's David. I also have Zoran with me. Do not jump up! I repeat, do not jump up!"

David glanced at Zoran with a mock-worried expression on his face. "You think he's got a woman in there?"

"It's just Brandy," Hawkins answered. "She's started jumping up on me whenever I get home. I think she misses me. I'm trying to break her of the habit."

"Seems to be working," David joked.

"It'll be okay, don't worry," Hawkins said. Then he turned back to the door and called out, "alright Brandy! We're coming in!" With that he pushed the door open and jumped inside to face 195 pounds of canine onslaught.

After Hawkins managed to calm Brandy down, and wipe the doggy slime from his face, he filled her bowl with more than a pound of chow. As the massive canine dived on the bowl and began vacuuming up the food, Hawkins realised, once again, that all was okay in his dog's little world. *What a life*, he thought.

Then he tended to his human friends waiting in the converted kitchen-dining-lounge area in the basement of the house by providing each of them with a thick, tarry espresso coffee. It was the ritual of the preparation that normally relaxed Hawkins. And the pleasing, comforting aroma of coffee pervaded the expansive room. But on this occasion it was lost on the three scientists. It was masked by an over-riding sensation of apprehension for their female colleague.

"Okay, why the seeds?" Hawkins jumped right to the crux of the matter as he settled into the stiff-backed sofa next to Zoran. David reclined almost flat out with feet up in Hawkins' favourite leather lounge chair.

"Dunno," David said as he tilted his head forward and sipped from his espresso. "Maybe it was a prestige thing. Maybe they just wanted to be the proud owners of the oldest ancient plants ever cultivated."

"Doubtful," Hawkins commented. "Any declaration that they even had the plants would not only be an admission of guilt for the theft, but also for the more serious crimes of murder and kidnapping."

"Then maybe they were taken for some rich psycho's private collection," David said. "Or by an agency that auctions unique or rare antiquities out to the highest bidder. Ancient artefacts are stolen every day for that very reason."

"Could be," Hawkins mused. "But maybe they were taken for a more specific purpose."

"What do you mean, Jim?" asked Zoran. "Do have an idea?"

"Not yet," Hawkins responded.

"Maybe we should talk to someone who knows something about ancient plants," David suggested.

After a moment Zoran said, "why don't we ask Stanley? He showed a lot of interest in the jar containing the seeds. Also, he asked Lori and Pavlos to keep him informed about all of their progress with the seeds since that time."

"He did?" Hawkins said, sounding surprised. After a moment of consideration, that feeling became one of concern. "That's unusual for Stanley to bypass me like that."

"I did think it was a bit inappropriate," Zoran said. "I was going to tell you about it at the time but it slipped my mind."

Just then, a problem that had been nagging at David's clouded brain all morning suddenly resolved itself into crystal clarity. "Wait a second," he exclaimed, sitting bolt upright. "They wanted the plants!"

Hawkins and Zoran both looked with concern at their younger colleague, who seemed to have forgotten that they had already discussed that part.

"Yes we know, David," Zoran soothed. "That's what we've been talking about."

"No, you don't understand," David said. "The man in green mentioned the plants. But no one was supposed to have known that we had successfully germinated the seeds. That information wasn't released to the press. As far as anyone else knew, we had just found some very old, but very dead, seeds."

There was a moment of silence as Hawkins and Zoran mentally digested this piece of information.

Then David drove the point home. "Don't you see? They knew."

"They knew," Hawkins agreed, nodding.

"But... how?" Zoran wondered out loud. "The only ones who knew about the germination experiments were us and –"

"– Stanley," Hawkins finished for him.

"Of course," Zoran said, looking stunned.

"Bastard sold us out," David said, shaking his head.

"Maybe," Hawkins said. "But we don't know anything for sure. There could be a logical explanation."

"What do you suggest we do then?" Zoran asked.

"We need to find out who Stanley talked to," Hawkins said. "There might be some link or a lead that the police could use to track down whoever killed Pavlos and abducted Lori."

The telephone on the coffee table rang suddenly, calling a halt to their discussion. Hawkins leaned forward, plucked the receiver off its cradle and announced simply, "Jim Hawkins."

"Hello Dr Hawkins. Ian Sanderson here. I'm glad I caught you at home."

"G'day Inspector," Hawkins replied.

"Dr, we have obtained the security tape which showed the outside of the LMB building during the arrival and departure of the men. Can you and David come down to the station?"

"Of course Inspector. He's here with me now and so is Dr Zoran Radovic, a key member of the archaeological team involved in making the discovery."

"Bring Dr Radovic with you. After all, the more brains we have on this, the better."

As the name implies, Parkside police station is located across the road from the north-east corner of Parker's Piece. Hawkins knew the station well because of the weekly aikido courses that were held there for members of the police force. These special classes were usually taught by his sensei but Hawkins had often taken on the role when his teacher had other engagements. Hawkins usually enjoyed these classes because the men and women of the police force often asked insightful questions and posed challenging 'what if' scenarios. He believed that this helped to make a response to an attack more effective on the street, should the need ever arise.

After introducing themselves at the front desk, the three scientists were met by Inspector Sanderson, who ushered them to one of the small interview rooms upstairs. They were now seated around a well-used pine table, staring expectantly at a 21-inch flat screen monitor. Sanderson loaded the disc that he had obtained from Addenbrooke's security department into the DVD player and hit the play button on the remote.

They saw that the camera had been positioned so the entrance of the LMB was framed perfectly with a wide-angled aspect that also encompassed a significant portion of the roundabout in front. After nearly two minutes of what appeared to be a still image, a dark-blue or black-coloured Mercedes sedan appeared and pulled slowly into the exact same position where Hawkins had found himself later that same night. The time at the bottom right hand corner of the image indicated 11:01 P.M. The four sitting around the table watched closely as three tall Caucasian men in dark-coloured track suits exited the car and scaled the two flights of steps towards the entrance. None of the men looked around to check their surroundings. They simply walked straight up the steps to the entrance.

The three men were followed up the stairs by a shorter man with a darker complexion who was dressed in a dark business suit. Unlike the others, this man appeared to be more alert to his surroundings but without displaying any overt attention.

"That's the guy that decked me," David said excitedly.

Sanderson pressed the pause button on the remote. "David, this could be important. Last night you stated that this man appeared to have had some boxing experience?"

"Yes Sir," David replied. "And my guess is that he was top-ranked. He was good. Very good."

"Then we might just get lucky and identify him," Sanderson responded. "Especially if he fought professionally. There's bound to be information on him, somewhere."

David nodded thoughtfully.

"Can you point out the man who shot Mister Konstantinou?" Sanderson asked as he pressed the button, resuming play on the DVD machine.

"No problem," David replied leaning forward. After a moment, he tapped a ghostly figure on the screen with his index finger. "This is the guy."

Because of the distant wide-angle view, it was difficult to distinguish the man from the other two men in front. But David was certain. "He was not quite as tall as the other two men in the track suits. And he had a large, hooked nose which you can just make out. He also had a jagged scar on his face, but you can't see that on this image."

Sanderson nodded his thanks and acknowledged, "Okay, I think we're getting somewhere."

They continued watching as one of the men held up a small white card to the security scanner. After a moment, the man pulled the door open, looked around furtively and stepped inside the building. The others followed.

"They obtained an access card to the LMB," Sanderson interjected. "It belonged to a student named George McLeod who worked in the building. We questioned Mister McLeod this morning and he said that he didn't even know that his card was missing. He only discovered that it was not in his wallet when prompted during questioning. McLeod noted that it must have been stolen sometime during the period when he had left his wallet unattended the previous day while using the gym at the Leisure Centre near the hospital."

Hawkins marvelled inwardly that the police had worked so fast on the case. He thought that it boded well for a speedy and positive outcome. He couldn't have been more wrong.

Sanderson fast forwarded the DVD 11 minutes to the point where movement could be seen again at the LMB front entrance. One of the men opened and held the door, while another one of the men emerged carrying a familiar slender body over his shoulder like a sack of potatoes.

Hawkins stiffened involuntarily. "Lori!"

"Those bastards," David said. "It looks like she's... she's dead."

"Not likely," Sanderson said. "It would make no sense for them to carry away a dead body, having already left one upstairs."

David immediately felt foolish but nodded his agreement.

Then, they all perked up as the leader, the man who killed Pavlos, stomped out of the building holding a white bag close to his body.

"That bag most likely contains the seeds, plants and some of the other missing samples," Sanderson observed.

"That looks about right," David acknowledged.

The last of the men to leave the LMB was the Latin American. Hawkins noticed that the man appeared to gaze directly at the camera as he followed the others to the waiting Mercedes. Then the man's face darkened almost imperceptibly at the same time as the solidly-built brute carrying Lori dumped her into the rear passenger compartment of the Mercedes, banging her head against the door frame in the process.

"Bastard," David observed.

"Right," Zoran confirmed.

They continued to watch as the man who had carelessly tossed Lori into the car, jumped in next to her while another of the tall men squeezed in from the opposite side, in effect pinning her unconscious body between them. Then the leader climbed into the driver's seat and the Latin American sat beside him in the shotgun position. A moment later, the car pulled forward and continued around the roundabout until it moved completely off the screen. Only 12 minutes had passed from the time that the car had first arrived to the point when it left the scene.

"Have you been able to learn anything about the car, Inspector?" asked Hawkins. "I noticed that the registration plate was never clearly visible."

"No, we couldn't make out the registration but we will let the image experts see if they can pull it out for us. Meanwhile, we've sent out a description of the car and passengers just in case they have remained in or around the Cambridge area."

"What if they attempt to leave the country?" Zoran asked.

"At this point, with the scant information that we have to go on, there's little chance that we can do anything to prevent that," Sanderson said.

"I don't get it," David said. "Why did they snatch Lori?"

"Hard to say," Sanderson responded. "They might have taken her as hostage for insurance reasons or maybe they actually needed her for something.

"But what could they need with a molecular biologist?" David asked.

"I honestly don't know, David," Sanderson said. keeping his look neutral. "Just be thankful that they do seem to need her alive."

Sanderson's true meaning was painfully clear to the three scientists. The men who broke in to the LMB had already killed once that night.

Sanderson continued, "I'm afraid that without more to go on we can only hope to get lucky right now."

The three scientists exchanged looks.

Then Hawkins said, "Inspector, I think we might have something."

Chapter 16

Cambridge
July 8, 2007

    The earlier tempest had now completely relaxed its assault on East Anglia. The dark, rain-swelled clouds had either dissipated or disappeared over the north-western horizon, leaving in their wake an emerging blue sky with just a spattering of non-threatening fluffy, white cirrocumulus formations. The Earth and sky had felt fresh and cleansed at first but now the fierce summer heat was returning with a vengeance. Inspector Sanderson left the unmarked police car in the shadowy lower section of the Lion Yard car park while he and Hawkins walked the rest of the way through the stifling heat to the Department of Archaeology building on the New Museum site. They made their way past the centuries-old gothic architecture and the contrasting modern bicycle racks through the courtyard to the main building. Professor Stanley Green's office was located on the third floor of the magnificent left-hand spire. The two men headed up the stairs. When they reached the landing, they encountered Beryl McKinney, Stanley's Personal Assistant.
    "Hello Beryl" Hawkins began. "This is Inspector Sanderson of the Parkside police force. He needs to go over a few details with Stanley about the incident at the LMB last night."
    "Oh yes," Beryl responded with righteous indignation. "Shocking business! I heard that one of the students was killed. I really hope that you catch whoever did this Inspector."
    "We're trying to do that, Mrs. McKinney," Sanderson replied. "We think that Professor Green might be able to help us."
    "Good. Let me check if he's free," Beryl said as lifted the telephone and punched out a 5-digit extension.
    As Beryl spoke with Stanley over the telephone, Hawkins mentally tuned out the one-sided conversation. He was still mulling over the known facts of the case which so far didn't seem to follow any sensible pattern. The most invaluable aspect of their discovery should have been the mystery of the giant

mummy. But it was the seeds that had interested the thieves, an interest that appeared to be shared by Stanley.

Inspector Sanderson's first impression when they walked through the door of the large office was that Professor Green looked like a guilty man.

Green was the first to speak. "Come on in gentlemen. Beryl told me why you're here. I'll be right up front and tell you that I don't see how I can be of any help, but I'll be happy to try. Please take a seat."

Hawkins and Sanderson sat down in the two solid mahogany leathered-covered seats in front of Stanley's desk.

"Thank you Professor Green," Sanderson began by flipping open his small notepad. "First of all, let me just say that I've enjoyed watching your television series, *Time Investigators*. It's the highlight of my Sunday nights at home. It's incredible to think that there is still so much history lying in the ground below us."

"Why, thank you," Stanley said beaming. "We do try and make it interesting."

"Now regarding the incident," Sanderson immediately changed tact. "What is your exact role on the project?"

Stanley looked a bit startled by sudden shift in the inspector's attitude and the directness of question but he answered immediately. "I am head of Department and when Jim asked me to consult on the discovery at Wandlebury, I was only too happy to offer my expertise."

"And did you, in turn, consult with anyone else?"

"No, I didn't need to consult with anyone."

"Let me rephrase the question," Sanderson said in a business-like manner. "Did you inform anyone at any time about any of the discoveries in the tomb?"

Stanley looked like a rabbit caught at night in the headlights of an oncoming automobile. Sanderson knew the look. He had spent many years in learning how to read people. The answer to the question would be yes, but the man was now trying to decide how to deliver that answer with the least amount of self-incrimination.

Stanley's face flushed as he responded. "Well... uh yes. I had to inform one of our major benefactors in the United States."

"Name?"

"W. P. Merrick."

"The American billionaire?" Sanderson asked, now genuinely surprised.

Hawkins' mouth dropped open in shock.

"Yes, him," Stanley replied. "You see, he funds a lot of archaeological interests and projects throughout the world and we are one of the many."

Sanderson recovered his composure and resumed his line of questioning. "Okay, thank you for that. We need to establish what you told him and when it was said."

Stanley now grasped the implication behind Sanderson's question. "What? Do you honestly think that Merrick had anything at all to do with the break in?"

When Sanderson remained silent, Stanley explained, "but that's crazy? He's one of the richest people on the planet. He owns half of the equipment and most of the discoveries here, anyway. Why would he steal something that already belongs to him?"

"At this stage we have to consider every possible suspect, including Mister Merrick and you of course," Sanderson replied. "Please answer the question."

Stanley's face had turned two shades darker pink. He was clearly angry now. But he finally sighed and admitted, "I've kept him informed about all of the discoveries in the tomb and the results of all of the experiments carried out on the artefacts on, more or less, a daily basis."

Hawkins couldn't believe what he was hearing.

"Did Merrick show interest in any of the artefacts in particular?"

Stanley briefly considered stalling, but he knew it would come out one way or another. "Yes, the seeds."

Sanderson paused and then said, "did he ask you to report back to him specifically about any experimental progress made by Mister Konstantinou and Dr Davis regarding the seeds?"

"As a matter of fact, that was my idea," Stanley came clean, now realising that all of the Inspector's questions were going to be this blunt.

"And how did you obtain the information?"

"I asked Konstantinou and Davis to report to me directly," Stanley answered, while glancing apologetically at Hawkins.

"Isn't that a bit unusual, Professor Green," Sanderson chided. "That doesn't seem like the traditional way of carrying out a scientific investigation."

Stanley looked properly chastised by now. But he said nothing.

"Anything else you want to admit, Professor?"

"You mean, did I also inform Mr Merrick that Konstantinou and Davis had germinated the seeds?"

"Exactly."

"Yes."

"When?" Sanderson asked without mercy.

"July 5th, around 9 o'clock... I think," Stanley said.

"I'll need to see that e-mail," Sanderson said. "And the others."

"I'll get Beryl to print them out for you."

"That'd be nice, thank you." But Sanderson wasn't finished yet. "Why did you do this?"

"I didn't do anything illegal, Inspector," Stanley said with an attempt at defiance in his voice.

Sanderson replied evenly. "Please answer the question."

Stanley's attempt at redemption evaporated with a sigh. "Money. A million US dollars."

Sanderson was quiet as he jotted down some notes and made some obvious underscores on the page with short, slashing motions. Then he asked, "for what exactly?"

"Merrick is obsessed with archaeological discoveries that could be linked to the *Book of Genesis*," Stanley began. "Especially those that reference legendary plants with healing powers."

"So you believe that these seeds that were actually found on British soil, are described in the Bible?" Sanderson asked.

Stanley fixed Sanderson with a penetrating glare. "It's more likely that the seeds come from the Middle East based on the Cuneiform inscriptions. And the translation has some direct references to specific elements of *Genesis*."

Hawkins suddenly tensed. He knew that he shouldn't speak up according to the game plan that Inspector Sanderson had set out with him, but this was too much. "You have the translation?"

Stanley sighed. "I got them yesterday."

Hawkins was stunned.

Sanderson acknowledged Hawkins' timely intervention with a slight nod and turned his attention back to Stanley. "What did the translations say?"

"There were two short phrases," Stanley answered. "The first was a reference to the Nephilim —"

"The what?" Sanderson interrupted.

"The fallen ones," Stanley answered, as if that explained everything.

Hawkins felt the room suddenly grow clammy.

Sanderson showed no outward reaction. "And the second phrase?"

Stanley replied without hesitation. "The Tree of Life."

Hawkins and Sanderson left the main Building in the Department of Archaeology and walked the short distance across the cobbled rectangular courtyard to the auxiliary building housing the labs. Sanderson wanted to view the giant mummy and the other artefacts first hand. He suggested that it might help him by providing useful insights into the investigation.

After ascending the stairs to the labs on the second level, Hawkins unlocked a small secure lab with a reinforced steel door and admitted the inspector. Before them, on an over-sized roll-away table, lay the giant in all its magnificence. The withered body practically filled the room with its enormous proportions. Hawkins thought it was more amazing each time he viewed the giant corpse.

Sanderson's jaw dropped. "This is incredible," he marvelled.

Next, Hawkins showed the Inspector some of the mysterious artefacts that had been found with the giant. Sanderson was most impressed by the shape and size of bronze sword. After asking permission, he hefted the massive weapon with two hands on the hilt and found that it was even heavier than expected. "I guess that one would need the strength of a giant to use that in battle," he remarked.

Hawkins agreed. "Biblical references suggest that Goliath's sword weighed in the region of 11 pounds. This one is closer to 13."

"Amazing," Sanderson observed.

Finally, they examined the 'Adam and Eve' jar which was stored separately in the rear of the main lab because it was still undergoing some analyses. Peering inside, Sanderson noticed that there were about a dozen brown, slug-shaped objects lying in the bottom of the jar.

"That's all of the remaining seeds," Hawkins said.

But for Sanderson, it was almost like an anti-climax. He said, "you know I find it hard to believe that this is what the thieves were after. Compared with the other discoveries that you and your team have made, this seems so unimpressive."

"I thought so at first too. But now I'm not so sure. Maybe the seeds are the most important factor of all."

"Do you believe that these are really seeds from the Tree of Life?" Sanderson persisted.

"At this stage, I don't know what to believe," Hawkins said. "But it appears that somebody thinks so."

"Point taken," Sanderson said.

Chapter 17

Cambridge
July 8, 2007

Zoran Radovic found the rumbling drone of the 900 cubic centimetre engine soothing as he glided past the architectural wonders of the Cambridge town centre on the Triumph. He felt separated from the real world in his armour-like helmet and leathers. It was almost as if he could view the world as an outside observer and nothing could touch or harm him.

His mind churned over all aspects concerning the discovery of the mysterious tomb and the uncanny series of events that had transpired since then. Like the others, he was sick with worry over what might have become of Lori. And the revelation that Stanley Green had at least been partly responsible for the events leading to this had shaken them all to the core. Zoran had been surprised to learn that Stanley had actually gathered and released information about the jar containing the ancient seeds to the American billionaire. Even if Stanley was correct and the jar contained seeds from the Tree of Life, Zoran guessed that these could only be of a symbolic or religious value to the thieves. So why had they gone to such extreme lengths to obtain them? Whatever the case, he decided that Stanley could not possibly have been involved in what had occurred at the LMB, at least not directly.

Like the others, Zoran had at first been thrilled with his role in what they had come to refer to as the scientific discovery of a lifetime. Very few archaeologists or geologists ever made it big with their chosen careers, but it seemed as if the possibility of a successful future had suddenly become guaranteed for all of them. They had simply been in the right place at the right time. But that had suddenly turned into the wrong place last night with the theft of the seeds, the death of Pavlos and Lori's kidnapping. To make matters worse, the police had so little to go on.

He throttled along Gonville Place past Parker's Piece and then had to break suddenly at the pedestrian crossing for a gaggle of tourists who had ventured out to cross the road. While he was waiting, feet down and motorcycle idling, he turned to gaze at the Cambridge youth scattered around the park. Just as the red light changed to flashing amber, he lifted his feet and accelerated smoothly away lest the sight of the scantily clad females cloud his thinking. He didn't notice the jet-black Mercedes S 600 Saloon waiting to turn right at the next traffic light until he pulled up to a stop right behind it.

It suddenly struck him like a bullet to the brain that it looked like the Mercedes that was used for the break-in at the LMB. His heart began pounding like a jackhammer. From his vantage point behind and slightly to the side of the automobile, he could see that the two occupants bore a similarity to the men that he had seen on the security DVD just this morning, but he couldn't be certain. At any rate, he didn't think that these two had noticed him and, besides, it was unlikely that they were even aware of who he was, since his face was safely obscured underneath his helmet.

The traffic light went through its sequence from red to amber to green and the Mercedes turned right into Mill Road. Zoran eased the motorcycle into gear and cruised slowly behind the car trying to look invisible in his all too conspicuous yellow and black leathers. The two vehicles quickly passed the Parkside Swimming Pool and then entered the narrowed section of the road hemmed in by a continuous stream of small shops and businesses. As usual for the university town, the road was swarming with foreign students on bicycles, some even riding on the wrong side of the road.

After becoming aware that he was probably following a bit too closely, Zoran decided to pull up to the curb and let a little distance build between the two vehicles. He resumed the chase after three cars and multiple bicycles had passed him. He could easily see the Mercedes traversing the humpbacked railway bridge as he followed from about 100 yards behind. But when he reached the top of the bridge himself, he couldn't see the car anymore. He realised with a sudden stroke of panic that he had either lost the car, or it turned off somewhere while it had been hidden from his view by the arched bridge.

He accelerated down the bridge and swerved momentarily into the oncoming lane to pass the car immediately in front of him and managed to get past some of the swarming cyclists as well. As he approached Cavendish Road just beyond the bottom of the bridge, he glanced left and spied the Mercedes picking its way cautiously between the tightly packed parked cars. He turned into the road and pulled over to the edge and waited. From this position he could see that the car appeared to be making its way to the end of the road which dead-ended at the bottom.

Then he saw the car pull partly up onto the kerb and park in front of a mid-terrace house. Zoran kicked the motorcycle into gear and slowly edged forward. Although he was still about 100 yards away, he was just in time and near enough to see both occupants enter a brown Victorian house fronted with large bay windows. He stopped where he was and pulled over to the kerb again. He knew what he had to do next.

Chapter 18

London Heathrow Airport
July 8, 2007

Hawkins settled into the spacious premium economy window seat of the Boeing 747-400, mentally preparing himself for the flight to New York. The doors to the aircraft were closed and the plane began to taxi towards the runway. The cabin personnel went about their well-practiced task of pointing out the emergency exits and describing the use of seat belts, oxygen masks and life vests.

He was a well-seasoned traveller and normally didn't mind flying, as long as the journey wasn't too long in duration. Flights from the UK to Sydney, for example, typically lasted around 21 hours broken into two separate flights and Hawkins found this almost too much to endure. By comparison, the short flight to New York was a stroll in the park.

It had been a last-minute decision and he had barely made it to Heathrow Airport on time for the flight. Following their discussion with Stanley, Hawkins and Sanderson had decided that the best course of action was a face-to-face meeting with William Merrick, himself. The objective was to find out what the aged billionaire knew about the case. Information was their only hope in trying to track down the people who had taken Lori. And Merrick was their only lead. He was also a potential suspect.

Since New York was clearly outside of Sanderson's jurisdiction, Hawkins was the most likely choice for the initial interview with Merrick. The best line of contact was through Stanley since this was already well-established. When they approached the Professor with their request, he had jumped at the chance, apparently more than happy to try and make amends for his earlier questionable actions.

True to his word, Stanley had easily convinced Merrick to meet with Hawkins. The billionaire had sounded appropriately sympathetic to the cause and even said that he would do everything he could to help bring the perpetrators to justice.

Sitting next to Hawkins was an American woman with big hair who reminded him of Oprah Winfrey. After the pilot's announcement for the cabin crew to take their seats for take-off, the woman turned to Hawkins and said "I'm sorry to impose this on you but could you hold my hand for this? This is only my second flight ever and things didn't go so well on the first."

Hawkins gulped inwardly but, to prove that chivalry was not dead, he said "of course." He stretched his right hand across the arm rest and offered it to her palm-side up.

She grabbed it tightly with her left hand and gushed, "thank you."

Hawkins noticed that she had a charming smile.

"The last guy I sat next to, on my way over here, refused to do it," the woman said in a can-you-believe-it whisper.

"That's terrible," Hawkins said. He hoped his face didn't betray anything other than sympathy.

As the plane accelerated, shuddering down the tarmac, the passengers were pressed back into their seats due to the increase in g-force. Hawkins felt the woman's grip tightening around his fingers like a vice. Then the ground fell away as the plane cleared the runway and headed for the open skies. It was then that the woman closed her eyes and emitted a sustained whimpering moan. Some of the nearby passengers glanced over in obvious amusement at the terrified woman and her poor boyfriend.

Hawkins just sat quietly in his seat, with his face turning several shades of darker in sheer embarrassment. He tried to remember how long the flight took to reach New York. He would have even preferred the one to Sydney right now.

Chapter 19

Cambridge
July 8, 2007

Zoran wasn't sure if the men that had been driving the black Mercedes were the ones they were looking for so he pulled out his cell phone and called someone who might be able to help.

A voice answered almost immediately. "Hello, Davy the human punch bag speaking."

"Uh…Davy… David," Zoran faltered. "Is that you?"

"Who were expecting to answer my phone, Tony Blair?"

"Where are you?" Zoran asked.

"Starbuck's in the Grafton Centre. I thought a steady infusion of caffeine might help to ease the pain."

"All right, stay put and I'll be right there."

"I'm not going anywhere," David replied.

Zoran jumped on his motorcycle and shot over to Starbuck's in 5 minutes flat. After ordering a latte for himself and another espresso for David, he sat down and attempted to calmly fill him in on the encounter. Even though he was still wearing the bandage on his head, David looked remarkably healthy after what he had been through. He listened silently to Zoran's story as he cradled the espresso thoughtfully in both hands. When Zoran had finished the tale, David placed his empty cup down carefully on the table and said, "let's go."

Zoran rode with David on the back of his motorcycle to Cavendish Road and they parked against the kerb, about 150 feet from the house. They decided to wait until the occupants showed some sign of themselves. Neither David nor Zoran felt that it was worth going to the police with any information until they were certain of the facts. To pass the time while they waited, the two scientists engaged in an animated discussion.

"I spy with my little eye something beginning with B," David said.

"Badger," Zoran called out tentatively.

"Do you actually see a badger?"

"No, but...," Zoran trailed off.

"You have to be able to see it," David patiently explained.

"Big house?" Zoran asked, still not quite getting it.

"Well, that's another guideline that I should have mentioned. You can only use nouns. 'Big' is an adjective...I think."

"Blonde," Zoran offered.

"Wha –? Do you see a blonde?"

"Yes, walking away behind us. She just came out of the house with the black door."

"And very nice from my point of view," David commented. "But the word is not blonde."

"Bug?"

"No, but you're getting warm."

Zoran paused for a moment, smiled, and then said, "Beetle. You spied a Volkswagen Beetle."

"Correct. In fact, in America they call it a Volkswagen Bug instead of a Beetle. So, you actually had it with your last answer."

"So that puts me in the lead and – "

"Sssssh," David interrupted abruptly. "I spy someone coming out of the house."

"Is it one of them?" Zoran asked quietly.

After a moment, David hissed, "yeah. That's the guy that Pavlos was scuffling with when the other bastard shot him."

Lori Davis was alive. She had been a prisoner now for 18 hours. She was still nauseous and had vomited bile regularly from the massive dose of chloroform they had used to incapacitate her, but otherwise in good health. They hadn't even bothered to tie her up. They just left her in the confined space of the attic with a small cup of drinking water and a warning not to call out. There was a low wattage bulb with a pull chain overhead to give her some light but her captors hadn't been foolish enough to leave her cell phone with her. They must have searched her while she was unconscious. A chilling thought.

Although she was terrified, she had mentally examined every possible reason why they had taken her. So far, they hadn't told her anything. She expected that at any moment they would finally decide to kill her or do worse things that didn't even bear thinking about. After all, they had gunned Pavlos down in cold blood and probably the same to poor David.

She had regained consciousness about 5 or 6 hours ago. She had sensed her own breathing and felt the hard wooden surface beneath her, and her eyes popped wide open when the ugly man with the scar had shaken her. She recognised him immediately as the one who had shot Pavlos. Then she threw up on the man's shoes.

Soon afterwards, she had overheard one of them talking German on the telephone below her to a man called 'Herr Schmidt.' The only words that she could make out chilled her to the bone – 'töte sie' and 'nach Basel'. She knew these meant 'kill her' and 'to Basel'. Then she heard the varying sounds of dialogue and laughter from a television program. It took her a few minutes before she could identify it. And when she did, she couldn't believe her ears. Her captors were watching *Friends*.

Her only hope was to escape, somehow. She looked around the attic to see if there was anything that she could use. She tried to slow her breathing so she could think clearly. Without really knowing why, she pulled the chain turning the light off and let her eyes adjust to the darkness. After a minute or so, she felt that she could see a narrow sliver of daylight on the far slope of the attic ceiling. After another minute she was certain. There was an opening. She switched the light back on when she heard a door slam downstairs. Someone had either come in or left the house. Whatever she was going to do, she had better do it soon.

"Are you sure that's him?" Zoran asked.

"Yeah," David replied. "That's the guy."

They both watched as the man strode to the Mercedes and pressed the key remote to unlock the car.

"I'll call Inspector Sanderson," Zoran said as he pulled out his cell phone.

David tensed. He wasn't sure if they had enough time as they watched the man walk out into the road to get to the driver's door. They couldn't wait for the police to get there. They had to do something fast. He did the only thing he could think of –

Frank Bader was reaching for the door handle when he caught sight of something out of the corner of his eye. He glanced up and noticed a man jogging fast down the street in his direction. He looked back at the car and reached for the handle again but something was wrong. He jerked his head back up again in shock. He recognized the man! He also realised that the man wasn't jogging. He was running straight at him!

David slammed rugby style into the larger man, who emitted a muffled, "scheisse," as they tumbled to the tarmac-covered road. David fumbled for position and managed to remain on top. The man underneath him had taken the brunt of the initial pounding and scraping force from the road. He was injured badly, but he was still immensely powerful. He managed to grab the loose material around the shoulder of David's shirt with one hand and somehow twisted free with the other.

Zoran stared in silent horror when he realised what was about to happen. He dimly noticed that no one had answered his telephone call and now he had been referred to voicemail. Then he saw the glint of a long knife in the man's freed hand. He dropped the phone to the ground with a clatter and sprinted ungainly down the road to help David.

While working on her escape, Lori's scientific brain was thinking about the fight-or-flight reflex. This was also known as the 'acute stress response' because animals can react to dangerous threats with a powerful discharge of their sympathetic nervous system. This reaction triggers the release of hormones which increases the heart rate and breathing, thereby maximising the flow of oxygen to the muscles. This prepares the animal for one of two options: they can either face the threat and fight or avoid the threat and take flight.

The only other time in her life that she had felt such fear had been when she was 13-years old. She and her younger brother

Tommy had been on a family vacation in Pismo Beach, California. They were both surfing the waves near the pier, lost in the moment as their father and mother watched intermittently from the shore. They had surfed 7 or 8 waves when they saw several bullet-shaped sea lions beside them. The next terrifying moments would be etched forever in her memory.

As Tommy began paddling to ride the next large wave, his surfboard was suddenly jolted from something beneath the surface and he cartwheeled into the water. It was almost as if the board had hit something large like a submerged rock. But when Lori saw the huge dorsal fin sticking out of the water above where Tommy went down, she knew with heart-wrenching fear what it was. She felt sickened and terrified when she saw the huge grey fish shaking something beneath the surface. Without thinking she paddled her board, splashing furiously towards the monster. When she got close enough, she slipped her hand down towards the sheath strapped to her right calf, pulled out the 8-inch diver's knife and dove into the water.

She bumped right into the writhing left flank of the shark. She was sure the creature sensed her presence but considered her to be of no consequence. By some primal instinct that she never understood, she reached out with the slender muscular fingers of her left hand and grabbed hold of the shark's exposed gill slits. The shark's skin had felt like sandpaper as she stretched forward and plunged the knife into one of its soulless black eyes.

The shark's reaction was as violent as it was swift. It immediately shook its great body and then swam out to deeper water like a torpedo. Incomprehensibly, she had driven it away and she hoped that it would die. Then she turned and saw the red billowing cloud in the water surrounding her little brother's torn wet-suited body, she knew with grim finality that she had been too late to save him.

By this time, everyone on the beach had realised what was happening in the water and left their towels to approach the surf area. Lori could see both of her parents knee-deep in the water, extremely distressed and shouting to her, as the last of the remaining surfers and swimmers returned to shore. Three burley lifeguards swam out to her, one of them dragging a rescue board. But Lori stayed right where she was. She wouldn't leave her brother in case the shark came back.

When the lifeguards reached her, they were faced with a distraught teenage girl. They spent several minutes pleading with her to leave the body, but she was adamant. She shook her head continuously and screamed, "No!" But gradually, through her tears, she began to realise it was hopeless.

Just when the chief lifeguard thought he was going to have to club her unconscious to get her out of the water, he was finally able to encourage her to return to the beach with him and to the waiting arms of her parents. The other two lifeguards brought back the larger pieces that could be found of Tommy's body using the rescue board.

Later, when the newspapers described the incident, Lori was hailed as a heroine. The headlines of one paper read:

Teenage Girl Drives off 12 Foot Great White Shark that Killed Her Brother

The article went on to say:

The size of the shark had been estimated based on the area of the bite wounds on the 11-year-old victim, Thomas Davis. Experts from The Department of Fisheries and Game suggested that the shark had mistaken the boy for one of the sea lions that were also present that day. This was most likely due to the similar coloration of the sea lions and the grey wet suit that he had been wearing. His 13-year old sister, Lori Davis, who valiantly drove the shark away, had been wearing a bright pink wet suit.

Of course, she didn't feel like a heroine. All she felt was a tremendous sense of loss. *If only I had been nicer to him*, she thought. *If only I had let him get his way once in a while.* But it was too late for her to tell him how much she really loved him, even if he was a brat most of the time. All of these thoughts fuelled her resolve. Now she had to get out of this house.

David was in pain. His bruised ribs had been re-injured as he fell with the German brute to the ground. The only consolation was that he didn't think it would kill him. The knife that was flashing towards his head would do that.

His instincts took over. He quickly thrust his left arm upwards and grabbed the man's knife hand tightly by the wrist and used his body weight to force it back down to the pavement. Then he snapped out a powerful right-handed punch that exploded into the German's cheek bone, driving his head down into the pavement. There was a sickening crack as the back of the man's head impacted the ground with a deadly force.

The man dropped the knife and lay still in the road with a pool of blood spreading slowly from the back of his head.

David pushed himself up from the man and groaned, clutching the right side of his rib cage, as Zoran arrived on the scene.

Zoran noticed that an old woman across the street was peeking through her window in shocked horror. He wondered how she would later recount the incident to the police.

"I think he's dead," Zoran said quietly.

"I think you're right. But he wasn't a very nice man." David paused for a second and asked, "did you get through to Sanderson?"

"No, and I think I dropped my phone near the bike."

"Doesn't matter," David responded. He caught the peeping woman's attention, gave the universal extended thumb and pinkie sign for telephone, and mouthed the word 'POLICE' to her.

She disappeared from the window in a flash.

David turned back and gazed at the man that he had left lying in the road. "If this guy's dead he won't mind us using him for a minute longer, will he?"

"Use him for what?"

"This," David grunted as he struggled to pull the man's limp body up and across his shoulders for makeshift version of a 'fireman's carry.' His ribs caused him minor discomfort, but he was beyond the pain barrier now.

Zoran watched with a mixture of surprise and horror as David lumbered with the large body over his shoulders straight toward the ground floor front bay window of the house that the man had come from. Then without pausing, David twisted sideways, yelled, "BANZAI!", and launched his human cargo through the window.

Driven by the terror of impending death, Lori worked as quickly and as quietly as she could. It took her three minutes to widen the aperture in the roof by 6 inches using her fingers to pull and scrape at the loosened boards. But that was as far as she got. The rest of the boards were stuck tight. Determined not to give up, she got a good grip and used her entire body weight to exert more force.

Nothing.

Her shoulders and arms burned with lactic fatigue and her fingers were raw and bleeding. She knew that she had to keep trying but it was hopeless. She couldn't do any more. Then she thought of her brother. And whether miraculously real or strangely imagined, she heard a tiny voice somewhere in her mind. *Come on Lo, you can't give up!*

She looked down at the thin boards that she had already pulled down. *You're supposed to be smart!* An idea came to her. She could use one of the boards that she had already pulled down. She picked up one of the sturdiest pieces and, using all of her strength, she began to pry another board away.

Hurry up!" The voice in her head was getting louder.

Time was running out. She used the board now to smash upwards furiously, no longer caring about the noise. Before she knew it, she had widened the aperture sufficiently so her slender body might just squeeze through. She pulled the broken slate roof tiles through the opening to clear the way.

She reached up through the opening and took a strong grip. Just then she heard another noise from outside on the street. It sounded to her like a crazy man yelling in Japanese, and this was followed soon after by the loud sound of breaking glass. She pulled herself up. That was when Scarface burst up through the attic door.

The body crashed heavily through the window. Heinrich Meyer jerked upright from the chair in front of the television in surprised horror as he saw the body of his partner thump onto the hard wooden floor along with clattering pieces of shattered glass. Although Heinrich was momentarily stunned he snapped his head up to look at the shattered window frame and was surprised by someone wearing a headband climbing through it. It was the dark-haired man that they had encountered in the lab last night.

"Here's Johnny!" the man announced.

Heinrich quickly reached inside his coat to his underarm holster, yanked out his pistol, flicked the safety lever into the off position and aimed in the general direction of the man's head. He pulled the trigger.

Lori just managed to scoot through the opening and pull her legs through as Scarface crab-walked towards her. The man shouted in thick accented English, "you come back, or I shoot you!"

Lori was splayed out precariously clutching for a hand hold on the steep sloping roof. She had to find a safe way down. In a feeble attempt to buy some time she yelled out the first unfriendly German phrase that popped into her head. "Nein, scheissekopf."

The man poked his head through the hole she had made and grinned at her, displaying his crooked yellow and brown-stained teeth. Then he pointed a large black pistol at her and said, "so, you are not coming back?"

Without thinking, Lori let go and slid down the roof towards the street 25 feet below.

Chapter 20

Cambridge
July 8, 2007

While still outside the window, Zoran heard the loud crack of the gun firing and cringed as David's head twitched violently from the impact of the bullet. Then he watched in abject despair as David's limp body crumpled forward into the house. Before he had time to react, he caught a glimpse of something above him accompanied by a splintering sound and someone grunting in exertion. He was stunned. It was Lori!

She had appeared above him hanging from the flimsy plastic guttering on the front edge of the roof. He watched helplessly as she kicked her legs in a desperate struggle to gain some purchase on the outside wall of the house. The piece of guttering that she was hanging from had broken away and was slowly bending down and outwards. Then she fell.

Simultaneously, Zoran lurched forward with his arms out. By some miracle her feet struck the sloping roof-like top of the ground floor bay window that projected out from the wall, slowing her descent, and altering her trajectory. This gave Zoran enough time to position himself below for an insane attempt to catch her. But he hadn't really thought it through.

Her left buttock struck his up-stretched arms at a speed of 15 feet per second and her right foot impacted his leather-protected chest, knocking him to the ground. He somehow managed to cushion the rest of her fall as they landed together in a tangle of arms and legs in the small courtyard garden in front of the property.

"Nice catch," Lori managed. She wasn't aware that her face was streaked with tears.

Zoran was winded but managed a nod of acknowledgement. Then he croaked, "run! To my bike!"

Together they scrambled up from the garden and bolted for the motorcycle. Zoran leapt onto the front portion of the saddle and started the ignition as Lori jumped onto the small space behind him. He reached back and handed her his helmet which she pulled on, gave the thumbs up sign and clutched him firmly around the waist. As she turned back to look at the house, she saw Scarface and another man burst through the door and run to the Mercedes. Both men were brandishing handguns. "Go!" she shouted.

Zoran kicked the motorcycle into gear, and they shot up the road against the one-way system like an angry bumble bee. Lori risked a backwards glance and saw the bulky jet-black Mercedes reversing crazily up the road after them. Almost immediately the driver skilfully swerved the car backwards into the first crossroad and skidded to a halt. Then he rammed the car into forward gear and turned sharply back onto Cavendish Road in pursuit.

Cavendish Road had been built as a narrow lane in the time of the horse and carriage, giving Zoran's motorcycle the clear advantage. If another car were to turn into the road, he and Lori would be able to get past it by manoeuvring onto the pavement, but the wider Mercedes would be blocked. That didn't happen.

In a matter of seconds, Zoran and Lori reached the junction to Mill Road and turned right, swerving around oncoming traffic over the railway bridge and toward the Police Station. Lori looked back and saw that the black car was close behind them, drawing angry responses from other motorists as it rudely weaved around slower cars heading up the bridge, alternately accelerating and braking to stay with the motorcycle.

Just as Zoran and Lori crested the bridge, they spotted a police car racing in their direction with siren whooping and lights flashing. The two of them waved to attract its attention but it kept on going. Zoran assumed that it was heading back to Cavendish Road in response to a call, most likely from the old woman who had observed the incident in the street.

The Germans saw the police car and slowed their conspicuous vehicle dramatically to avoid attracting attention. Then, after the police car cleared the bridge, the driver of the Mercedes stamped the accelerator to floor and continued the high speed pursuit.

The motorcycle was now about 50 yards ahead of the Mercedes, with three cars in between. Zoran powered his bike up the narrow road crowded with pedestrians, cyclists and automobiles. Lori looked behind them again and saw that the Mercedes had somehow moved past two of the cars and was rapidly closing the distance.

The motorcycle screamed up to the junction toward the end of Mill Road where the two riders were confronted by a brief shock – a long queue of cars waiting at the traffic light. Without hesitation, Zoran swerved quickly around the stopped cars and ran through the red light, causing several cars to brake suddenly. He then throttled the Triumph diagonally across the junction towards Parker's Piece, jumped the kerb and aimed for the pedestrian access point through the wrought iron fence on the corner.

As Zoran skilfully man-handled the motorcycle past the fence and onto the Piece, Lori twisted around and marvelled at the chaos that they had left at the junction behind them. Somehow the Mercedes had also managed to get past the cars to the accompaniment of blaring horns, tangled traffic, and considerable shouting. The black car turned left onto Gonville Place, whereupon it cruised slowly down the road and its two passengers glared menacingly at the couple on the motorcycle.

Unaware of what was happening behind him, Zoran accelerated along one of the pedestrian pathways toward the middle of the Piece. He noticed that the foreign students were still out for the evening sun and some of them were even cheering him on, without even knowing what was really happening.

He finally stopped the motorcycle at the centre point where the Piece's two crossing pathways converged. Then both he and Lori gazed in confusion along the full length of Gonville Place looking for the Mercedes, which had somehow vanished. As they heard the sound of more police sirens, Zoran said, "we have to get back to the house."

"Why? We just got away from there." Lori took that moment to hug him tightly from behind. "I was so scared that I almost forgot to thank you for what you did."

"Lori, we have to go back for David," Zoran said soothingly.

"David is alive?" she asked with renewed hope.

"He was with me but one of those guys shot him when we came to find you."

"No!" Lori screamed in anguish.

Zoran couldn't think of anything to say. He turned the bike around and they headed back in the direction that they had come from across the Piece.

As they pulled up and parked outside the house, three police cars were already on the scene. Scores of pedestrians also lined the road craning their necks to see into the house with the shattered bay window. Zoran and Lori quickly explained who they were to one of the police constables standing outside the residence on crowd control duty. After a moment the policeman nodded as if acknowledging the potential importance and then ducked into the house to relay the information to his supervisor.

While they were waiting, Zoran and Lori watched an ambulance coming down the road with its lights flashing. Then, a tall red-haired policeman with three chevrons on each of his shoulders came out of the house to meet with them.

"I'm Sergeant Condron," he pronounced in an authoritative tone. "I understand that you were involved in this situation?"

Sensing problems, Lori took the lead in the discussion, using her feminine charms to their advantage. "Yes Sergeant. I'm Dr Lori Davis who was abducted from my lab last night by the men in this house."

It was clear that Condron recognised the name and the incident by the sudden change in his demeanour. "Yes, I know about that. Can you tell me what happened here Dr Davis?"

"My friends rescued me from the house, but there were injuries in the process," Lori summed up the situation quickly.

"Officer," Zoran interrupted. "Our colleague was shot. He fell just inside the window."

The conversation stopped as the paramedics rushed into the house carrying a roll away stretcher.

Then Sergeant Condron said seriously, "I have one dead and one alive just below the window on the living room floor lying in a pile of broken glass."

"Which one is alive?" Lori asked, choking back tears in anticipation of bad news.

Zoran remained silent. He had a sinking feeling in the pit of his stomach.

"The one who already had stitches in the back of his head," Condron replied. "That kid is either accident prone or damn lucky. The bullet just grazed his head, but it must have knocked him senseless."

"David!" Lori gasped.

At first, Zoran was stunned. Then he stuttered choking on his emotions, "that's David - David Englehart, Sergeant. I thought the gunshot had killed him because he went down so quickly."

"I'm no doctor but I think he'll be fine," Condron offered.

Zoran considered that for a moment before responding. "I guess he must have a hard head."

"Indeed", the Sergeant added.

Chapter 21

Virgin Atlantic flight VS001
July 8, 2007

Around 3,500 miles away, Jim Hawkins was in trouble. The woman he had sat next to on the plane had talked non-stop for the entire flight. At one stage he had even put on his headphones and eyeshades and pretended to be asleep, but she kept right on talking. He gave in after a few minutes and subjected himself to even more of her turbulent family history. Her name was Florence. She was a trial lawyer, which mostly involved negotiating settlements with the opposing legal team. Very rarely was it like what you see on TV, as in big celebrity cases. Next Hawkins had learned that her sister, Yolanda, was a wafer thin 110 pounds because she had never learned to cook properly. Her brother, Cassius, was a no-good bum who had once appeared on an episode of the Jerry Springer Show entitled, 'Chillin' with Strippers.' And Florence's deadbeat husband had left her last year for a catwalk model. "Can you believe it?" She asked.

Hawkins said that he couldn't.

Just as she began to list more of the shortcomings of her estranged husband, the pilot announced that they were on final approach and could all passengers ensure that their seatbelts were fastened, their seat backs were in the upright position and their trays stowed correctly. The announcement seemed to take the steam out of her as if she suddenly remembered that 'she was in an airplane, several thousand feet up in the air. As New York City grew bigger through the cabin windows, she turned to Hawkins and said through strained teeth, "can you?"

Hawkins smiled and offered his hand. He would be safe on the ground soon.

Chapter 22

New York City
July 9, 2007

"Crikey!" Hawkins gasped as he sprang upright in bed. It took him a moment to realise where he was, an executive suite at the Warwick Hotel in Manhattan. He scanned the room and then flopped back down and stared at the ceiling. He always had weird dreams when he travelled to different time zones. He thought it might have something to do with the fact that dreams were often more vivid following a period of sleep deprivation. But this was worse than ever. Maybe it was because his mind was haunted by the succession of disturbing events that had occurred over the last few days.

Shortly after his arrival in New York he had called Zoran and learned the good news about their incredibly foolish, but daring, rescue of Lori from the men who had taken her. He had breathed a sigh of relief when he heard that Zoran and Lori had come through the episode in relatively good health and that David had suffered only a minor wound to the head from a glancing bullet. *What was it about that kid's head?* After exchanging a few more pleasantries, Hawkins had ended the call by suggesting that Zoran try to refrain from any further heroics, unless absolutely necessary. Zoran told him not to worry. He was hanging up his superhero cape for good.

But Hawkins was worried. He knew this wasn't over. It was more important now than ever to find out what the hell was going on. Perhaps he would find some of the answers here. He gave up trying to go back to sleep when he noticed the faint murmur of traffic sounds from the street below. Midtown Manhattan was beginning a new day. He stumbled out of bed to the bathroom and had a quick cold shower to liven himself up using the most effective method at his disposal. Then he brushed his teeth and got dressed in his dark charcoal grey business suit for the day ahead. It wasn't every day that one got to meet a billionaire.

He decided to walk from the hotel for his 9:00 A.M. meeting with Merrick as it was only about 6 or 7 city blocks to the billionaire's Park Avenue penthouse and the morning air would help to revive him. As he crossed 6th Avenue, he noticed a Starbuck's. He went in and ordered his usual Grande latte, but this time with an extra shot of espresso. Then it happened, as it always did in the United States. On this occasion, the guilty party was the attractive young dark-haired girl that took his order, who reminded him of the actress, Liv Tyler.

"Ooh, you're English," she said excitedly.

Hawkins tried not to hurt her feelings. "No, I'm actually Australian, but I do live in England."

"I knew it," the girl said.

"But you just said I sounded English."

"Yeah, but Australian was my first thought," she said in an attempt to appear worldly-wise.

"Really?" Hawkins said, playing along. "That's very astute. Australian and English are very similar accents. To be able to distinguish them from each other is quite a feat." As he heard himself saying this, he hoped that there were no other Aussies or Brits in the coffee shop who might have overheard his sacrilegious proclamation.

The girl beamed with pride. "Your drink will be ready at the end of the counter Sir. You have a great day!"

"You too," Hawkins responded.

Hawkins arrived at the building housing Merrick's penthouse suite 5 minutes before 9 o'clock. The security guard behind the counter in the ornate lobby waved him onwards past the desk toward a private elevator. Hawkins noted with some disquiet that the opened doors revealed an aged attendant who appeared to be waiting for him. He was never quite sure whether he was meant to tip such people merely for the sake of pressing a button that he was perfectly capable of pressing himself. Maybe the attendant's presence was also for security reasons he mused, giving the man the benefit of the doubt. When the elevator arrived on the penthouse floor and the doors opened onto a small hallway of Merrick's penthouse, Hawkins decided on a compromise as he stepped out of the elevator. "I'll get you on the way down."

The attendant stared blankly straight ahead as the doors closed in front of him.

Strike one, Hawkins thought as he turned and pressed the buzzer for Merrick's suite. Almost immediately, the solid wooden door was pulled open by a middle-aged woman dressed in a stylish business coat and a medium length skirt.

"Hello, Dr Jim Hawkins I presume?" the woman greeted him with a broad smile. "I'm Mister Merrick's Personal Assistant, Mildred Honnemacker."

Hawkins beamed a smile back at her. "G'day."

"He's waiting for you in the library. Follow me please."

Hawkins stepped into the room feeling slightly anxious as Mrs Honnemacker closed the door behind him. Then he followed her swaying form through the spacious hallway decorated with various ancient artefacts including some spectacular Egyptian, Assyrian and Sumerian sculptures. Hawkins observed silently that it was an astoundingly priceless collection. He also wondered if any of the pieces had been acquired illegally. They came to an opened doorway and Mrs Honnemacker ushered him into the cavernous library, which was dominated by several more artefacts, hundreds of antique books and a very large and intricate Persian rug.

Sitting in a wheelchair, behind a large mahogany desk, was a very old man. His face was heavily lined and leathery, and his few wisps of white hair were in complete disarray. His eyes were dimmed by cataracts and his skin had a grey pallor. But he still looked imposing – just as a man worth about 20 billion dollars would do.

"Mister Merrick. This is Dr Jim Hawkins," Mrs Honnemacker said, breaking the ice. Her introduction enabled Hawkins to snap out of the spell that he found himself under. He felt like a delinquent schoolboy, standing in front of the headmaster.

"Dr Hawkins, come in and take a seat please," Merrick said in a friendly, slightly quavering voice. "Forgive me if I don't get up, but I find it rather difficult these days."

"Thank you," Hawkins said as he made his way to one of the leather wing-backed chairs facing the desk.

As Hawkins eased himself down, Merrick asked, "would you care for a beverage Dr Hawkins?"

"I don't suppose I could get a café latte?"

"Of course, I have everything," Merrick said. He turned his attention back to Mrs Honnemacker who was waiting at the opened door. "Mildred, can you please ask Carol to whip us up a couple of lattes please?"

"Right away Mister Merrick." She turned and left the room.

Then the billionaire said, "well Dr Hawkins, I believe that you and your colleagues have some suspicion that I had something to do with the incidents connected with the theft of seeds from the Laboratory of Molecular Biology, in Cambridge?"

Strike two. He envisaged that this could go quite badly. He had to play it very carefully with this man. Trying to sound unruffled, he responded, "at this stage we have no idea who was involved. The reason that I am here is to find out if you have any information that could help with the investigation."

Merrick smiled, almost as if Hawkins had just passed an important test. "What do you want to know?"

"Through your knowledge on this area, and as a man of some... uh... means, we were hoping that you might be able to suggest any possible... suspects." Hawkins realised that he would never make a good policeman. He didn't have the right persona."

"Where would you like to start?"

"The seeds," Hawkins answered. "Professor Green has already told us that you were specifically interested in the jar containing the seeds," Hawkins said. "And, by coincidence, that same jar was of primary interest to the thieves."

"That's not a coincidence, Dr Hawkins," Merrick replied evenly. "Mankind has been looking for something like this for untold millennia."

"Looking for what exactly?"

"The Tree of Eternal Life," responded Merrick.

Hawkins almost choked on his coffee. "But surely that's just a legend," he managed. "And the tree was merely symbolic for the acquisition of knowledge."

"Wrong tree," Merrick said.

"Sorry?"

"You're thinking of the wrong tree," Merrick explained patiently. "According to the *Book of Genesis*, Jehovah planted many trees in the Garden of Eden including the Tree of Knowledge, the tree you referenced. But there was another called the Tree of Life. The fruit from this tree makes the eater immortal. It's confusing since Jehovah banished Adam and Eve after they had eaten from the Tree of Knowledge to prevent them from learning about the importance of the Tree of Life. God then sent an angel to guard the entrance to the garden so mankind would not return and eat of this tree and become like a god."

"But surely those are just figurative stories," Hawkins opined.

Just then, a young woman, who Hawkins guessed must be Carol, brought in two steaming mugs containing the café lattes for Hawkins and Merrick.

Upon Carol's departure, Merrick resumed the discussion where they had left off. "I'm not so sure. There is an abundance of corroborative evidence which suggests that there could be some truth to the stories. The Tree of Life of Garden of Eden fame was believed to have flourished in the Zagros Mountains between Iran and Turkey. But there are many other legends throughout the world about a miraculous tree that could bestow eternal life to those who ate the fruit. The ancient Greek gods were thought to have gained immortality by eating ambrosia, the so-called 'food of the gods.' The sagas of the Norse gods describe an immortal ash tree called Yggdrasil. There are Chinese legends about a tree that bears a peach every 3,000 years that bestows immortality upon the one who eats it. And on the other side of the world, the ancient Mayans had depictions of an equivalent Tree of Life on some of their monuments."

Hawkins was aware that many similar legends were common in both the Old and New Worlds.

"The ancient Persians believed in an ethereal domain called the 'Aryan Expanse,' which was inhabited by beings described as being beyond death. This expanse could have been an actual geographical location located to the south of Mount Elburz, home of legendary winged gods called the Simurgh. These were giant beings credited as being the teachers and healers of Mankind. The land below the mountain was covered by a vast inland sea containing a central island on which could be found two sacred trees. The first of these was known as the Tree of All Seeds. The second was known as the Gaokerena Tree, which had healing properties and conferred immortality to those who ate its fruit."

"Just backing up a bit," Hawkins interposed, "could you explain more about these 'winged' gods?"

"Of course," Merrick answered. "The legend of the Simurgh might have originated with the shaman-like priests who dressed in vulture feathers. In the 1950s, two American palaeontologists excavated a cave near Shandihar in Kurdistan where they found the wing bones of large predatory birds buried and covered in red ochre. These were dated to around 9,000 BCE. A study of the bones showed that they were comprised of different species of vulture, bustard and eagle."

Merrick continued. "As with your discovery, the wing bones showed signs that they were still in articulation when they were buried, and they had clearly been hacked away intact from the birds' bodies by a sharp implement. This led the palaeontologists to conclude that the wings had been worn as part of a ritualistic costume, similar to that used by the vulture shamanist cult of Catal Huyuk, in Turkey, almost 2,000 years later.

"And now for the important point of all of this," Merrick said. "It is highly likely that these bird shamans were mistaken for supernatural beings. This is not surprising since they possessed advanced technology including the knowledge of astrology, metallurgy, agriculture, and the healing properties of certain plants and other natural substances. Some scholars have even suggested that the stories about these beings may have led to the Biblical accounts of angels. This possibility has been suppressed or deemed heretical by most world religions. But there are many accounts of these winged beings well before the writing of the religious scriptures. For example, there is an ancient Sumerian tablet which bears an inscription referring to a race of winged demons created by the gods who waged war on an un-named king for three years. Another Sumerian tablet describes the descent of the goddess Ishtar into the underworld where she encountered giant men covered with feathers, who ruled the world from the days of old. There is also an ancient Hindu legend that describes a half giant, half eagle called Garuda, who stole a goblet containing the secret of eternal life from the gods. Your discovery Dr Hawkins provides supportive scientific evidence for some of these legends."

"Evidence?"

"Yes. For one, there is the image on the jar depicting the scene from the Garden of Eden and then, of course, there is the translation of the script on the clay tablets."

Hawkins stiffened at this. "You know about the translation?"

"Yes, Professor Green told me."

Hawkins silently mulled over Stanley's latest act of duplicity.

Merrick carried on. "The scene on the jar depicts the Garden of Eden with a tree as the focus of attention. We know this is meant to be the Tree of Life because that is one of the phrases imprinted on the clay tablets. Then there is the image of the giant pointing out this tree to the couple, a scene reminiscent of the role ascribed to the serpent in the Book of Genesis. The inscribed word Nephilim tells us exactly who this is. He is one of the fallen ones."

Hawkins recalled this term from the talk that he and Sanderson had with Stanley. "Fallen ones?" he asked with some trepidation.

"Fallen angels," Merrick said.

Hawkins remained silent.

Merrick clarified. "As in Azazel, Beelzebub and… Lucifer."

Chapter 23

New York City
July 9, 2007

    Hawkins realised that he must have been looking at Merrick as if the man had sprouted an extra head.
    Merrick continued his explanation without seeming to notice. "The *Bible* says that an entire legion of angels was thrown out of Heaven for transgressions such as stealing from the gods. One of the things that they took with them was the secret of eternal life. I know how difficult this is to accept Dr Hawkins, but it is written in the *Bible* and other religious texts. Furthermore, a passage from the *Book of Genesis, Chapter 6*, says something even more incredible and often ignored by Christian readers: the offspring of angels and mortal women were the giants."
    Hawkins' mouth dropped open in surprise.
    Merrick tapped a few keys on the computer keyboard in front of him and clicked the mouse a few times. "I'll project the verse so you can see what I'm talking about." A 60" widescreen monitor sprang to life on the left side of the library and showed the relevant passage:

'And it came to pass, when men began to multiply on the face of the Earth, and daughters were born unto them, that the sons of God saw the daughters of men that they were fair; and they took them wives of all which they chose. There were giants in the Earth in those days: and also after that, when the sons of God came in unto the daughters of men, and they bare children unto them. The same became mighty men which were, of old, men of renown.'

    Merrick added, "the sons of God fell from grace and were cast out of Heaven by powerful archangels loyal to Michael. The outcasts were referred to as the Nephilim, from the Hebrew root word 'Naphal' which means to fall. The word has also been translated simply as 'giant.' And the phrase 'men of renown', implies that they had famous names, suggesting that they are known through our legends.

"The *Book of Enoch*, which does not form the Canon of Scripture for most Christian Churches, states that the sons of God not only chose human wives but they also gave away the secrets of Heaven. They taught humanity the science of astrology and acquainted them with mathematics and the wonders of medicinal plants. They also taught men how to work the metals of the Earth to create swords and knives.

"When God looked down from heaven and saw the bloodshed and lawlessness caused by their transgressions, he sent the faithful angel Uriel to tell Noah of a coming deluge that was meant to erase the evil ones from the world. Only Noah and his family who had remained pure would be saved. But the plan didn't work. There were other survivors.

"Some of the survivors were the remnants of the giants. They are mentioned in many places in the *Old Testament* after the great flood. The Book of Genesis refers to them as the Rephaim. The Book of Deuteronomy references races of giants known as the Emim and the Anakim. A passage from the Book of Numbers describes an encounter between Moses's people and men of great stature. The most famous of all was from the Book of Samuel about Goliath and his epic battle with David. Besides his size, Goliath may have been such a feared opponent because of the advanced metal armour and weapons that he possessed."

Hawkins uncharacteristically let his latte begin to grow cold as he became absorbed in Merrick's narrative.

"From the evidence of the inscriptions, the vulture's wings, the advanced architecture, and weaponry, it appears that you might just have discovered one of these lost giants. Perhaps he even had a legendary name. Anyway, that's what the people who entombed him believed and they clearly had knowledge and skills that were far ahead of their time."

"But why would anyone be interested in the seeds?"

"Of course, they may not be after the seeds *per se*," Merrick answered. "They're interested in the tree that the seeds might still be capable of producing and, more specifically, the fruit of this tree and its purported benefits."

Hawkins asked, "assuming for the sake of argument that this tree really existed, can you think of anyone who might have been involved in what happened in Cambridge?"

"You sound just like a policeman Dr Hawkins," Merrick said smiling. "Well, let's assume that the crime was motivated by money, as most are."

Hawkins nodded.

"Then an obvious suspect would be any large pharmaceutical company working on life extension, like my own. Most are investigating natural or ancient remedies as potential new drugs. Merrick Incorporated has already laid out significant capital investigating natural products such as extracts from exotic plants acquired from around the globe. The acquisition of a readymade life extension drug would save millions of dollars in research costs alone, not to mention what it would do for the company's share prices."

Hawkins was surprised that Merrick would cast aspersions so quickly in his own backyard.

"What do you know about this area of research?" Merrick asked.

"Not much," Hawkins answered truthfully. "I'm aware that cells have some sort of molecular clock involving the telomeres which limits the number of times they can divide." He was pleased that he had absorbed at least some of Lori's lecture on this subject. "After this point, cells stop dividing, and this leads to aging and death of the entire organism." Hawkins stopped and sipped from his latte, effectively letting Merrick know that he couldn't go into much more detail. But then he remembered something else. "In fact, our molecular archaeologist, Dr Davis, tested the length of the telomeres from the giant's muscle cells and the telomeres appeared to be completely intact."

Merrick's eyes blinked in uncharacteristic surprise. After a momentary silence, he asked, "are you certain?"

"Of course, the tests would need repeating," Hawkins allowed.

"But Dr Hawkins, that might be proof that the Tree was more than just a legend."

Hawkins started to say something but checked himself.

Merrick continued, excitedly. "This suggests that the giant had not aged as we do, and may have been alive for hundreds or even thousands or years when he was finally killed."

Hawkins felt his flesh crawling. "But that's impossible," he said thinly, realising that he had just given an automated sceptical response ingrained in him after so many years of scientific training. "But aren't there other factors besides the telomeres which limit human life expectancy?"

"Of course, you're right," Merrick admitted. "Just to clarify, life expectancy and lifespan are not the same things. Life expectancy is the number of years that an organism can expect to live based on an average taken from the population. The life expectancy in most developed countries is now around 77 years. So, I am living on borrowed time. Lifespan, on the other hand, is the maximum number of years that an organism of a particular species can live. For humans, this appears to be around one 120 years. In fact, the longest confirmed human lifespan was attributed to the French woman Jeanne Louise Calment, who died in 1997 at the grand old age of 122 years.

"Put simply, aging is caused by progressive damage to the cells. There are many causes of this damage currently under investigation by scientists, but most agree that the finger of blame for the increased decrepitude and tumour susceptibility of aging organisms, points to the mitochondria. The mitochondria convert food molecules into energy and, like any production factory, they are not completely efficient and can generate considerable waste products that are bad for the environment. These waste products cause cellular disruption which, in turn, leads to increased susceptibility to degenerative diseases and cancers. It is no coincidence that most cancers, for example, are diagnosed after the age of 55 and most other diseases such as diabetes, heart disease, osteoporosis and arthritis are more likely to manifest themselves with old age.

"One effective means of improving mitochondrial efficiency and warding off the ravages of time is by simply modifying the amount of food molecules that enter the system. A reduction in caloric intake has been shown to increase mitochondrial efficacy and thereby minimize the damage caused by oxidative stress. This appears to work by activating a protein called Sir2 which causes animals to switch from growth mode into one which favours repair. The results of this are spectacular. Rats and mice placed on a low caloric diet live healthier and longer lives.

"Another protein called Daf2 has been identified in lowly roundworms and this does the opposite. It accelerates aging. This protein operates as a master switch inside cells, controlling a cascade of other proteins that impede the cellular repair mechanism. By genetically knocking out this protein, researchers have produced worms with slowed metabolism and greater stress resistance. The net effect was that these mutant worms lived to around twice their normal lifespan.

"But with all of this knowledge, the benefits of improved nutrition and the advantages conferred by improved public health systems and modern medicine, there is still that 120-year age limit in humans that we simply cannot go beyond. And you might be surprised to learn that this limit is specifically referred to in the *Bible!*"

Hawkins blinked.

Merrick clicked the computer mouse three times and a passage from the *Book of Genesis, Chapter 3*, appeared on the screen:

And Jehovah God saith, 'Lo, the man was as one of Us, as to the knowledge of good and evil; and now, lest he send forth his hand, and have taken also of the tree of life, and eaten, and lived to the age.'

Merrick summarized, "this passage states that the gods were worried after man had eaten from the Tree of Knowledge, because he would learn that he could also eat from the Tree of Life and become immortal, like them. "Now take a look at this next passage from Genesis, Chapter 6 which describes man's eviction from the Garden of Eden."

And Jehovah saith, 'My Spirit doth not strive in man -- to the age; in their erring they are flesh: and his days have been a hundred and twenty years.'

Hawkins was stunned. How was it possible that the limit of the human lifespan could be spelled out so precisely in a religious text that was thousands of years old?

"Before the flood," Merrick continued, "Adam and his descendants had very long lives. The *Bible* states that Adam himself died at 930 years, Noah was 950 and Methuselah lived to be an impressive 969 years-old. Also, the famous Sumerian King List contains the names of numerous individuals described as demigods who lived incredibly long lives before the occurrence of a similar cataclysmic flood. But after the flood, lives were drastically shortened. In the time of David, for example, the ages of the Kings were listed as only 40 to 70 years.

"These sources suggest that at one time, men might have had access to something which gave them longer lives. But after the fall from grace, the gods somehow limited the maximum lifespan to 120 years."

Hawkins asked, "are you saying that the gods did this by limiting access to –?"

"– The Tree of Life," Merrick finished. "That's what it says in the *Bible*."

"But that would suggest that they were more advanced, at least in their medical abilities, than we are even today," Hawkins observed.

"There are many who believe precisely that," Merrick said. "There is a great deal of evidence which suggests that the so-called gods were most likely members of an advanced civilization who spread their culture to the more primitive societies of the time. This concept of a common source of civilization explains why many of the world's myths are universal, such as the ones about gods, giants and a massive flood that wiped out the largest part of humanity.

"After the cataclysmic flood, some of the giants who survived took their knowledge with them, including the secrets of eternal life, and they scattered to the four corners of the world. We hear of their exploits in the legends of many ancient civilizations including the Egyptians, Sumerians, Assyrians, Inca, Maya, Aztec, and several other North American Indian tribes. The descriptions were always the same, bearded white men of very large stature who came from across the water. They were known as the bringers of civilization and credited not only with teaching men the special skills of agriculture, engineering and writing but also the knowledge of mathematics and astronomy. They were known by famous names, such as Osiris, Dionysus, Viracocha, Quetzylcoatl and Kukulkan, and they were represented by symbols of the snake, or the feathered serpent!"

Hawkins readjusted his posture in the chair. The similarity of the symbolism to the Biblical serpent was not lost on him.

"These universal legends might explain the many reported findings of giant human remains around the globe like your own recent discovery, Dr Hawkins," Merrick continued. "And I'm sure you are aware that there have been hundreds of other reports on this subject from all over the world."

Merrick took Hawkins' silence as agreement.

"Over the last 200 years, for example, amateur excavators found giant remains regularly in American States renowned for their high concentration of burial mounds or similar structures. Although most of the tombs were plundered and the contents effectively lost, numerous accounts of the giants' existence were left behind."

Again Merrick, tapped some keys on his computer followed by a couple of mouse clicks to reveal a long list with the title 'Giant Human Remains' at the top:

In his book, The Natural and Aboriginal History of Tennessee, author John Haywood describes "very large" bones in stone graves found in Williamson County, Tennessee, in 1821. In White County, Tennessee, an "ancient fortification" contained skeletons of gigantic stature averaging at least 7 feet in length.

Ten skeletons "of both sexes and of gigantic size" were taken from a mound at Warren, Minnesota, 1883. (St. Paul Pioneer Press, May 23, 1883) A skeleton 7 feet 6 inches long was found in a massive stone structure that was likened to a temple chamber within a mound in Kanawha County, West Virginia, in 1884. (American Antiquarian, v6, 1884 133f. Cyrus Thomas, Report on Mound Explorations of the Bureau of Ethnology, 12th Annual Report, Smithsonian Bureau of Ethnology, 1890-91).

In Minnesota, 1888, were discovered remains of seven skeletons 7 to 8 feet tall. (St. Paul Pioneer Press, June 29, 1888).

In 1911, several red-haired mummies ranging from 6 and a half feet to 8 feet tall were discovered in a cave in Lovelock, Nevada. In February and June of 1931, large skeletons were found in the Humboldt lake bed near Lovelock, Nevada. The first of these two skeletons found measured 8 1/2 feet tall and appeared to have been wrapped in a gum-covered fabric similar to the Egyptian manner. The second skeleton was almost 10 feet long. (Review - Miner, June 19, 1931).

Merrick said, "I also came across another recent account on an obscure website when I was researching mining operations in California. Merrick tapped a few more keys and the screen changed to display the following:

Lompoc Record, June 30, 1959. The skeleton of a giant man over 8 feet tall was discovered by local youths in a granite tomb in the foothills of Lompoc California near the Johns-Manville diatomaceous earth mines. Along with the skeleton were found several stone tablets containing undecipherable hieroglyphic writing, a bronze axe head, decorative beads and shells. The skeleton and the artefacts have been sent to the Smithsonian Institution for further analysis.

"No follow up studies on this discovery were ever published by the Smithsonian Institution," Merrick said.

"Why is that?" Hawkins asked

""It is difficult to know with any certainty," Merrick replied. "But there have been several accounts on how the Smithsonian might have covered up certain bits of archaeological evidence in the past. Most of this appears to have involved cases that contradicted the accepted dogma on man's origins or presence in the Americas."

Merrick explained, "In classifying all of the information found in the New World in the late 19th century, the Smithsonian director John Powell and his co-workers adhered to the isolationist viewpoint. This means that they did not believe in any contact in the New World before the voyages of Columbus. But the evidence that consistently turned up indicated that the Americas were also populated in by tall Caucasians and other ethnic groups before this and even in prehistoric times. Because this contradicted their preconceived beliefs, massive amounts of information on visitations by European, African, and Middle Eastern peoples were falsely catalogued, lost, or purposely destroyed. Of course this included all traces of giants." Merrick stopped talking and took a sip of his now cold latte.

Hawkins' head was reeling from the twists and turns that their lively discussion had taken over the past hour. "Mister Merrick," he said, "you've described several groups including drug companies, the Smithsonian Institution and even organized religion that could have had the motivation and the means of carrying out what happened in Cambridge. But I have the sense that you don't really think it was any of those."

"Merrick responded with a sudden tiredness in his voice. "Although we can only make vague guesses about what might have occurred in Cambridge, there is one group that I have thus far neglected to mention that may have been involved in the Lompoc incident.

"What group is that?"

Merrick hesitated and then gave his answer. "Nazis!"

Chapter 24

Basel, Switzerland
July 9, 2007

Gerhardt Schmidt was 11 years old in 1939 when he joined the Hitler Youth movement. Neither he nor his parents had any say in the matter since it was required by law. The objective of the movement was to train future Aryan supermen and soldiers who would serve the Third Reich faithfully. Physical and military training took precedence over scientific and other forms of education. The youths in the camps learned to use weapons, built up their bodies by physical training and even gained knowledge of military strategies. A certain amount of cruelty of the older boys to the younger members was tolerated and sometimes even encouraged, as it was believed this would help to harden them and weed out the weaklings.

Because of his slight and pale appearance, Gerhardt had been targeted for bullying right from the start. One day after a hard training session on the obstacle course, two older boys had made fun of his lack of physical prowess and his weedy body. Later, they surprised him in the showers and began taunting and pushing him around. His apparent helplessness and the fact that he did nothing to stop the abuse was a significant source of amusement for the other boys. Their fun resulted in considerable pain for Gerhardt when he was pushed with an extra degree of roughness, causing him to lose his footing on the soapy floor. He fell, cracking his head on the tiles. None of the boys bothered to help him as he lay with blood dripping from his head onto the floor, mingling in a small pool of pink water around the drain. He was finally taken to the infirmary by one of the team leaders when it became apparent how seriously he was injured.

Gerhardt lay in the infirmary for the next two days while the other boys carried on with their training. He had received a concussion from the fall and his head was now bandaged to cover the 7 stitches used to close the wound. Everyone thought and even expected him to give up and quit the Youth Movement when he got out of the hospital. But as he lay there, Gerhardt wasn't thinking about quitting. He was plotting his revenge. He even snuck out of the hospital for several hours on both nights to get everything ready.

Three days later he was back in training and the same two boys began to pick on him again. This time, Gerhardt challenged them to meet him down by the lake after dark. He told them that he would fight them there one after the other if they were brave enough to come. The boys agreed that they would hold off beating on him until then.

Later that night, the two boys headed off alone down the trail that led from behind the barracks to the lake. As they came round the final bend they saw Gerhardt standing in front of the lake shimmering majestically in the light of the full moon. They left the trail and approached him, puffing out their chests and clenching their fists. Gerhardt was just waiting there, apparently relaxed. One of the boys must have had a bad feeling that something was wrong. He reached out to touch the other boy as a warning, but it was too late. Suddenly they were both falling into the earth. They screamed first in fear and then in pain as they landed a split second later. This was followed shortly after by breathless crying noises and a soft gurgling sound.

Gerhardt walked to the edge of the formerly camouflaged 10-foot-deep pit and surveyed the results of his handiwork. Both boys had been impaled by several of the wooden spikes that he had painstakingly sharpened and jammed into the soft earth at the bottom of the pit. He didn't say a word. He just watched the life ebb from the bodies of the two boys as their blood spilled to mix with the mud in the bottom of the pit. They both stared up at him wide-eyed until they finally died around 10 minutes later, within 30 seconds of each other. Then Gerhardt went back to the barracks and went to bed. He fell into a deep sound sleep.

The bodies were found the next day. Many of the boys knew what had happened, but none of them said a word. And no one ever bothered Gerhardt again.

By 1943, Nazi leaders began turning the Hitler Youth into a military reserve force to counterbalance the heavy losses that their forces had been incurring. The Youth were formed into the 12th SS Panzer Division Hitlerjugend, which saw action against British and Canadian forces during the Battle of Normandy. Over the next few months, they gained a reputation for fighting with wild ferocity and outright fanaticism. Gerhardt was one of the most dangerous and behaved like he was possessed by demons on the battlefield. He claimed that he had personally killed or maimed at least 40 of the Allied forces by the end of the conflict.

Then the war ended and the Fuhrer was dead. The dream appeared to be over. The Allied forces disbanded the Hitler Youth as a part of the Nazi Party. Several members of the organization were accused of war crimes but because they were children, few or none were prosecuted. The real criminals like Gerhardt Schmidt were simply released.

Everything and anything to do with the Nazi Party was now shunned as the German government attempted to prevent the formation of any new movements by a process called denazification, a procedure insisted upon by the Allies. But this program was not entirely successful owing to bureaucratic shortcomings. The failure was due primarily to the fact that ex-Nazi members or sympathizers were not purged of their opinions or even their outrageous conduct. Several former members of the fanatical Hitler Youth, like Gerhardt, retained their ideology and their belief in the superiority of the Aryan race. And they quietly plotted in secrecy for their return to a position of power.

In the post-War years, they joined forces and slowly developed an underground network of Nazi organizations that would one day stretch across every continent except Antarctica. Their tentacles even reached into the noblest of institutions including banking, medicine, publishing, and education. They amassed billions of dollars through both legal and illegal means.

The goal of the organization had always been the same: to ensure the survival of the master race and its eventual return to power. To this end, Schmidt developed his own niche. He would carry on the work of the SS-Ahnenerbe which had been commissioned in the 1930s to research the ancestral heritage of the Aryan race. Through careful study of Old-World texts from the rise of Sumer and Gerzeh in the 4th millennium BCE to the expansion of the Persian Empire in the 6th century BCE, along with research into New World civilizations from the appearance of the Olmecs in 1,500 BCE to the fall of the Aztecs in 1521 AD, he pieced together what he believed was the true history of the Aryans. Along the way he developed an exceptional talent for manipulation and intimidation, and he often used this to get others to do his bidding. This sometimes necessitated the 'disappearance' of some of these people once the task had been completed. But Schmidt was attempting to do something of great value. Surely that was worth the sacrifice of a few lives.

Chapter 25

New York City
July 9, 2007

    Hawkins considered the possibility that Merrick had lost his marbles. "Nazis?" he asked carefully.
    "More like neo-Nazis," Merrick allowed.
    Hawkins took a moment to absorb this information. "But what were Nazis...or even neo-Nazis...doing in small town America during the 1950s? And why would they be interested in stealing a giant or any of the other artefacts for that matter?"
    "Good questions," Merrick commented. "They were looking for what they believed to be their heritage."
    "Heritage?" Hawkins asked, finally feeling the effects of jet lag kicking in.
    "The Aryan race," Merrick specified. One of the main tenets of Nazi supremacy is the belief that they were descended from a master race of giants called the Aryan who built a civilization that dominated the world about 10,000 years ago. There is some difference of opinion, but most believers say that the Aryan race originated in the Caucasus Mountains of south-western Russia. From there, the Aryan spread out and gave rise to Europeans, Iranians and northern Indians who shared the same Indo-European root language. Nazis claim that the civilization eventually declined because inferior races mixed with it but the remnants survived in distant refuges such as the Americas and Asia.
    "Hitler became obsessed by these ideas. He became interested in the occult. He believed in reincarnation, the lost continent of Atlantis and the idea that the early myths of battles between giants and gods were actually vague memories of a disaster which destroyed the Aryan civilization. Along with these beliefs, Hitler and his henchmen sought out legendary items which were thought to wield enormous power such as the Spear of Destiny, the Holy Grail, the Ark of the Covenant, and the Tree of Life. They carried out extensive archaeological and

anthropological expeditions to far off lands including Egypt, Tibet, Greenland and even Antarctica. Of course their quest didn't end at the completion of World War II. It is still ongoing in the shadows, spearheaded by neo-Nazi groups throughout the world."

Hawkins asked, "but why do you think the thieves could have been Nazis...or neo-Nazis?"

"Good question," Merrick said. "As far as the incident in Lompoc is concerned, there are actually two pieces of proof. Firstly, one of the so-called archaeologists who removed the artefacts from the site spoke English with a German accent."

"But the possibility that they were German doesn't necessarily suggest they were members of a Nazi organization," Hawkins noted.

"Agreed," Merrick said. "But the second item of proof is more compelling. A witness found a small piece of physical evidence that was dropped at the site, something that was highly suggestive of Nazi involvement."

"What was the evidence?"

Merrick replied, "a Hitler Youth Dagger!"

On the street below, two men sat in a pearl white Cadillac Eldorado. The taller, more senior man sipped from a brown paper cup containing a barely palatable black sludge that passed as coffee while the younger man simply sat and stared straight ahead. The men were listening over a speaker to the conversation in Merrick's penthouse suite. This was possible because most of the rooms in the suite contained electronic surveillance devices, which had been planted there the week before. Up to now, neither man had been interested in what they had been hearing upstairs. In fact, much of the language was technobabble and gobbledygook and of no real importance to anyone. However, both men glanced at each other with obvious surprise and interest when Merrick mentioned the Nazi Knife.

"The individual who found the dagger is now a retired police officer named Peter Blake," Merrick said. "He and his friend

Brian Sullivan spied on the so-called archaeologists carrying out the excavation in the Lompoc hills. Blake and Sullivan were both 14 years-old at the time.

"According to Blake, there were a lot of strange things going on during the actual excavation and the archaeological techniques that were used were not strictly kosher. It might be worth your while to speak with him personally and to Mister Sullivan to get their stories firsthand."

Hawkins could see the sense in that suggestion. Besides he knew that even though David and Zoran had somehow miraculously rescued Lori, whatever was going on was far from over. "Okay," he agreed. "Anyway, I guess this is the only real lead that we have right now."

Merrick smiled and said, "I can arrange for my private jet to take you there, Dr Hawkins. At least, you can travel in comfort."

Hawkins thought briefly on his recent inbound journey. He accepted Merrick's offer without hesitation.

Chapter 26

Cambridge
July 9, 2007

Two men dressed entirely in black moved confidently past the banana yellow motorcycle, propped on its kick stand near the empty bicycle rack. The taller of the two, a large man with closely cut blonde hair, chiselled features, and a lantern jaw, cast a furtive glance about the cobbled grounds. The man with the jagged scar below his left eye regarded the motorcycle with distaste. They entered through the front door unobserved. Once inside the cavernous stone lobby, they paused to ensure the adjoining ground floor corridor was clear of pedestrian traffic. Then they quietly ascended the curving granite stairway leading to the upper levels. They reached the landing for the labs on the second floor. After walking along the short corridor past three closed doors, they stopped, scanned their surroundings once more and entered Jim Hawkins' lab.

Both men saw that the lab was devoid of people, as it should be at this time of night. But as they moved deeper into the nearest bay, they noticed a diffuse glow coming from the opened door of a small office, situated in the left-hand corner of the lab. This signalled the presence of at least one occupant. They looked at each other and silently agreed on a last minute adjustment to their plans. The man with the scar crept toward the light, reaching for his HK Volkspistole.

Zoran Radovic reread the e-mail message that he had been working on to make sure that he was satisfied with the wording. In many ways, the electronic mail system was the ultimate form of communication. Messages could be sent and received almost instantly across the world in the blink of an eye. But it was this property that sometimes worried him. Once they were sent, there was no way to take back a message that contained inappropriate words or phrases, whether they were intended or not. This could sometimes lead to problems. Many an e-mail had been sent and received that led to misunderstandings. But like all great inventions, one had to take the good with the bad.

Satisfied with the wording he clicked the mouse once, sending the message out into the ether. He hadn't spoken or written to his mother in ages and wasn't sure why he felt compelled to do so just now. Maybe it had something to do with the terrible events that had occurred over the past few days. He hoped that his little sister Valentina would be able to help their Mother work the computer. Both his parents were dinosaurs when it came to the rapidly evolving world of technology.

He now turned back to the task at hand, surfing the net to research everything he could find on ancient seeds and plants. He was so intent on checking the top 10 hits of his search that he didn't immediately notice the dark presence looming in the doorway to the office.

Suddenly, he caught a glimpse of the shadowy figure in his peripheral vision. He quickly turned his head only to be confronted by the face of evil, regarding him almost thoughtfully. The man was holding a large black pistol with a silencer screwed on to the end of it. And it was pointed right at him.

The man spoke in thick accented German, "you have caused us much trouble Dr Radovic."

Zoran didn't say a word. He knew there was no escaping what was about to happen. He didn't want his last moments to be wasted on this man. Instead, he tried to disappear. He imagined that he was sitting astride Dragi, wearing his helmet and leathers. Maybe this would protect him. He turned his thoughts inward and embraced his life and friends. He thought about his parents, his sister, his two little nieces, everyone, and everything.

The man with the scar on his face noticed Zoran's introspective composure and realised that he would receive no satisfaction from this killing. After a momentary pause, he simply pulled the trigger once and the black cannon spat out its deadly projectile into the victim's skull.

Zoran rocked back from the impact. A lightning bolt exploded in his skull, igniting all of his brain cells. Then his nervous system collapsed. His upper body crumpled, and he fell forward onto the keyboard of the computer and his mind was consumed by darkness....

Inspector Sanderson found David propped up in bed in a private room of the Addenbrooke's Accident and Emergency Ward. Lori was perched faithfully beside him in a Spartan plastic chair, where she had been for the past hour.

David noted Sanderson's entrance with a broad grin on his face, "Inspector, we have to stop meeting like this."

"It would help if you started wearing a Kevlar helmet," Sanderson replied. "You're a lucky fellow. One inch further over and I don't think even your skull could have deflected that bullet."

David smiled and said, "I do feel lucky. It reminds me of that guy, I think he was a forest ranger, who was struck by lightning more than 30 times and managed to survive every time."

Lori spoke up. "David, that ranger didn't think that he was lucky. In fact, he felt unlucky because he had been hit so many times by such a freak occurrence as a lightning strike. He eventually committed suicide."

"Can't say much for your bedside manner," David observed.

Sanderson smiled at the exchange. "If you're both up for it, can I get you to go through what happened at the house? There might be something important that we missed."

Lori began. "Unfortunately, I don't really remember anything from the point where they shot poor Pavlos until I woke up in the attic. I remember one of them squishing me from behind, pressing a chloroform-soaked cloth to my face. It must have put me out for hours."

"How do you know it was chloroform?"

"I know what it smells like," Lori answered. "We use it routinely in the lab as a solvent when preparing DNA."

Sanderson nodded. "Do you have any idea why they took you?"

"Not a clue," Lori said. "After they shot Pavlos, and I assumed they had also killed David, I guess I expected them to kill me too. I'm surprised they let me live."

"Did you hear any conversation in the house?"

"Some," Lori answered. "But, unfortunately they spoke in German, so I didn't get much."

"That's okay," Sanderson said. "What do you think you heard?"

"A name... Herr Schmidt," she said. "One of them was speaking to him over a telephone. I think it was a cell phone because the voice kept moving. Then I recognized the words for 'kill her' and I started to panic."

Sanderson noticed that she still looked shaken. "Did you hear anything else, Lori?"

"Yes. I heard him refer to Basel, as in the Swiss city. Do you think they might be taking the seeds there?"

"Could be," Sanderson answered.

"Uh... I don't think so," David interrupted.

"What do you mean, David?" Sanderson asked.

"The head police guy on the scene at Cavendish Road said that they found a bag containing the seeds and small plants on the dead man. They were in his coat pocket."

"But if they no longer have them —" Lori started.

Sanderson was stunned. He blamed himself for not getting back on the case sooner. "They might try again!" he said completing Lori's thought process.

"But the rest of the seeds are being stored in the Archaeology Lab," David said, "along with the mummy and the other artefacts."

Lori's heart suddenly became a pounding drum. She blurted, "I think Zoran is there now, at the lab. He said he had to check up on a few things."

The urgency of her tone induced Sanderson into action. "What's the number?" he asked, snapping out his cell phone. After David told him, Sanderson rapidly punched in the number and put the phone up to his ear. His call elicited 8 rings and then went to voicemail.

David and Lori looked on in silence.

Sanderson stopped the call and punched in a two-digit number, connecting him with the police station.

Sergeant Condron and three other members of the police force arrived at the lab 5 minutes later. They found the body slumped over the computer keyboard in the office. The gunshot wound to the forehead was sickeningly obvious and a pool of blood had collected and congealed over most of the desk. Some had spilled onto the thinly carpeted floor. One of the young policemen was violently sick in the office waste bucket. He apologized to his comrades when he had more-or-less recovered his composure. But most of them had also felt physically ill by what confronted them. It was one of those things that you could never prepare for.

Condron offered comfort. "That's okay, Maloney. It's a difficult sight for anyone to see, even a policeman. It shows you are human."

Maloney smiled weakly.

Another one of the officers, a tall willowy woman named Georgia Sinclair, asked the obvious question. "Why did they kill him? He was obviously no threat. He was just sitting at the computer, working."

"That's a good question," Condron said. "Can you and Salim check out the lab to see if anything is missing? The Inspector mentioned a ceramic jar and seeds."

Sinclair raised an eyebrow at this and said, "of course, right away." She waved a 'let's go' signal to Constable Salim and they moved into the lab. They paid cursory attention to each row of lab benches as they progressed their search pattern moving outwards from the office. At first it was difficult to assess the situation due to the clutter typical of most scientific labs. However, when they reached the bay furthest from the office, they found broken fragments of a ceramic jar.

It was clear to them that the jar had been hurled to the ground purely for the sake of smashing it or to gain easy access to the contents. There was no sign of anything resembling seeds, but surely that couldn't be very important. After all, there was a dead person in the next room. Nothing else in the lab appeared to have been disturbed. Sinclair and Salim reported their findings to Condron.

Sergeant Condron nodded his thanks. He called for the coroner as well as more officers to help set up the crime scene. After that he went back into the office to look once more at Dr Radovic's body. With a heavy heart, he called Inspector Sanderson.

Lori and David reacted to the news in different ways. Lori simply broke down and wept. She slumped on David's bed with her breaths coming in heaving sobs. Thoughts of Zoran flashed fleetingly through her mind. The latest images were the strongest – the way he had helped her to escape from the house on Cavendish Road. He had rescued her just like a knight in shining armour on that ridiculous yellow motorcycle of his. She felt her heart wrenching from the sudden pangs of grief. They would never see his smiling face again.

David, on the other hand, felt like a vice had tightened around his head. Although he felt the same pain as Lori, he was also overcome with anger. Why were the seeds so damn important? So far, the cost had been the lives of two of his friends and he had also very nearly lost his own life twice. More than anything, he needed to do something "Let's find these bastards Inspector."

Sanderson nodded but his expression lacked confidence.

Chapter 27

Airspace over north-western Arizona
July 9, 2007

    Hawkins stared out the elliptical window of the Gulfstream 200 jet at the magnificent panorama of the Grand Canyon below. The scene reminded him of pictures that he had seen of the stunning surface of Mars. The red, brown, and copper hues mingled over the wrinkled tapestry of the landscape in ways that no photograph could ever capture. It was Mother Nature in all her glory. To Hawkins it was a desolate wasteland.

    The news of Zoran's death had left him numb. When the solitary air hostess had handed him the cell phone and said a call had just been relayed from Inspector Sanderson in Cambridge, he knew it was bad news. But listening to the Inspector say the words out loud, made it all too real.

    His thoughts turned to what he was now trying to accomplish by gallivanting across the United States. His obsession with finding the men behind this was no longer just about the seeds. It had become something far more important. It was now about finding the monsters who had kidnapped Lori and took the lives of Pavlos and his best friend.

    Sanderson's voice, cracking with interference from the tenuous connection, dissolved his reverie. "Lori and David are okay, but both were badly shaken by the news. I have assigned a police guard for each of them, just as a precaution."

    Hawkins reflected on the underlying meaning of Sanderson's words. Their lives were now at risk.

    "You should be aware that David wants to pursue the ones who did this to the ends of the Earth," Sanderson continued.

    Hawkins didn't admit that the same thought had occurred to him. "I'll speak to him, Inspector. And to Lori."

    "That's a good idea," Sanderson said.

    "Inspector, could you make sure that Zoran's motorcycle is brought to my house for now? I think he would have wanted that."

Sanderson felt the pain over the telephone. Although it was against protocol, and the motorcycle was still considered part of a crime scene, Sanderson answered. "I'll see what I can do."

The Leer jet touched down gracefully at the small airport in Lompoc just after 5:00 P.M. local time. Hawkins emerged from the sleek airplane and clomped down the short flight of steps with the dynamism of a zombie on Prozac. The gleaming white limousine that Merrick had arranged to meet him had pulled up onto the runway approximately 50 feet from the jet's final resting place.

The driver was either incapable of speech or had decided that silence was the best policy. He didn't say a word to Hawkins as he put the archaeologist's small bag into the vehicle's cavernous trunk. He was a large, stiff, muscular man who presumably also doubled as a bodyguard. He drove Hawkins from the airport to a district containing hotels and small businesses. These were situated along Lompoc's main thoroughfare, signposted as 'H Street,' but was actually a continuation of the Pacific Coast Highway. The driver left him at the Lompoc Quality Inn with a brief affirmation that he would be back at 9 A.M. to pick up him up for the short drive to Peter Blake's house.

Hawkins checked in to the hotel in a daze and went immediately to his room on the second floor in an attempt to catch up on his sleep. But after undressing and climbing into bed, he tossed and turned for several hours. He dozed occasionally, but his thoughts kept returning to his friends in England. He finally drifted off to sleep sometime after midnight. The last thing he could recall was an image of Zoran, riding tall over a hill on his motorcycle. He was waving.

On the far side of the hotel parking lot, two men watched and waited in a rented plain Ford sedan.

Chapter 28

Lompoc, California
July 10, 2007

With a population of more than 40,000 people, Lompoc was not exactly a small town, at least not anymore. The city had expanded in the 1970s and 1980s due to its links with the nearby Vandenberg Air Force Base, home of the 30th Space Wing and the Western Launch and Test Range. Vandenberg's prime location on the northern Pacific Ocean and its position relative to the jet stream made it possible to launch satellites into polar orbits. Vandenberg was responsible for launching military and commercial payloads and for testing intercontinental ballistic missiles. In the early 1980s it was being outfitted as the West Coast Space Shuttle launch and landing site to complement the existing facility at Cape Kennedy, in Florida.

To support the massive incoming work force required for this challenging venture, thousands of new homes and businesses were constructed in Lompoc and surrounding areas, and investments were made in accordance with the promising future of the town. The West Coast Space Shuttle program was on schedule to begin operations in October 1986. But on January 28th that year, the US space program experienced a major setback. The space shuttle Challenger exploded over Cape Kennedy approximately 73 seconds after launch due to what would later be determined as a faulty 'O ring' on one of its solid rocket boosters. All 7 crew were killed in the explosion, including a New Hampshire school teacher. The investigation into the cause of the explosion led to grounding of the remaining shuttle fleet until it was deemed safe to fly again. The effect on the city of Lompoc was devastating. The West Coast Space Shuttle program was cancelled. This decision led to an economic recession and the closure of several businesses. The chance for a prosperous future was lost, at least for the time being.

Apart from the Shuttle Program, Lompoc wasn't exactly famous, but it did have an interesting history. The first settlers in the valley were predecessors of the Chumash Indians who occupied the area for around 10,000 years before European contact. The establishment of the Mission La Purisma Concepcion in 1787 by Father Fermín de Lasuén marked the first European settlement of the area. La Purisma was the 11th in a chain of 21 missions established throughout the Golden State. The mission was destroyed by an earthquake in 1812 and then re-built approximately 4 miles north of the original site.

The Lompoc Land Company was formed in 1874 with the purchase 43,000 acres for the purpose of establishing a temperance colony. The city was incorporated in 1888. The completion of the West Coast Railway between San Francisco and Los Angeles in 1901 provided the impetus for the growth of the fledgling town. Fields were cleared for production of agricultural products. But it was the production of flowers that took off in the biggest way. Now, the valley is famous for the sheer number and variety of flowers that flourish there, and it is also the site of an annual flower festival which attracts thousands of visitors from near and far.

In 1923, the worst peacetime naval disaster occurred near Lompoc off the breezy coastal region known as Honda Point, with the loss of 7 destroyers and the lives of 23 sailors. It was thought that the shipwrecks were caused by localized oceanic disturbances following a massive earthquake that occurred across the Pacific Ocean in Japan 6 days earlier.

In 1940, Lompoc became the fictional site of what was to become a classic film called *The Bank Dick* starring William Claude Dukenfield, also known as W.C. Fields. *The Bank Dick* was Fields' last major film role and has been deemed 'culturally significant' by the United States Library of Congress.

Lompoc also contains one of the world's largest known deposits of diatomaceous earth, a naturally occurring sedimentary rock that can be pulverized into a fine white powder. Diatomaceous earth is essentially comprised of silica and the fossilized remains of diatoms, a type of hard-shelled algae. It has several useful applications including as a filtration aid, a mild abrasive in products such as toothpaste, a mechanical insecticide, an absorbent for liquids, and as a component of dynamite. The deposits are located in the southern hills of the town where the diatoms and other creatures of the ancient seashore left their corpses. It was near these deposits that the remains of several other extant and extinct species had also been discovered including those of lions, bears, fish, whales, mammoths and… *a giant man.*

Aside from the part about the giant man, these facts were contained within the information pamphlet in Hawkins' hotel room. He had mentally added that to the list. He mulled over the town's short, but interesting, history as he sat waiting for a waitress to take his order at the Denny's Restaurant which was located within walking distance of his hotel. He loved the portions and variety of foods available in American breakfast restaurants. It was one of the things that Americans did well.

Hawkins' waitress, an athletic-looking young college-aged girl, approached him to take his order. "Have you decided on what you want this morning?" she asked in the usual overly friendly American waitress spiel.

"Yes please," Hawkins said. "I'd like the Denver omelette, with a short stack of pancakes, two pieces of dry brown toast and a half-carafe of orange juice."

"Oh, cool accent," she gushed. "Are you from England?"

The limousine pulled up outside the lobby of the Quality Inn at 9:00 AM. The chauffer hopped out and held the back door while Hawkins ducked inside and allowed himself to be swallowed up by the spacious leather backseat. Silent Bob, as Hawkins had decided to nickname the driver, manoeuvred the car around the circular drive and onto the Pacific Coast Highway. Their first destination was a drive-through Starbuck's Coffee shop that Hawkins had noticed earlier when he had walked to breakfast. Silent Bob eased the car through the narrow lane, ordered at the speaker, then paid for and collected Hawkins' first caffeine infusion of the day from the girl at the sliding window.

Then they resumed the journey and headed across town. Hawkins sipped from his latte as he gazed at the odd mixture of modern and century-old architecture going by. When they reached the town's largest junction at the intersection of 'H Street' and 'Ocean Avenue,' they turned right and then immediately left onto the next street as they headed for the southern rim of the valley. They rolled past several residences and a large, rectangular red brick Catholic Church and then the road suddenly became a scenic highway that cut through the rolling foothills.

Hawkins noted that the gently meandering road was lined intermittently by various homes, some of which were of the sprawling ranch style that he liked so much. After a few more minutes, Silent Bob slowed, turned off the main highway and brought the limousine to a halt in a driveway that provided access to an impressive ranch house.

The spacious property consisted of a white smooth-plastered single-level house with traditional Spanish style low-pitched clay tile roofing. The forward grounds were decorated with various western implements and tools, including 19th century wagon wheels, a rustic plough, and several wooden barrels. The house was flanked on the left by a small orchard of orange and lemon trees and on the right by a grove of cacti of numerous shapes and sizes. Towards the rear, the property was bounded by a large creek, which carved its way deeply into the landscape. Beyond the creek, the land merged seamlessly into the inclining hills that formed the eastern wall of the canyon.

As Hawkins stepped from the limousine, a tall man resembling a rugged 19th century cowboy emerged through the large wooden front door of the ranch house. Although his hair had mostly turned to grey, he was in amazing shape for a man in his 60s. He had crystal clear, discerning eyes and a ramrod straight posture that complemented his slim muscular physique. He sported a red plaid shirt and blue Levi jeans over well-tanned cowboy boots. The man raised his hand in greeting and called out, "Howdy. You must be Dr Hawkins."

Hawkins nodded and walked towards the man's outstretched hand. "G'day, call me Jim!" He grabbed Blake's large, calloused hand.

"And you can call me Pete. Am I right in thinking you're Australian?"

"That's right," Hawkins answered, silently thankful.

"From where, exactly?"

"Sydney."

"Great city," Blake said. "Been there three or four times."

Hawkins knew then that he and Blake would get along just fine. Close up, Hawkins could see that his face was only slightly weathered with small wrinkles that looked more like laughter lines. It was face that could be trusted.

"Well, I guess we have a lot to talk about. Why don't you come in and we'll start with coffee?" Blake said.

"You just said the magic word."

"I remember that day in 1959 just like it was yesterday," Blake said with a faraway look in his eyes. "My best friend Brian and I could see almost everything from the ridge above the plateau where the so-called archaeologists were busy unearthing the sarcophagus. I had my suspicions about them since they didn't seem to be working with enough care and were far too rushed at every stage of the procedure. If anything, they appeared more like treasure hunters. After they got the lid open, they worked for a while longer and then one of them climbed inside and removed the contents of what looked like two ceramic jars."

"Were there any markings on the jars?" Hawkins asked.

"Yes. Both jars contained pictures, but we weren't close enough to make these out. However, Brian and I both recognized a symbol that appeared as part of a repeating pattern around both jars, and it scared the Dickens out of us."

A chill went up Hawkins' spine. "Swastikas?"

Blake paused for a moment, assessing Hawkins carefully with probing eyes. "Yep, several of 'em. How'd ya know?"

Hawkins quickly updated him about the similar symbols they had found on the jar in Cambridge.

Blake's reaction to this news was straight and to the point. "Well, I'll be corn-cobbed and hogtied."

Hawkins decided he would have to write that one down.

Blake went on, "Brian and I never told anyone about the swastikas. We didn't think they would believe it. After all, no one believed us about the giant."

"Did you learn about their likely significance later?"

"Yes. We learned in school that the swastika was originally an important symbol in many eastern religions and was associated with the earliest known civilizations."

Hawkins added to that, "that's right. It appeared over a great expanse of time and over a large area stretching from southeastern Europe into many parts of Asia."

"So how did the symbol get to England, and to here?"

"You ask good questions, Pete."

"Part of being a cop."

"There are two possibilities," Hawkins began. "The first is that the swastika arose here independently as part of the ancient Chumash tradition. There is plenty of evidence to support this since the same symbol has been associated with many other Native American tribes, particularly those of the Southwest. The second way is by diffusion."

"So, the appearance of the symbol in the New World might stem from contact with people, perhaps giant ones, from the Old World?" Blake said, correctly interpreting Hawkins' use of the word 'diffusion.'

"You're not an amateur archaeologist, by any chance?"

"More like armchair. I watch the *Discovery Channel* a lot."

Hawkins smiled at that. "The possibility of ancient contacts between the Old and New Worlds has been the subject of much debate over many years in the archaeological community. But the evidence is becoming insurmountable that there was indeed contact, and this led to strikingly similar archaeological and artistic developments in widespread parts of the world."

"Like the appearance of pyramids and mummies on both sides of the Atlantic Ocean?"

"Exactly."

"Anyway, sorry that I got us off the subject," Blake said. "I could talk about this subject until the cows come home. I should get back to telling you about the discovery."

Hawkins realised that he had also drifted from the main topic. Blake was a natural talker with a wide range of knowledge.

"After the archaeologists were done for the day, Brian and I climbed down for a close look," Blake resumed. "What we saw changed my world forever. The image of that giant lying inside the sarcophagus would haunt my dreams for many years afterward. And after the news coverage of your discovery in England, it was like living through it all over again."

"Why?"

"The two discoveries were almost identical," Blake answered. "The large granite blocks, the giant, the weapons, and the jars, all seemed so very similar. But the age that the two giants were buried might be different."

"Why do you say that?"

"The tomb you discovered in Cambridge was dated at 5,500 years ago. But in Lompoc, we overheard the geologist say that it was 8,000 to 10,000 years-old, based on the overlying strata."

Hawkins was stunned. "That's incredible. That could mean that the giant, and maybe others of his kind, interacted with the indigenous ancient tribes of the area, such as the Chumash, and whoever came before them."

Blake said, "I did some research and found that there are Indian legends about a race of very tall, warlike people living in the area. The legends say that the giant men were sometimes helpful. They taught the Indians agriculture and other useful skills, but they also had a dark side. They were cannibals!"

Hawkins felt an eerie *deja vu* sensation as if his skin was crawling with ants.

Blake carried on. "The Chumash believe that this area is haunted by the spirits of the giants, and they stay away... so as not to anger them."

"What happened after you and Brian discovered what was inside the sarcophagus?"

"We ran. We told Chief Thompson about the body. But when we returned to the site the next day with him and his deputy, and our brothers, it was gone."

"Gone?"

"The Chief reckoned the scientists must have returned to the site during the night and removed everything."

"But was a report ever filed? Was there ever any follow up work done at the site?"

"No. At least I don't think so. The Chief called the Smithsonian but was unable to learn anything. First, they told him that the scientists had disappeared. We learned later that three of them had been killed in Washington DC when the plane they were flying in crashed into the Potomac river. The skinny German man, who seemed to be in charge, disappeared completely as if he never existed. The Smithsonian found no record of who he was or how he came to be assigned to the project. Then they claimed that, because of all this, the artefacts had either been lost or misplaced. To make matters worse, Brian and I returned to the site about a month afterwards and everything else was no longer there."

"You mean that the sarcophagus itself was gone?"

"Not a stone," Blake said. "The area where it had been standing was completely flattened and looked like it had been dug over. We searched around for hours just trying to find some trace to prove to ourselves and others that it had been there, but we turned up nothing."

"Unbelievable."

"That's what was so worrying and so disappointing about this. I guess that if I hadn't already found the Hitler Youth Knife, there wouldn't have been any proof at all. I discovered it just after Brian and I had snuck down to the pit to see what the archaeologists had uncovered inside the sarcophagus and there it was, lying in the dirt. I figured that the German man must have dropped it without realising. I didn't tell the Chief or anyone else, but I did show it to Brian a few months later. I eventually gave it to him as a memento of our shared experience. I think Brian still has it on display in his living room to this day."

"What do you think it means?"

"The knife?"

"Yes."

"As strange as it might sound, my policeman's instinct tells me that Nazis were here and they were looking for something."

Hawkins remained silent.

"It wasn't the giant *per se*," Blake said. "Although, that was probably what attracted their attention in the first place. No, it must have been whatever was in those jars. They took those first." Blake went on. "But only one of them seemed to know what they were looking for. And after he found it, he must have arranged the deaths of the other three to cover his own tracks."

"And that's when the case went cold?" Hawkins asked.

"Maybe," Blake answered. "But more than likely, the Chief just forgot about it. He wasn't exactly a patient man."

"Do you think there's any chance of picking up the trail again?"

"Only if the same people were involved in the crime in Cambridge," Blake answered. "But that's a major stretch considering that there are almost 50 years between the two incidents."

"Suppose there is a connection between the two," Hawkins posed. "What would you do next?"

Blake paused for a moment and regarded Hawkins with speculative eyes. He said, "then I would recommend three potential starting points. First, visit the site here to see if you can detect any archaeological lines of evidence that we might have missed. I would be more than happy to take you there. Second, speak directly with Brian who might be able to recall some important detail that I left out. And third, go to the Smithsonian Institution and see if you can track down what become of the relics from the Lompoc site. You probably won't find anything, but your inquiries might rattle a few cages, and you never know what might jump out at you."

Hawkins thought about the suggestions for approximately three seconds before he responded. "Shall we take a look at the site first?"

"I thought you'd never ask. But first, can you tell me about what happened in Cambridge?"

The classic sports car accelerated smoothly around bends of varying acuteness through the canyon. The perceptible changes in g-force felt good to Hawkins as Blake expertly handled the metallic blue and white 1967 Shelby Mustang like a skilled rally driver. After two miles, Blake edged the sleek vehicle off the road onto a small dirt lay-by, causing a cloud of dust to billow around the car like a desert sandstorm. A large eucalyptus tree stood sentinel next to a barely discernible trail on the edge of the lay-by. After the two men stepped from the car and approached the trailhead, Hawkins noticed that something had been carved into the trunk of the tree:

Brian Sullivan
Tim Sullivan
Tony Blake
Pete Blake

June 28, 1959

Although the etchings had been overgrown by almost 50 thin layers of eucalyptus bark, they were still visible.

"Boys will be boys," Blake commented, gazing fondly at the tree. "I think it was Brian's idea. He always did have a sense of drama."

Hawkins just smiled as they walked past the tree and hiked up the faint trail towards the site. They were equipped with two sets of trowels and spades that they had taken from Blake's shed in case any minor excavation work was required. After nearly 20 minutes, they came to a small plateau on the hill side.

Even after 5 decades of continuous erosion, it was obvious to Hawkins that there had been something there. For the most part, the land had been reclaimed by the chaparral shrubbery that blanketed most of the hillside. But the landscape still showed the scars of the old excavation.

"Is this where you found the sarcophagus, Pete?" Hawkins asked as he pointed to the large hollow in the middle of the plateau.

"Yes. I didn't think that there would be any sign of it after all this time."

"It would be next to impossible for anyone to put all of this back without leaving some trace," Hawkins observed. "At any rate, this would have been a perfect spot on the mountainside for a tomb. This natural plateau would have offered good stability."

"Makes sense," Blake said. "Where should we start?" he said raising his spade to emphasise the fact that he was referring to the digging.

"Let's look around first. We can start by searching below the site along the downhill slope. It's possible that run-off from the mountain could have carried any missed objects down the hill, if they weren't buried too deeply."

The two men searched diligently along the downhill slope for almost an hour, periodically stopping to dig into the surface with the tools. They unearthed the occasional pottery shard, but these were Chumash in origin. Next, they turned their attention to the depressed area on the plateau itself. It was obvious to Hawkins, from the wide areas of loosely packed soil, that the site had been excavated and then partially filled in. After another two hours of searching, they found nothing of any significance. It had been picked clean. Whoever did this had gone to great lengths to make sure that not a trace of evidence would ever be found.

The two men gave up and returned down the mountain trail to the car. Upon passing the eucalyptus tree, Hawkins reached into his pocket, pulled out an object and set to work on the tree.

At first Blake gazed in wonder and then his face broke into a broad smile when he realised what Hawkins up to. There was now a new etching on the tree, above the original:

Pete Blake
July 10, 2007

Chapter 29

Lompoc, California
July 10, 2007

Hawkins left Blake's house just after two o'clock and was chauffeured back to the drive-through Starbuck's by Silent Bob. On this occasion, he went inside for a much-needed snack. In an attempt to avoid any misguided questions about his nationality, he ordered his steak and cheese sandwich along with a café latte using a put-on American accent. But to his ears, it came out sounding like a bad impersonation of Huckleberry Hound. He was sure that the young girl who took his order could barely suppress the urge to giggle. But his tactic worked. She didn't ask any questions about his origin.

He chose a soft corner chair so he could quietly go over the facts of the case while eating his lunch. He often resolved the most nagging problems using this munch and think approach. He slowly chewed his way through the sandwich as he created a mental list of the salient points:

1. A stone sarcophagus at least 8,000 years-old – containing a giant skeleton – discovered in Lompoc in 1959.
2. There is a strong possibility that the jars in the Lompoc tomb were robbed... of something.
3. The giant and all artefacts were removed from the site and then subsequently lost, misplaced, or stolen.
4. Three of the scientists involved in investigating the site were killed under mysterious circumstances.
5. The main suspects: Nazis?

He sipped his latte and then meticulously carried out the same mental operation for the Cambridge discovery:

1. A tomb – 5,500 years-old – containing a similar giant skeleton – discovered in Cambridge, in 2007.
2. Also present in the tomb: numerous advanced Bronze Age weapons, dried human meat and bones from the wings of a griffon vulture.
3. The tomb also contained jars, possibly similar to those in Lompoc.
4. The contents of the jars – this time known to be seeds – were stolen.
5. In the process, two of his friends had been killed, one beat up and shot, and another kidnapped.

6. *The main suspects: Nazis?*

He gazed at his now empty plate and cup on the table. Although the discoveries were similar, he still wasn't sure what to do next. He sighed ordered another latte, this time in a take-away cup for the short walk back to his hotel.

Calvin Hagler and Ray Crowther, aged 20 and 19 years respectively, had lived lives that some might consider all too common for those coming from Los Angeles' poorest districts. They had both joined the same street gang in their early teens and they saw immediate and violent action. While still in their mid-teens, they had already killed 5 people between them and they progressed steadily upward through the ranks of the gang as their exploits became more widely known. But after this, life became too dangerous. After two or three near misses it was Calvin who had the bright idea that they should get out of LA with their cajones still intact, and Ray agreed.

Their move took them to Lompoc, California. That was where Ray's older cousin Michael lived with his family. In Lompoc, Ray and Calvin used their expertise garnered on the streets of LA to good effect in a town that was simply not ready for the likes of them. Calvin's extracurricular activities ranged from shoplifting, to carjacking and street fighting. Ray occasionally resorted to armed assault and robbery. However, both missed the good old days. That was why they were both excited about this new job of killing some guy they had never even heard of.

Earlier that day they had met the German man with the prominent scar who had invited them for a coffee, promising them some interesting business and big bucks. Neither of the youths showed any reaction when they were told that all they had to do was waste some guy and make it look like a robbery. Then, they were told to stab him through the heart. They were not allowed to use guns because that would attract too much attention. When Calvin said that he never went anywhere without a piece, he quickly changed his tune when he learned that they would earn 1,000 dollars each if they successfully carried out the task in the manner requested. It would be easy money.

Calvin waited patiently at Denny's restaurant drinking filter coffee while watching for their man to return to his hotel. Then he noticed the guy strolling past the restaurant carrying a Starbuck's cup. The man seemed to look around as he walked. It was obvious that he was a stranger to the city. Calvin whipped out his cell phone and punched in his partner's number. When Ray answered the call, Calvin said, "he's on the way."

"Roger alpha team," Ray called out with military precision. "Beta team on the move."

"Cut out that John Wayne Green Beret crap and be serious man," Calvin chastised. Then he smiled into his phone and said, "alpha team out."

Not willing to risk bodily harm by running across the Pacific Coast Highway, Hawkins opted for the relative safety afforded by the traffic lights and pedestrian walkway at the junction. After crossing the wide road, he took a swallow from his latte and headed toward his hotel. Just as he passed Denny's he noticed a tall young black man in a leather coat emerge quickly from the restaurant. Hawkins' alarm bells started ringing. The weather was far too warm for a coat and the man appeared to be trying hard to look inconspicuous.

Hawkins hoped that he was just over-reacting and wrung out from jet lag. He cut through the vacant lot that served as a short cut to the hotel. The man was following him. Hawkins edged round the back of a brick building when another man stepped out in front of him. As Hawkins stopped short he realised that the first man was now right behind him. *Not good.*

The man in front of him pulled out a long knife held with the blade side pointing upwards, the correct orientation to maximize damage. The man with the knife said, "looks like we got ourselves a winner here, Cal."

Hawkins momentarily froze as he noted that both men acted like they had done this before, and they meant business. Also, they were both larger than him. The man in front of him was easily 6'3" and 220 pounds while the man behind, Cal, had to be at least an inch taller and 30 pounds heavier.

"Man, I told you no names," Calvin said as he pulled out his own shiny knife.

"Aw, it doesn't matter," the other said.

That was when Hawkins knew that they intended to kill him.

Parked at a safe distance away in their rented Ford, two men watched the scene through powerful binoculars.

"Think we should get involved?" The younger man asked his partner while not taking his eyes off the three men in his field of view.

"Won't be necessary," the large older man replied, lowering his binoculars and turning towards his partner.

"Okay, you're the man."

"Yes, I am. Now shut up and let me concentrate." He turned back to the scene and raised the binoculars to his eyes.

Ray took control. "Give us your –"

Hawkins pulled the lid off his latte and chucked the steaming contents into his attacker's face. Not aikido, but effective nonetheless.

Ray screamed as he reflexively patted his scalded cheeks and eyes with his hands, including the one holding the knife.

Hawkins wasn't finished. In one continuous motion he reached out with both hands and grabbed Ray's upraised knife arm firmly by the wrist and elbow as he twisted to the side.

As Calvin lunged forwards, Hawkins heaved Ray into the path of the knife. Hawkins winced as Ray was impaled through the right side of his throat. He hadn't intended for that to happen, but he couldn't stop to worry about that now.

""You stabbed him!" Calvin said as he watched as his friend slump forward to the ground and roll onto his back.

Hawkins felt sick. But he had a bigger problem right now and that was standing right before him holding a bloodied knife.

"You should help your friend," Hawkins said. "He's lost a lot of blood already."

Calvin looked momentarily thoughtful and then lunged at Hawkins with the knife extended before him, stepping over his friend in the process.

To Hawkins, everything happened in slow motion. He stepped to the side and came forward as Calvin was mid-step over Ray and he grabbed Calvin's outstretched arm around the wrist. Then he slammed his other arm on top of the young man's forearm. Without stopping, he snapped a powerful lock on the trapped wrist. The entire movement lasted one second and elicited an equally rapid response from Calvin, he grunted and dropped to his knees.

"Ow, ow, ow... ow," the Calvin cried between gritted teeth. It felt like his wrist would snap at any second.

But Hawkins stopped the pressure at just the right point. Then he lowered his body while keeping Calvin's entire arm locked into his chest. The net result was that Calvin shot the rest of the way to the pavement to try and escape the pain. That was Hawkins' objective, to take him down. He then used his right hand to slip the knife from Calvin's hand and tossed this a safe distance away across the gravel.

Calvin was now pinned face down with his right arm extended unnaturally backwards in Hawkins' grip. Any movement caused the young hooligan intense pain. "Lemme go help Ray!"

Hawkins peered over at Ray and saw no movement. "I think it's too late."

Calvin grunted.

"Do you have a mobile phone, Calvin?" Hawkins asked.

For a moment Calvin thought about lying but then the kung fu dude with the funny accent tightened his hold and Calvin felt that his shoulder muscles could tear at any moment. "Course I do. What kinda fool'd be caught without one these days."

Hawkins let that comment slide and asked, "where?"

"Inside coat pocket..." Calvin gasped. "But I can't move."

"That's okay. I'll get it."

He reached under Calvin's heavily muscled torso with one hand while maintaining the hold with the other. The phone was where Calvin said it would be. Hawkins drew it out and punched the key pad three times with his thumb.

"Who ya calling man?" Calvin asked exasperated.

"The police." Hawkins had dialled 911, the American emergency services number. "Meanwhile, you have some explaining to do."

"I ain't telling you nuthin' man," Calvin said through gritted teeth.

The call was answered and Hawkins paused in his discourse with Calvin to give the details to the dispatcher. After disconnecting, he said, "now Calvin... are you going to talk to me?"

"I ain't sayin' nothin'."

Hawkins tightened his grip to exert more pressure on Calvin's shoulder. He said, "that's okay. We'll just wait for the police. They should be here in about 10 minutes."

Calvin agreed to talk.

The police arrived on the scene three minutes later with red and blue lights flashing and tyres skidding to a halt on the loose surface. This was followed by a large red and white ambulance that pulled next to the police car around 30 seconds later. Hawkins turned his captive over to a young policeman who promptly slapped the handcuffs on Calvin and assisted him into the back of the police car. The paramedics examined Ray's body and determined that he was dead on the scene.

One of the policemen, a stocky Hispanic man with a moustache, questioned Hawkins while the other more junior officer took notes. Hawkins lied and said that it appeared as if the two men were planning to rob him. He told the truth about the rest of the incident but it became clear to him that the police were not going to let him go easily and would have to take him in for further questioning.

Just then a blue and white Shelby Mustang pulled to a stop behind the police car and Pete Blake emerged onto the scene.

"Whaddaya got here, Sanchez?" Blake asked casually.

"Hi Chief," Sanchez responded. "Guess you've been monitoring the police radio again?"

"Just can't seem to stay retired," Blake responded.

Sanchez explained the situation to his former boss. Because the robbery had led to the death of one of the perpetrators, they would have to take Hawkins in.

Blake said that he could vouch for Hawkins. He added that they should let him go on his way for now. Sanchez agreed reluctantly. Then the police and the paramedics made preparations to leave the scene.

"Thanks Pete," Hawkins said when the officer had turned and walked back to his car. "I didn't know that you were the head honcho here at one time."

"Yes, but I actually retired last year. The problem is that I still get too interested when things like this happen in my town. I think there's more to this attack than a simple robbery. And I think you know that too."

"It seems that way. While I was waiting for the police I took the opportunity to chat with our friend there. Turns out he and his partner were put up to this by a German man with a scar."

"Did he tell you under duress?"

"Well, I was kind of holding him down."

The two men in the Ford put down their field glasses.

"Well Jones, I think the situation just got hot."

"So what do we do next?" Jones replied.

"Continue to watch and wait. Sooner or later we'll get the lead we've been waiting for."

Hawkins returned to his room at the hotel shortly after 8:00 that night. He looked around and he could tell that the maid hadn't been in there since early in the morning. However, after closely inspecting a few well-placed items, he knew without a doubt that someone else had been in the room.

Chapter 30

Basel Switzerland
July 11, 2007

Manuel Rodriguez sat in the hard leather chair and shuddered inwardly at the sight of the red flag on the panelled wall before him. The flag was plain except for the central white circle containing a black symbol. The symbol was an equilateral cross with its four arms bent at right angles, pointing in a clockwise direction. It was one of the oldest symbols on the planet for good luck and well-being. In Hinduism, Jainism, Zoroastrianism and Buddhism it was deemed to be holy. It has appeared on ancient art forms in many countries throughout the world including Japan, China, Azerbaijan, India, Israel, Greece, Italy and Britain. The renowned explorer Heinrich Schliemann discovered similar motifs in the ruins of ancient Troy, in Turkey. In the New World, it was important to Native American tribes like the Navajo, Hopi, and Apache.

Although Manny might have appeared relaxed to the casual observer in the dimly-lit room, there was at least one large butterfly at work on his stomach. He wasn't unnerved by many people in the world, but the man sitting across from him at the large mahogany desk beneath the Nazi flag was a glaring exception. It wasn't that this man was physically imposing. In fact, he was barely average in height, emaciated and pale. It was because the man seemed to radiate a cold, dark malevolence. And there was something very wrong about his eyes. They seemed blank. It was almost as if there was no soul behind them.

Manny had first seen those eyes more than 25 years before in Mexico City, when he had been a mere youth of 16. At that time, Mexico had been facing a crisis of unprecedented proportions. The economy was reeling from the shock of a severe recession. Beset by falling oil prices, higher world interest rates and skyrocketing inflation, the value of the peso had plummeted. But like many emerging market countries, the

Mexican government tackled the problem by orchestrating a temporary solution known as a 'liquidity crisis.' In order to secure new foreign loans and debt forgiveness, they offered incentives for wealthy nationals and foreigners to empty out the nation's official reserves. Since the peso had become so untenably overvalued, the exchange rate for its conversion into hard currency guaranteed massive profits for those that participated. The vultures came from near and far to scavenge the dying carcass of the Mexican economy. The net result was that billions of dollars in pesos were laundered into foreign accounts.

Several years afterward, Manny had begun to suspect that the man behind the desk had been one of those vultures. But it wasn't until much later that he had worked out something even more startling, the main reason for the man's presence in Mexico City at that precise time. It had been about artefacts and it had been about William Merrick. Manny was now fairly certain that nothing had happened by chance and he had been an unwitting pawn from the beginning.

It had begun with boxing. He had just won his 14th straight professional match at the Arena Mexico by a spectacular first round knockout. The pale man in the dark suit had been there in the audience. Manny noticed him because he stood out easily from the rest of the crowd and was obviously a stranger to the city. Also, the man had regarded Manny with a strange look of assessment. But Manny thought no further of it on that occasion.

Manny was unbeaten in the ring. He had disposed of all his opponents by knocking them out in three rounds or less. This was due to his lightning fast reflexes and speed in the ring. Most of his victories resulted from using this speed to avoid being hit while at the same time delivering fantastic flurries of punches of his own before his beleaguered opponents could even react. But when the man that he had just beaten died a few days later from brain damage, everything changed. He had realised that he just didn't possess the necessary killer instinct to carry on. So the Green Flash hung up his boxing gloves and never set foot in the ring again.

But then he was faced with a big problem. He would no longer have the benefit of the boxing prize money for paying the substantial monthly rental fees on his small apartment. He was forced to fall back on the few paltry pesos that he earned every two weeks from his tour guide job at Teotihuacan. But this wouldn't be enough. Not by a long shot. He had needed to find some way of making more money or he and the three other orphans, his dearest friends, would soon be back out on the streets again.

Then an opportunity presented itself. The pale man from the boxing arena had approached him almost as if he knew about Manny's negative cash flow issues. The man, who called himself Schmidt, had offered Manny the irresistible sum of 1,000 US dollars just for carrying out one simple task.

Schmidt explained that Teotihuacan was far older than the historians claimed and had actually been built by a lost, highly-developed civilization. The Aztec name Teotihuacan translated as 'the place where gods were created.' The layout and construction of the city was simply magnificent. One thing was certain: it had been built by a civilization with advanced architectural and engineering skills. Starting at the northernmost Pyramid of the Moon, the wide Avenue of the Dead extended southward for an impressive 2.5 miles past the majestic Pyramid of the Sun, Temple of the Feathered Serpent and many other smaller temples, pyramids and platforms.

There had been many strange discoveries, mostly surrounding the Pyramid of the Sun, to lend support to Schmidt's claim. In 1971, archaeologists found that the giant pyramid had been built over a natural cave that had been enlarged from a natural lava tube. It was clear that the cave had been used as a sacred place long before the pyramid was constructed. But as with most ancient sites, the contents of the cave had been almost completely looted, probably in pre-Columbian times. One of the most baffling discoveries about the Pyramid of the Sun concerned the massive sheet of Brazilian mica that had been removed from the top level of the structure and sold by an unscrupulous site-restorer in the early 1900s. To date, no one has come up with a sensible answer as to why the builders had imported this particular type of mica to the site considering that other varieties of this mineral were available in the area. But the greatest enigma was why the builders had employed mica in the first place considering that its main use in modern times is as a high-voltage electrical insulator.

Schmidt had told Manny that much less was known about Teotihuacan's second largest structure, the Pyramid of the Moon. But local archaeologists speculated that it might contain several smaller structures and chambers from a much earlier period. This theory turned out to be correct when, in the summer of 1981, a hidden chamber was discovered by local workers who tunnelled into the base of the pyramid on its western face. The chamber was a perfect square, measuring just over 11 feet on each side, and was found to contain greenstone figurines, obsidian blades, pyrite mirrors, conch shells, the remains of 8 birds of prey and at least one other artefact, the one that Schmidt wanted.

Manny didn't stop to consider the fact that what he was about to do was illegal. He justified his actions based on the knowledge that he wasn't doing it just for himself. It was also for the welfare of three other lives that depended on him. So later that night, he stole into the colossal pyramid through the newly dug passageway. He reached the chamber after only 20 feet at a point where the tunnel bent sharply to the right. He entered at the nearest corner which had partially collapsed and noticed immediately that at least some of the artefacts had been left *in situ*, presumably so their exact positions could be recorded the next day. He would leave all of these undisturbed, except for the one object that he was there for. After only a minute he found the partially uncovered metallic object reflected in the glow from his small flashlight. It was lying next to the wing bones from several large birds. He remembered the Aztec's legend that their gods had told them to build the city where they saw an eagle and serpent. He felt a slight pang of guilt as he used the trowel that he had brought with him to chip the object completely away from the cement-like earth. He could feel the spirits of his ancestors watching him as he brushed the dust away from the strange, surprisingly heavy artefact. What he beheld took his breath away.

It was an encrusted device comprised of numerous gears that varied in size, similar to those found in 18th and 19th century clocks. But this object was at least 2,000 years-old. It was an orrery, a mechanical device for illustrating the positions of the planets around the sun in a dynamic manner. He recalled from his readings that the Greek philosopher Posidonius had constructed one of the first orreries which showed the diurnal motions of the sun, moon and the 6 known planets. Strangely, the one that Manny held in his hands showed more than 6. It appeared to include the outermost planets of Uranus, Neptune and maybe even Pluto, none of which can be detected with the naked eye. But the ancients were not thought to have developed the technology to make such far-reaching observations of the solar system.

He carefully placed the bent and broken object into his backpack and disappeared into the night. After delivering the goods to Schmidt, Manny tried to forget about it entirely. He simply got on with his life and was just happy that he would never have to deal with the likes of that man again. And with the money that he had received, he could hold the apartment and live comfortably for at least another two years. But it wasn't to be.

A few months later, Manny had the seemingly fortuitous meeting with William Merrick and then he began working for the famous billionaire in New York City. And then, just a few months after that, Schmidt had contacted Manny with his demands. He wanted information from time to time on Merrick's archaeological exploits and any new scientific developments by Merrick Incorporated. The 'or else' was not said directly but Manny knew that Schmidt could expose his role in the theft from the Pyramid of the Moon. And there was also another thinly-veiled threat – the one against Manny's friends back in Mexico City. Manny had been sending money to them regularly until they could survive on their own. He wondered how Schmidt had discovered this. It was obvious that Schmidt was a force to be reckoned with.

In effect, Manny became a corporate mole. For more than 20 years he fed Schmidt various pieces of information in betrayal of Merrick, who was like the father he never had. As far as archaeology was concerned, one of the most striking projects involved the discovery of three bronze trees in Sechuan, China, which were dated at more than 3,000 years-old. One of the trees was 14 feet tall and contained a strange bird-like creature at the top and a dragon situated at the base. In between the two figures, orbs of fruit hung from the branches. It had 'disappeared' from the site less than one week after the initial discovery. At the time, Manny had wondered about the significance of the tree and the intended symbolism. Now he knew.

Manny knew that whatever Schmidt and his organization were up to, human life meant nothing to them. They had killed the young Cypriot scientist who had bravely attempted to resist them on the night when they had first stolen the seeds. This had caught Manny off guard but he reacted instinctively in trying to spare the lives of the other two scientists. After a brief scuffle he managed to use his boxing skills to render the young dark-haired man unconscious, although he did not go down easily. Then he tactfully suggested that Dr Davis could be worth more to them alive since her expertise might be helpful in cultivating the plants.

His thoughts turned to the nature of Schmidt's organization. He knew that it was difficult to determine the worldwide extent of today's neo-Nazi institutions as they tend to operate in secrecy. This allows them to recruit and raise funds without interference. The current knowledge of neo-Nazi activity indicates a presence in nearly every western country with strong connections across international groups.

Manny drew his gaze away from the flag back to Schmidt. The man's eyes appeared even darker than the surrounding gloom. But there was something else worrying Manny, something that he couldn't quite identify.

Schmidt was speaking. "We have enough of the seeds to continue the project, assuming that we can get them to grow.

Your assistance in this matter has been greatly appreciated as usual Manny. But I need you for something else now."

After a moment's hesitation, imagining what he would really like to say to this man, Manny simply responded, "I thought it was over."

"Just one more small thing."

Manny sighed inwardly. "What would you like me to do?"

"Go back to the United States and assist in operations there. Dr Hawkins has been making a nuisance of himself, running all over and asking troublesome questions. I want you to take care of it."

"Take care of it?" Manny asked.

"I want this to be finished. Reinhard is going to accompany you to make sure it is done properly."

"That man is a cold-blooded killer," Manny said.

"Precisely," Schmidt acknowledged with a smile.

Defeated, Manny rose to leave. "Do you believe in karma, Mister Schmidt?"

"You mean the sum of everything that an individual has done, is doing and will do? And how all actions have a consequence which can transcend different lifetimes?"

"That's right," Manny nodded. "And if there is such a thing as karmic justice, you will no doubt return in your next lifetime as a snake."

"Very amusing," Schmidt said, calmly leaning forward into the light. "But I won't be going anywhere for quite some time."

As Schmidt's features became visible, Manny realised with a muted intake of breath what had been bothering him before. But now he thought that it must be some trick of the light. That face – *It was impossible.*

Chapter 31

Lompoc, California
July 11, 2007

Hawkins stepped from his hotel room and inhaled. The morning mist had mostly dissipated leaving the air lightly scented with flowers from the nearby fields. The rising sun had thrown the impressive rolling mountains to the south into stark relief against the deep-blue background of the cloudless sky. The city nestling below the hills gave the impression that it belonged as a permanent fixture of the landscape. But at the same time, Hawkins imagined what it must have looked like to the earliest inhabitants, thousands of years in the past. Perhaps it had been a paradise.

Hawkins had tried to contact Brian Sullivan to set up a meeting but had received no answer to any of his telephone calls. Since Sullivan did not appear to have a voicemail service, Hawkins couldn't even leave a message. However, Blake had told him that Brian and his wife Susan were avid gardeners and spent most of the time cultivating their one and half acres of land on the edge of Lompoc near the Mission. Hawkins decided that he would just go to the house.

Like Blake's place, the Sullivan residence was of the traditional Californian ranch style. The property was a sprawling single storey dwelling with an elevated two storey section in the centre of the building, housing a massive front entrance. The roof was covered in red Spanish tile and the white washed walls were sparsely draped in bougainvillea vines with pinkish red hanging bracts. The property was fronted by a small grove of olive trees which overhung the long white brick driveway, leading to an expansive paved area surrounding the house.

The rear of the property contained a small wooden barn and several demarcated plots which were obviously dedicated to distinct botanical interests. This area led on to the wild coyote brush, live oak, walnut and sycamore trees which lined the bluff overlooking the corridor of the Santa Ynez river bed 100 yards in the distance.

Silent Bob pulled the limousine to a stop in front of the house and Hawkins climbed out and made his way toward the front door. He passed a black Dodge Dakota pickup truck and a grey Mercedes-Benz S430 parked in front of the house.

He rang the ornate bell that was situated to the side of the large walnut double front door and waited. He distinctly heard the faint *bing-bong* of the bell inside the house, but there was no answer. He walked around to the back of the house to see if the Sullivans were in the rear garden. But a quick scan of the area revealed no one in sight. So he called out in the friendliest I-am-not-an-intruder voice that he could manage, "helloooo! Mister Sullivan, Missus Sullivan. Anyone home?"

The only answer came from a dog barking somewhere in the distance. Hawkins decided that he would check out the barn before giving up. He couldn't see anything resembling an entrance on the wall facing the house so he moved to go around to the side. As he rounded the corner of the building he stopped suddenly. This was not strange because anyone would stop suddenly if they had been pounded by a sledgehammer in the solar plexus. Hawkins lost all of the air from his lungs and doubled over in pain. He saw what appeared to be stars against a hazy red background and was fairly certain that he was on the verge of blacking out from the pain. After what seemed like a few minutes but was actually only 20 seconds, he was able to draw enough air back into his lungs so that he could stand upright again.

The old grey-haired man that had hit him was just below average height but he was built like a Rottweiler on steroids. Hawkins noticed that he actually smelled like one as well. He looked like he hadn't shaved for at least a couple of days and, from the malodorous aroma that Hawkins was now experiencing, the man had probably not bathed for at least that same length of time. Hawkins could now see that the man had not actually used a sledgehammer to hit him after all. Apparently, he had only used his right hand which he still held tightly curled into a massive veined fist. The man's broad shoulders and powerful looking arms appeared like they had been honed from years of hard manual labour combined with endless hours of pumping iron in the gym. The burning maleficent look in his eyes seemed to scorch the earth before him. When the man spoke, Hawkins could see that he clearly had not read the book which professed that Californians normally go out of their way to be courteous and kind to foreigners.

"Who the hell are you?" the old man snarled with spittle forming around the edge of his mouth.

Hawkins wondered for a second if the man might be rabid. He was at a loss for words and found it difficult to come up with any sensible response to the question. He managed to get out, "my name is Jim Hawkins and I –"

"Whaddya doin' on my property?"

"I'm looking for Brian Sullivan. Are you him?"

"That's me. But I don't like strangers comin' onto my property. Now beat it."

Hawkins suspected that there was something else behind the man's eyes besides the obvious fury. *Was it fear?*

"I am a friend of Pete Blake's," Hawkins said, hoping that this would soften Sullivan's mood a little.

Sullivan's eyes narrowed. "I don't care if you're a friend of George Dubya Bush. Now get the hell offa my land!"

Hawkins started to respond when Sullivan took a step forwards and moved like he was going to hit him again. Hawkins quickly held up his hands, palms forward and said, "okay, I'm going." With that Hawkins turned and walked away.

Sullivan's eyes narrowed as he watched the man leave.

After Hawkins climbed into the back seat of the limousine with his hand held to the upper region of his gut, Silent Bob suddenly turned to him and spoke. "Did I just see that old man punch you in the stomach?"

Hawkins paused in momentarily shock since it was the first time his driver had attempted a conversation of any sort. "That was no old man. That was a stubborn old kangaroo in disguise and he's got a mean kick."

"Who is he? He looked like a nutcase."

"Well he's certainly not a charter member of the Lompoc Welcome Wagon. But there's something that's not right here. He looked more scared to me than anything else."

The driver manoeuvred the limousine out of the drive onto the main road and said, "did you get a look inside the barn?"

The question derailed Hawkins for a moment. It was not one he had expected to come from this quiet man. "No. I never got the chance." He paused for a moment deep in thought and then said, "why do you ask?"

"Well, there could have been someone in there. Someone not very nice, who could have been forcing the old man's co-operation."

Hawkins couldn't hide the shock from his face. He thought that something was wrong about the situation besides Sullivan's unfriendly reception. But there was also something else on Hawkins' mind now. "What's your name?"

"Vincent Magliatti. Call me Vince."

"Vince, what else do you do besides drive for Mister Merrick?"

Vince took a moment before he responded. "I'm also a bodyguard... of sorts." He smiled sheepishly at Hawkins in the rear view mirror. "But I'm getting a bit past it now."

Hawkins looked at the powerful build of the mid-50ish man in the front seat and decided that he could still take care of himself.

Vince continued. "I was a Navy SEAL during and shortly after the Vietnam conflict. You know, Sea, Air and Land?" He paused for any reaction from Hawkins. There was none.

"We were trained to analyse situations before we took any action. We had to make sure we weren't rushing blindly into a trap. More often than not, this approach helped to save countless lives, including ours."

"So what's your analysis of the situation?" Hawkins asked.

Vince told him.

Back in his room at the Quality Inn, Hawkins placed several calls to Cambridge. He received no answer at either of the labs in the LMB or the Department of Archaeology, so he dialled the number for his own residence. He had asked David to look in on Brandy from time to time and suggested his student could even stay there, if he wished.

The call was answered on the third ring. "Hello, Jim Hawkins' residence," David's voice answered.

"Hi David, Jim here."

"Hey, how's it going over there in Long Pock?"

"That's Lompoc," Hawkins pronounced it as l-o-m-p-o-k-e, just like the locals. "It's a Chumash Indian word meaning 'little swamp'."

"Yeah? Sounds great. Hey man, that dog of yours eats like a horse on cannabis."

"I hope you haven't been over-feeding her."

"No," David replied just a little too quickly. "You didn't actually want that 6 pounds of prime rib you had in freezer, did you?"

"David, don't you know that you should never let big dogs over eat? She's going to get fat."

"Well, it was either that or your furniture. We caught her licking your favourite leather chair this morning."

"We?"

"Yeah," David answered. "Me and Lori. Sanderson thought it would be a good idea for us to stay in the same place until this whole thing blows over. And your place does have four bedrooms... and a decent liquor cabinet."

Hawkins was happy that Sanderson was looking out for their welfare in his absence. "And how is Lori?" he asked.

"Still a bit shell-shocked like the rest of us. It's hard to believe that Zoran is really gone."

"I know," was all that Hawkins could think to say.

"Speaking of Lori," David began, "we were both thinking that we should come to the US of A and join you in whatever it is that you're trying to do."

"I'm not so sure that's a good idea," Hawkins cautioned. "It might be dangerous."

"You sound just like my mum. Anyway, we're probably in just as much danger here as we would be over there."

Hawkins couldn't argue with the logic. Besides, he could use David's help for part of his plan. "What about your work? And Lori's?"

"Jim, you know as well as I do that this story goes way beyond what we found here."

"Okay," Hawkins gave in to David's surprisingly well thought out argument. "I'll soon be heading to the Smithsonian Institution, in Washington DC. Maybe you two could meet me there."

David covered the phone and mumbled something, obviously gaining approval from Lori. After a moment he came back on. "We'll be there, Doc. We'll try and get a flight out of Heathrow tomorrow morning."

"Are you both sure about this?"

"Yeah, we're sure," David said confidently. "Besides, you're now officially out of alcohol."

"I think he could be on to something, at last," Reeves mumbled between mouthfuls of a Taco Bell Burrito Supreme. He and Jones were sprawled out on the front bucket seats of the Ford, parked below Hawkins' room. The room had been bugged and the telephone tapped so they were now able to carry out live eavesdropping. Reeves reached forward to tweak the audio knob, lowering the volume now the conversation had finished. The two of them had also managed to plant 5 micro-thin NAVSTAR GPS tracers for real-time tracking of Hawkins' movements. These had been secreted in some of Hawkins' personal items including his travel bag, ballpoint pen, wristwatch, sports jacket and spare shoes. The tracers were accurate to within two feet almost anywhere on the globe. The signals were transmitted to a cellular modem that Reeves had in his possession as well as to the central NSA tracking station in Fort Meade, Maryland.

"Why do you say that?" Jones asked, politely lowering his Chicken Soft Taco as he asked the question.

"The Smithsonian Institution," Reeves aborted his next bite of the burrito to retort. "That's gotta be the key."

"What do you mean?" Jones asked, already tensing for Reeves' predictably impolite response.

Reeves didn't disappoint him. "Didn't they tell you anything before you landed this assignment?" As he articulated the words, a large chunk of burrito flew from his mouth and landed on the dashboard of the rental car.

"They didn't give me too many details," Jones replied, pretending not to have noticed the incident with the burrito. "Why don't you tell me? We've got time."

"Yeah, you're right there," Reeves sighed.

When he had been brought up to date, Jones said, "I think that I'm gonna take up heavy drinking."

"Join the club."

Hawkins placed another call to Cambridge. This one was to Inspector Sanderson. The call was answered on the first ring and they had exchanged a few pleasantries about the weather conditions in Cambridge versus Lompoc. It was raining in the former and sunny in the latter. Hawkins informed Sanderson about his plan to go to Washington DC the next day and that David and Lori would be meeting him there.

"Inspector, I think it would be a good idea if David brought the rest of the seeds to Washington."

"Are you sure?"

"They might come in handy. Perhaps as a bargaining chip."

"It may also have the opposite effect," Sanderson said.

"We'll have to take that chance. Things are already getting weird over here."

"Trouble?"

"You could say that. First, I was attacked by two men, but I managed to scrape through. Then I was beat up by an old man with halitosis. To top that off, I think someone's been following me ever since I got here."

"Maybe you'll be safer in DC."

"I doubt it."

"Me too."

"So what do you think?"

"Well, your last idea to swap the ancient seeds for ordinary palm seeds was a good move. The thieves probably don't even know that the ones they took from the Archaeology building are useless. I'll go along with you on this as well."

"Thanks Inspector. Will there be a problem with customs?"

"Don't worry. I have connections."

"Why that sneaky son of biscuit eater," Reeves sputtered, projecting more burrito particles onto the dashboard.

"He switched the seeds," Jones said with raised eyebrows. "Smart move."

"So those Nazi Kraut bastards don't have nothin' then." Reeves summarised.

"Guess not," Jones replied, wisely refraining from pointing out Reeves' usage of the mixed slurs and the double negative.

"It sounds like he could be on to us," Reeves said. "We have to be careful not to underestimate this guy."

"Are we going to DC then?"

"Wherever he goes, we follow," Reeves said. "Besides, that's where the seeds will be."

Hawkins' telephone conversations were also captured by the ECHELON network and relayed again to the appropriate operatives in the intelligence agencies where they were flagged for further action. As before, copies of the conversations were also siphoned out of the supposedly secure system to be received by another equally determined party.

Seven hours later, two men who had spent the previous 5 hours on a train journey from Basel, boarded a 747 at Charles de Gaulle Airport in Paris, France. The plane was bound for the United States capital.

Chapter 32

Lompoc, California
July 11, 2007

    In the late evening twilight, Hawkins and Vince returned to Brian Sullivan's house. This time the only vehicle that was present in the driveway was the black pickup truck. Hawkins noticed that a dim light shone through the large front window on the left side of the door. Hawkins left Vince sitting in the car and crept up to the window. He was momentarily worried that he would be illuminated by a safety light that would flash on at any second, but that didn't happen. He peered through the window at a sizeable living room with white walls containing expensive looking paintings and photographs, a shiny brown-tiled floor and polished wooden furniture. But the room showed a mild degree of clutter as if it hadn't been tidied for a least a couple of days.
    Sullivan was sitting in a chair in front of the television, the source of the light. But he wasn't watching what was on, which appeared to be a local news program. Instead, he was sitting forward on the edge of the chair with his head down in his hands. He still appeared to be unshaven and was wearing the same clothes that he had on earlier that day. On the table before him was a half empty bottle of Jack Daniels. There was no glass.
    Hawkins moved to the door and rang the bell. A moment later, Sullivan opened the door and simply stood there. Then, in a lifeless alcohol-laden voice, he said, "Mister Hawkins, I thought we had an understanding?" Without waiting for a response, Sullivan turned his back on Hawkins and returned to his seat. It was the actions of a man who believed that there was nothing in the world that could hurt him. Not anymore, anyway.
    Hawkins hesitated and then stepped into the house. He noticed that the room had a slight smell of whiskey and body odour. Against his better judgement, he closed the door behind him and approached the chair which contained the slumped form of Sullivan. "You're not going to hit me again are you?" Hawkins asked, only half joking.

"Just don't give me any reason to. But I don't give a donkey's behind anymore. Just state your business and leave."

"I want to know why you acted the way you did this morning," Hawkins said.

Sullivan replied succinctly. "Never mind. Now beat it"

Unperturbed, Hawkins continued. "I came to ask you about the discovery that you and Pete Blake made back in 1959, in the hills of the canyon."

Sullivan's eyes widened at this, but he said nothing. He reached forward and took a massive drink of Jack Daniels straight from the bottle. Then he smacked the bottle back down on the table. Hawkins noticed that the level had gone down by at least an inch. Sullivan sank back in the chair as if Hawkins wasn't there.

Hawkins hesitated and then decided to change his approach. "Pete Blake said that he gave you a knife? A Hitler Youth Knife that he found at the site?"

Sullivan still didn't answer, but he lifted his head and his eyes flicked to a small display cabinet on the wall by some photographs.

Hawkins looked closer and noticed that the cabinet contained a few items of military paraphernalia such as old medals, a hand gun and two grenade pins. But there was also a conspicuous empty space with a trace outline of an object than had once been there.

"They took it didn't they Brian?" Hawkins thought that it felt right to use his first name even though Sullivan hadn't told him that he could.

Sullivan now moved to sit upright and nodded.

"Where's your wife, Brian?"

The grizzled old man shifted as if he was going to stand and take another swing at Hawkins, but then he sat back down.

"They took her too, didn't they?" Hawkins asked

Sullivan looked up at this, but didn't respond.

"They came to see you, didn't they? Hawkins continued. "They claimed that they were a US government intelligence agency and were here about the discovery that you and Pete made, didn't they?" Hawkins carried on without waiting for an answer. "After they got the information that they wanted from you, they told you that you couldn't tell anyone else about it in the interests of national security. When you said you doubted that they were US intelligence and refused to co-operate, their request turned into a threat. Then after all of this, they took the knife so you would no longer have any evidence of what happened back in 1959 and they took your wife to guarantee your silence."

"Yes, they did all of that, more or less," Sullivan said now looking directly at Hawkins. "They took her. She was all I had, the only important thing anyway."

"What are you going to do?"

Sullivan looked up sharply. "Nothing, I'm gonna do what they said. They'll kill her otherwise. Although I'm thinking now that they will probably kill her no matter what happens."

Hawkins didn't dare respond. He knew that this was probably right. *What was one more person to add to their list?*

Sullivan was looking at Hawkins again, his forehead wrinkled and his eyes focussed as if he had just realised something important. He blinked away the tears that had begun to well up in his eyes. "You...you're a spy aren't you? You work for some agency. English, from the sounds of it. You're after the people that took Sue aren't you?"

Hawkins winced at this. Sullivan was wrong on all counts. However, he felt the need to give Brian some kind of hope.

"I'm just an archaeologist," Hawkins said apologetically. "I came here because I was interested in what you found, from a scientific point of view."

Sullivan turned his head slightly to get a better look at Hawkins, squinting so that fine wrinkles appeared around his bloodshot eyes. "Naw, you're not just an archaeologist. You don't look like a scientist."

"What's a scientist supposed to look like?" Hawkins asked, genuinely interested in the man's impression.

"Not like you anyway. You're much more than that. I can tell."

No sense arguing with the man, Hawkins thought. He said, "okay, Brian. Whatever you say."

When he saw the look of hope on Sullivan's face, he couldn't help himself. He spoke without thinking. He divulged a secret that he swore he would never divulge to anyone. "I was a Commando working with the British SAS during the first Gulf war. I handled covert assignments."

"Did you ever come under heavy fire?" Sullivan asked, suddenly interested in Hawkins' credentials.

"Yes, on my last mission before the end of the war. Six of us were ambushed by an Iraqi platoon."

"What happened?"

"Three of us were killed. I got out alive when we were rescued by friendly Apache helicopters. None of the Iraqis were that lucky."

"I was in 'Nam during Operation Rolling Thunder in '65 and '66," Sullivan said, trading exploits.

Hawkins recalled that 'Rolling Thunder' was a code name for the sustained bombing campaign against North Vietnam. It was meant to destroy the will of the North Vietnamese to fight, to annihilate industrial bases and air defences, and to stop the supply of equipment and men down the Ho Chi Minh Trail. But, if anything, the will of the North Vietnamese grew even stronger.

"I was with the First Cavalry Division as part of the 'mopping up' operation," Sullivan continued. "We killed over 1,000 Viet Cong by continually marching through the area after bombing missions. One time we came under heavy return fire when the VCs had dug themselves in around the remnants of one of their SAM sites. They were waiting for us and they had laid some wicked traps in the jungle. Two of my buddies were killed right by my side.... I couldn't even –" Sullivan stopped suddenly. Small tears tracked down his cheeks.

Hawkins wasn't sure what Sullivan was going to say next but he knew that it must have been a painful memory. He leaned forward and put his hand firmly on his shoulder. He paused and thought for a moment before speaking. "I'll try to find your wife,

Brian. If I find her, I'll bring her back to you personally." Hawkins bravado sounded lame, even to his own ears.

But Sullivan actually smiled. He wiped the tears from his face with the back of his thick wrist and said, "can you do that Mister Hawkins?"

"I'll try," Hawkins said, now wishing he hadn't said anything.

"What am I thinking?" Sullivan said as he sprang up from the chair. "I'm coming with you."

Hawkins said gently, "no Brian. Your fighting days are over. You have to stay here and wait for her. They might try and contact you again," he said convincingly. "You have to leave this in my hands."

"I suppose you're right," Sullivan said as he sat down again. "I would probably just get in the way."

"Don't worry Brian, it will be over soon. She could be back before you know it."

Sullivan smiled as if he was imagining the moment. "Alright, but I won't be able to sleep until I get her back."

"You might want to use some of that time to clean the house, shave, have a shower and change into a fresh pair of clothes," Hawkins suggested.

"Guess I must smell kinda ripe then?"

"Put it this way, I would burn those clothes if I were you."

Sullivan smiled. "You take care, Mister English Agent. I'm sorry I hit you earlier."

Hawkins patted Sullivan affectionately on his powerful shoulder. "Me too, Brian." He turned to leave. But then the thought occurred to him that he had to put one thing right. He couldn't let Sullivan go on believing something that wasn't true.

"Brian, one more thing -"
"Yes?"
"I'm Australian."

Hawkins met Pete Blake at Starbuck's the next morning. In the two days that Hawkins had been in Lompoc, every server in the place had come to know him as a regular. He didn't have the heart to let them know that he was leaving soon and would probably never return.

Blake and Hawkins talked about the incident that had occurred at the Sullivan residence. Blake said he would look after his lifelong friend, as he always had. Hawkins said that he would take Blake's advice by trying to follow up on what had become of the artefacts that had been taken from the tomb in Lompoc. They discussed the possibility that there had to be some traces left somewhere.

"You might have to dig deep," Blake said.

"Is that an archaeology joke, Pete?"

"Blake said, "in all seriousness, there might be some clues to be found at the Smithsonian Institution. They might have filed the artefacts away in a place where they are not readily accessible because of the circumstances under which they were acquired."

"Makes sense."

"Because of the bureaucracy that you're likely to encounter, it won't be easy to get at this information. You'll have to talk to the right people."

"Any idea who?"

"You'll just have to poke around and see what kind of response you get. You know… see what jumps out at you."

Thinking over the past couple of days Hawkins realised that he had probably had some success with that strategy already.

Chapter 33
Basel, Switzerland
July 11, 2007

Basel is the third most populous city in Switzerland with around 170,000 inhabitants within the city limits and nearly 10 times that in its urban area. Situated on a significant bend in the River Rhine, where the French, German and Swiss borders meet, it functions as a major industrial nexus for chemical and pharmaceutical industries. This strategic location has also led to a long history of settlement in the area. Basel's foundations go back to prehistoric times with the establishment of a Celtic site. This was followed by construction of a Roman base in 44 BCE, which stood for three centuries. After this, the city passed successively to the Alemanni, the Franks and Transjurane Burgundy until it was finally incorporated into the Holy Roman Empire in the 11th century. In the 15th century, it became the focal point of Christendom with several important events including the election of the last antipope, Felix V. Shortly afterwards, Pope Pius II endowed the University of Basel, where notables like Hans Holbein the artist, Paracelsus the alchemist and Erasmus the theologian, taught. In 1501, Basel separated from the Holy Roman Empire and joined the Swiss Confederation as its 11th state.

The modern city of Grossbasel lies on the steep left bank of the Rhine while Kleinbasel, lies on the lower right bank. The two parts of the city are joined by 4 ferries and 6 bridges. The first bridge was erected in 1225 AD and for several centuries it was one of the few ways to cross the Rhine and was, therefore, of strategic importance. Originally, the portion of the bridge that lay on the side of Grossbasel was constructed of stone, while the section on the side of Kleinbasel was made of wood. The bridge has since been constructed entirely of stone and named Mittlere Rheinbrücke. It contains 7 archways with a small chapel situated in the middle. The arches of the bridge are bounded by small medieval balconies, with excellent views of the river and city. It was on one of these balconies that a fuming man, with a beet-red face and wildly stomping feet, appeared to be undergoing major cardiac arrest.

Schmidt shouted angrily to himself, cursing Dr Hawkins for switching the seeds, and waving his arms for frustrated emphasis as a strolling, arm-in-arm couple passed by. The bewildered couple had to shuffle quickly out of range to avoid being caught by a flailing arm or flying spittle. After several minutes of this rant, Schmidt pulled the latest batch of stolen seeds from his pocket and turned his burning gaze on them. He couldn't remember the last time that he had felt such utter animosity toward anything or any person.

He should have known that the seeds were counterfeit when they had been delivered to him. They looked subtly different. But someone had deliberately altered them to make them look ancient. It was that meddlesome archaeologist who had discovered the tomb. Because of him, the next phase of the project was in jeopardy. Schmidt hurled the seeds into the river. As he watched the small useless pellets splatter and disappear into the dark rolling waters below, he swore that he would stop at nothing to obtain the authentic seeds and make sure that Dr Hawkins would die painfully. And the opportunity to accomplish both of these tasks might just have presented itself. Dr Hawkins' telephone call to his young colleague in Cambridge had given away the information that the real seeds were being transported to Washington DC. Perfect.

So Schmidt had ordered Manny and Reinhard to go there to see if they could acquire these seeds and dispose of Hawkins and the others at the same time. But he had already underestimated the archaeologist once. What if this was another ruse? He decided that he would also send someone back to Cambridge to determine if any or all of the seeds were still being hidden there, somewhere. As for Schmidt himself, he needed to return to his project.

Chapter 34

Arlington Virginia
July 12, 2007

    The lobby of the Hyatt Regency was buzzing with the typical guests enjoying the nightlife along with attendees from the aftermath of two different conferences that had taken place in the hotel. There was also a continuous stream of similar guests checking into the hotel for the Biometric Consortium Conference which would be starting there at 9:00 A.M. the next morning. If events followed the usual pattern, things would probably not begin to quiet down for at least another two hours.
    Jill Pierce had made the hasty decision to work at the hotel during her summer vacation to earn a little extra money before starting her sophomore year at the University of Virginia. But she was beginning to wonder if she wouldn't have been better off spending her vacation time with the rest of her college friends at the beach. She had been on duty since 8:00 P.M. and was already tired. She was unsettled when a tall man with a facial scar approached the desk. Still she managed to put on her best 'be-courteous-to-all-guests' expression and beamed, "can I help you, sir?"
    "Ja, can you give me room number of Doctor James Hawkins please? I have important slides for his presentation tomorrow."
    "I'm sorry but I can't give you the number. Standard hotel policy, you understand –" When the man started to develop a malignant look in his eyes, she quickly added, "but I can call his room for you."
    The man looked puzzled and then appeared to make up his mind about something. "No, it is okay. Can you check computer. See if he is here?"
    "Yes, hold on a second." She turned and tapped away on her keyboard and after a moment the details popped up. She peered at the flat screen monitor and read out, "yes, Dr J. Hawkins checked in this evening at 10:00 P.M."

"Can I leave CD, has slides on it, so it can be taken to Doctor Hawkins' room?" Without waiting for an answer, the man pulled out a small case from his inside coat pocket.

Did I just see a gun? She wondered, with some alarm. "Certainly, we can do that," Jill said, using her eager to help voice. She decided that she would do well not to get on this man's bad side. "Let me just get an envelope to put it in." She turned and entered the large office attached to the reception area to fetch an appropriate envelope. Then she returned with this to the desk.

The man was gone and he hadn't left the disc. Then, Jill looked at her monitor and noticed that it was turned slightly from its normal position. The listing 'Dr J Hawkins - Room 732' was still highlighted. *Oh crap.* She looked around and saw that the other girl on duty, Alice, was still busy with a customer. She decided not to tell anyone about the incident.

After travelling back to the East Coast of the US in Merrick's jet, Hawkins had checked into the Hyatt Regency in Arlington, Virginia. He chose this hotel because of its proximity to Ronald Reagan National Airport and it had easy access into the heart of Washington DC via the Metro Rail. Almost immediately after carrying his small bag into the executive suite room, he collapsed onto the bed. He was so tired that he had forgotten to use the dead bolt and chain locks on the door. Even though he was a well-seasoned traveller, the back and forth coast to coast trips had effectively turned him into a zombie. But he had to allow for the possibility that he was also suffering the after effects from the three shots of Aberlour Scotch Whiskey that he had on Merrick's well-stocked airplane. He was asleep within 5 minutes.

Reinhard stepped out of the elevator on the 7th floor. The hallway was empty except for the silver service trays that had been disposed of onto the plush-carpeted floor outside several of the rooms, awaiting pickup from hotel staff. Taking his cue from the sign posted near the elevator landing, he turned left and headed down the hallway to room 732. He took out his newly-acquired silenced HK pistol, flicked the safety off and re-holstered it ready for action.

He stopped walking when he reached the room and listened at the door for any signs of movement within. The only sound that he could hear was from a television somewhere down the hall. He pulled out a small computerized card and inserted this into the key slot of the door. The card was attached by a flat wire to a microprocessor which was now carrying out a high speed search for the key code. After one minute, the processor gave an audible beep. He pulled the card out and the light on the door lock flashed green.

Hawkins was in a deep sleep when his eyes snapped open. He had been dreaming about relaxing on a beautiful beach, somewhere in California. Then he heard a strange beeping sound on the beach. He wondered if the alarm on the table by his bedside had been left on. Maybe it had been set for this unusual time by the last occupant. But then he realised that alarms didn't usually sound like that. It had been a single tone. *Had the noise been part of his dream?* He didn't think so. Something was wrong. Then he heard another noise and he knew that it was not a dream. Someone was in the hall.

With the green light still on the door lock, Reinhard quietly twisted the knob and eased the door open. He was pleased to notice that Dr Hawkins had not deigned to use the internal locks. Reinhard had found that people rarely did. It made his job much simpler. He pulled his gun out and rushed into the darkened room. Moving quickly in the dim light, he ran to the foot of the king-sized bed, and emptied three bullets into the bed in a spread pattern to maximize coverage.

Chapter 35

Cambridge
July 12, 2007

Sanderson sat in his office at Parkside Police Station and gazed with unwavering attention at the open file on his desk, going over, and over, the existing evidence on the case. The department had several versions of crime-solving software for computer-aided searches that he could have used instead. Most of these were capable of finding linkages among data elements and highlighting key information. But these relied heavily on the amount and integrity of the data entered into the system. But that was a problem here. They had so little to go on. In addition, Sanderson was a strong believer in intuition. This was something that still could not be duplicated by a computer. And right now his intuition was telling him that he was missing something.

He had seen it all over the years. He had his fair share of failures and triumphs. It was through these cases that Sanderson had slowly but surely learned the best methods for catching the bad guys. Sometimes this required a bit of luck, but one had to be prepared to take advantage of this. Sanderson found it intriguing that the biggest crimes were often solved by good police work and acting on the smallest of details. One just needed to know where to look.

So here he was on a hot July evening in Cambridge still searching for clues. Although the case was proving difficult, Sanderson knew that it could easily turn out to be the most important of his career. But he could only act on this case by offering local support, since the multifaceted crime had already transcended international borders. Tracking down the criminals would also require the intervention of the British Secret Intelligence Service, MI6. But that wouldn't stop him from doing everything he could to help.

He had a few pieces of information to go on. Most of these had been gathered from the house on Cavendish Road that the criminals seemed to use as an operation centre. After a great deal of paper chasing, Sanderson managed to work out that the house had been set up originally in 1967 through Cambridge University for use by visiting European scholars. However, it turned out that no scholar had lived there for the past 5 years. They would need to get hold of the complete list to confirm that. Sanderson tracked down the name of the leasing agency but found that this no longer existed. He did learn that the house had been purchased originally by a company based in Basel, which appeared to have interests all over the world. Sanderson immediately saw the connection with Lori Davis' comment that she had overheard regarding the same Swiss city.

The police had also recovered a passport and credit cards from the man David had killed in self-defence, as well as the stolen seeds. The man was identified as Frank Bader, a banker from Berlin who had no discernible criminal record, at least according to the databases that Sanderson had access to. Several sets of fingerprints had also been found in the house although none of these were identifiable. He hoped that MI6 would have more success.

Sanderson looked up from the folder and rubbed his wrinkled forehead with his thumb and index finger. Another headache was developing. He wasn't sure if it was a result of the seasonably humid weather or if it was from the tension of trying to make headway on this baffling case. He decided that he needed to go home. His wife was beginning to think of him as 'the strange man that sometimes comes here to sleep.'

As Sanderson shut down his computer and stood to leave, his thoughts suddenly turned to Dr Hawkins. He wondered how the archaeologist was getting on.

Chapter 36

Arlington Virginia
July 12, 2007

Reinhard peered closely at the bed that he had just shot to pieces as his eyes became more adjusted to the partial darkness. *What the hell?* There was nobody in there! Other than the possibility that Dr Hawkins had not returned to the room from a night out, Reinhard considered the slim chance that his entrance into the room had been detected and the occupant might have managed to find a hiding place. He quickly whirled around and pointed his gun at the entrance to the bathroom behind him and slipped smoothly inside. He passed through the outer chamber and peered into the shower area. *No one there.*

He moved back into the room's small entrance hallway and flicked on the lights. He decided that he had to search the entire room but he had to move quickly in case someone had heard the shots. He had used a silencer but that only reduced the sounds somewhat. He also had to remain on guard in case Dr Hawkins was hiding somewhere and waiting to leap out at him.

He rushed over to the large floor-to-ceiling window and threw the curtains open to expose the elegant covered balcony. *Empty.* Then he carried out a quick search of all the other typical places that a person could hide in a hotel room, such as under the bed or in the wardrobe. But he was wasting time. He decided that he had already been in the room too long and rushed out of the door. Glancing up and down the still empty corridor, he swiftly moved back to the elevator. He had to get out of the building. There was always tomorrow.

When he heard the beeping noise, Hawkins had rushed into the outer chamber of the bathroom which was situated right next to the front door of the room. He had to be ready for almost anything. When the door opened he would have to work out some way of dealing with the intruder or intruders. But the door to his room had never opened. The noise that he had heard came from the room directly opposite his, on the other side of the hallway.

Hawkins had booked two rooms just in case someone was on to him now that he was back on the East Coast. Although he had purchased both rooms with his credit card, only room 732 had been registered under his name. Whereas the room opposite, where he was actually staying, had been booked under the name of Maurice Fluber, the first name that had popped into his head. Hawkins had explained to the pretty receptionist that his colleague Dr Fluber, would be arriving later on that night but Hawkins would be paying for the room for him. The tactic had saved his life.

Hawkins peered through the peephole across to the opposite door as the intruder finally left room 732. The man with the scar seemed to look right at him as if he could see through the peephole. But then he turned abruptly and disappeared down the hallway.

As he was unarmed and suffering from jetlag, Hawkins decided to try and go back to sleep. He would leave his investigation of what the gunman had been up to until the morning. He hoped that there wasn't going to be any mess that he would have to explain.

Chapter 37

Washington D.C.
July 13, 2007

    Hawkins emerged along with a surging tide of humanity into the blazing hot summer day from the relatively cool shelter of the Smithsonian Metro Station. Squinting in response to the intense solar glare, he slipped on his Serengeti Aviator sunglasses and surveyed the grounds of the Mall around him. Immediately to his right was the Freer Gallery of Art and he could see the massive structures of the Natural History and American History museums ahead of him on the far side of the grassy plain. The lofty obelisk of the Washington Monument pierced the sky, beyond the trees to his left.

    The National Mall is a long rectangular open park in the centre of Washington DC. It stretches from the spectacular Lincoln Memorial on the eastern bank of the Potomac River to the majesty of the United States Capitol Building further to the east. The Washington Monument was positioned more or less in the centre of the rectangle. Other notable features include monuments and memorials dedicated to Thomas Jefferson, Franklin D. Roosevelt, Albert Einstein, both World Wars, and the haunting black granite wall of remembrance, displaying the names of the 56,000 young Americans who lost their lives in the Vietnam War.

    The Mall was originally conceived by the French-born American architect, Pierre L'Enfant. It is one of the most popular areas in Washington DC for tourism. Since its inception at the beginning of the 20th century, it has been the site of many significant political events and rallies. These include the March on Washington on August 28th in 1963 that featured Martin Luther King's famous 'I Have a Dream' speech, the Vietnam War Moratorium Rally in 1969 and the March for Women's lives in 2004. On this particular day it was a haven for the somewhat less austere activities of jogging and sunbathing.

The Mall is also the location of the world famous Smithsonian Institution. This is comprised of 19 different museums and 7 research centres. Nine of the buildings are located along the northern and southern edges of the Mall, bounded by Constitution and Independence Avenues, respectively. The impressive headquarters of the Institution is situated on the southern flank of the Mall adjacent to the Freer Gallery and serves as an administrative and information centre. The building is constructed of red sandstone in Romanesque-Gothic style, giving rise to its nickname, 'The Castle.' Located outside the building is a bronze statue of Joseph Henry, the Institution's first secretary, while just inside the entrance is the crypt containing the remains of James Smithson, the British mineralogist and original benefactor of the Institution. This was where Hawkins had arranged to meet David and Lori.

He spotted the two of them standing somewhat conspicuously in front of the small sepulchre. David sported a white bandage around his head, looking like a 1960's hippy, and was dressed in dark blue jeans and a lime green T shirt emblazoned on the front with white text that read: 'IN MY DEFENCE – I WAS LEFT UNSUPERVISED.' Lori was wearing tight white trousers that accentuated her long legs and a lavender-coloured tube top.

Hawkins called out, "G'day you two." He shook David's hand and patted him on the back. Then, without thinking, he gave Lori a hug and a light peck on the cheek. Up to that point, he hadn't realised how nice it was to see both of them safe and sound. He aimed to do everything that he could to keep it that way. Even if that paradoxically meant exposing them to further danger.

"So," David began without any formality, "what's the plan?"

"We're going to focus on the Lompoc angle. We need to find some answers about the giant and other artefacts that were removed from the site in 1959. There may be a connection between this and what happened in Cambridge last week."

"How?" David asked. "That's a gap of almost 50 years."

"I'm not sure yet."

David nodded but said nothing.

"Did you bring the you-know-what's with you?" Hawkins asked.

David answered, "yeah, they're in a safe place. But, why bring 'em here? Isn't that...well, dumb?"

"We might be needing them."

David's eyebrows arched quizzically. Lori interjected. "Do you really think that the artefacts from Lompoc were brought to the Smithsonian?"

"Maybe," Hawkins answered. "Like in Cambridge, the thieves might only have been interested in the seeds that were also found there. It's conceivable that the giant and the other artefacts could have been locked away and then forgotten in one of the Smithsonian warehouses."

"But even if we somehow manage to locate these artefacts, what would that tell us?" David asked.

"Probably nothing. But I'm hoping that our inquiries and a bit of poking around will help draw them out in the open."

"Draw them out?" David repeated.

"That's the plan."

David said, "I hate to sound like the sensibly cautious one here, but that sounds like it could be kinda dangerous."

"Not as dangerous as waiting around for them to come after us," Hawkins answered. He gave them both a quick update on the events that occurred over the previous few days in Lompoc and the hotel in Arlington. "At least by poking around, we're calling the shots, which should give us some advantage."

David nodded but both he and Lori looked uncertain.

Hawkins said, "as a starting point, I've arranged an appointment with the Assistant Collections Manager of the Natural History Museum warehouse for 5:00 P.M."

The three of them walked across the grassy expanse towards the Museum of Natural History on the northern side of the Mall. This imposing edifice was constructed in neoclassical style, with an ornate facade on the Mall side composed of a large stepped entranceway and 6 enormous fluted columns. Hawkins recalled that this museum claimed to hold more than one 125 million specimens of animals, plants, fossils, rocks, meteorites and cultural artefacts. However, it wasn't clear how many of these were kept in storage in the warehouse which lay beneath the museum or in any of the other mysterious Smithsonian holding facilities scattered along the Eastern Seaboard.

The three scientists entered the building and were immediately faced with the magnificence of the two-storey rotunda that served as the central hub of the museum. The room was dominated by the centrepiece of the museum's fantastic collection, an elevated display of a giant African elephant with ears aggressively fanned and trunk raised as if it were charging toward an unseen enemy. The lethal-looking pachyderm was more than 12 feet tall at the shoulder and had tusks at least as long as the average human male.

Standing in front of this display, seemingly unaware of the monster behind him, was a Nigerian man of average height, embracing a blue notebook high in front of his chest. He had a slender build, thinning hair and wore glasses with inordinately thick lenses. He had obviously been scanning the crowds when his head seemed to lock onto the approaching threesome. Then, his face lit up in sheer joy as he lurched towards them with his right hand outstretched in greeting.

"Dr Hawkins and friends," the man called out in a surprising deep booming voice. "I am Azubeze Asante, the Assistant Collections Manager."

Hawkins reached out and shook Asante's' hand. "Thanks for agreeing to meet with us Dr Asante. These are my associates Dr Lori Davis and my PhD student, David Englehart."

Asante beamed, displaying ivory white perfectly straight teeth. "It is a pleasure to meet you all. Everyone around here calls me Beze. My full first name sounds too much like I am sneezing." He erupted into deeply-resonant, joyful laughter with the cadence of machine gun fire, "*ha-ha-ha*."

Hawkins said, "it's a deal. And you can call me Jim."

David and Lori followed suit by offering the same first name courtesy.

"I am aware of your amazing discoveries of the giant and other artefacts in Cambridge. It has created quite a stir around here, as you can imagine, *ha-ha-ha.*"

The three visitors found themselves grinning broadly in sync with Asante's infectious laughter.

"Beze," Hawkins started, "we were hoping that you could help us with something related to that. Is there somewhere that we can sit down and talk?"

"Yes my friend. Just beyond the dinosaur exhibit is a small café. Maybe you would all like to have a drink? The café has some fine freshly-ground coffees from all over the world."

Hawkins smiled and said, "couldn't hurt."

The four settled into a booth in the café with their drinks in front of them. Hawkins told Asante about the discovery and theft of the other giant and artefacts in Lompoc and how this actually predated what had occurred in Cambridge by 5 decades. "We think that one of two things happened," Hawkins said. "The first possibility is that some of the pieces, including the giant, were whisked away to some unknown destination, probably never to be recovered. The second, and the one we are hoping for, is that they were locked away in one of the Smithsonian warehouses where they might have remained for the past 48 years."

Asante looked frozen.

Hawkins continued. "If they are here somewhere, is there some method that could be used to... uh locate them?"

Asante snapped out of his trance. "First of all, let me say this is absolutely incredible. I thought your discovery was impossible enough on its own, but now you are telling me that there were two giants. I think I will be even more shocked later when I have time to think about what this means. But, in answer to your question, I am sorry to say that it would be next to impossible to track down these objects. The Institution has steadily acquired an average of 10,000 items every week for the past 160 years. You can imagine that it would be extremely difficult to look after even a fraction of these items and categorize them efficiently.

And, like most museums, the vast majority of these are kept in storage, inaccessible to the general public.

"There is an ongoing project to catalogue artefacts that were brought in before the days of electronic archiving. But this is a daunting task considering the staggering number of artefacts and limited manpower on hand to tackle the problem. At the rate we are going, it could take another 30 years at least. But of course there are other problems. It is unfortunate, but true, that many older artefacts were never logged in at all. Countless items were either lost in storage or even destroyed. It would be intriguing to find out what has been stored away and forgotten in the darkest corners of the many museum warehouses."

"Why don't we just take a look?" David asked.

Asante belted out another deep belly laugh. "Where would you like to look my friend? There is just too much. Even I would not know where to begin."

"There might be a way," Lori interjected.

"Do you have an idea, young lady?", Asante asked.

"Maybe," Lori said looking thoughtful. "We might not need to locate the artefacts directly."

"What do have in mind, Lori?" Hawkins asked.

"What if we used the new archiving system to locate items that were brought in during the summer of 1959? There is a chance that all of these, including the Lompoc artefacts, could have been stored together in the same approximate place for lack of any other method."

After a momentary pause and a brief nod, Asante said, "by George, it is worth a try.

"Beze, will you help us?" asked Hawkins.

"Of course," Asante answered grinning broadly. "I am dying to see these artefacts."

Chapter 38

Washington D.C.
July 13, 2007

    They returned to the museum after dark. Asante had managed to come up with some potentially useful information using Lori's search strategy. Most of the items collected in July 1959 were stored in a massive Smithsonian warehouse situated in Suitland, 6 miles outside of Washington DC. The four of them took a taxi to the warehouse.
    On the journey, Asante sat in the front seat with the driver, while Hawkins, David and Lori occupied the cramped rear seat. The conversation was kept to a minimum as Hawkins busied himself with something that neither David or Lori could fathom. They looked on with raised eyebrows, in puzzled silence.
    In the moonless night, the warehouse building was imposing and sprawled over an entire city block. Flanked by Hawkins, David and Lori, Asante talked with the lone guard outside the building. After a few moments of raised voices, the red-faced guard granted them access to the building. From the reluctance displayed by the man, Hawkins presumed that this constituted a major departure from the daily routine.
    As they entered the building, the lights clacked on incrementally from left to right revealing the incredible expanse of the building's interior. Hawkins was reminded of the final scene from the film *Raiders of the Lost Ark*, in which the powerful religious artefact that Indiana Jones had been searching for was crated and 'filed away' in the giant government warehouse, probably never to be seen again.
    From their vantage point on an elevated platform overlooking the football stadium-sized building, they could see that approximately half of the room was comprised of row upon row of large stacked wooden crates and the rest was taken up by dozens of enormous bookshelf-like cases containing thousands of packed objects. Hawkins noticed the familiar tang of warehouse odour that carried a subtle hint of wood and dry air.

Apart from Asante, each of them resembled open-mouthed blow fish as they surveyed the scene before them.

"I know that this looks daunting my friends," Asante said, "but I think we have vastly narrowed down our search. According to the records, there were many objects collected during the early part of July in 1959, coinciding with the approximate time that the Lompoc artefacts went missing. It appears that most of these have been stored unprocessed in row 87, section 9B. We can begin our search there."

For the first time, Hawkins noted the stencilled yellow numbers below them on the concrete floor of the warehouse at the head of each row of crates and shelves. Going by the digits that he could see stretching into the distance, he guessed that there had to be more than 100 rows. He was thankful that Asante had managed to narrow their search area to what was hopefully only a small section of a single row. "We better get started then," Hawkins suggested.

Asante led the way as they trundled with echoing footfalls across the building to the beginning of row 87. They turned into the long deep canyon of crates and boxes and marched forward, until they reached the section posted '09-B' on an elevated placard. The letters 'A' and 'B' indicated whether the objects of interest were placed on the left or the right side, respectively. Mounted above each section was a security camera which sent a clear message, *we are watching you*. Hawkins did the arithmetic and, assuming that there was one camera per section, he calculated there must more than 1,000 of these covering the building.

They surveyed the scene before them and their shoulders slumped in unison. Section 09-B stretched easily over 100 feet in length and soared more than 25 feet over their heads. It appeared like a giant bookcase containing several tiers of broad shelves, which housed thousands of boxes and crates of all sizes and shapes. Rollaway ladders were placed at the end of each section to facilitate access to objects stored above head height.

They began their task, each armed only with a small crowbar. Then David noticed something. He said, "some of these crates have stencils or markings on them. Why don't I get on the ladder and someone could roll me along back and forth, while I scan the various levels looking for anything that might indicate that the contents came from Lompoc."

"Excellent idea," Asante exclaimed.

The search began in earnest. Lori wheeled the ladder incrementally along while David, perched like a lookout on the mainmast of an 19th century sailing vessel, scanned the crates and boxes for any relevant markings, starting with the uppermost level of the stacks. Most of the crates bore stencils which indicated they contained items recovered from Indian burial mounds scattered along the Mississippi and Ohio River Valleys. Others appeared to originate from the vast region spanning the Great Lakes to the Gulf of Mexico. So far, David hadn't spotted anything that looked like it was from California. He kept Lori and the others updated by calling down to them periodically.

After 30 minutes, Asante and Hawkins had gone through approximately two-thirds of the lower level, having stopped occasionally to open some of the crates for direct inspection. David and Lori had completed their rolling scan of the top row without finding anything of relevance. Then David descended several rungs on the ladder to view the next level of the stack and Lori began wheeling him in the opposite direction. After traveling about one quarter of the distance, David glimpsed something that caused him to do a double take. "Hold it!" he called down to Lori.

"Found something?" Lori asked.

"A crate with 'Chumash 07-1959' printed on it. That was the name of those Indians in Lompoc wasn't it?"

"That's right," Hawkins answered.

"Want me to open it here?" David asked.

Hawkins glanced at Asante who was already nodding in agreement. "Go for it, David," Hawkins called.

David systematically set to work on the lid with his crowbar and within 30 seconds he had it opened. The others could see him carefully slide the lid to one side, lean forward and peer within. "Huh?" he exclaimed.

"What is it David?" Lori asked.

Hawkins and Asante had joined her at the base of the ladder. They all looked upward expectantly.

Then David said, "looks like US Civil War stuff."

Down at ground level, Hawkins and Lori looked questioningly towards Asante.

"As I feared my friends, much of this has not been catalogued with the greatest attention to accuracy."

Hawkins looked up again and called, "what's actually in the crate, David?"

"Well, there are four swords. They have long curving steel blades with leather-wrapped handles and brass hilts."

"Cavalry sabres," Asante affirmed.

"There's also some grey uniforms and hats," David added. "I guess that means this is Confederate stuff. And there's also a bayonet and a few black iron balls."

"Cannon balls," Asante corrected.

"Hey!" David called. "There's another one right next to it."

David was now fixated on a massive crate standing next to the one containing the Civil War items. "It also has 'Chumash' stencilled onto it," he called down to them. "But I won't be able to open this one. It's jammed in too close to the shelf above it."

"Don't worry my friend. I will get a forklift so that we can transfer it down here." With that, Asante dashed off.

About two minutes later, a large yellow forklift truck appeared at the head of the row piloted by a determined-looking Asante. He raced the vehicle down the aisle towards them accompanied by the high pitched whine of the high-revving engine. Just when Hawkins was beginning to wonder if the metal monster was out of control, Asante expertly swerved it into the area below where David was perched. Without any preamble, Asante operated the clunking mechanism and expertly raised the tines to the approximate level of the crate. Then he nudged the vehicle forwards so that the tines slid easily into the two-inch gap beneath the crate.

The other three looked on and marvelled at Asante's surprising display of forklift expertise.

The Assistant Collector pushed a lever forward to elevate the fork a few more inches and simultaneously tilted the mast backwards to prevent the load from slipping. Then he reversed the vehicle, drawing the crate clear from the shelf.

Now that the crate had been freed, they could all see that it was approximately 10 feet long and 4 feet wide.

Asante finished the job by lowering the large load to the ground and then withdrew the vehicle so that it was standing 10 feet away. He climbed out and joined Hawkins and Lori by the crate.

David remained up on the ladder gazing along the row to see if there was anything else of interest that he might have missed.

In row 86, less than 40 feet from the scientists, Reinhard felt the smooth grip of his pistol as he crept forwards. He was followed by two brutish-looking men who could easily have won first and second prizes in an ogre-of-the-month contest. They also carried pistols. The three Germans were followed by Manuel Rodriguez who had declined to carry a weapon. He moved in silence compared to the other heavy-footed men.

Only moments ago they had heard the sound of a forklift manoeuvring down the next row where the scientists were. They could also occasionally see the scientists moving through the gaps created by the open plan shelving. *They must have found it*, Reinhard thought. He could also make out the faint murmur of voices, but couldn't quite hear what was being said. He decided to give the scientists one more minute and then he and his men would move in and take them by surprise. He turned and used hand signals to convey his intended plan to the three men behind him. They all nodded their heads in agreement. They moved around into the next aisle as a unit.

Asante and Hawkins quickly began to pry open the lid of the crate with the crowbars. After a few seconds they had levered out all of the nails, each yielding their grip on the crate with a loud squeak. Together, they lifted the heavy cover away, placed it to one side and peered inside the crate. They could see a large off-white coloured tarpaulin covering...something. Lori edged next to Asante and Hawkins while David watched the scene from his perch on the shelf. The young PhD student had climbed from the ladder into the space that had been taken up by the crate.

There was a moment of expectation as Asante peeled back the cover. What they saw took their breath away. Even though they had seen it's like before, Hawkins, David and Lori were still stunned. Asante uttered a deep guttural sound and then staggered back in shock, almost falling over.

Sticking to the shadows along the edge of the aisle, the three Germans and Rodriguez had edged to within 100 feet of the scientists. Although they had been unable to hear most of the conversation, they could see that their quarry had found what they were looking for. Their orders for this mission had been simple – find out where the real seeds were, obtain these at all costs and kill all of the scientists. Reinhard looked forward to the killing part.

The four men moved forward still using the shadows created by the incomplete lighting of the warehouse. The Germans flicked their pistols' safety switches into the off position. Manny started to follow...then he froze.

Two enormous human feet encased in a clear plastic sheet confronted the scientists. Each foot was easily 18 inches long and displayed 6 gnarled toes. The dried skin appeared like wrinkled parchment.

"Incredible," Asante commented as he stepped back to the edge of the crate, joining Hawkins and Lori. "I would not have believed it, had I not seen it with my own eyes. Let us see the rest of him." With that he pulled the cover completely off to reveal the length of the giant.

"I can't believe it," Lori exclaimed. "It looks almost exactly like the one in Cambridge. It's just about the same size, with 6 digits on its hands and feet. It even has the extra rows of teeth on its upper and lower jaws." The latter observation was apparent to everyone because the giant's mouth was locked wide open in a hideous grimace.

Lying to the side of the giant was a massive bronze axe. There were also numerous decorative items scattered throughout the crate including a few seashells and pierced beads. But Hawkins' eyes were drawn to something else, two objects positioned on either side of the giant's grotesque head. Hawkins reached into the crate and gently removed the one nearest to him. It appeared to be a carbon copy of the 'Adam and Eve' jar that they had found in Cambridge. It had the same figures, the tree and the swastikas. He noticed that neither jar was sealed. Just then, Hawkins was suddenly struck by an ominous feeling. He turned to Asante and said quietly, "Beze, tell me again how you knew to look here for the crate."

Asante looked confused. "I searched the electronic database by the date of acquisition, just as Lori suggested." Then his face darkened. "But you know it was the strangest thing. I noticed that someone else was looking for the same item just the day before. There was an electronic update notice telling me that the file had been accessed."

Hawkins looked at Asante and felt sick. It was a trap. And they had walked right into it.

Unaware of anything untoward, Lori asked, "is there anything in those jars?"

Just as Hawkins opened his mouth to respond an authoritative voice rang out from somewhere up the cavernous aisle.

"Hold it right there! NSA!"

Chapter 39

Washington D.C.
July 13, 2007

Azubeze Asante had never had a gun pointed at him in his 37-year lifetime. And now he had two of them aimed in his direction. It was not a nice feeling. He realised with gut-wrenching finality that any moment could be his last. He was petrified. Yet, somehow, he found the words to speak.

"What are you doing here?" he challenged in his deep booming voice.

Lori was surprisingly unworried by this latest development. Maybe she was just getting used to it. The past three or four days had been filled with guns, theft, murder and even motor vehicle chases. *Besides,* she thought, *the National Security Agency were the good guys... weren't they?* She reasoned that there must be some kind of misunderstanding, and nobody would come to any harm.

She couldn't have been more wrong.

David watched the scene unfolding below him in quiet fascination. He had a perfect view of the proceedings from the space recently vacated by the large crate. Since nobody was pointing a gun in his direction, he reckoned that his presence had so far gone undetected. He decided that he would take no action until he could work out just what the hell was going on.

Hawkins was no stranger to having guns pointed, or even fired, at him. But most of this experience came from his experiences in Iraq. He stood quietly trying to centre himself, breathing in and out. This also helped him to take in his entire surroundings.

"Don't make any sudden moves and no one will get hurt," the tall burley agent with the blonde crew cut called out. "Everyone put your hands up and back away from the crate."

The three scientists complied.

The agents stepped forward into the light. Hawkins noticed that the man who was issuing the orders held his pistol supported with two hands while his body was positioned sideways, minimizing his profile. The other man had adopted the exact same posture. *They are obviously government trained*, Hawkins reasoned. He also recognized from a distance that the weapons were most likely Beretta 92Fs, standard issue of the US military and intelligence agencies.

"Where is the warehouse security guard?" Asante asked in a loud authoritative voice. "How did you get in here?"

Hawkins noticed that the younger agent looked uncertain at this question. But the other man, obviously the more senior of the two, looked unflustered and determined.

"I think you know the answer to that question," the agent replied.

Hawkins' spine was tingling violently. He now knew what was wrong. He had to do something. He started to drop his hands and speak but the big agent shifted his aim so that it was pointing directly at his chest.

"You make one more move and I'll drop you!"

Hawkins moved.

Three shots rang out in rapid succession.

Chapter 40

Washington D.C.
July 13, 2007

    Two of the bullets caught the tall agent in the abdomen. The impact sent him sprawling backward and he fell heavily to the concrete floor. It was going to be a terrible death over the next 10 to 15 minutes of his life. It would have been much better if the bullets had actually killed him outright. The acids from his punctured stomach were already leaking into his abdominal cavity, and he was being poisoned from within. The third bullet clipped his young partner on the left shoulder, tearing away flesh but not inflicting any serious damage. After gently touching his shoulder to test the wound, Jones made a decision that saved his life. He immediately flung himself to the floor next to his dying partner, just as two more shots rang out and splintered the crate that he had just been standing next to.

    Hawkins started moving a split second before the gunshots erupted from behind them. He grabbed Lori firmly around the waist and pulled her quickly to the ground behind the giant crate on the side opposite to their new antagonists. Without pausing, Hawkins called to Asante who was standing like a petrified deer in the line of fire. "Beze Move!"
    Asante had felt the bullets buzzing through the air on either side of him like supersonic insects. He thought that he would know what to do in a situation like this. But that misconception had developed from the comfort and safety of his own living room while watching Bruce Willis and Samuel L Jackson on the movie channels. This wasn't anything like those movies. But Hawkins' voice jarred him into action. He immediately dropped to the floor as two more shots rang out, narrowly missing him. Asante folded his arms across his chest like a museum mummy and rolled frantically towards the edge of the crate. If it hadn't been such a serious situation, Asante's mode of attempted escape would have appeared humorous.

Tactically, Asante's rolling motion was a good idea. It was fast and it lowered his profile making it more difficult for the unknown shooters to target him. But the gunmen were now moving forwards to improve their odds and three more shots rang out, clipping the concrete floor just behind him. The flat trajectory caused one of the bullets to ricochet causing small fragments of concrete to spatter like miniature projectiles into Asante, decimating his lower leg below the knee. His cry of pain echoed throughout the warehouse.

Hawkins lunged from behind the crate like a scuttling crab, grabbed Asante by his shirt collar and pulled him to safety. No sooner had he ducked back down when another shot struck the crate near his head, sending wood splinters spraying through the air. He could feel the gunmen drawing nearer as he whipped off his thin coat and tied the arms tightly around Asante's leg. Asante was still conscious but appeared to be in a state of shock. Hawkins motioned to Lori to apply pressure to the pulsing wound as he racked his brain for a plan.

This was the first gun battle that Jones had been in. It wasn't like the intensive training that he went through at the academy. He was scared to death. He realised that if he didn't do something fast it was all going to be over far too quickly. The last few shots had been concentrated on the crate where the scientists were now taking cover. The gunmen had left him and Reeves alone for the moment sprawled on the floor about 50 feet from the crate. Glancing over, he could see that his partner was struggling in his last throws of life. Reeves' chest was heaving and his breaths were growing increasing more strained and raspy. His eyes were closed tightly as if he were trying to shut out the nightmarish situation around him. Jones had to act. He reached out, grabbed his partner by the shoulder and began dragging him inch-wise to the edge of the aisle. Maybe they could find cover in between some the larger crates.

"Danny!" Reeves had his eyes open. It was the first time that Reeves had ever used Jones's first name. "Leave me –" He suddenly choked and shuddered in agony.

Jones's eyes went wild with horror. "Simon, I can't."

"I'll be dead no matter what," Reeves smiled, although it was clear that he was in intense pain. "You have to –" Again he stopped due to a violent tremor that shook his body. "It's your only chance. Hurry!"

Jones choked back the sudden feeling of emotion and nodded. *Why had Reeves been such a dickhead all of this time?* He couldn't believe that he had chosen his last few moments in life to show that he was human after all. Jones sprang to his feet and moved diagonally forwards to where a large crate was jutting out from the rest of the stack and took what little cover it afforded. His movement didn't appear to attract any attention. He closed one eye and pointed his gun at the tall gunman now moving swiftly towards the crate shielding the scientists.

Hawkins could hear the gunmen behind them, moving steadily closer. Two more bullets slammed into the crate and he heard something shatter inside the enormous box. *There goes one of the jars*, he thought. This brought to mind a frightening possibility that he had ignored so far, the bullets can come right through the crate.

He noticed a frantic movement ahead of him as the young, dark-haired NSA agent scrambled for cover behind the edge of a long crate. His partner was no longer moving. Then Hawkins saw the young agent raise his pistol and he fired two shots directly over their crate at the approaching men behind. He could tell by the sound that neither shot had hit anything.

Almost immediately, two return shots splintered the edge of the crate next to the agent's head. The young man lowered his profile by dropping into a crouched position. Then another barrage of gunfire erupted around him and he was nicked by another bullet. Part of his left earlobe was now missing. But the agent bravely held his position.

Just then the gunfire stopped and an accented voice rang out in the cavernous warehouse. "Dr Hawkins, there is no escape. We can kill you any time. You have something that is ours. Hand it over and we will let you, all of you, leave here."

Hawkins had no doubts the man was telling the truth, there was no escape. But the man had lied when he said he would let them leave if they gave up the seeds. The stakes were too high. From the proximity of the voice, Hawkins could tell that the gunmen were close to the crate. Whatever he was going to do, it would have to be now.

At that moment, he thought of David. His student's secluded position on the shelf must have shielded him from the gunmen's view. Then at least he might get out of this situation alive. But knowing David's impetuous nature, Hawkins worried that the young man might just give himself away by attempting something crazy.

Hawkins touched Lori on the shoulder and gave her a look that was meant to convey the idea that everything would be okay. She sent a heart-wrenching look back at him and shook her head. He started to rise.

Reinhard saw Hawkins emerge from behind the crate and knew that he had won. He would give the order to kill all of the others now and they could hold the leader of the scientists until they had the seeds. Then they would kill him as well. But that would have to wait until they were sure where the seeds were. Reinhard knew there were none to be found in the jars from the crate. Schmidt had told him that these had been removed many years before. They were only here for the seeds from Cambridge that Dr Hawkins had hidden somewhere. If they were lucky he might even have brought them here. His reverie was interrupted by something moving high above their heads. Then a voice shouted a single crazy word.

"GERONIMO!"

Two 10-pound Civil War cannon balls hurtled downward and struck one of the gunmen simultaneously on the top of the head and the right shoulder. A third ball missed and struck the floor at the man's feet cracking the cement. The effect of the first ball on the man's head was devastating. His skull was instantly caved in and the resulting sharp splintered bone fragments penetrated his cerebral cortex. The second ball shattered all three of the major bones that made up his shoulder joint beyond repair. He dropped the gun and collapsed backward.

When they realised with horror what was happening, Reinhard and the other gunman flinched reflexively and covered their heads to avoid the same fate as their fallen comrade. This allowed David time to throw two more objects down. These were Civil War cavalry sabres. One landed where David had intended, within the crate, but the other just caught the edge and clattered to the concrete floor behind it.

David shouted, "Jim! The crate!"

Hawkins didn't hesitate. He reached into the crate and snatched up the sabre. Without another thought, he rushed toward the nearest gunman.

Jones was stunned by what had just transpired. He saw one of the men turn toward Dr Hawkins, who was now brandishing a sabre, of all things. The other man was firing upward where the airborne attack had come from. Jones realised that it was now or never. He glanced back at his partner. He knew it was over for Reeves. He turned back to the unfolding scene. *This is for you partner.* He broke cover and ran toward the melee.

At the same instant, the tall German wheeled towards Hawkins who was closing in on him rapidly.

Hawkins adjusted his angle of approach so that the man's massive body was blocking his partner's potential line of fire.

As the big man zeroed the gun in on Hawkins' head and his finger began to pull the trigger, the archaeologist lunged sideways and whacked the man's wrist hard with the flat side of the blade, effectively dislodging the weapon. The shot went wild as the gun clattered to the ground.

The man clutched his wrist in pain and he uttered a few obvious curses in German, some of which Hawkins recognised. Then the man seemed to recover and resigned to attack with or without a weapon. He put his head down and stomped toward

Hawkins in an insane attempt to get inside the range of the sword.

Hawkins stepped backward, raising the sword high over his head, and let the man charge at him. Just when it seemed as if his attacker was about to bulldoze him into the concrete, Hawkins swung his right leg further back and brought the brass hilt of the sword straight down on the man's head where the base of the skull joined the top of the neck, or what would have been a neck if the bull-like man actually had one.

The man shrieked in agony as he lost his balance and crashed head first into a large crate on the opposite side of the aisle. Then he sprawled into a heap on the floor in a condition that was somewhere between unconscious and dead.

Hawkins didn't have time to care which.

Now the last gunman was just standing there, leering at him. For the first time, Hawkins could see the man's face clearly. There was a long jagged scar running down his left cheek. Scarface! This was the man who had killed Pavlos and most likely Zoran.

Scarface raised his weapon. He couldn't miss. But then he smiled. He turned abruptly and pointed his pistol at Lori. "Ready to watch the lady die?" the evil voice taunted as his finger tightened on the trigger.

Jones was running flat out when he saw the last remaining gunman shift his weapon from Hawkins to the young lady. From the finality of the man's gesture, Jones knew that the girl was as good as dead if he didn't do something. He skidded to a halt 20 feet from the crate, took a wide stance and raised his weapon. He saw the gunman's eyes go wide in surprise. Then three things happened simultaneously.

Jones pulled the trigger on his pistol repeatedly.

David, who had returned to his perch on the shelf, let go with another cannonball.

Hawkins, recognizing that he had no chance to cover the required distance in time to save Lori, sent his sabre spinning towards the killer's torso.

The results of the threefold assault were devastating. Four bullets slammed into Scarface's torso, tearing through several vital organs. The cannonball clipped the left side of the gunman's skull, jarring his head suddenly and unnaturally to the right and cracking two cervical vertebrae. The spinning sabre slammed point-first, after two complete rotations, behind the man's right shoulder causing his gun hand to jerk upwards. Although Scarface's finger completed his brain's last orders and pulled the trigger, the bullet merely struck the ceiling of the warehouse, 50 feet over their heads.

Propelled mostly from the force of the 4 bullets, Scarface fell backward and his gun hand flopped in an extended arc over his head. This action sent the gun skidding backwards along the concrete floor. He was dead by the time he hit the ground.

After a moment of stunned silence from the survivors in the warehouse, David's voice called down from above. "Did we get him?"

The scene in the warehouse wound down to a sedate pace in the aftermath of the battle. Adrenalin levels of the living returned to near normal. David climbed down from the high shelf to join his friends standing with Agent Jones around the crate.

It was the first occasion that Jones had to look in the crate and he was spellbound. It was clear that there was a lot more to this situation than what he had been told during his mission briefing.

Lori sidled up to him and put her hand on his shoulder. "Thank you for what you did. I was sure that he would have shot me if you hadn't intervened."

Jones turned two shades darker at Lori's touch, shook his head and smiled. "It was a team effort."

"He almost got me as well," David chimed in. "I felt one of the bullets go right past my nose."

Hawkins said, "it was a close call for all of us. Good thinking with the cannonballs, David." Then he stooped and checked on Asante's condition. "I think that Beze has gone into a state of shock. Can you call the emergency services Agent Jones? We need to get someone here very soon." Then Hawkins pulled out a large piece of tarpaulin from the crate and covered Asante to keep him warm.

Jones nodded his agreement and flipped open his cell phone. He punched in the number and gave out the necessary information to the dispatcher. Then he flipped the phone shut and turned back to Hawkins. "I'll need those seeds Doctor. It's a matter of national security."

Hawkins noticed from the man's tone, that it was not a request. "So are you the ones that have been tailing me ever since I arrived in this country?"

"You know about that?"

"And are you the ones who also entered my hotel room in Lompoc and planted those listening devices and GPS tracers in some of my belongings?"

Jones looked crestfallen. "How did you –?"

Hawkins suddenly felt sorry for the National Security agent. It was clear that the agency expected him to put his life on the line for a cause but without giving him all of the necessary facts – including information on Hawkins' military background.

Jones continued, "but that doesn't change the fact that you have to turn those seeds over to me."

Hawkins didn't have time to respond. This was because another voice rang out from the other side of the crate and interrupted their conversation.

"I am afraid that's not going to happen."

Chapter 41

Cambridge
July 13, 2007

    Willy Schrader had been watching Dr Jim Hawkins' house for nearly 8 hours. In that time, he had seen no one enter or leave the premises. He was certain no one was home. He had been with the organization for over 10 years after being recruited in Berlin as a novice burglar who had just run afoul of the law. He had been caught by the police after his 8th robbery. He was sentenced to two years in Tegel Prison but this was commuted to three months followed by a one-year probation. The reason he received a light sentence was mainly due to the fact that he had not used a gun during the robbery and it was his first offence, as far as they knew, anyway.
    He hated prison and swore to himself that he would go straight when he got out. On the day of his release, he embarked on a new career path. But then came the lucrative offer from Herr Schmidt. The man had approached him while Willy was working behind the counter, taking orders. After Schmidt received his two Big Macs, fries and medium Coke, he asked Willy to join him in the corner booth. Schmidt told him he was aware of Willy's criminal past, including jobs the police did not know about. When Willy started to rise from the table in protest, Schmidt asked him if he would like to earn 500,000 Euros per year using his talents. Willy sat back down.
    After agreeing to Schmidt's offer, Willy walked out of MacDonald's and never returned. The jobs for Schmidt always entailed stealing artefacts from collectors. Willy reasoned that the items should have been in museums anyway. Over the years he had recovered such artefacts as cylinder seals and clay tablets from ancient Sumer and Assyria, inscribed pottery from Asiatic and American Indian civilizations and even some Mayan codices and eerie crystal skulls that had originally been recovered from temples in the jungles of Central America.

For this job, he was tasked with finding out whether a Cambridge archaeologist had stashed away some ancient seeds somewhere in the house. Schmidt had told him the seeds were of tremendous importance and a bonus of an entire year's salary was his, if Willy could recover them. Having determined that the house was clear, he jumped over the back fence and walked across the lawn towards the rear door. He had already spotted the house had no burglar alarm. *Piece of cake*, he thought. After quick inspection of the door lock, he began to systematically apply a shiny set of small utensils to the key hole. He was inside the house within 30 seconds.

Sanderson was sitting at his desk eating a late lunch of tuna on granary bread when the call came through. He was told about a possible break in and a barking dog at Dr Hawkins' house on Hills Road. He rushed out the door leaving his sandwich. When he arrived at the scene he saw that a police car was already in the driveway next to Hawkins' Camaro, and the front door of the house was open. As Sanderson emerged from his car he heard the deep booming bark of Hawkins' dog. He guessed that whatever had happened here was not over yet. He entered the front door and called out, "Spencer! Prescott!"
"In the living room Inspector," a crisp voice replied.
Woof! Gruff!
Sanderson found the two officers in the downstairs reception room with their hands on their hips, shaking their heads and gazing at the spectacle on the floor. A thin acne-scarred man lay sprawled on his back with a well-chewed yellow Frisbee lying partway on his head. He appeared to be conscious but in discomfort. The massive Great Dane that had its two front paws planted on the man's chest, apparently trying to encourage him to get up and throw the Frisbee.
Woof! Woof!
Sanderson noticed that every time the dog barked and wagged its tail, the man on the floor closed his eyes tightly as if hoping it would all go away. The man also had a considerable amount of doggy drool on his face.

Sanderson opened the conversation with one of the officers. "Besides the obvious, what have you got here, Spencer?"

"Looks like a break in Inspector, just like you predicted."

Gruff!

Spencer continued. "We were watching the house as you asked and observed the subject enter through the rear. It looked like he picked the door lock using a set of skeleton keys. We haven't had a chance to examine these yet since they are most likely in his pocket, and we can't get to that. We moved in as soon as he entered the house but, after a few seconds, we heard a loud scream followed by barking. Then we entered the room and found everything pretty much as you see it."

Gruff!... Rurr!

The dog was completely fixated on the terrified man lying on the ground. The massive canine looked like it couldn't comprehend why the man wouldn't get up and play.

"I don't think he's a dog lover," the other officer, Prescott, commented dryly.

The three policemen turned back to watch as a large drop of drool snaked down from the dog's massive jaws and landed on the man's upper chest, discolouring his shirt. The way the man started to squirm, one would have thought that it was actually battery acid that had splattered on him. Nevertheless, they couldn't help but wince in empathy for the burglar's predicament. So far the man had not yet spoken a single word.

Sanderson said, "did you check the rest of the house?"

Woof!

Spencer replied, "no, but we don't think that he had time to get very far. The dog must have been on him immediately."

"Just the same, I'll have to check," Sanderson said. "While I'm gone, why don't one of you see if you can entice the dog into the back yard with the Frisbee while the other places the intruder under arrest?"

"I'll give it a try," Prescott said looking slightly worried. He began to approach the dog cautiously, slightly bent at the waist with his hands on his knees. "Want to play Frisbee? There's a good girl. Yeah, who's a great big Scooby Doo good girl?"

Sanderson shook his head in wonderment, left the room and went straight for the downstairs kitchen. As he was descending the stairs he heard the cadence and volume of Brandy's barking increasing in obvious excitement.

Gruff! Gruff! Rurrr! ...Woof! Woof! Gruff!

Either the dog is eating everyone in the room or Prescott is having some success with the Frisbee, Sanderson chuckled to himself. He entered the spacious kitchen-dining-living area in the basement. As he looked at the room conversion for the second time he thought that Dr Hawkins had done a grand job of it. It was like a home within itself and he remembered that Hawkins had told him that he had spent most of his time down there. The living room had a large widescreen television equipped with a digital satellite receiver which seemed to be the focal point of the furnishings, consisting of two leather recliner chairs, a medium-sized sofa and a large coffee table. The dining area was done in a tasteful diner-booth style consisting of a large U-shaped leather bench and an oval polished pine table.

Through the basement kitchen window, Sanderson could see into the rear garden. He spotted Officer Prescott and Brandy clearly having fun with the Frisbee. The rules appeared to be simple and it was clear who was boss. Prescott would loft the Frisbee lightly away from him and Brandy would break into a gallop, leap into the air and catch the floating disc in mid-air. Brandy would then prance back to Prescott with her head held high and the Frisbee in her mouth covered in saliva and fresh bite marks. Then the process would be repeated.

The kitchen area was nicely fitted out with a double stainless steel sink along with a gas stove, a microwave oven and an antique white refrigerator that was covered in hundreds of tourist magnets which Hawkins must have acquired while travelling all over the globe. One of the nicest features of the kitchen was the large walk in pantry in the corner. He opened the pantry door and looked inside. His eyes went directly to the large storage area on the floor. It took a moment for the shock to register but then he reeled back in horror.

Brandy! What have you done?

Chapter 42

Washington D.C.
July 13, 2007

The man who had spoken emerged from the shadows. He was holding Scarface's gun.

"You!" David proclaimed. "I was wondering when you would turn up."

The man started to say something when Agent Jones made a surprisingly fast move for his gun. The man was even faster. In a blur, he drew a bead on Jones before the agent's hand had travelled even half way to the weapon in his shoulder holster. "Stop Agent Jones, I don't want to shoot you!"

Jones did a decent impersonation of a statue.

"Good. Now while you're there, please remove your pistol and throw it into the crate, along with any other weapons that you might have on you. And please move very carefully."

Jones scowled but complied by tossing his gun into the crate.

The man nodded his approval, obviously trusting that this was the only weapon Jones had at his disposal. Then he turned to David. "Do you have any weapons on you, young man? Any more cannonballs perhaps?"

David smiled mischievously but shook his head.

The Latin American man then fixed his attention on Hawkins. "Now Doctor, if you would be so kind as to collect the pistol belonging to the man you disarmed earlier and carefully throw that into the crate as well."

Hawkins stooped to retrieve the gun, flipped on the safety switch and tossed it into the crate.

"Thank you. Now please put the lid back on the crate and seal it."

Hawkins picked up one edge of the heavy cover and, with David's assistance, manoeuvred it back into place on top of the crate. They each banged in a handful of the nails that protruded from the lid, using their crowbars as hammers. When satisfied the crate was effectively sealed, they placed their crowbars on top of the lid and stepped back with the others. Everyone wondered what was coming next. They wouldn't have long to wait.

The man bent down, placed his own pistol on the floor, stood upright again and then smartly kicked the gun with the side of his foot so it went spinning behind him towards the rear of the warehouse.

"What is this?" Jones said, taking a forward step.

Hawkins stepped in front of Jones, blocking his path. "Wait. Let's hear what he has to say."

The man acknowledged Hawkins with a nod and said, "I do not like guns. There has been enough death and injuries here today. I just want the seeds. Then I'll be on my way."

"We have no seeds, Mister…?" Hawkins answered, inviting the man to fill in the blank.

"Rodriguez. I work for William Merrick."

"Then Merrick is behind all of this," David blurted out.

"No. Merrick knows nothing about this. There are others involved."

"Who?" Jones interrupted.

"No more questions. Tell me where the seeds are, Dr Hawkins."

"I already answered that question. Besides, I thought you and your people already took what you needed."

Rodriguez actually smiled at this. "The first batch stolen from the molecular biology lab was recovered by the Cambridge Police Force. The second batch taken from the Department of Archaeology was not the genuine article. You should know that Dr Hawkins, since you're the one who switched those for ordinary seeds."

Agent Jones showed no reaction to this, while Lori and David looked on in open-mouthed in surprise.

But now Hawkins knew where Rodriguez had got his information from. He had to keep him talking. "Did you kill Zoran?"

Rodriguez appeared to be physically jolted by the question. "I'm not a killer." He gestured toward the body of Reinhard lying behind him. "It was the work of this man. He also murdered the young Cypriot in the LMB, and the guard outside this building."

"It doesn't matter if your finger wasn't on the trigger," Hawkins said. "If you were with them, you are also responsible."

Rodriguez didn't respond. He had to get things back on track and end this quickly. The authorities would be there all too soon. "Where are the seeds, Doctor? I know you asked David to bring them to Washington."

"You've been listening to my telephone conversations," Hawkins noted calmly.

Rodriguez said nothing.

Then it was Hawkins' turn to do something unexpected. He knelt down, hoisted his left trouser leg and pulled a transparent bag containing small, brown, pellet-like objects from his Argyle sock. He stood and placed the bag on top of the crate.

Jones stammered, "no, you can't!"

"Don't worry Agent Jones, it won't be that easy." As Hawkins stepped back from the crate he was now holding a US Civil War cavalry sabre.

Rodriguez regarded Hawkins stoically. After a moment he seemed to make up his mind. He stepped back to Scarface's body and pulled the other sabre out from between the killer's ribs. Then he turned and walked slowly towards Hawkins. "Are you sure you want to do this?"

Hawkins wondered the same thing. But he had to make it look good for his plan to have any chance of working. He said, "if you can get past me, the seeds are yours."

Jones muttered to David and Lori in the background, "this is the weirdest night of my life."

"This is fairly typical for us," David commented.

"Do you think he knows what he's doing?" Lori asked.

David looked thoughtful for a second. "Not a chance."

They all turned to watch.

Quicker than the eye could follow, Rodriguez lunged forward.

Almost immediately, Hawkins realised that he had bitten off more than he could chew. Rodriguez's single handed frontal assault with the sabre was brilliantly executed and he seemed to move faster than a striking cobra. Hawkins barely had time to sidestep the lightning quick attack using the flat edge of his own sabre to cover his escape. Then Rodriguez turned and was on him immediately, slashing at his sword – not at his body.

He's not trying to kill me Hawkins realised. *At least for now.* Hawkins' experience enabled him to see the move coming and he managed to parry the blow using a circular motion of his own sabre. He initiated an instantaneous counterattack by fluidly continuing the motion with a quick sweeping slash aimed at Rodriguez's forward leg. Unlike Rodriguez, Hawkins wielded his sabre with a two-handed grip for greater power. But this introduced two potential problems. Firstly, it effectively reduced his reach. The second problem resulted from the fact that the sabre's hilt was only designed to fit a single hand. This meant that his hands were forced into an overlapping grip, impairing the efficiency of his strikes.

Rodriguez reacted almost instantaneously to Hawkins' blow by withdrawing his leg with cat-like agility, but not before the tip of the blade sliced through the fabric on his trousers, narrowly missing flesh.

Then Hawkins followed up with a powerful slashing onslaught that had Rodriguez scurrying backward.

But Rodriguez managed to disperse the ferocity of the attack using his speed. Then he seemed to recover and launched his own campaign, swishing his sabre in a blur or short back and forth strokes.

The repeated loud clanging sound of steel crashing into steel resonated throughout the warehouse as Hawkins deftly parried Rodriguez's powerful strikes. Instead of moving backward, Hawkins circled to the left and attempted to escape Rodriguez's blade. Then Hawkins sprang backward and absorbed a powerful strike which caused Rodriquez to overstretch and partly lose his balance.

Hawkins took advantage of the mistake by pinning the man's sabre down and he immediately lunged in for another attempted strike.

Rodriguez barely managed to pivot to the side and draw his blade back in front of him.

But Hawkins wasn't finished. He lunged in again for a pounding assault on his opponent's sword. The sheer force of the blows kept Rodriguez on the defensive as he just managed to ward off the flurry of strikes from Hawkins' sabre. Then a long flicking strike penetrated Rodriguez's defence, nicking him on the cheek.

This only seemed to energize Rodriguez. He suddenly darted forward and slashed with a long single-handed stroke that glanced off Hawkins' wrist.

Hawkins quickly glanced down to check the wound. He noticed that it was only a minor scrape but it still stung. And now he had another problem. He was beginning to tire and his arms were growing heavy. He was also worried about the battering that his sabre was taking due to the continuing force of his own blows and in parrying those of Rodriguez. The weapon that he had picked up from behind the crate was in poor condition. He had to finish this before it was too late.

He knocked Rodriguez's sabre to the side with a powerful downward stroke and then pressed his advantage by lunging toward his opponent's torso with a straight thrust. His movement was easily parried as the two weapons met with a resounding clash midway between them. This was the response that Hawkins was looking for. He pressed forward so the crossed sabres were forced upward as he released his left hand from the weapon and leapt deeply behind the Latin American and roughly grabbed the side of his coat near the pocket.

The movement would have unbalanced most people, but Rodriguez was not like most people. He reacted instantly by driving his right elbow into Hawkins' sternum causing the latter to release his grip on the coat. Rodriguez twisted away and turned back to face his opponent.

Hawkins was momentarily winded by the blow but he didn't want Rodriguez to know this. He immediately came in for a direct attack using repeated downward slashes as Rodriguez stepped back and attempted to parry the blows.

That was when Hawkins decided to end it. He needed to get the timing just right or he could soon be in a lot of pain – or worse. His next thrust caught Rodriguez just below the right knee, opening a small gash in his trousers and drawing more blood. Then Hawkins drew his sabre back with the blade held flat.

Like a tiger pouncing on its helpless prey, Rodriguez brought his own weapon down on Hawkins' extended blade snapping it into two pieces. The broken tip clattered noisily on concrete.

Even before the shock registered on those watching, both men stepped back. Each showed the signs of having been through a fierce battle. Hawkins regarded his enemy with some trepidation since he was now effectively unarmed. He hoped that he had gambled correctly.

Just then the discordant sound of multiple sirens could be heard from the opened front entrance of the warehouse.

Rodriguez reacted by rushing to the crate. He snatched the bag, turned and ran.

"Hey!" Agent Jones shouted as he started forward in a half-hearted attempt to stop the man.

But Hawkins, still panting from the brief battle, barred Jones' way with an out-stretched arm. "We have to let him go."

"But can't let him get away with those!" Jones warned.

Hawkins said, "don't worry Agent, you guys will catch him."

Jones gazed at him in disbelief.

David and Lori looked on, completely lost.

"And you'll get the man who's behind all of this," Hawkins continued. "But now let's get Beze to a hospital."

Chapter 43

Santa Barbara, California
July 14, 2007

Santa Barbara is a mid-sized picturesque city on the California coast, around 60 miles south-east from Lompoc and 80 miles north-west from Los Angeles. This stretch of south-facing coastline is known as the 'American Riviera' because of its many affluent residents, pleasant Mediterranean-like climate and rugged natural beauty. In keeping with the Spanish heritage of the city, much of the architecture adheres to the mission-style, consisting of white buildings with unadorned surfaces, limited fenestration and low-pitched clay tile roofs. The atmosphere of the city is enhanced by arched facades, enclosed courtyards, beautifully landscaped parks and long white sandy beaches framed by postcard-quality palm trees. The Santa Ynez Mountains rise dramatically behind the city with some peaks topping 4,000 feet.

In the early 1900s, Santa Barbara was the film capital of the world. For more than a decade, over 1,500 films were made there and it became a hangout for legendary stars such as Charlie Chaplin, Douglas Fairbanks and Mary Pickford. It was also the home of California's oldest and wealthiest families with most of the money coming from cattle ranches that still surround the city. In the 1980s, Santa Barbara became more open to the tourist trade thanks to President Ronald Reagan who visited his large ranch regularly in the nearby Santa Ynez Valley. The President's trips were well-covered by the press and enticing pictures of the city and surrounding areas were broadcast to the world. Today, Santa Barbara still welcomes the rich and famous although most of the money now comes from technology and the Hollywood influence. Notable celebrity residents include the likes of John Travolta, Kevin Costner and Michael Douglas.

The unassuming Los Hermanos Plant Nursery was situated in the foothills of the Santa Ynez Mountains approximately one-mile north of Santa Barbara's Mission. The large billboard in front of the small Spanish-style office of the nursery claimed it specialized in California native plants along with trees, shrubs, vines, perennials, ornamental grasses and aquatic plants from around the world. The facility consisted of several small buildings and greenhouses along with a variety of covered and open stalls displaying their wares. In the early evening, the cool ocean breeze carried the scent of pine trees along with that of the various herbaceous and flowering plants.

In a small annex behind the main office, a fuzzy tan-coloured rodent sat on Gerhardt Schmidt's palm, wrinkling its pink nose. Going by appearances alone, it was nothing out of the ordinary. It was an archetypal, young and vigorous *Mus musculas*, known throughout the world as the common house mouse. Schmidt placed the miniscule animal into the steel mesh cage with extreme carefulness that could almost be mistaken for affection. A small plaque on the wire chamber identified the occupant in black bold letters as '8'. Once back in its sawdust-covered home, the energetic rodent scurried to the food dispenser in the corner. Without missing a beat, it began to tuck in to the mixture of cereal grains containing the chopped fruit additive.

Schmidt gazed at the tiny creature with clinical detachment. He wondered if it sensed anything unusual about its own existence. Did it feel different compared to others of its kind? But why would it? From the time it was 1 year-old, it had been caged alone. It couldn't have any recollection of its 7 other littermates who were used as control subjects. There was no way it could have known that all of its brothers and sisters had died of old age 38 years before!

Schmidt walked with Manuel Rodriguez and a tall blonde-haired man named Dieter. They made their way silently past utility buildings, open areas containing bedded plants and greenhouses of various sizes and shapes. Schmidt cradled the small white bag that Rodriguez had given him. "Manny, you have no idea how important this is."

"Important enough to be worth the lives of three more of your men?" Manny said. "And the lives of a security guard and a government agent who were unfortunate enough to get in the way?"

Schmidt scowled. Nobody questioned his judgement. And not only had Rodriguez challenged him, he had done so in front of one of his men. Schmidt glanced over at Dieter but realised that the tall robotic man didn't even appear to be listening. He would keep his anger in check. "Yes. All of them and more."

The three men stopped at a 10-foot high cyclone fence topped with tightly coiled strands of barbed wire. It seemed oddly out of place in the otherwise welcoming environment of the nursery. Dieter reached out with a key and opened the heavy padlocked gate, the hinges squealing in protest. Ahead lay a gravel- and grass-covered compound containing a small weathered greenhouse and a red brick utility shed.

"Where are we going?" Manny asked.

"There," Schmidt replied, gesturing at the greenhouse.

Manny had no doubt that Schmidt would soon try and kill him. But he had to see this. He started forward after the slender German, followed closely by Dieter. From the outside, the greenhouse appeared to be ordinary and unimpressive.

The three of them entered the angular glass building. Then Schmidt stood back and smiled as he watched Manny scan the room. There was only one object there. A small tree. Examining it closely, Manny realised that it had an unusual, other-worldly appearance. It looked like a miniature palm, although it was slightly twisted like a meandering vine. The rough and stumpy wooded trunk gave rise to an extensive arborisation of branches and twigs that culminated in leaves which were almost as long and thin as palm fronds. Amongst the leaves, dangled several small yellowish fruits that were slightly wrinkled and glistened as if they were wet or oily.

"You are looking at something which has probably not existed on this world for thousands of years," Schmidt intoned. "It has been known by many names throughout the ages, but you are probably more familiar with the one given to it in the *Book of Genesis*."

Manny didn't respond. He already knew this.

Schmidt said, "the seeds that produced this tree were almost 10,000 years old. I acquired them many years ago in a small town not far from here."

"How were you able to grow this from seeds that were so old?" Manny asked.

"It was not difficult. The hard outer casing of the seeds must have rendered them resistant to severe conditions, even to the passage of extreme time. But even so, we managed to produce only one plantlet that survived into adulthood. This tree is the only one of its kind."

"Why not take offshoots from the mature tree and produce more?" Manny asked.

"That doesn't work. I think the tree was designed so that it cannot be reproduced by traditional cloning methods."

"Designed?"

"Yes. You might be looking at one of the earliest examples of selective breeding or perhaps genetic engineering on the planet. Someone must have taken specific measures long ago to ensure that this tree cannot be mass-produced."

"But genetic engineering has only been possible for the past 30 years or so."

"Ah yes," Schmidt said, rolling his eyes. "The typical view that we currently represent the pinnacle of civilization on this planet. Like so many others you give no credence to the fantastic achievements of some of the great civilizations of the past."

Manny remained silent, thinking.

"As a Mexican Catholic, you probably believe everything you read in the *Bible*," Schmidt snorted. "Have you never considered the possibility that the gods and angels described in those passages were just men? Albeit men who were relatively advanced compared to the more primitive societies of the Middle East and southern Europe? Wouldn't the primitives have looked upon these men as gods because of their advanced skills of metallurgy, shipbuilding and architecture as well as their knowledge of agriculture, astronomy and their possession of medicines that can heal the sick or dying?"

"But why go to all this trouble to bring back this species of tree? Why is this one tree so important?"

Schmidt shook his head and smiled. "Look at me Manny!"

"I'd rather not."

"Manny, how old do I look?"

"I guess around 55."

"That is not what I asked. How old do I look?"

"Less than 40," Manny answered reluctantly. "35 maybe."

"Good. Although you were right. I am older. But much older than you think."

Manny looked closely at Schmidt's features.

"I was born in the year 1928," Schmidt added, "that makes me 79 years-old!"

Manny felt his heart suddenly skip a beat. *Could it be true?*

"But how?"

"The fruit, of course. Since the late 1960s, I have eaten approximately one piece per month. It has been enough to slow my biological clock and keep me looking and feeling like a young, healthy man somewhere in his early 30's. Although I can't be certain, it might have actually caused the clock to turn backwards."

Manny peered again at Schmidt's wrinkle-free face, looking for any sign of plastic surgery or any other indication that it was some kind of bizarre trick. There was nothing obvious. Putting his disbelief aside for the moment, he asked, "how does it work?"

"We think it produces a factor that stimulates the continual renewal of cells in the body, perhaps by activating the proliferation and differentiation of stem cells."

"If this is true, you should give it to medical science," Manny said. "It could help to cure untold diseases associated with aging. People could live longer, healthier lives."

"A typical fool's answer," Schmidt snapped. "Do you realise the chaos that would ensue if everyone started living longer? The planet would suffer from massive overpopulation which could have widespread social, health and ecological impacts. There would be increased war, famine and illness related to the extreme overcrowding. Societies would have to completely change their structure. There could be no more pensions and the world's economies could collapse. And there would be the ethical and political issues regarding who should have access to life extension and who should not."

Manny found it ironic that Schmidt, of all people, was citing ethics in his argument. "Most scientific advances have their advantages and disadvantages. They can be used for good or evil. You should let someone else decide what to do with it. Something of this potential importance should not be under the control of just one person. You can't play God."

Schmidt responded with vehemence. "I can assure you that my plans will serve a far greater purpose than simply helping the pathetic weaklings and other inferior beings who should be weeded out of society anyway."

"Plans?" Manny dared to ask. He knew that Schmidt had only revealed as much as he had for only one reason.

"It is of incalculable value for the next phase of our operation. A drug that can eliminate aging will enable us to control a large portion of the world's economy. Since most of the world's diseases strike the aged, it could make pharmaceuticals a thing of the past. We could hold these companies and entire governments to ransom. Imagine the power that would give us."

Manny didn't miss the subtle glance that Schmidt gave to Dieter. Just as the pistol emerged from Dieter's overalls, Manny stepped forward and immobilized his gun hand while simultaneously delivering a devastating right cross to the German's head, shattering his cheek bone.

Dieter toppled unconscious to the ground, never really knowing what hit him. The un-fired gun fell harmlessly from his grasp, clattering noisily on the concrete floor.

"I forgot just how fast you are," Schmidt commented.

Manny stepped forward, causing Schmidt to flinch and step back. "My work for you is finished now," Manny said, calmly. "My debt has been repaid many times over. If I ever see you again, I'll not hesitate to kill you."

Schmidt said nothing. He simply stood and struggled to appear defiant as Manny turned and left the greenhouse.

Schmidt looked down at the damage to his henchman, who was now moaning in agony on the floor of the greenhouse. This could be more difficult than he anticipated. He would have to find another way of getting rid of the troublesome Latin American. He could not afford to miss again.

Manny walked along the rough wooden planking toward the outermost section of the busy pier. Down below, he could see the slick, shiny grey bodies of three or four dolphins, sliding through the rolling waves. A small Mexican boy suddenly cast his fishing line with the grace of a new-born buffalo, almost catching the clothing of the old-time angler next to him with a loosely-baited hook. From the edges of the pier, several barely-visible lines of monofilament curved down into the swirling waters tended by would-be anglers of all sizes and ages.

As Manny reached the pier terminus, a mid-sized brown pelican settled onto the flat wooden railing in front of him with a slow, dramatic flutter of wings. Manny stepped to the side, giving the creature its space, and looked down into the green murky depths of the timeless Pacific. His mind processed the events that had just occurred in the greenhouse. The attempt on his life told him everything he needed to know. He pulled the cell phone from his pocket and punched at the key pad rapidly sending a single-worded text message:

NOW.

He prayed it was not too late. He looked at his Seiko Black Dive Watch and watched 25 seconds tick by. Then his phone beeped, prompting the pelican to take off in an ungainly spasm of its long wings. Manny gazed at the screen and noted the simple reply:

OK.

Chapter 44

Airspace over Nevada
July 15, 2007

"Man this is the only way to travel."

"David, if you say that one more time I might just get airsick all over you," Lori threatened from the seat next to him.

David flinched in mock alarm and quickly inched away from the potential splash zone. Lori had a valid point but no one was going to take this away from David. His eyes still shone with excitement as he craned his neck to take in the luxurious passenger cabin of the Gulfstream 200 once again. He patted the armrest of his almond-coloured leather chair as if it was a faithful Labrador. The spacious interior was fitted elegantly with 8 identical passenger chairs, in front- and aft-facing configurations, along with a three-place leather divan that was moulded perfectly to the arched starboard cabin wall. The remainder of the cabin was tastefully finished with cream-coloured leather headliner and sidewalls, sleek polished burl elm side-panels and tables, and a light diagonal diamond-patterned wool carpet. The amenities featured a full service galley, an enclosed aft lavatory and an entertainment and communications system that included TV monitors, DVD and video players, a telephone and high-speed internet access. David turned and gazed out the window at the spectacular shoreline of Lake Mead and muttered loud enough to be heard over the high-pitched whine of the engines, "I've got to get me one of these."

Lori shook her head in a 'what-are-we-going-to-do-with-him' fashion.

Hawkins announced, "I think we need to go over our plan."

"So you're finally gonna tell us what's going on?" David asked.

"We're going to visit a plant nursery."

"Huh?" David grunted.

Lori said nothing.

"First thing we need –"

Hawkins stopped speaking when he noticed the stewardess approaching from the rear of the jet with a cell phone in her hand.

"Sorry to interrupt Dr Hawkins," the stewardess said while handing him the telephone. "Inspector Sanderson is on the line." The diminutive woman smiled and returned to the rear of the cabin.

Hawkins immediately felt a knot of disquiet tightening in the pit of his stomach as he stood, moved to the front of the cabin and raised the phone to his ear. Sanderson wouldn't call unless something had happened.

"G'day Inspector, how are things in Old Blighty?" he ventured.

"Hello Dr Hawkins," Sanderson's voice sounded strained. "I'll come straight to the point. There has been a break in at your house. The perpetrator entered through the back door."

Hawkins felt ill. *His house?* Fearing the worst he asked, "how's my dog? Is Brandy okay?"

"Just fine," Sanderson said, quickly easing Hawkins' anxiety. "In fact, she's the one who actually caught the would-be thief before he could do anything. She must have been on him as soon as he came through the door."

Hawkins smiled at that. "She has been known to jump up on people from time to time."

"You don't say? We found her standing on the man's chest when we entered the premises. He was so petrified he looked moments away from cardiac arrest."

"She probably just wanted some attention. Was he hurt?"

"Not as such. His ribs were a bit bruised where she stood on him and his head was completely drenched in drool. There may also be a little bit of emotional scarring, and we don't think he likes dogs anymore, if he ever really did. But of course that's the least of his worries now."

"Did you find out who he was working for?"

"We're still questioning him about that. So far he hasn't said anything else but the repeated words 'grosser Hund'. Apparently it means –"

"– big dog," Hawkins finished for him. "German. He must be working with the same people who stole the seeds."

"That's the angle we're working on."
"So I gather he didn't find anything?"
"Well...," Sanderson hesitated, "there was one problem."
"But he couldn't have had any time –"
"Not the burglar."
"You mean...?"
"Brandy. She must have been hungry."

As the plane made its final approach into Santa Barbara Municipal Airport, Hawkins picked up where he left off. "We're going to pay a visit to the Los Hermanos Plant Nursery. That's where the seeds were taken."

"How could you possibly know that?" Lori asked.

"Yeah," David added. "Did we miss something?"

Hawkins thought this was a good time to come clean. "I planted a microdot GPS tracer in one of the seeds taken by Rodriguez."

After a moment of stunned silence, David said, "so that's what you were fiddling with in the back of the taxi on the way to the warehouse."

Hankins said nothing.

"But I don't understand," Lori said. "Where did you get this device from?"

"The NSA."

"But we didn't even meet Agent Jones until after we got to the warehouse," Lori said.

"It was before that, in Lompoc."

Lori and David looked blank.

"I suspected someone was watching me so I planted breadcrumbs at key locations in my hotel room before I went out. When I returned I discovered that almost all of these had been disturbed."

"You made a low budget burglar detector?" David asked.

"Yes," Hawkins said. "But they were not burglars. In fact, their intentions were to leave something there – tracking and listening devices. After discovering they had been in my room, it was only a matter of time to uncover where they had placed these. Then I appropriated two of the tracers for my own use."

"So why were the NSA following you?" Lori asked.

"Because they believed that I could eventually lead them to the people who took the seeds."

"So the US government is in on this?" David asked.

"Yes, as a matter of national interest. Agent Jones actually told us that in the warehouse."

"But why?" David persisted.

"I think they were mostly interested in ensuring the seeds didn't fall into the wrong hands."

"How do you know all this?" David asked. "Are you some kind of spy or something?"

"No, just an archaeologist."

David looked doubtful. "So what else can you tell us?"

"Well, I'm fairly certain that most of our e-mails and telephone conversations have been monitored from the beginning."

David and Lori looked as if Hawkins had just told them he was from outer space.

"They can do that?" David asked, amazed.

"Yes, and they have been able to since the Cold War years," Hawkins said. "They can intercept all electronic and digital forms of communication almost anywhere in the world. They have probably been on to our discovery since Stanley first notified William Merrick with his e-mail message."

"They can really listen in on all of our private telephone calls and read our e-mails?" David asked in an exasperated tone.

"Yes, but they probably only do so for a select few," Hawkins answered. "All of the captured communications are searched by powerful computers for the use of combinations of key words and phrases, such as bomb, White House, invention and discovery. Most ordinary messages would actually pass through the system and remain un-flagged since they would not be of interest to national or international security."

Lori asked, "how about the people who stole the seeds? How did they find out?"

"I'm guessing that they either had someone working inside the intelligence network or they somehow managed to breach the system," Hawkins said.

"And you knew about this all along?" David asked with a puzzled expression on his face. "But you made telephone calls to us and sent e-mails containing sensitive information. Wouldn't they have intercepted those too?"

Realisation suddenly dawned on Lori. "That was part of the plan. He knew they were listening and fed them misleading information."

Again, Hawkins said nothing.

"So that's how they found out the last batch of seeds were fake," David said. And that's how they knew Lori and I brought the real seeds with us to Washington DC."

When Hawkins didn't respond immediately, another thought occurred to Lori. "We didn't bring the real seeds did we?"

"No," he said apologetically. "They weren't real."

"You used us and the seeds to lure the bad guys out in the open," David said. "Sneaky!"

"It was the only plan I could come up with on short notice," Hawkins offered. "Sanderson and I hid the real seeds in the bottom of one of Brandy's bags of dog food. But after the attempted burglary, Sanderson checked on our stash and discovered that Brandy managed to break into the Pantry where the bags are stored, tore the bag to shreds and ate every single morsel inside. Nothing resembling a seed was left."

David said, "guess that means you'll be following her around the garden for a few days with a plastic baggie."

"What about your last telephone call from Inspector Sanderson?" Lori asked. "Aren't you worried that they will find out the real seeds are in your house…I mean in your dog?"

"It's unlikely," Hawkins said. "That call was made over a secure iridium system with end-to-end encryption."

David looked thoughtful. "You are a spy."

Chapter 45

Cambridge, England
July 14, 2007

    The 8-man crew drove back hard with their legs propelling the sleek craft smoothly up the River Cam. Sanderson marvelled at the skill involved just in maintaining the balance of the carbon fibre boat while the long and lean occupants worked in unison like a multi-limbed organism to power it through the water in sync with shouted instructions from the slender female coxswain nestled in the rear. From Sanderson's vantage point atop the bridge, the long white boat resembled a giant stick insect flicking along the partly algae-matted surface of the river.
    The Midsummer Common footbridge near the Fort St George Pub was one of Sanderson's favourite spots along the river. There was just something about looking down on the slowly flowing water that calmed his mind. Maybe it was because of the slight difference in perspective afforded by the unique angle on the river that enabled him to concentrate more easily on the smallest of details and come up with previously unseen connections. At this moment in time, he was concentrating very hard. It was that house on Cavendish Road again. He sensed that he was missing something important.
    Another boat passed under the bridge, again crewed by 8 men but this time with a small male coxswain. They appeared to be winding down from a short and furious sprint, most likely after practicing their start from a dead stop. Most of the boats on the river were out honing their racing tactics in preparation for the Town Bumps which would be taking place the following week. Sanderson watched as the slowing boat narrowly missed cutting through several ducks.
    Just then, his thoughts were disturbed by the muted dulcet tones of Beethoven's *Fur Elise* emanating from his coat pocket. He snatched his cell phone quickly and noted from the screen that the caller was Sergeant Condron. He gently pushed TALK

with his thumb, held the phone up to his ear and said, "hi Matt, whaddayagot?"

"Just routine Chief. We finally got the list of all the residents who stayed in the house on Cavendish Road. It goes back 4 decades."

"Anything of interest," Sanderson probed.

"Don't think so, Sir. The records show what appears to be a list of bogus or assumed names but, of course, we're digging deeper."

"Why do you think the names are bogus?"

"We've run down a few of them who were in fact scholars, but none of them have ever been to the UK. There are also a few other names that belong to Celebrities."

"And you're sure that none of them have ever stayed there?"

"Not unless you think big shots like Chris Tarrant and Simon Cowell would slum it in a dingy Victorian house on Cavendish Road."

"Point taken."

"However, there was one other name, a home-grown celeb, who was associated with the house for 6 months during 1967."

"What was the name?" Sanderson murmured, only partly focussing on what Condron was saying.

"Oh, it was that Professor who does the program about digging up Britain's past...."

"You don't mean –?"

"Yes. Let me see.... I don't really watch the show myself...."

Sanderson could hear papers rustling as Condron searched for the name. His gut was wrenching.

"Here it is," Condron said. "Chap named Stanley Green."

Chapter 46

Santa Barbara, California
July 15, 2007

The spotless Lincoln Town Car limousine pulled into the unpaved parking lot of the Los Hermanos Plant Nursery, drawing the attention of some late shoppers like moths to a flame. The 'celebrity effect' took over as most of the customers stopped dead in their tracks so they might catch a glimpse of a local superstar. However, an audible groan spread throughout the small crowd when they saw the elderly Mediterranean-looking driver emerge from the car who opened the near door for the three ordinary passengers in the rear. These were nobodies. The two non-descript but good looking male passengers wore jeans and bright-coloured tee shirts while the attractive surfer-chick wore tight white trousers topped by a turquoise blouse.

"Shouldn't we have guns or something?"

Hawkins looked at David for a long moment and said, "you'd probably end up shooting yourself in the foot."

"And I would probably end up shooting him in the foot," Lori said, continuing the dialogue from a Hollywood film from the 1980s that none of them could quite remember the name of.

Hawkins smiled. He recognized the nervous banter that was commonplace for troops on the eve of battle. He had experienced it first-hand several years before. He just hoped for a better outcome on this occasion. "Just be careful at all times. We're not really sure who or what we're dealing with here."

"Which is why we should shoot first and ask questions later," David said, persisting with the gun strategy.

"You must have seen too many John Wayne films when you were growing up," Hawkins commented.

"Actually... it was *Roadrunner* cartoons," David replied.

"That explains everything."

Lori went straight to the main reception area of the nursery accompanied by Vincent Magliatti. The ex-SEAL had insisted on staying by her side during the potentially dangerous mission. He had a daughter who was around the same age as Lori. Ordinarily he would have relaxed his guard when he saw the two young Latin American women who were on duty behind the registers. But his SEAL instincts remained on high alert.

"Hello! Welcome to Los Hermanos," the nearest of the two girls exclaimed. "How can we help you today?"

Lori was momentarily taken aback. She had forgotten how overly-friendly Americans could be when greeting customers in commercial shops. She had unknowingly become acclimatised to the less sociable British approach during her short time in Cambridge. "Is the manager or owner here today?"

The second girl looked with undisguised suspicion at Lori. "Do you have a complaint or something?"

"Oh no," Lori answered quickly. "I just need to speak to someone about shipping in some foreign plants." She tried to keep her request general but out of the ordinary so the girl would accept that it needed to be dealt with by somebody with a greater authority.

From the attendant's expression Lori could tell that she had approached this in the right way. "Well...," the girl began, "the manager is off the site right now but the owner of the nursery just happens to be visiting from Switzerland. Maybe you could talk to him about this?"

At the mention of Switzerland, Lori's blood turned cold. A short, "yes please," was all she could manage.

"I'll call him for you," the girl offered. She picked up the telephone and tapped out a 3-digit extension. After speaking briefly with someone on the end of the line she hung up and said, "Mister Schmidt will see you now. He's in the office right behind this building."

Hawkins and David headed for the small greenhouse on the edge of the nursery grounds, the location of the stolen seeds. Hawkins knew this through the assistance of Agent Jones, who had used the cellular modem and high-resolution satellite imagery to localize the signal from the GPS micro-tracer that Hawkins had planted in one of the seeds.

They made their way around medium-sized greenhouses, display areas and a number of plant shoppers. When they reached the apparent edge of the nursery's grounds, their forward progress was impeded by a locked Cyclone fence topped by razor wire. The greenhouse stood about 60 feet beyond the fence next to a small red brick utility building.

"Seems they don't want just anybody poking around in there," David observed.

"Hmmm," Hawkins grunted. "Guess we're in the right place."

"What are we gonna do?"

In answer, Hawkins pulled out a pair of heavy duty wire cutters from his back pocket.

"I see you came prepared."

"Don't give me too much of that Boy Scout credit. The fence was obvious from the NSA satellite images."

"Speaking of the NSA," David said, "do they know the seeds in the greenhouse aren't the real ones?"

"I didn't get around to telling them that part. I wanted to make sure we had their cooperation first."

"You're a very deceitful man," David noted.

"Thanks. Now, are you going to help me cut through this fence?"

"What if it's alarmed?"

"David, you should know me by now," Hawkins admonished.

"What?"

"That's what I am counting on."

It happened almost too quickly. It was hard to believe that after all of the difficulties that they had been through that they had found the man they had been looking for just by asking a few simple questions. At first glance, Mister Schmidt seemed harmless enough, sitting almost delicately at his desk across from her and Vince. He was thin and slightly pale with a youthful look. He appeared to be completely unimposing. That is, until one looked in his eyes. She had the strangest sensation that Schmidt could see right through her. It was almost as if the man had been expecting them to come to the nursery that day. That was the moment Lori realised that this little ploy of theirs could end very badly. Maybe she should just make up some excuse and she and Vince would walk out of there. But then she remembered that this could actually be the man who was ultimately responsible for the killing of Pavlos, Zoran, Agent Reeves and countless others. Just as she was about to say something she realised that Schmidt was speaking.

"I hear that you are interested in importing some special plants from abroad," he opened in a cordial business-like tone.

Lori decided to go with the plan that Hawkins had outlined on the final portion of their journey to Santa Barbara. "Yes, trees."

Schmidt's eyes narrowed at this. "Trees?"

It didn't escape Lori's attention that this struck a nerve. So far, Hawkins' plan appeared to be working. "Yes, we're looking to bring in some Judean date palms."

Schmidt appeared to be almost scowling now. "You are mistaken. The Judean date palm has been extinct for two millennia."

Lori was aware of this. Her statement had been designed to provoke a telling response. The potential problem was it might be working too well.

"However, there are now a few of those trees in existence thanks to the amazing achievement of Israeli scientists who managed to cultivate some of the preserved seeds found in the Arabah desert. That makes these the oldest known seeds ever to be successfully cultivated. But, of course, this doesn't even come close to what you and your colleagues achieved using seeds several thousand years older, found in the Aryan tomb in England, Dr Davis."

How stupid of her not to realise that he would know about her. He must have known straight away who she was despite her now seemingly childish idea of introducing herself by a false name. Her heart became a drum. She looked across at Vince and saw that he was starting to rise from his chair. The big man had also realised that the jig was up.

Almost at the same time, the door burst open and two men rushed into the room brandishing silenced pistols. Vince moved like a speeding freight train to the nearest gunman, grabbed his gun hand and drove his elbow upwards into the man's nose. The effect was instantaneous as the shattered fragments of nasal bone and cartilage were driven into the frontal lobe of the man's brain and he collapsed like a 230-pound rag doll on the hard wooden floor. But the years had dulled Vince's reflexes. He turned toward the second man and moved to draw out his own service revolver from the holster mounted below his right kidney when he realised it wouldn't be fast enough. The man's sleek pistol suddenly spat out two slugs of deadly poison which tore into Vince's chest and neck.

Lori watched in horror as the kindly man who had sworn to protect her fell to the floor, rolled onto his back and looked up at her with apologetic eyes. He issued his last gasp of gurgling breath through the hole in his neck and died side-by-side with the first gunman. She swallowed the bile rising in her throat and saw that the man who had shot Vince was now pointing the same pistol directly at her.

Never having moved from his chair, Schmidt said, "it was good of you to come right to me my dear. I thought we were going to have to come looking for you. I wonder if your other friends are here as well."

Lori didn't speak. They had disastrously underestimated their opponent. She was disgusted to note that Mister Schmidt didn't seem to be concerned in the slightest that Vince and one of his own faithful bodyguards were now lying dead, spilling dark red blood onto the floorboards.

Hawkins used the wire cutters diligently to create a large L shape in the Cyclone fence. Just as the task was completed, an announcement came over a Tannoy loudspeaker system stating that Los Hermanos Plant Nursery would soon be closing and would all patrons kindly make their way to the cash register with their purchases. Hawkins pulled the loose section away from the fence allowing David to scurry through, then climbed in after him. According to their newly-hatched plan, Hawkins moved toward the greenhouse and David ran to the outbuilding.

Hawkins found the greenhouse door unlocked and entered swiftly. He was surprised at how small the space appeared now that he was on the inside. He noticed that it was occupied by a small tree along with several small pots that appeared to have been freshly-planted with something. *The seeds?* Then his attention flicked back to the strange tree, bearing the small yellow fruits. *Could it be?*

He didn't have time to ponder the significance of what he was looking at any further as saw through the translucent panes of glass that David was smashing through the padlocked door of the outbuilding using a medium-sized stone. Hawkins saw the broken lock fall to the floor and he watched David successfully open the door. He turned back to the tree for another look when he noticed out of the corner of his eye that David remained standing stock-still in the now opened doorway of the utility building.

Hawkins left the greenhouse and found David gazing into the outbuilding with his hands on his hips, shaking his head in apparent confusion.

"What's in there?" Hawkins said from behind.

David turned and looked at his mentor. "Just some standard garden tools, a couple of gasoline drums, a plastic container of motor oil, an industrial-sized lawn mower, some large burlap sacks containing God-knows-what and a cobweb-covered case containing a dozen empty bottles of that crappy German wine, Liebfraumilch."

"That's all?" Hawkins asked.

"Oh yeah... and a little old lady with a bag on her head."

Chapter 47

Mexico City
July 14, 2007

The noise suppressor, often referred to erroneously as a silencer due to the impression that it completely 'silences' any firearm, was screwed slowly onto the Mk 12 SPR sniper rifle. In reality, the cylindrical attachment only reduced the sound of most weapons to a pneumatic snapping noise, similar to that of a powerful staple gun. And then the supersonic ammunition used in this case produces additional noise in the form of a small sonic crack when the projectile breaks the sound barrier during its flight to the target. But this did not worry the shooter.

The suppressor had other benefits besides noise reduction. And these were important to him. It also dispersed the sound and reduced flash from the muzzle of the rifle by as much as 90 percent making it difficult for anyone to pinpoint the source of the bullet. Thus, the suppressor did not make the sniper silent, but it did make them relatively invisible.

With a muzzle velocity of 3,000 feet per second, the 5.56 × 45 mm NATO cartridge with the military ball bullet can penetrate approximately 15 inches into soft tissue under ideal circumstances. Only two rounds were loaded into the rifle's magazine, the shooter was that sure of his abilities. He slowly focussed the Mid-Range/Tactical Illuminated Reticle Dayscope mounted on the weapon. After 6 seconds the crosshairs were locked on the target. "Like shooting fish in a barrel," he whispered to himself.

The sights were adjusted once more. The rifle barrel moved, tracking the target. The operator breathed gently in and then out. His forefinger squeezed the trigger gently.

Isabel Gonzalez scrubbed vigorously to remove the slightly-encrusted rice from the large iron pan. The non-stick receptacle was not living up to advertised potential. But she never let that sort of thing disturb her. She was happy. Family nights like this were special to her. The paella had been a big hit, as it always was, with her two teenage daughters Maria and Anna, and with her wonderful husband Jorge who she had now been blessed with for almost 20 years. Now that dinner was finished, Maria and Anna would spend the next hour or so grinding through their homework and Jorge would be camped in front of the television watching *Boxeo Mexico*. It was more or less the same every Thursday night. Perhaps later they would all play some poker before the girls' bedtime.

She gazed out through the kitchen window at her reflected image as she often did when reminiscing. She could see that there were only a few lights on in the brown apartment block directly across the way. She thought for a moment that she had just seen a flash of light from a window somewhere above her but it was probably just her imagination or a reflection from a passing automobile.

Then she heard the sounds of the boxing program from the salon. Of course this brought back memories of her youth and the teenage boy that had helped her and the others so long ago. It had changed everything. It was amazing that life had turned out so good for her after such unpromising beginnings. God had blessed her.

The high velocity round tunnelled through the night air and entered the target's head just above the left ear blowing out the other side of the head in a heterogeneous spray of blood, bone and brain tissue.

Chapter 48

Santa Barbara, California
July 15, 2007

Wolfgang Huber noticed the amber light flashing silently beneath the monitor. The fence of the secure compound had been breached. He notified Schmidt immediately but was surprised by his leader's seemingly calm response. It was almost as if the man had been expecting something like this to happen. Schmidt had ordered Wolfgang and another man named Carl to the enclosure to deal with the infiltrators. The last man, Dieter, would remain behind to help Schmidt watch the girl.

Hawkins peered past David into the building. From the small amount of light coming through the now open door, he could make out most of the building's contents. It was exactly as David had said, including the little old lady with a bag on her head. She was tucked away in a corner, sitting on a crude vinyl-covered chair with a coarse burlap sack pulled down over her head. Her ankles and wrists were tied by a thin rope to a metal support post that ran from the ceiling to the floor. Her upright posture and shallow breathing told Hawkins that she was still alive. Hawkins stepped inside and told David to keep an eye out.

David nodded and manoeuvred to a position just inside the door frame, giving himself a panoramic view of the compound.

Hawkins squatted down in front of the woman and pulled the sack gently from her head. Now freed from the slightly putrid covering, her deeply wrinkled eyes blinked rapidly and then morphed into a tight squint against the harsh light penetrating the building from the outside world. Hawkins felt his blood boil when he saw that a thick strip of duct tape had been plastered firmly over her mouth. With the utmost care he reached for the corner of the tape and began to peel it away. He was surprised to see her regarding him with eyes that were unafraid. "Mrs Sullivan?" he ventured as he carefully pulled the tape from her mouth and dropped it to the ground.

"Why yes, how did you know?" the woman said in a subdued squeaky voice.

"I've been looking for you."

"Did Brian send you?"

"That's right."

"I hope he's been okay. That man's completely helpless without me to look after him."

Hawkins smiled. "I'm sure he'll be alright now."

"Looks like your friends are here," Schmidt gloated.

Lori said nothing. She was being watched closely by the man who had killed Vince. She couldn't help but wonder how the beastly man had acquired the contusion to his cheek bone but she took some pleasure in the fact that it was newly acquired and obviously painful. His left eye twitched constantly and he frequently brought up his hand to touch the bruised area.

Schmidt continued, "it is fitting that you should all die together considering the trouble you have caused me."

Lori remained silent.

Although he appeared to be in complete control of the situation, Schmidt was worried. There was something about this Dr Hawkins that unnerved him. He had never met anyone who was so hard to kill. The archaeologist had already managed to escape certain death situations at the hands of his henchmen not once, but three times. Then there was that crazy student of his, who had already survived a beating from Manny and a gunshot wound to the head. The two of them seemed to have as many lives as a cat.

Through the translucent glass panels of the greenhouse, David could see two men dressed in blue overalls and brandishing weapons, moving forward. It looked to him as if they had been cast from the same mould with similar powerful-looking physiques and identical short haircuts.

David alerted Hawkins to their presence with a single word. "Trouble."

Hawkins looked unperturbed. "How many?"

"Two, with pistols."

Hawkins turned to Mrs Sullivan and assured her that everything would be okay. Then he asked her to move back into the corner away from the door.

"If you've got any clever ideas, now would be a good time," David interrupted.

Hawkins paused a bit too long for David's current state of unease. Then he said, "how are you at making cocktails?"

"What... like Margaritas?" David asked, incredulous.

"No. The Molotov variety."

"Petrol bombs?"

"Why not? We've got everything we need right here."

David looked around at the contents of the well-stocked shed and nodded in understanding. "You got it Wiley Coyote. Let's blow up some stuff!"

"Doesn't the Coyote usually blow himself up?" Hawkins replied.

Carl and Wolfgang crept to the edge of the greenhouse and found it empty of trespassers. Both men were seasoned veterans, having a total of 15 kills between them over the 6 years that they had worked for Schmidt and the organization. Almost in tune with each other, they looked beyond the glass structure and saw that the door of the utility building, where they had left the old lady to die, was wide open. With a wave of his pistol, Carl motioned to Wolfgang to move in. They crept around the greenhouse and began to edge forward.

David leapt from the building and flung the first fire bomb with all his strength. Given its low trajectory, the flaming bottle skipped off the hard ground between the two gunmen like a stone skimming over water and crashed into the greenhouse shattering an entire side panel. The bottle itself did not break immediately until it struck the internal concrete floor, splattering the gasoline that it contained over an amazingly wide area. Bright orange flames tinged with black smoke erupted around the newly-planted tubs.

The reaction of the two gunmen was well-disciplined. Although the flaming petrol bomb had only narrowly missed them, they both dropped immediately to the ground and let loose with a barrage of gunfire at the doorway of the brick building with their Heckler and Koch pistols. Most of the bullets struck the outside of the door frame, chipping away sizable chunks of the brick wall. Only two of the shots made it in through the door but no one inside the building was hit.

"This reminds me of that final scene from Butch Cassidy and the Sundance Kid," David said. "You know the one where the two of them are taking cover in a barn and they're being shot at by the whole Bolivian army, just before they were both killed?"

Hawkins pointed out, "this is just two guys. And we're not gonna die. That is, if you learn how to throw these things right."

"That's the way I was taught to throw a cricket ball, low and hard."

"You need to get more arc into it so the bottle shatters when it hits."

"Got it," David acknowledged, "more arc."

Hawkins reached down to pick up a 'cocktail' and David did the same. "You first," Hawkins offered. "Aim for the one on the right. I'll take the one on the left."

David nodded, lit the rag using Hawkins' packet of hotel matches, jumped from the doorway again and let loose a powerful throw at a steep upward angle of around 45 degrees. The result was spectacular. He had thrown the bomb high enough, but he had thrown it too far. The flaming bottle sailed over the gunmen and smashed through one of top panels of the greenhouse. It shattered as it impacted the greenhouse's concrete floor. The resulting eruption of flames spread toward the tree. He summed up his latest effort. "Crap!"

As Wolfgang turned to look at the developing inferno within the greenhouse, Carl fired three more shots that only hit the doorframe of the outbuilding. Just then he saw a man dart into the open doorway and launch another bottle in their direction. Carl squeezed off one more shot and then watched in horror as the flaming weapon came soaring through the air, targeting the rocky ground directly in front of him.

The bullet fired by Carl's gun tore through the fabric of Hawkins' shirt burning a small gash through the skin of his triceps muscle. The grazing wound stung but Hawkins barely registered the pain. The glass bottle shattered on the stones about three feet in front of the man who had shot at him, causing hundreds of pieces of gravel and the flaming fuel to splatter directly onto the man's face, shoulders and upper torso.

As if possessed by a fire demon, the stricken man sprung up from his prostrate position on the ground and emitted a blood-curdling banshee-like scream and began to flail about in search of a way to extinguish himself.

The other gunman now struggled to maintain his composure. He looked on and shuddered as his partner fell back to the ground and writhed in agony as he was consumed by the flames. In one surprisingly humane act in the life of a brutal killer, he fired two bullets into his partner's head to end the suffering. Then he turned and ran back to the burning greenhouse, pulled out his cell phone and pressed a single button.

For a second, Lori thought Schmidt was suffering from a major stroke. A moment earlier, she watched him pick up the telephone on the desk after a single ring. He had begun speaking with someone when his jaw stopped moving and his eyes began to bulge. Then he started making an unintelligible gurgling noise and his face turned bright red. "Get to the tree!" he shrieked. "It is more important than your own life." He slammed the telephone down and appeared to look around the room for someone to shoot.

Having a good idea that she could be the likely target, Lori shrank back into her chair and tried to become invisible.

After looking like he was still capable of spontaneous human combustion, Schmidt let off some steam by knocking a small cage containing a mouse to the floor and then he appeared to make up his mind about something. He turned to the other man and said, "Dieter. Carl is dead and the greenhouse is on fire."

"Should we call the fire department?" Dieter asked.

"No, idiot! We have to tend to it ourselves. Go now! I will follow with the girl."

Dieter grunted his acknowledgement and made for the door.

Schmidt turned and looked back at Lori with eyes that could ignite paper. He pulled her roughly upright and pressed a sinister-looking knife against the side of her neck so the razor-sharp point was on the verge of breaking skin. As the knife flashed past her eyes, she thought she saw an image of a red swastika on the black handle.

Schmidt spun her around so he was now behind her with the knife still pressed against her neck and said, "if anything happens to that tree, you will feel this knife slice through your carotid artery. Then you will feel nothing at all."

Lori had no doubts that Schmidt meant every word as he roughly escorted her out of the office onto the grounds of the now deserted nursery. She breathed a sigh of relief that he hadn't appeared to notice that a small scalpel-like box cutter, which had been lying on his desk, was no longer there.

Hawkins and David watched as the frantic man ran into the greenhouse, which was rapidly becoming a blazing inferno. Hawkins suddenly realised what the man's intentions were. "David, cover me! I've got to get in there."

"Are you crazy?"

"Probably."

"What about me?"

Hawkins said, "take care of Mrs Sullivan… watch out for more bad guys."

In response, David stooped and picked up another fuel bomb.

Chapter 49

Mexico City
July 14, 2007

The discordant wail of police sirens cut through the night. It was a sound that was heard all too often in the heart of Mexico City where 8 million people clustered tightly together for their daily sustenance. The long-term residents had become accustomed to the bustling, chaotic city and its high rate of crime, although most were still unnerved by the constant reminder of the crimes committed on their own doorsteps.

Isabel Gonzalez had come close to dying that night. She had heard the loud crack followed by the dull thumping sound of flesh and bone crumpling onto the hard balcony floor. A tall Caucasian man dressed in black lay dead on the terrace outside her kitchen window. Dark coagulating blood, fragments of skull and pink brain matter had sprayed in a diffuse splatter over her favourite potted flowers and the ivory white tiled surface of the balcony. A handgun lay just beyond the body's fingertips, under the white plastic deck chair that she had used two hours before in catching the last warming rays of the evening sun. Tears rolled down her cheeks as she gazed at the horrible reminder that the world could sometimes be a terrible place.

Jorge gently rubbed her shoulders and offered soothing words of comfort. She touched his hand to let him know she was okay and then sat down on the small kitchen chair. She waited anxiously for the moment when the girls completed their studies. They would soon emerge innocently from their bedrooms and discover this scene from hell. Perhaps Jorge could head them off. But the police would soon be there. She shuddered as she asked herself the questions once again. *Why had this man been on their balcony? Why did he have a gun? And who had killed him?* She wondered if she would ever know.

Francisco Espinosa sped down Avenida Chapultepec in the crimson Alfa Romeo Spyder Veloce. The case containing the disassembled weapon rested diagonally across the black bucket passenger seat. He was careful not to exceed the speed limit and risk calling attention to himself. He felt at ease now he had passed the remains of the colonial era aqueduct on the left side of the road. He had put enough distance between himself and the apartment block. His pulse had finally returned to its normal rate of around 60 beats per minute, although it had never really risen much higher than that.

Around a minute later, he turned into a small side street and eased the car to a stop. The centuries-old forest and castle crowning the summit of Chapultepec hill loomed in the distance, silhouetted against a crimson sky tempered with wisps of purple clouds. At the foot of the hill, a cluster of massive Cyprus trees swayed gently in the evening breeze. He left the car idling and pulled out his cell phone.

Francisco had watched the assassin climb the three stories on the outside of the plain brown apartment block up to the balcony. Then he observed the man watching and waiting for the right moment to carry out his deadly task, just as Francisco waited for his. The same man had been given the order to kill two others that night. All three of the targets had one thing in common – they had been friends of Manuel Rodriguez a long time ago. Francisco knew all of this because he was one of the three. But he had guessed correctly that Isabel would be the first target because she had meant so much to Manny. And there was no doubt in Francisco's mind that a man like Schmidt would have known this. The CIA Special Projects agent slowly tapped the too small keys on the tiny cell phone, composing his short message. Then he pressed send.

DONE.

He breathed a long sigh of relief and tucked the phone away. The rest was now up to Manny. He gently eased the car into gear and disappeared into the night.

Chapter 50

Santa Barbara, California
July 15, 2007

Hawkins sprinted toward the body of the dead gunman. After skidding gracefully to a stop on the loose stones, he tried not to look at the man's still smouldering corpse as he searched for his objective – the gun. It wasn't in plain sight so he reasoned with some disquiet that it must be lying under the man's grotesquely-burned carcass. He had just steeled his nerves for the gruesome task of turning the charred remains over when something occurred to him. It was unlikely that the man had been in a state of mind to hold on to his weapon while he was running around like a burning torch. So he dashed to the position where the man had been lying prior to being struck by the fire bomb. The gun was there!

Hawkins knew something about firearms. This particular model was issued two years after he had left the service but it was still basically familiar to him. The Heckler and Koch USP 40 had a magazine capacity of 13 cartridges. After a quick estimate of how many shots had been fired, he guessed that there were at least three bullets left. He hefted the weapon and dashed toward the burning greenhouse.

Wolfgang Huber questioned his own sanity as he stood beside the raging inferno. The normally hot interior of the greenhouse was made even more unbearable due to the additional heat generated by the spreading flames. The large number of wooden benches, tubs and tools inside the structure merely added fuel to the fire, and the tree was in imminent danger of being consumed.

When Wolfgang was younger, he had been a reserve fireman for the Santa Barbara County Fire Department. Despite that experience, the only means that he could come up with to fight this fire were the two small black extinguishers mounted just inside the entrance of the greenhouse. One of the cylinders had a green triangular symbol on it, indicating that it was a 'type A' water extinguisher. He knew that it would be risky using this against a combustible hydrocarbon-based fire, since the compressed water it ejected would most likely cause the flames to spread. Instead he grabbed the 'type B' foam-based extinguisher marked with the red square, pulled the release pin and stepped toward the flames. Just as he began spraying, the man he had been shooting at burst through the door behind him holding Carl's gun. Wolfgang immediately stopped spraying and thought about reaching for his own weapon.

"Keep going," the man said waving the pistol. "You're doing just fine."

Wolfgang considered his options. Then he nodded, turned back to the fire and resumed spraying. Others would be coming soon anyway.

From his vantage point inside the utility building, David saw another man in blue overalls running headlong into the compound on the far side of the greenhouse. The man was holding a gun and looked determined to use it. His destination was unmistakable, the greenhouse. David needed to warn Hawkins. He could only think of one way.

He had to get this one right. This time, he needed to actually throw the fuel bomb completely over the greenhouse or he could end up adding to the danger that his mentor was already facing. But David was worried because the first two that he had thrown appeared to be drawn to the greenhouse as if the glass structure was a giant bottle magnet.

He closed his eyes, took a deep breath and pictured the throw ahead of time. He opened his eyes and lit the petrol-soaked rag that he had used to stopper the bottle. Then, employing a bowler's run-up to gain the maximum momentum, he flung the flaming cocktail as hard as he could.

Hawkins watched as the tall blonde-haired man used up the last contents of the small extinguisher on the raging fire. The man's efforts had been mostly wasted as the spray had only seemed to redistribute the existing flames without greatly diminishing them. If anything, the heat from the blaze now seemed more intense than ever. It was also becoming more difficult to breathe since the air inside the greenhouse had grown choked with poisonous black smoke from the burning plant pots.

Hawkins noticed that some of the leaves and the base of the tree itself were beginning to erupt in flames. The small tree didn't stand a chance. "Quick, use the hose to wet the tree!" Hawkins coaxed the man. He hoped that this might offer some protection and prevent the tree from being burned too severely.

Surprisingly, the man took the order from Hawkins without question. He dropped the now empty foam extinguisher and ran through the spreading flames for the long coiled hose pipe attached to the sink spout in the rear of the greenhouse. He turned the water on and pressed his thumb into the emerging stream at the end of the hose to generate more pressure. Then he systematically began to douse the leaves of the tree with the stream of water while he looked nervously around at the blazing firestorm. It would be suicide to remain in there much longer.

Hawkins now saw that the situation was hopeless. To make matters worse he had just noticed something else. A stack of bags containing fertiliser lay directly in the path of the advancing flames. This could be disastrous due to the explosive potential of fertiliser with its typically high content of combustible organic matter and nitrates. Hawkins' newfound worries were interrupted by the sound of breaking glass and the whoosh of a small explosion outside the greenhouse.

Dieter caught a glimpse of the flying bomb through the corner of his eye just before it struck. The bottle whizzed past his head and shattered on the ground 6 feet behind him. Most of the flaming fuel from the bottle splattered away from him. *What the hell is going on here?* He looked angrily around to see where the homemade bomb had come from when he spied the charred remains of what once was a human body between the greenhouse and the utility shed. *Carl?* Then, just in front of the utility shed, he noticed a man's figure that appeared to be in the final act of throwing something. Dieter's heart stopped. Another bomb was flying toward him.

This one struck the ground and shattered just in front of his right foot. At 31 years of age, Dieter thought he had witnessed or experienced all manner of assaults. He had been shot at, stabbed, punched and kicked. He had even been attacked with a machete on one occasion. But none of that compared with this. Not only did fragments of the shattered bottle tear into his leg like hot burning missiles, but his overalls were engulfed simultaneously in burning gasoline.

He screamed from the immediate, intense agony. The level of pain was like nothing he had ever experienced before. Despite this, he had the presence of mind to throw his gun down, kick his shoes off, drop to the ground and begin pulling the burning overalls from his body. While still screaming, he ripped the burning one-piece garment down and over his feet in what must have been world record time and dashed it away from him. Then he patted and rubbed his bleeding and burning leg with his large hands, smothering the remaining flames. He was okay.

But then he looked up as a shadow moved across the sun to the left of where he was sitting. A young man was standing there with his hands on his hips and he was smiling.

"You know you could get arrested for public indecency dressed like that," the man pointed out in a clipped British accent.

Dieter realised with sudden horror that, in his haste to get out of his burning overalls, he had failed to consider that he was only wearing his brief yellow Betty Boop bikini underwear.

"Especially with legs like those," the man added.

Schmidt approached the compound clutching Lori's shoulder while still holding the knife to her neck. He couldn't believe his eyes. The door to the outbuilding was wide open. There was Carl's horribly burnt body lying dead in the compound. Dieter was sitting on the ground stripped down to a rather effeminate pair of banana yellow underpants. And there was Hawkins' student standing over Dieter. He was sporting a blue tee shirt with the Clint Eastwood expression 'MAKE MY DAY' emblazoned upon it.

But none of this gave him much cause for worry. It was the burning greenhouse that made him snap. Just as he made up his mind to abandon the girl and run foolishly into the burning building, the greenhouse door burst open and Wolfgang staggered out and sagged to his hands and knees. Schmidt gazed in disbelief as his henchman was stricken by a violent hacking cough and then spewed the contents of his stomach on the compound floor. Ten seconds later another man emerged from the greenhouse. Dr Hawkins!

The archaeologist looked to be in better condition than Wolfgang, but he was still coughing uncontrollably. Schmidt saw that Hawkins held a bag in one hand and a gun in the other which he aimed non-to-steadily at Wolfgang.

Schmidt suddenly came to his senses and shouted, "go back inside! Get the tree or the girl dies!" He held Lori tightly from behind and made it clear with physical gestures alone that he wouldn't hesitate to use the knife that he was holding to the side of her neck.

But before Hawkins had any time to decide on his next course of action, the greenhouse was rocked by a series of booming mini-explosions that caused several of the remaining glass panels to shatter outwards.

Schmidt cried out in anguish. "AUTSCH!"

The tree and the new seeds were now certainly destroyed. He let the knife drop away from the girl as his body visibly sagged in defeat. It was over. But Schmidt's feeling of pain was quickly replaced by an uncontrollable rage. His eyes bulged and his hands shook as he brought the knife back up to Lori's neck.

Chapter 51

Santa Barbara, California
July 15, 2007

Manny walked briskly along the undulating palm tree-lined path among the occasional inline skaters, cyclists and joggers. He inhaled deeply the cool evening air that wafted in gently from the harbour. It sharpened his senses and his resolve. He had just received Francisco's single-worded message which told him that the danger had passed, and Isabel was safe. He was now free to act.

His only problem now was transportation. The nursery was a good two miles inland from the beach and he needed to get there fast. But having walked so far along the beach on his stroll, he realised that he would never make it back in time to make use of the rental car he had left at the Hotel Marmonte.

His thoughts were suddenly interrupted by a raucous engine noise. It was then that he took notice of two teenagers on a grassy knoll in front of a tall palm tree. Both were clad in multi-coloured leather gear while they tinkered with a lime-green Kawasaki KX250 dirt bike. One of the boys probed the bike's carburettor with a screwdriver as the other twisted the throttle repeatedly, testing the tone of the small engine. Disbelief was evident on the faces of other beach dwellers in the vicinity at the sheer audacity of the intrusion on their peace and quiet. Indeed, the repetitive, ear-splitting, low- to high-pitched roar would have been irritating almost any time and anywhere.

It was music to Manny's ears. He quickly checked to see how much money he had on him, counted out 10 one hundred dollar bills and strode up to the boys.

"Hi," he said. "I need a big favour."

Chapter 52

Los Angeles International Airport, California
July 15, 2007

Los Angeles International Airport is the 5th busiest airport in the world for passenger traffic. It serves 87 domestic and 69 international destinations in North America, Latin America, Europe, Asia and Oceania. Its location on the Pacific coast, 15 miles south-west of the city of Los Angeles, places it close to some of the major sights of the area such as Hollywood, Universal Studios, Venice Beach and Disneyland. It is also within two hours driving distance of other major Californian coastal cities including San Diego to the south-east and Santa Barbara to the north-west.

Virgin Atlantic Flight 23, an Airbus 340-300, touched down on the two-mile long concrete runway with a squeal of tires and a puff of smoke. The CFM56 Turbo Fan engines whined deeply as the pilot applied reverse thrust, slowing the great metal beast abruptly to a more manageable speed with a nerve-wracking shudder from the flexible airframe. "Welcome to Los Angeles," the British flight attendant announced in the usual cheerful airline hostess manner. "The temperature is 79 degrees Fahrenheit and the local time is 6:47 P.M. Please remain seated until the aircraft has come to a complete stop and the seatbelt sign has been turned off."

Even though he had flown through 8 time zones, Professor Stanley Green felt relaxed and refreshed. The flight from London Heathrow had lasted 11 gruelling hours but he had managed to sleep for most of that in a spacious and comfortable first class cabin seat. It was an easy thing for a man to do if he had a clear conscience. He realised now that he had blundered by sending those e-mails to Merrick about the seeds and several other aspects of the discovery. He had been motivated by the money Merrick had promised. But it would have stopped there. He would never have allowed Merrick Incorporated to come into physical possession of the seeds. That would have severely undermined their plans. So when that Columbo-like Inspector from the Cambridge police force had questioned him, Stanley had convincingly played the part of a simple, yet greedy old scientist. And the fool had believed it.

Neither Sanderson nor Dr Hawkins would have any idea about his past. Stanley's father had fought in the war. He had been a fighter pilot who was killed when his Messerschmitt ME 262 Turbojet was gunned down in April 1945 over Normandy by British Supermarine Spitfires. But Stanislaus Grünberg, who had been only three years-old at the time, always remembered this. When he grew to be a young man, he joined one of the Neo-Nazi movements. His first instincts were to show the world that Hitler was right and that the Germanic people were the true descendants of the master race. But then he met Gerhardt Schmidt, who convinced him that it was best to bide his time and wait for the right moment. That was when Stanislaus changed his name and moved to England. Over the next 40 years, he built up a solid reputation as world-renowned scientist specialising in the ancient civilizations of Biblical times and eventually as a television celebrity on a widely-watched program devoted to unearthing Britain's past. He was ideally positioned to help the organization execute its long term plans.

The Airbus lumbered to the terminal like a drunken elephant. The enormous wings flexed with every bump and dip on the tarmac. As requested, Stanley remained seated until the aircraft lurched to a stop and the overhead light depicting a belt and buckle flicked off. After the 5-minute wait, the doors were opened and he joined the other passengers in shuffling off the aircraft through the angular umbilical-like skyway and into the busy terminal.

Stanley was pleased to see that the queues at passport control were shorter than usual for the entry into the US. He reckoned that he would be through in less than 10 minutes. When his turn came at the counter, the bored inspector scanned his passport and then fingerprinted and photographed him as is now the normal procedure for processing Non-Americans entering the United States. Stanley thought he detected a change in the agent's composure but the processing was completed and the man waved him through.

He breathed a sigh of relief as he walked on, chiding himself for worrying. But he tensed when he saw the two tall men in suits converging on him like heat-seeking missiles.

"Passport please," one of the two men ordered in a neutral tone, his hand outstretched waiting.

"But... I've already been through passport control," Stanley said feebly.

The other agent held up his badge emblazoned with the picture of an angry-looking eagle with a red, white and blue shield across its breast. "National Security Agents," he said robotically.

"What?"

"Your passport, Professor Green!"

After a momentary hesitation Stanley's composure sagged and he proffered the flimsy booklet. Then the agents ushered him away.

Chapter 53

Santa Barbara, California
July 15, 2007

    Lori heard Schmidt roar with rage and she knew that she only had a split second to react. She let gravity take over and dropped to the ground. Immediately she felt the breeze from Schmidt's knife as it sliced through the empty space where her head had been a split second before.
    Not anticipating that his target could be anywhere except impaled on the edge of his knife, Schmidt lost his balance and fell forward.

    Hawkins' heart missed a beat when he saw the knife arcing toward Lori's neck. But, remarkably, Lori escaped by dropping to the ground like a rag doll and she slashed Schmidt's leg with what appeared to be a small knife. Then Hawkins saw the wiry man regain his balance quickly as he looked at Lori in open-mouthed shock. Schmidt pressed one hand to the bleeding wound on his thigh while pointing the knife, almost accusingly, at Lori with his other hand. Without speaking he lunged in for another attempt.
    Hawkins was struck with a sick feeling of helplessness when he realised there was only one hope of saving her. He raised the gun, aimed in the vicinity of the man's torso and squeezed the trigger. Click!
    Empty, he realised with a jolting shock. The gunman had used up all of the bullets after all. In the next heartbeat, he dropped the gun, stuffed the bag that he had been holding into his coat pocket and ran toward Lori at a full sprint. He wouldn't get there in time.

    At the same instant, and about 100 feet away, David quickly considered going for the gun lying near the man sporting the bikini underwear. But by the time he reached it and worked out how to fire the damn thing, it would be too late. He had to do something else. "Hey, Betty Boop!" he called to the man.

Dieter looked up at David but said nothing.

"Sit tight!" David suddenly crouched low and punched the man hard on the jaw. "Gotta go," he said pointlessly to the now senseless man slumped on the ground. He turned and started to move towards Schmidt and Lori. Then he saw something that made him stop dead in his tracks.

From her awkward position on the ground, Lori lashed out again with the tiny blade as Schmidt lunged toward her. Her swipe narrowly missed his pelvic region but her clear intent caused him to recoil backwards. It was a momentary respite.

Schmidt recovered his aggressive stance quickly. Despite his emaciated, pallid appearance, he seemed to move with the speed and power of a finely-tuned athlete. He narrowed his eyes and was coiled and ready to strike out at the girl for the final kill. Instead, he stopped and turned toward the entrance of the compound. His eyes opened wide in fear.

Manuel Rodriguez raced through the gate on the Kawasaki dirt bike as if he were Evel Knievel gathering speed for an impossible jump. The high-pitched roar of the over-revving engine sounded like a chainsaw gone wild. The bike's knobbly tires bit into the uneven surface holding the machine true and steady as it bore down on the thin man at more than 50 feet per second.

Having regained his composure, Schmidt steeled himself as he turned and faced the threat as a matador confronting a charging bull. He held the long knife at eye level and waited for the right moment to move. Just when it appeared as if the bike was going to plough right through him, he darted to the side and executed a vicious strike toward the rider's head. But he wasn't fast enough.

Manny saw the sharp steel flashing through the air. He instinctively reached out and deflected Schmidt's knife arm as he simultaneously heaved the motorcycle sideways so he was thrown clear. He landed hard on his left side, jarring his shoulder, arm and hip, as well as tearing a sizeable gash in his Collezione Italia green jacket. At the same time, the skidding rear wheel of the bike slammed into Schmidt's legs.

Schmidt's shins were shattered as his legs were knocked out from beneath him and he was hurled through the air like a crash test dummy. His flying, rotating body slammed unceremoniously face first onto the hard stony surface of the compound 20 feet from the point of impact. As the dust settled on the scene, Schmidt remained where he had fallen. A bright crimson pool oozed from his neck. The bloodied Hitler Jugend knife lay next to him.

Hawkins and David arrived on the scene almost simultaneously. Both were open-mouthed at what they had just witnessed. Hawkins guided Lori gently to her feet and felt her trembling almost uncontrollably with either fear or relief. This quickly turned into a powerful embrace as she squeezed his ribs almost tight enough to cause damage.

Hawkins pulled back and asked, "Vince?"

Lori had tears in her eyes as she shook her head and said, "he gave his life for me."

Manny sprang upright and quickly dusted his clothes off. He noticed from Schmidt's awkward position and laboured breathing that the evil man was in a very bad state. Manny felt neither remorse nor happiness.

Almost in slow motion, Schmidt shifted his head and looked up at the man who had thwarted his plans with a stunned expression that quickly morphed into a look of outright hatred. He struggled for breath and tried to speak but no words came out. The fire seemed to ebb from his eyes. The rivulet of blood flowing from his neck pooled on the hard stony floor of the compound.

Manny just watched as Schmidt died.

Agent Jones and the retired policeman pulled cautiously into the parking lot of the nursery two minutes behind Rodriguez. Pete Blake's eyes were riveted to the LCD screen of the laptop. He raised his eyebrows in surprise. "He's stopped."

"What, completely?" Jones quizzed.

"Yes."

"Something's happened," Jones said. "I don't like it." He peered over at the computer on Blake's lap and then made up his mind. He stamped on the accelerator with his foot and the car responded by bursting through the closed front gates of the nursery. They could both see the dark tendrils of smoke rising above the fenced compound ahead of them.

Jones pulled the car to a screeching halt behind the last building on the nursery grounds and immediately scrambled out the door, drawing his gun. He could see Rodriguez standing over a motionless body. "Stay here Pete!" Jones commanded.

Blake didn't respond as Jones bolted for the opened gate of the compound. He continued watching for three seconds then climbed out the car and ran after Jones.

The inferno of the shattered greenhouse provided a hellish backdrop as Manuel Rodriguez stood over Schmidt's lifeless body. There were fewer flames now as black smoke curled into the sky from the broken shell of the structure. Lori's senses were still reeling from her close encounter with death and the daring rescue by someone that they had previously considered to be their nemesis. She, Hawkins and David approached cautiously.

Lori was the first to speak. "Thank you for what you did."

Manny looked up at them with a dazed expression as if he had just awakened from a dream. "He had to be stopped."

"Looks like he's stopped for good," David observed.

"But why didn't you do something before?" Lori asked.

"It wasn't the right time."

Hawkins asked, "how long have you worked for the intelligence service?"

Manny was stunned. "How did you find out?"

"I suspected when we were duelling in the warehouse. You were holding back."

"You call that holding back?" David protested. "He almost killed you."

"Sorry for my deception but I was forced to operate in secrecy," Manny said. He had gambled that the discovery in Cambridge was the key to unravelling Schmidt's organization from within and, at the same time, to closing the book on a long dark chapter in his own life.

"So you're actually one of the good guys?" David asked.

"I was trying – "

The blistering piece of lead that tore into Manny's flesh came from somewhere behind them.

A split second before, Jones had temporarily lost sight of the scene as he dashed around the last prefab structure in front of the compound. His anxiety grew in proportion to the amount of time his view was obscured by the building. After all, Rodriguez was his responsibility. As soon as he cleared the building and had a clear shot, he didn't hesitate. He fired his weapon.

The three scientists watched in muted horror as Rodriguez, jolted by the impact of the bullet, fell to the ground.

"No!" Hawkins shouted.

But Rodriguez only groaned, rolled to his haunches, pressed a hand to his bloodied shoulder and regarded the young agent who had shot him with calm acceptance in his eyes.

Hawkins saw that Rodriguez had only a minor wound to his shoulder. Most likely, the bullet had passed clean through. Then Hawkins made a decision. He said something that drew surprised reactions from everyone.

"Rodriguez, there's a GPS tracer in your pocket."

"But how…?" Rodriguez started. Then realisation dawned. "During our duel…when you grabbed my coat?"

Hawkins nodded with a guilty expression on his face. Then he took the small bag from his coat and handed it to the man in the torn, blood-soaked suit. "You'll know what to do with these."

Rodriguez accepted the bag and raised his eyebrows questioningly. But once it was in his hands, he knew what Hawkins meant.

"Thank you. I will do my best."

He struggled to pull the motorcycle upright using his one good arm. He stepped carefully onto the saddle and kick-started it back to life. Then he released the clutch, throttled up and shot across the compound like a streak of lightning.

Blake had grabbed Jones from behind and pulled the NSA agent's gun hand down to prevent him from firing again. But it was unnecessary. Jones had already realised his folly.

"I thought he was attacking them," Jones said weakly.

Blake could feel the agent shaking. "Don't worry partner," he said, patting his shoulder. "The man seems to be okay, anyway."

"I was aiming for his heart. I could have killed him."

"But you didn't. Now you'd better call the emergency services. We could have a real situation on our hands if this inferno spreads to the shrubs in the foothills."

"Thank goodness I'm a lousy shot," Jones said as if he hadn't heard. Then he plucked out his cell phone and made the call.

Over the next few minutes, Jones learned that the tree had been destroyed and his mission had been technically accomplished. He checked on the two surviving gunmen. One had just regained consciousness and was suffering from third degree burns on one leg. The other had inhaled so much smoke from the burning greenhouse that he was still periodically subjected to violent fits of retching. Jones also needed to make sure that neither man had any further weapons at their disposal. This was only a formality for the man in the Betty Boop underpants since there weren't many places where he could have hidden one.

"So who was this guy anyway?" David asked.

Everyone had now gathered in the vicinity of Schmidt's lifeless body. Mrs Sullivan gazed around at the aftermath of the chaos in the compound as if she saw this sort of thing every day.

"He was the leader of a multinational Neo-Nazi movement," Jones replied. "His organization has long been suspected of illegally appropriating precious and important artefacts from archaeological sites across the globe. The theft of the ancient seeds was one of their projects."

"But why?" David persisted.

"We don't know for sure," Jones confessed. "But we do know that he wanted the seeds because of what he believed they were. And, on the off chance that he was correct, they would have had a very powerful weapon in their hands for obvious reasons. That's why we had to stop him and attempt to confiscate the seeds. At least they were destroyed in the fire."

Hawkins looked down at his shoes.

No one had noticed Pete Blake step away from the group. He was looking down at the dead man's body with a curious expression on his face.

Then the sounds of multiple sirens permeated the evening air as the Santa Barbara emergency services could be heard drawing near. The nursery would soon be swamped with policemen, fire fighters and paramedics.

Blake returned to the group. "Do you know his name, Agent Jones?"

"Well, we have an alias, Gerhardt Schmidt."

"Why do you think it's an alias?" Hawkins asked.

"Because the real Gerhardt Schmidt was born in 1928," Jones stated matter-of-factly. "This man is far too young to be him."

"It's not an alias," Blake said.

After a moment of stunned silence, Hawkins asked, "how do you know that, Pete?"

"Because this is the same man that Brian and I saw in 1959."

Chapter 54

Santa Barbara, California
July 15, 2007

The golden eagle circled the edge of the field effortlessly on the uneven rising column of warm air. Its keen eyes constantly scanned the tall grasses and open patches on the sloping ground for any movement that didn't belong. It had eaten earlier but the thought of living food so near made it eager for more. It knew something was there. The great bird of prey twitched its primary feather on the left wing tip and smoothly circled back along the length of a chain-linked fence flanking the field. Sustaining itself in level flight now, the eagle slowed until the wind was a whisper in its feathered face. There! Coming straight forward, partly camouflaged against the brown earth, a small furry creature scurried with reckless abandon. The eagle paused, tilted its long flattened wings, arched its neck downward and reduced its altitude like a commercial jet positioning itself for a runway landing.

Number 8 moved sporadically in short bursts across the ground. He had been free now for the first time in his inordinately long life for just over an hour after its cage had crashed to the ground and the door popped open. The smells, the dirt, the grass, the breeze were all wonderful. This was what he had been missing. The thrill of exploration. He headed back toward the grass when a large shadow rushed toward him from above. Then his small body was suddenly crushed with pain as something ripped him from the ground and bore him skyward. *Something sharp cutting into his flank, squeezing hard. Rushing air. A flash of light. Release... at long last.*

Chapter 55

Lompoc, California
July 15, 2007

The metallic-blue Shelby Mustang slipped like a wraith through the late evening twilight. The last road sign indicated that they were now less than 6 miles from Lompoc. Blake was driving with Mrs Sullivan sat comfortably in the shotgun seat of the mid-sized sports car, while Hawkins, David and Lori bunched together like sardines in the rear. Although the sun had set an hour earlier and darkening clouds were forming ahead of them, the temperature still hovered in the mid-80s. Blake had both windows rolled down generating what Californians commonly referred to as 2-70 air-conditioning. This was known otherwise as two windows down at 70 miles per hour.

"Uggh...I just swallowed an insect," David announced.

"That'll teach you to keep that mouth closed," Lori teased as her hair was swept back by the wind.

"We could roll 'em up," Blake shouted over the rushing noise. "But the aircon's not working."

"It's fine for me," Lori said.

David said, "I need the protein anyway."

Hawkins smiled. He was pleased to hear the light-heartedness after what they had all just been through. It was a good sign that there would be no emotional scarring. In David's case, that was probably not a factor anyway. The kid never seemed to let things affect him. Mrs Sullivan appeared to be as unperturbed as if she were at an afternoon tea party. Even Lori, after her recent close encounter with death, was coping as well as could be expected.

He had spoken to Inspector Sanderson via telephone just before they left Santa Barbara. The Inspector told him a joint MI6 and NSA operation had raided Schmidt's headquarters in Basel. A total of 23 men had been arrested and charged with numerous international crimes including transport of illegal antiquities, drug manufacture and trafficking, and illegal weapons trade. The authorities had confiscated numerous artefacts that represented the pinnacle of Old and New World civilizations, 150 pounds of heroin, several chemical compounds that still required identification, and 5 types of biological or chemical weapons. But the most disturbing factor of all for Hawkins had been learning that Stanley had been taken into custody at Los Angeles airport as one of the key members of this same organization. Then there was the enigma of Gerhardt Schmidt. Was it possible that this was the same man behind the tomb robbery in Lompoc almost 5 decades ago?

The temperature dropped significantly as the Shelby emerged from the foothills into the outskirts of Lompoc. A mass of dark, threatening thunderheads rolled over the hills into the valley and the sensation of static electricity and the scent of ozone permeated the night sky. Blake shifted down to third gear as the first drops of rain began to fall. The low frequency noise from the car's engine was strangely resonant with the deep rumblings of the building thunderstorm.

Mrs Sullivan sat silent and erect in the seat next to Blake, hands folded across her lap and seemingly oblivious to the brewing storm. The car crossed the concrete highway bridge spanning the Santa Ynez river bed situated approximately a half mile from the Sullivan residence. A broad smile was fixed on her face and her eyes sparkled as she peered through the windscreen for the first signs of her home.

Blake turned off the main road into the long driveway and brought the Shelby to a halt next to Sullivan's black pickup truck. Mrs Sullivan stepped elegantly from the car while Hawkins climbed from the back seat and joined her. The two linked arms and then walked leisurely toward the house. The massive front door opened and a sturdy-looking figure appeared.

Hawkins hoped that Brian had remembered to clean the place.

Chapter 56

New York City
August 23, 2007

The morning gloom dissipated as the dawn gradually penetrated the mahogany-slatted Venetian blinds, illuminating Merrick's Art Deco-styled Park Avenue penthouse like an Egyptian solar temple. Manuel Rodriguez sat at the smoothly-polished pine breakfast table savouring the one cappuccino that he allowed himself each day. He always liked to rise before the morning sun. It was the best time to catch up on his thinking.

After leaving Santa Barbara, he had embarked on a cross country journey by bus and train. He paid for all stages of the trip using cash so his movements couldn't be traced. He stopped for a day in Las Vegas Nevada at an old friend's private clinic to have his shoulder seen to. He discarded the green suit and Armani shirt since these had tell-tale holes and other suspicious signs of damage, including the darkened stains of his own blood. He travelled the rest of the way to New York in a Green New York Jets jersey that he purchased from a sports paraphernalia shop.

Upon finally arriving back at Merrick's penthouse suite in Manhattan, the old billionaire had literally welcomed him with open arms. Strangely, Merrick didn't question him on his whereabouts but Manny suspected that the old wizard probably knew something. But there was a secret that Manny did manage to keep. There were 7 pieces of fruit in all, although most had been partially burnt. After making a few discreet inquiries with the scientists at Merrick Incorporated, Manny quickly came to realise that there wouldn't be enough material to carry out proper scientific testing to identify the active ingredients. Whatever miraculous secret the golden fruits held would soon be lost to the world forever.

As he had done every morning for the past month, Manny prepared Merrick's breakfast. This typically consisted of a special blend of muesli with chopped exotic fruits of various kinds. The fruits that Merrick liked best were papayas, mangoes, pomegranates, pineapples and lychees. But Merrick didn't know about the other ingredient that Manny had been incorporating into the mix over the past few weeks in sparing amounts.

Manny took the cereal into Merrick's spacious room along with the morning editions of the *New York Times* and the *Financial Times*. The billionaire was already sitting up in his bed, propped on two giant pillows. The glow from the morning sun illuminated his features. To Manny, it seemed the wrinkles were less pronounced and the eyes were less rheumy. *But was it just a trick of the light?*

"Morning Sir," Manny said as he handed Merrick the tray.

"And a fine one it is as well," Merrick replied.

"You are looking well today," Manny ventured as he watched Merrick take the first mouthful of cereal.

"Strangely, I'm feeling well," Merrick replied, looking bemused. "I've been thinking...."

"About what Sir?" *Does he suspect something?*

"Maybe we should meet with Dr Hawkins. He's here in Manhattan for the Annual Archaeological Society meeting, presenting a paper on their discovery of the two giant mummies. Why don't you reserve my old table at Stella for the three of us?"

"Of course Sir, but are you sure you're up to this?"

"Make it for 8:00 P.M."

Manny didn't trust himself to say anything more.

Jacques de Villipin, the maitre d' and manager of Stella, one of the most expensive restaurants in mid-town Manhattan, looked around the elegant room in satisfaction. It was a good crowd for a Thursday night in August, just a week or so to go before the end of summer when the midweek dining normally starts to taper off. There were a number of regulars in, along with several faces that he had never seen before. Most people usually came in and ordered the cheapest items on the menu, presumably just so they could claim that they had dined at the famous restaurant. But tonight there were a number of big spenders in the house. The most notable of these was William

Merrick, the fourth richest man in America. Merrick had taken his usual seat at table 7 along with his two companions, his immaculately-attired aide, Manuel Rodriguez, and another handsome gentleman that looked familiar. De Villipin thought he might have seen the man on television.

As the evening in the restaurant wore on and de Villipin went about his duties, a nagging thought gradually developed. Before tonight, he had not seen Merrick in the restaurant for several months. He had heard the billionaire was rarely seen in public anymore due to his rapidly fading health. In fact, de Villipin was sure he had read somewhere that the old man's body was riddled with cancer. He recalled this specifically because the article ended up by speculating who would inherit Merrick's fortune since he had no living family or other potential heirs.

When it came time for their desserts, de Villipin went to their table personally to see if they had any special requests. As far as Merrick himself was concerned, de Villipin recalled that the man never ordered desserts. But he had to ask for the sake of Mister Rodriguez and the other gentleman. The two younger men ordered the tiramisu, the restaurant's specialty. The gentleman also ordered his second café latte of night. De Villipin noticed that he had a slight Australian accent. *Most Americans would probably think he was English*, he thought to himself with measured satisfaction. And then something happened that took him by surprise. Merrick ordered a large portion of the key lime cheesecake. De Villipin saw that this had also taken Rodriguez aback.

When Merrick noticed that he and cheesecake were now the centre of concerned attention, he smiled. "What's the matter? Can't an old man order a dessert without alerting the anti-cholesterol squad?"

Rodriguez and the other man smiled broadly.

Then Merrick said, "After all, you only get to be old once."

Chapter 57

Cambridge, England
September 1, 2007

The dog days of summer are typically the hottest and most humid time of year. These days are a phenomenon of the northern hemisphere and are so named because they occur from July to September when the dog star Sirius, the brightest star visible from Earth, can be seen rising before the morning sun. The ancient Romans believed that increased temperatures occurred during this period because Sirius added its heat to that of the sun. Ancient authors claimed that during the dog days, the sea boils, wine turns sour, people become febrile, animals grow languid and dogs, in particular, begin to turn mad.

It was an easy matter for the residents of Cambridge to understand how at least some of these claims could be true on the unbearably hot and sultry September afternoon. Outside temperatures were soaring in the high 90s Fahrenheit. There is a well-known song by Noel Coward which states that 'only mad dogs and Englishmen go out in the midday sun.' And yet, two Englishmen, one Australian and a massive Great Dane stood in the blazing sunlight as they all stared at the same spot on the ground in the garden. The scene was almost comical as the expressions on the men's faces ranged from complete bewilderment to flat out amusement, contrasted with the 'what did I do?' look of their canine companion. Any observer who wasn't clued in to the specifics of the situation would find it strange that the object of their communal attention appeared to be a dried up pile of dog faeces.

Growing out of the pungent amorphous mass, were two small sprouts about 4 inches high. David immediately recognized these for what they were because he had seen their like before in Lori's laboratory. "I don't believe it," he said. "Right here in your back garden."

"It's incredible," Inspector Sanderson said.

"It's all thanks to Brandy," Hawkins responded.

Hearing her name spoken, the dog let out a muffled, *woof!* Hawkins elaborated. "After she broke into the pantry and ate everything inside the bag, the seeds must have passed right through her digestive system relatively intact over the next few days."

"Who's a good girl, Brandy?" David called over to the dog.

Gruff!

"Well, I'll be darned," Sanderson said. "Of course you'll have to move the shoots to a greenhouse, or something, so they can survive the coming winter."

"I plan on building a small one right here in the garden."

"So what are you going to do if they continue to grow?" Sanderson asked.

"I hadn't thought that far ahead. But it would be best if we kept this to ourselves for the time being. We all know what trouble these things can cause."

"Agreed," Sanderson said.

"Me too," David chipped in. "Besides, I need some time to recover before I can go through anything like that again. But there's one thing I don't get...."

"What's that?" Hawkins asked.

"How did these manage to grow in your back garden of all places? We had to cultivate them in a lab."

"It was probably a combination of things," Hawkins said. "The temperature, humidity and soil conditions might have been contributing factors. Also, many seeds grow better after passing through the gut of an animal. However, the key factor was most likely the application of an exceptional natural fertilizer."

"Ah, good ole dog poo," David summarized.

Epilogue

Cambridge, England
September 2, 2007

Jim Hawkins massaged the polish carefully onto the front faring of the motorcycle. After a final brisk, circular rub, he stepped back and stood motionless for several seconds admiring the powerful sweeping curves and bold angles of the fine piece of British engineering. The motorcycle's bold contours were accentuated by the sunlight dancing over its surface. Somewhere in the brightness, he imagined that he could see the ghostly image of Zoran.

The heat wave had enticed many of Cambridge's residents to venture out and enjoy the sunshine for what would probably turn out to be the last opportunity of the year to expose bare skin. Throughout the afternoon, there had been a continuous stream of open-topped convertibles, casual and serious cyclists, and scantily clad pedestrians heading toward the city centre. Hawkins found the simple task of polishing his Camaro and Zoran's motorcycle therapeutic while he watched this small part of the world going by.

His attention turned to the sleek chocolate brown Camaro parked almost protectively next to the motorcycle. The Beach Boys haunting melody *When I grow up* emanated from the Sony sound system that he had installed in the space where the car's original radio had once sat. As always, this particular song made him think about his own life. The polish that he had applied to the Camaro had left such an amazing glossy finish that he could actually see his reflected image, albeit somewhat distorted, in the smoothly curving passenger-side door. He found himself peering closer at the reflection of himself for any signs of age such as grey hair, wrinkles and spreading waistline that would someday begin to take hold of him, just as it had for all of humanity for countless millennia.

But what if aging could be averted? What if people could live to the age of Methuselah? Would life be any better, or worse?

Maybe it's the shortness of life that forces one not to miss opportunities and not to waste precious time. For the first time in many years, Hawkins found himself feeling excited about living for the moment.

His thoughts were suddenly and rudely interrupted by the sound of a passing Volkswagen convertible beeping its horn. As the car drove slowly past his house, he could see that the culprits were three young males who had been calling out to a particularly striking female jogger. As the would-be Casanovas carried on cruising down the road to seek out another victim for their charms, Hawkins glanced at the subject of their attention. She wore a flaming orange Lycra outfit that was nicely filled out in all the right places as she jogged lightly along the pavement in his direction. Then he felt his pulse racing as the vision in Lycra stopped at the bottom of his driveway.

"G'day!" Hawkins said, quickly recovering from his surprise.

"G'day yourself," Lori called back, now bending slightly and putting her hands on her knees as a means of catching her breath. After a moment she straightened and asked, "have you been away? I must have jogged past your house every day for the past week trying to catch your attention."

"I just got back from New York yesterday."

"That explains it. How's your arm?"

"If I cut down on the fire-bombing, sword fights and gun battles, it should heal up just fine."

"Sounds like a good plan," she smiled.

Hawkins smiled. "Can I interest you in a café latte?"

"No thanks."

He was floored.

Her smile widened. "Haven't you noticed that I don't drink coffee?"

"Uh… no."

"I'm a tea drinker," she said. "Earl Grey if you have it."

Dr Paul Charles Guest (BS, MS, PhD) is a research scientist from Cambridge, England. He has worked in both academia and the pharmaceutical industry and published more than 300 scientific articles, 3 magazine articles and 18 non-fiction books in the areas of psychiatry, metabolic and neurodegenerative diseases, virology, stem cell biology, medical technology, age-related diseases, and life extension research. The Genesis Factor is his first novel.

Printed in Great Britain
by Amazon